Praise for *Sorrowland*

"*Sorrowland* is gorgeous, and the writing, the storytelling, is magnificent. This country has a dark history of what it's willing to do to Black bodies, and Rivers Solomon lays that truth bare in a most unexpected, absolutely brilliant way."

—Roxane Gay, author of *Hunger*

"A stirring sense of the epic animates this striking novel . . . This capaciousness is echoed in the sheer range of *Sorrowland*'s timely preoccupations . . . Its frame of reference is generous—in some ways, it's clearly rooted in Afrofuturism, owing plenty to Octavia Butler, but it nods as well to *Giovanni's Room*, Robin Hood and folklore from multiple cultures . . . Solomon's audacity lies in imagining at least some of those wrongs not only remembered but put right, and in dreaming up powers potent enough to make it so."      —Hephzibah Anderson, *The Guardian*

"Riveting and harrowing . . . [*Sorrowland* is] gorgeously written and sure to be one of my favorite books of the year."

—Margaret Kingsbury, *BuzzFeed*

"*Sorrowland* contains so much wisdom and insight, wrapped in passion and fury and tenderness."

—Charlie Jane Anders, author of *Victories Greater Than Death*

"Rivers Solomon has once again created an engrossing, emotional, and original read with pages that demand to be turned. The writing is visceral and soul-clenching. The characters—bold, creative, and memorable. The action—heart-stopping. This is imaginative storytelling at its finest. Once I started *Sorrowland*, I could not put it down until I reached the end. And then I wanted more!"      —P. Djèlí Clark, author of *Ring Shout*

## ALSO BY RIVERS SOLOMON

*The Deep*

*An Unkindness of Ghosts*

## Rivers Solomon
### *Sorrowland*

Rivers Solomon writes about life in the margins, where they are much at home. In addition to appearing on the Stonewall Honor list and winning a Firecracker Award, Solomon's debut novel, *An Unkindness of Ghosts*, was a finalist for Lambda Literary, Hurston/Wright Legacy, Otherwise (formerly Tiptree), and Locus awards. Solomon's second book, *The Deep*, based on the song by the Daveed Diggs–fronted hip-hop group clipping., was the winner of a 2020 Lambda Literary Award and short-listed for Nebula, Locus, Hugo, Ignyte, Brooklyn Public Library Literary, British Fantasy, and World Fantasy awards. A refugee of the transatlantic slave trade, Solomon was born on Turtle Island but currently resides on an isle in an archipelago off the western coast of the Eurasian continent.

# RIVERS SOLOMON

 MCD · PICADOR   FARRAR, STRAUS AND GIROUX   NEW YORK

# SORROWLAND

MCD

Picador

120 Broadway, New York 10271

Originally published in 2021 by MCD / Farrar, Straus and Giroux

First paperback edition, 2022

Grateful acknowledgment is made for permission to reprint
the following previously published materials:
Excerpt from *The Snowy Day*, by Ezra Jack Keats, used by permission
of the Ezra Jack Keats Foundation.
Excerpt from *Giovanni's Room*, © 1956, by James Baldwin. Copyright renewed.
Used by arrangement with the James Baldwin Estate

Photograph of forest by Richard Oriolo.

The Library of Congress has cataloged the MCD hardcover edition as follows:
Names: Solomon, Rivers, author.
Title: Sorrowland / Rivers Solomon.
Description: First edition. | New York : MCD / Farrar, Straus and
    Giroux, 2021
Identifiers: LCCN 2020053564 | ISBN 9780374266776 (hardcover)
Classification: LCC PS3619.O43724 S67 2021 | DDC 813/.6—dc23
LC record available at https://lccn.loc.gov/2020053564

Paperback ISBN: 978-1-250-84926-7

Designed by Abby Kagan

Our books may be purchased in bulk for promotional, educational, or business
use. Please contact your local bookseller or the Macmillan Corporate and
Premium Sales Department at 1-800-221-7945, extension 5442, or by email at
MacmillanSpecialMarkets@macmillan.com.

Picador® is a U.S. registered trademark and is used by Macmillan Publishing
Group, LLC, under license from Pan Books Limited.

For book club information, please visit facebook.com/picadorbookclub or email
marketing@picadorusa.com.

mcdbooks.com • Follow us on Twitter, Facebook, and Instagram at @mcdbooks
picadorusa.com • Instagram: @picador • Twitter and Facebook: @picadorusa

1  3  5  7  9  10  8  6  4  2

*To everyone I will ever be, and ever was.*

*Author's Note*

This story takes place on stolen land. While *Sorrowland* is set in a United States with a speculative and amorphous shape, the geography and settings explored are based on areas traditionally stewarded by the Tonkawa, Caddo Nation, and Lipan Apache in what are colonially known as Central and East Texas, as well as on lands historically inhabited by various Plains nations with shifting territories, including the Apsáalooke/Crow, Oceti Sakowin/Sioux, and Arapaho, in what settlers have designated Wyoming and Montana. No story of the so-called United States is complete without an understanding of its foundation on genocide and dislocation, nor without acknowledgment of the Indigenous people still here fighting the ongoing occupation.

I wrote this book in England, a single nation among many in Europe responsible for genocides not just on Turtle Island but countless worldwide. I hope that even as *Sorrrowland* delves into the pain these colonial states have wrought, one might see the joy, triumph, and humor of those who resist, resist, resist. That said, there is no mincing words about some of the darker themes in this book. Note discussion and instances of racism, misogyny, self-harm, suicidality, and homophobia, inclusion of animal death and explicit violence, and references to sexual violence that have taken place off the page.

I hope you find in this book whatever it is you need right this moment.

PART ONE

KINGDOM PLANTAE

# 1

THE CHILD GUSHED out from twixt Vern's legs ragged and smelling of salt. Slight, he was, and feeble as a promise. He felt in her palms a great wilderness—such a tender thing as he could never be parsed fully by the likes of her.

Had she more strength, she'd have limped to the river and drownt him. It'd be a gentler end than the one the fiend had in mind.

Vern leant against the trunk of a loblolly and pressed the child naked and limp to her chest. His trembling lips lay right where the heart-shaped charm of a locket would be if she'd ever had a locket. "So that's how it's gonna be, hm? Win me over with lip wibbles?" she asked, and though she was not one to capitulate to bids for love, this baby had a way about him that most did not. There was courage in his relentless neediness. He would not be reasoned out of his demands.

Vern reached for the towel next to her. With what gentleness she could muster, and it wasn't enough to fill a thimble, she dragged rough terry over the baby's mucky skin. "Well, well," she said, cautiously impressed, "look at you." Vern's nystagmus and resultant low vision were especially troublesome in the waning light, but pulling her baby close lessened the impact of her partial blindness. She could see him full-on.

He was smaller than most newborns she'd had the occasion to handle and had inherited neither her albinism nor her husband Sherman's yellow-bonedness. His skin was dark,

dark-dark, and Vern found it hard to believe that the African ancestry that begat such a hue had ever once been disrupted by whiteness. The only person Vern knew that dark was Lucy.

Viscous cries gurgled up from the child's throat but died quickly on the bed of Vern's skin. Her flesh was his hovel, and he was coming to a quick peace with it. His bones were annals of lifetimes of knowledge. He understood that heat and the smell of milk were to be clung to or else.

It was a shame such instincts would not be enough to save him. As much as Vern had made a haven here these last few months, the woods were not safe. A stranger had declared war against her and hers, his threats increasingly pointed of late: a gutted deer with its dead fawn fetus curled beside; a skinned raccoon staked to a trunk, body clothed in an infant's sleepsuit; and everywhere, everywhere, cottontails hung from trees, necks in nooses and feet clad in baby bootees. The fiend's kills, always maternal in message, revealed a commitment to theme rarely seen outside a five-year-old's birthday party.

Another girl might've heeded the warnings to leave the woods, but Vern preferred this obvious malevolence to the covert violence of life beyond the trees. To be warned of bad happenings afoot was a welcome luxury. People might've followed Vern off the compound when she'd fled if there'd been a fiend there discarding dead animals as auguries.

"Hush, now," Vern said, then, thinking it was what a good mam would do, sang her babe a song her mam used to sing to her. "*Oh, Mary, don't you weep, don't you mourn. Oh, Mary, don't you weep, don't you mourn. Pharaoh's army got drown-ded! Oh, Mary, don't weep.*"

Even though it was a spiritual, it wasn't a song about Jesus direct, which suited Vern because she hated music about the Christ. It was one of the few items on which she and her husband, Sherman, agreed. She nodded along to every sermon he gave about the ways the white man plundered the world under the direction of this so-called savior.

*Whole continents reek of the suffering that man has caused. Can you smell it?* he would ask. The congregation would shout, *Amen, Reverend Sherman, we smell it!* And then he'd ask, *Don't it stink?* And they'd say, *Yes, Reverend! It sure does.* And he'd ask, *But does it stink here, on the Blessed Acres of Cain, where we live lives removed from that white devil god of Abel and his followers?* The people would cry out, *No!*

According to Mam, there was a time when Cainites were less ardent about Reverend Sherman's teachings. His predecessor and father, Eamon Fields, was the congregation's true beacon. An early settler of the compound, arriving in the first wave, Eamon rose quickly from secretary to accountant to deacon to reverend. He was a stern man, violent, but for Cainites who'd been traumatized by the disorder inherent to Black American life, puritanical strictness held a dazzling, charismatic appeal. Sherman was not so hard as his father before him, which disoriented the brothers and sisters of the compound. In the end, he won them over on the pulpit, entrancing all with his passionate sermons.

*And do we dare abandon the compound and mingle our fate with those devilish outsiders?* Sherman asked.

*No, Reverend!*

*That's right, my beautiful brothers and sisters, kings and queens, sons and daughters of Cain. We stay here, where there is bounty. Free from the white devil dogs who would tear us limb from limb. Their world is one of filth and contradiction, poison and lies! Rich folks in homes that could house fifty, one hundred, two hundred, while the poorest and sickest among them rot on the street! Would we allow that here?*

*No!*

Sherman could make lies out of the truth—Vern had learned that much as his wife—but she full-believed her husband's fiery sermons about the Nazarene. She'd witnessed the curious hold Jesus had on people from her trips off the compound. Every other billboard and bumper sticker preached his gospel. Christ-talk made up the few words Vern could read by sight because they were everywhere in large print.

JESUS.

HELL.

SALVATION.

JOHN 3:16.

He was on T-shirts, bracelets, anklets, mugs. And that damn cross everywhere. The whole world outside the Blessed Acres of Cain seemed an endless elegy to Christ and his dying, his bleeding, his suffering. How come white folks were always telling Black people to get over slavery because it was 150 or so years ago but they couldn't get over their Christ who died 1,830 years before that?

Who cared if he rose up from the dead? Weeds did that, too. It wasn't in Vern's nature to trust a man with that much power. For how did he come to have it?

Her new babe would never have to hear a thing about him. Vern would sing only the God-spirituals. She didn't believe in him, either, but at least there was an ineffability to him, a silence that could be filled with a person's own projection of the divine. Not so with Christ, who was a person, a particular person.

*"God made man and he made him out of clay. Put him on earth,*

*but not to stay. Pharaoh's army got drown-ded. Oh, Mary, don't weep!"*
sang Vern.

Sherman didn't abide music about Jesus at the Blessed Acres of Cain, but he let Vern's mother listen to it in the wee hours when no one else on the compound could hear.

*"One of these days bout twelve o'clock, this old world gonna reel and rock. Pharaoh's army got drown-ded! Oh, Mary, don't weep."*

Vern's words slurred as she succumbed to fatigue, though she was not so tired as she might have been. The last stages of labor had come on with the quickness of a man in want of a fuck, and with the same order of operations, too. A sudden demand, a vague series of movements, a driving push toward the finish, followed by Vern's immense relief when it was all over. Birthing had been no more trying than anything else in her life, and this time, at least, she had a baby boy to show for her trouble.

Or baby girl. Vern's mam had predicted a son based on the way Vern carried her belly, but now that the child was here, Vern didn't bother checking what was between its legs. The faintest impression of what could've been a penis pushed against her belly, but then it could've been a twisted piece of umbilical cord, too, or a clitoris, enlarged from birth much as Vern's own had been. Perhaps this child, like her, transgressed bodily notions of male and female.

Vern liked not knowing, liked the possibility of it. Let him unfold as he would. In the woods, where animals ruled with teeth and claws, such things mattered not a lick. There were no laws here in this wild land, and wasn't it better that way? At the compound, Vern saw how girlfolk and boyfolk were, what patterns they lived out as if notes on a record, their tune set in vinyl, rarely with variation. Even Vern's best friend, Lucy, recalcitrant to the marrow, would call her a man when Vern, against compound edict, wore pants to muck out the animal pens or took a straight razor to her thick, coarse sideburns, longer than many men's.

Did it have to be such? Was it always so? Or was it much like everything back at the Blessed Acres of Cain? A lie.

Vern's babe was just a babe. Guided by scent, he found his way to her breast the way many a child would, his head bobbing as he squirmed toward her nipple. "You'd think I hadn't been feeding you from my very own insides these last eight and a half months," said Vern, teasing, but she didn't resent him his hunger. No child of hers could ever be a sated thing.

It was evening, but only just. Mam said that children born of the gloaming were destined to wander; that was why Vern's mind had always been so unquiet. *You got more opinions than sense*, Mam had said.

Vern had doomed her newborn to the same fate, but she would not apologize for it. Better not to belong at all than belong in a cage. She thought to name the child Hunter for all the searching in his squeezing fingers and hunger in his heart, but then what if her mam really was wrong and he was a girl in the end? A girl named Hunter. It gave her a pleasant zing to think of the impropriety of it.

Back at the compound, she'd be made to name him after a famous descendant of Cain. Malcolm or Martin or Frederick, perhaps Douglass or Eldridge. Vern's little brother was Carmichael for Stokely, and among her peers, there was Turner for Nat, Rosa for Parks, Harriet for Tubman.

Vern herself was named for Vernon Johns, the scholar and minister who'd preceded Martin Luther King, Jr., at Dexter Avenue Baptist Church.

Lucy had complimented Vern on the name when she'd first come to the compound with her parents. *It's unique. No one's heard of that Vernon man. I'm getting tired of hearing all these African American Greatest Hits names. This way you can be your own person.*

If Sherman had his way, he'd name the child Thurgood, but Vern could not do that to her kin.

"Abolition?" she said, testing how it felt on her tongue. "Lucy?" she whispered, surprised by how much it hurt to speak that name aloud. "Lucy." It'd anger Sherman to no end if she named his sole heir after the girl who never yielded to him once, and Vern lived to anger Sherman.

Vern licked her lips hungrily, overcome with a wave of inspiration. When the child was old enough to ask after a father, Vern would say it was Lucy. Raised in the woods, her little one wouldn't know all the ways that wasn't true. It was something she'd never hear the end of if Sherman were here, but then he wasn't, was he? "Lucy," she said one more time, then, "Lu. Luce. Louie?" searching out a variation that suited the fussy babe sprawled against her. "Lucius?"

None of the options felt suitable, and she frowned. Wild things didn't bother naming their offspring, and Vern was wild through and through. Her mam had always said so. A child in the woods didn't need a name, did it?

"I'll just call you my little babe," Vern said, planning to leave it at that, until she heard wolves in the distance making their wild noises to the night. There it was, a sensation of rightness. She didn't have many of those, so when they came, they were easy to recognize. "Howling," she said. "Howling. That's your name." He was her hungry, keening creature.

Just like her. Ravenous. For what? For goddamn what? There was nothing in these woods but darkness and a fiend who killed not for food or hide but for the pleasure it arose in him to end the life of something small. She'd fled the compound in want of something, and though she'd been gone for only a short while, she already knew she'd never find it.

⊠

THERE WERE NO WOLVES in these woods, not that Vern had ever heard of. Yet as her babe slept fretfully on her chest, lips still a-wobble over her areola, she heard their howling again, closer now than they'd been before.

Everybody at the Blessed Acres of Cain undertook thorough study of flora and fauna. There was none among them who couldn't name near every animal and plant and fungus, what to do with it, how to tame it, how to kill it, how to make from it all the stuff needed for life. Reverend Sherman insisted upon this knowledge.

Education as a tool of liberation was a philosophy that dated back to Claws, the precursor group to the Cainites. **C**oloreds **A**gainst **W**hite **S**upremacy.

Back when the Blessed Acres of Cain was just an upstart Black nationalist group without the renown of the Black Panthers or the reach of the Nation of Islam, the founders ran schools often focused on survivalism. Driven by revelations from God, they wanted their people to renounce white civilization any way they could.

If Black people planned to survive in a society antagonistic to their existence, they had to learn to be resourceful. Intimate familiarity with the land reduced dependence on the white economy. These philosophies were the impetus for the establishment of the compound. A swath of land would help foster connection with the earth. There was a belief that because the dirt was eons old, it possessed knowledge, and by eating it, people could share in that knowledge. Some of the early founders said it could impart visions. Eamon Fields had taken this small amount of mysticism and used it as a seed to form an entire religion, but there had always been and always would be a practical component of learning and doing and working.

So Vern knew all there was to know about wolves, what they sounded like, their behaviors, their mating cycles, their hunting patterns, where they lived, their place in recovering ecosystems devoured by the white man's fear and greed. She knew that the nearest wolf den was fifteen hundred miles from where she was.

How had she missed this? How had the very first sound of them not sent her heart into deathly contortions? She'd been too overtaken by the uncanniness of motherhood, with all its wetness.

The wolves that weren't there howled, on the hunt. Bewildered, Vern pressed Howling tighter to her chest and moaned. This wasn't supposed to happen, not out here. Hauntings were particular to the compound. Everybody got them back there. It was withdrawal, according to Eamon Fields, as still preached by Reverend Sherman. Detox. People on the compound lived lives removed from the poisonous influence of the white world. The psychic toxins that plagued the rest of humanity seeped out of them in the form of night terrors and visions violent enough that folks had to sleep strapped down.

But Vern had fled the compound going on two months ago. She was in the outside world now, supposedly swimming in toxins. These devils, then, unlikely as it was, were real.

Vern's little brother, Carmichael, had once done a project on the reintroduction of wolves to the Yellowstone region. Under one of Sherman's academic programs, young men could visit libraries off the compound. It was a recruiting technique. Black families saw how smart and cleaned-up Cainite boys were and wanted that for their own sons. Better the Blessed Acres than incarceration, they must've reasoned.

Carmichael's project had been about the dangers of white toxicity, how European settlers had hunted gray wolves dead, disrupting the ecosystem's balance. It took years of fighting to reintroduce them.

Maybe the Parks and Wildlife Services here had done the same in this area without Vern knowing. Wolves had been extirpated from this area, too.

Or wild dogs? Coyotes? But coyotes howled like dying witches, high-pitched and squealing. These chants were a sorrow song.

Vern tied Howling snug to her front with a piece of cloth. She braced against the tree to stand, legs unsteady from muscle strain and the weight of her still-big abdomen, uncontracted. Evening dew moistened the woods into a mire, and she had to mind her steps.

Vern walked eastward, away from the sound of the wolves. She touched every third or fourth tree to make sure she kept straight, each trunk marked with the carvings she'd made to find her way at night, when her vision was lowest. Her feet sank into the ground as she walked. Cool mud squeezed between her toes.

There was no path. With every step she cleared bushes and brush. Underfoot, leaves and vines and branches grabbed hold of her ankles. It was true dark now, with little light left from the setting sun to show which way was east.

More howling, and closer still. Vern forced her legs to move faster, heart racing. She wiped sweat from her temple, cheek, and brow. Despite the autumn chill, her swiftly beating heart and quickened breaths heated her body through.

"We're gonna be all right," she lied to her babe. Wolves didn't naturally prey on humans, yet here they were now giving chase.

Their wolfish whinnies rang just behind her. So fast they'd caught up. She could hear their devilish steps against the sticks and the mud of the forest floor. They were just behind, a few feet away, then inches.

Next, hot breath. Afterward, a tear at her ankles, casting her downward onto her side, her poor babe awaking with his own howl. A hot tongue slithered in her ear, burrowing in that cave of cartilage. It was as awful as a kiss.

"God of Cain," she said, out of habit, not devotion. Vern flung open her eyes. She would face her extinction and bear this hot, vicious undoing full-on. She'd watch their blurry shadows descend.

Vern's eyelids fluttered. She looked left. She looked right. She squinted into the forest dark.

There were no wolves to be found. Vern blinked and rubbed her eyes, but no sign came that she'd been chased down and bit at. With a crimped brow, Vern hushed her crying babe with pats on the back, aware she'd forgotten all about him during her death throes.

Vern snapped her head to the left at the sound of a dry leaf crackling.

"Who's there?" she asked.

A beam of light flared from the darkness, blinding her. The ground around her shifted, sections of soft mud flattening under a stranger's boots. Someone with a flashlight stalked toward her. With one hand to her babe and the other made into a visor on her forehead, Vern scooted backward in the dirt.

She could neither see the stranger's face nor make out more than a few details of his person, but slung over his right shoulder was a dead opossum dressed in pale pink overalls. The fiend had come.

"The wolves always flush out the runaways," he said, voice suspended in that liminal ether between growl and whisper.

Vern lay frozen before him, regaining her ability to move only at the sound of an animal stalking in the outskirts of her periphery. It beat the ground with heavy footfalls and crunched twigs and pine cones with its massive paws. Hungry, it snarled. The noise was enough to distract the fiend, and Vern tugged the knife from her nightgown's pocket and plunged it into his thigh. He cried out but didn't retaliate, staggering toward the animal instead.

Vern righted herself, hoisting up onto all fours and then to standing. She crouched as low as she could as she ran, trying to make herself invisible in the wild plant growth of the woods. She didn't hear footsteps behind her, but she kept running. She stumbled to a stop only when pain of breath-stealing magnitude twisted inside her belly. It squeezed like something alive inside her, wishing her dead, making it so. If the fiend was coming, there was nothing to do now but wait. Her life, Howling's life, that was all in his hands.

Overcome, Vern worked herself down to her knees, legs spread. The urge to bear down as hard as she could supplanted every other humanly want in her body. Not one to deny her baser self, she did as the urge commanded and pushed. And so, with one babe tied to her chest, placenta and all, she bornt another. The fiend surely heard her screams.

⊠

IT WAS A SORRY LOT she'd birthed her babes into. They had naught but Vern. Vern, fifteen years old, who was not yet so lost in teenagedom that she believed herself knowledgeable or anything approaching such. The world and all its troubles were as much unknowns to her as they were to her children. What more could she offer them but her milk, her skin?

With Howling and his twin strapped to her, Vern gathered wood and built a fire. It made her an easy find in the woods, but Vern had expended too much energy on being frightened this evening. Let the fiend threaten and taunt. She'd not be chased from her bit of earth with promises of harm. Only actual violence could unmoor her.

Vern made a lean-to once she'd finished the fire. She'd wait until morning light to journey back to her camp.

"Now, what to call you?" she asked her newest child, smaller even than the first, his breaths gasping and unsteady. Like her, he was albino. The babe's alabaster glow made him easy to see in the dark, a lantern in her palms.

"How about Feral?" she said, for no more reason than it sounded as rabid a name as his elder sibling's. It made her happy to give them such improper names, because there was nothing good about what was proper.

Vern wished to make every moment of her life a rebellion, not just against the Blessed Acres of Cain but against the world in all its entirety. Nothing would be spared her resistance.

Outsiders looked down on Cainland, convinced of their superiority. Whenever Cainites moved together in a group off the compound, distinctive in their uniforms, parents stared and pulled their children away. People called them a cult.

Vern wanted to know what made these folks so sure they weren't in a cult, too. A college kid had once walked up to Vern on a dare and asked, *Do you really believe in the God of Cain?*

Seconds ago, this kid and her friends had opened up a bag of food on top of a panhandler's head and broken out in laughter. Was that what she believed in? Was that her god? Laughing at the downtrodden and weary? Nobody at Cainland would do that.

Vern said as much out loud, and the teenager replied, *At least I'm not brainwashed.*

Seemed like she was to Vern. Little children who passed the homeless always stopped; if not to give, at least to look, to acknowledge. It was their parents who scolded them into looking away, ignoring, hating. People defended all manner of views inherited from their caregivers to the grave, all the while claiming to have reached these conclusions of their own sound minds.

So Vern vowed to eschew the outside world as much as she did Cainland.

She held each babe as she stood on shaking legs before the fire. Her nightgown rippled in billows around her. The pink fabric, warped by time, had the bleached-bloodstain hue of an overexposed Polaroid. No one could say it was a dignified birthing garment, but then birthing wasn't a dignified affair. One need only consider the sheer animal humiliation of the act: shit, mucus, sobs. O, what a thing to be reduced to your truest nature, to be once more a dog whimpering in the night, clinging to battle-worn pups, the vessel of your body transformed into a tunnel for viscera. At least in these lowly moments the world became absent of airs. There could be no tea-sipping with a veiny dark placenta sloshing out of you.

Vern crawled with Howling and Feral into the temporary woodland shelter, desperate for sleep that she knew wouldn't come without a fight. *The wolves always flush out the runaways*, the fiend had said. Had he put those sounds in her mind, then? Those feelings and smells? Meat-scented wolf breath and wolf slobber and wolf nails? She'd never had a haunting as full-on as that.

Vern huffed in disgust, sickened by her naivete. Distance from the Blessed Acres hadn't rid her of hauntings because everything Eamon or Sherman had ever said about toxins and withdrawal causing them was a fabrication. With her own two ears Vern had listened to her husband preach that nonsense and believed it. Foolery. She was no different than the Cainites who'd stood idly by at her wedding, sucking up Sherman's lies about Vern needing his husbandly guidance to save her soul. People said Vern was stubborn and hardheaded, but not stubborn and hardheaded enough to be immune to lies. She had proof now that the hauntings had nothing to do with withdrawal because she was miles and miles from Cainland, but it shouldn't have taken all that for her to know the truth. The visions Cainites had weren't society's toxins oozing out. They were toxins being put in. Had to be. That was all Cainland was, Reverend Sherman putting bunk into people's minds. Turned out he was doing it literally, too. Poisoning people. When she'd settled in these woods, Vern had thought she'd been the one to encroach on the fiend's territory, but he'd revealed his hand when he'd said what he said: *The wolves always flush out the runaways.*

He had to have followed her here on Reverend Sherman's orders. The dead animals were meant to scare her back to the compound. When that didn't work, he poisoned her mind with a haunting. He'd put something in the river water she drank from, something that was in the same water back at Cainland.

Vern reclined against the tree trunk that formed the base of the lean-to, babes on her belly. The curious quiet of November reigned. It was the season of shriveling and cadaverous light. So many creatures would die this coming winter, and Vern counted herself among them.

This recent revelation proved it. Escaping the Blessed Acres hadn't changed the most essential truth of Vern's being: a misfit in the Land of the Living, she'd always been a dead girl walking.

## 2

VERN SQUINTED at the fiend below. She watched him from her perch high in a shortleaf pine. He wore an oversized hunting cap, shearling-lined flaps protecting his ears against January wind.

She needed to be more careful. Just minutes ago she'd been on the ground, headed toward a trap to check it for meat. When she'd heard the fiend whistling, she had only a moment to dash up the tree to hide.

Howling and Feral slept on either side of her front, tied to her in a double pouch she'd made from a brain-tanned hide. Neither had yet made a peep, but they'd been napping now for hours and were due to awaken. If they did stir, she'd not be able to sway or rock them back into a lull. To do so would risk creaking the branch and alerting the fiend to her presence.

Vern berated herself for ever thinking her life would be free from harm by following in Lucy's footsteps and running away from Cainland. Things had a way of working out for Vern's best friend in ways they didn't for Vern. She wondered where Lucy was right now—surely not up no damn tree. No, Lucy was someplace living the life, probably sitting in one of those fancy big-screen theaters eating popcorn and slurping orange drink.

Lucy's escape from the compound had been carefully planned, and so it suited that her days now were lived less dangerously than Vern's, whose own fleeing had been a haphazard affair. Where Vern had sped away in the dark of night on a whim, Lucy had left midday. Her leaving had been arranged to fall on Juneteenth, one of the few non-Cainite holidays acknowledged on the forty-acre compound. The person who'd come for Lucy was taking advantage of the distractions of the celebration.

That day, a cloudless, sun-saturated sky had tethered Vern inside. She'd been in the attic of the temple since morning worship services. Her mother had tried to convince her to go outside, to put on her straw hat and sunblock, but Vern had felt the intrusive rays of the sun even through the window.

"I aint coming. You can't make me," Vern said.

Mam exhaled and wiped floury hands off on her apron before taking a seat next to her daughter. "Today's about freedom. That's something you actually care about. You sure you don't want to participate?"

"I'm sure," said Vern. She was freshly thirteen and no less full of preferences and opinions than she'd been since she'd hit age two, exhausting her mother with the force of her personality.

"Mrs. Casey made peach cobbler."

"So?" Vern asked.

"I don't want you being left out," said Mama.

"I like being left out," Vern said, exasperated by the utter ridiculousness of such a statement. "What if you were going to—I don't know—a torture carnival where everybody was supposed to try out different torture devices, and they was all, *Oh no, why don't you want to participate? Aren't you going to feel left out? Everybody's getting tortured but you!* It just doesn't make any sense, Mam."

"You can't keep locking yourself away like this." Mam shook her head and tutted.

"I'm locked away in Cainland. Might as well be locked up in here, too." Vern scooted away from her mother on the bed, drawing blood as she bit the inside of her cheek.

"You're not locked here. I don't see no doors."

"Metaphorical doors, Mam," said Vern.

"You know I can't make you. I could never make you do a damn thing. But I think you'll regret it. It's not a day to be alone.

Loneliness kills. Did you know that?" Mam stood up and put her hands on her waist. "Happy Juneteenth. Try, my sweet darling, to be happy for just once in your life. You might like it."

Vern sat on the window ledge for the duration of the carnival, her right eye squeezed shut and the left eye mashed up against her telescope. It had been a gift from Reverend Sherman for her astronomy lessons. She couldn't follow along without help seeing the night sky. He'd converted the attic into her study and observatory.

The fan in the corner of the room blew a few strands of Vern's golden hair onto her forehead, but most of her hair was crinkled and coarse enough that it stayed firmly put. Mam had hot-combed it last night in preparation for today, burning the hairs into silky straight compliance, but it was a hundred degrees and even with the ceiling fan and a smaller fan blowing right up against her face in the night, she had sweat it out before sunrise. By noon it had mostly reverted to its natural afro state.

Catching something in the corner of her eye, Vern tilted the telescope leftward toward the stables. Lucy was standing there talking to a woman, no one Vern recognized. Vern almost went to open the window and shout to Lucy, but the two had been fighting since Lucy's mam ran away from the compound a week ago. Caught in an eddy of grieving, Lucy rankled and sparked at everything, calling Vern names whenever Vern asked, *How are you?*

*That's a dumbass question, Wonder Bread.*

It was Vern's least favorite insult. Wonder Bread was what you called white folk. Vern wasn't white or anything close to it. Lucy only said it because of how much it made Vern's insides bleed with sadness to be compared to that just because she was albino.

Vern squinted through the telescope but couldn't see well enough, so she went to her drawer to get another gift from Sherman, her camera. She wound on an additional lens. After zooming in the camera, she took several pictures of the stables where Lucy and the stranger stood.

Vern hooked up her camera to her photo printer, hating herself for using it. She was the only one on the Blessed Acres allowed such luxuries. Sherman made exceptions to the self-sufficiency model when it came to Vern because he was trying to woo her. That man was desperate to be liked by her. She'd rather the cane than the syrup. His gifts were a lie and then some.

She paced the attic as she waited for the photos to print, walked as far as she could until she hit the wall. It was hard to imagine that Lucy's mam had really left, that she'd just kept going and going, like this place wasn't made of walls.

Experimentally, Vern drove her elbow back, preparing to punch through the recently finished plaster in the attic.

"One. Two. Three."

Nothing. She couldn't make herself do it.

"One . . . two . . . three."

She punched softly, then harder, then harder still, rubbing her knuckles down.

When the printer stopped clicking, Vern grabbed her magnifying glass from her desk and examined the printed-out photos. Mam thought the lengths Vern went to to get an eye on something were extreme, but Vern appreciated having such a thorough record of her life. Cainland was full of tall tales. Her pictures could give her a hint of what was true.

The first photo showed the woman and Lucy talking. In the next, Lucy was crying. In the next, the woman had wrapped her arm around Lucy's shoulder, pulling her along. In the last photo, the two were barely in the frame. Just slight gestures of animal forms.

Vern stood from her desk, knocking her chair down in her rush to get to the telescope. She looked through it—no signs of Lucy or her visitor. She moved the camera to the right and farther to the right and nothing, until the lens reached the road past the main gate, where a pickup truck was fleeing Cainland.

Vern didn't open the window and shout to the Cainites that Lucy was gone. She couldn't. Everybody here, whether they knew it or not, lived in the mouth of a great beast. As harsh as it felt to be left behind unrescued, Vern wasn't so lost in bitterness that she would ruin her friend's chance at escape.

Lucy's mother left but had sent someone back for her daughter, but Vern's mam? Well, she was still back at Cainland to this very day, probably doing her chores like a good Cainite woman, no thought for her daughter stuck up in a tree with her babes, a killer lying in wait down below.

Vern rested her head against the trunk of the tree, and Feral's lips gave a hint of a quiver. *No, no, no, no, no,* she mouthed.

He yawned silently. Howling, bless him, still slept soundly, the rumble of his sleepy snores inaudible over the noise of the woods.

Feral let out a small whimper. Vern tried to shift him so she could give him her breast, but the unsuitability of the position only frustrated him, and he started to stir awake. Vern plunged her nipple into his mouth. Still, the baby would not latch. He batted at her uselessly with his hands.

Out of options, she pressed her thumb and forefinger around her areola and squeezed, dropping milk into his mouth. Finally, Feral took the milk quietly and fastened his lips to her body.

But all Vern's fussing over Feral roused Howling. He rammed the sides of his fists into her chest. "Sh, sh, sh," she said as quietly as she could when his eyes gaped open. She couldn't wrassle both of them into a tandem feed up in a tree. She'd lose her footing.

"Sh, sh, sh," she repeated, grateful for the blowing wind.

Howling beat his head side to side, then, struck by the plight of not having fed in three hours, yowled. The volume of the shriek startled Feral into unlatching, and he released his own agonized wail.

"Quiet, babes," she admonished uselessly. Down below, the fiend cocked his head upward, his face a white blur at this distance. He pointed his rifle to the top of the tree, then fired. The roar scared a mess of kinglets and thrushes from the pines and shocked Vern into slipping from her perch.

She caught herself on a loose branch, the wood cracking beneath her weight. She released her grip and let herself fall onto a sturdier limb. As she heard the click of the fiend's gun cocking she inhaled a breath, checked that the babes were secure to her, then leapt into the neighboring shortleaf.

She crashed into one of the limbs but gripped tight so she wouldn't tumble downward. She weaved her way through the branches, counted to three, then jumped to the next tree.

The fiend followed from the forest floor, firing his rifle into the sky as he gave chase. Vern need only make it to the river, where she'd be able to navigate to the other side through the dense overhang of trees. She could lose the fiend while he waded and swam through the slow-moving waters.

Gun smoke scented the air with its sooty musk as shots rippled the air. What ten minutes ago had been a quiet winter morning was now a Fourth of July firecracker show. It only ever took a moment for life to break apart at the seams.

Vern heard moving water. Obscured though it was by lush greenery, the river chugged forward below. She counted one, two, three, then careered forward, prayerful that her feet would land on a bough or that her hand would catch one of the branches of the canopy drooped over the river. Her feet hit wood. Filled with thanks, she closed her eyes for a moment's benediction. It was a short-lived thankfulness. She lost balance, and the twig-like branches she had grabbed for purchase were too weak to support her.

Vern, babes in tow, fell to the river. With a splash, they went under before bobbing again to the surface. All three coughed up ice water. Vern couldn't see if the fiend was behind her, but she dove underneath and swam with the current, holding her breath for as long as she could and hoping her babes did the same.

Downstream, she broke the surface to gasp for air. The twins writhed in agony against her, alive. Seeing no evidence of the fiend, Vern swam to the bank on the opposite side of the river from where she'd started the day.

Howling and Feral, both their own shade of gray from the cold, coughed and sobbed. Vern smacked their backs hard until they spit up globs of water. Lost in wheezes, gurgles, and snorts, the babes refused to calm. No amount of rocking could convince them the danger was gone.

Vern staggered toward tree cover and collapsed into the undergrowth with a grunt. The impact disturbed the roost of a hidden woodcock, and it darted from its hiding spot in the thicket in a flustered tizzy.

Vern's throat, bruised by river water, trembled painfully as she spoke. The rest of her body was similarly afflicted. Her nails hurt. Her eyeballs. The woods, like a father whose mood suddenly turned soft again after a rage, comforted her through her aching. Fallen oak leaves and pine needles enfolded her and her wailing children. She lay back against a rotting loblolly log, its surface pillowy soft with white apioperdon.

At least something good would come from this day. Fried mushrooms for supper.

Welts streaked her face where branches had hit. Howling and Feral had been similarly assailed, their faces notched with tiny wounds. Vern's breath more even now, she held them both to her breasts. They quieted instantly, and while she thanked the God of Cain that the twins were alive, she thanked him more that they had finally stopped crying.

"That was something, wasn't it?" she said to the children, astonished by her tree-jumping. Had someone asked her when she woke up this morning if she could've done anything so daring and athletic, she would've said no. Her escape from the fiend had hardly been graceful, but that she'd done it at all was a feat that defied the bounds of her previously demonstrated capabilities.

Howling cooed at Vern, while Feral fed furiously. The air was rich with the sweet tang of persimmons, and when Vern tilted her head upward, she found herself beneath a canopy of the bright fruit. Overripe, one fell from its branch and half burst onto Vern's belly. She sat herself up. All around her, fallen persimmons lay squashed and busted on the forest floor.

This good fortune had all the trappings of a fairy-tale deceit, but she'd not eaten well in days, and besides, maybe she wanted to be fattened up by a hag. It'd be a relief to be eaten up, to never more have to run for her life.

She'd bite right into the frost-coated orange fruit and pay whatever price it asked of her.

### 3

SPRING CAME IN THE END, though the season did not carry with it hope for new life. April announced itself with a body. Howling, already crawling at five months, stumbled upon the fiend's handiwork during one of his morning wanders: a dead baby deer with a pacifier in its mouth. Vern had to stop Howling from plopping the binky out the corpse and between his own lips.

At least summer brought an end to the dreary dead fawn show, and Vern was able to get some work done. She tied one babe to her hip and the other to her back in a way that made it possible to walk ten or even fifteen miles to forage without tiring.

Blackberry season stretched long this year, sweetening the air like wine all through a dusty hot August. Her hands and wrists bled from the constant prick of thorns.

She carried pounds and pounds of wild berries in a square of cloth, four corners tied together into a satchel. Her treks lasted miles, and she was greedy with her takings. She gorged herself till it felt her belly might split, then put what remained in the sun to dry as stock for winter. Some she mashed into a gritty paste and cooked into leather over embers in the August noon sun, others she left whole.

She followed suit with wild grapes, red plums, and prickly pears. For savory fare, there were bearded tooth mushrooms, wild onions, and amaranth.

Vern always had a way of getting what she needed from the earth. Her eyesight made reading difficult, so back at Cainland she preferred classes that emphasized practical work. She'd gotten special permission from Reverend Sherman and the deacon board to spend half of each school day outside, better learning the land. She was killing rabbits with air rifles by age six, launching bullets into the fleeting blurs of their light brown bodies. She had to get closer than most in order to see them, but she was a patient hunter and a decent shot. Aiming was about the body. Not the eyes. She rarely used the magnifying scope Reverend Sherman had bought her.

Last fall, before the children were born, Vern had harvested sinew from the deer carcasses the fiend had left scattered, drying the muscle fibers in sacks. In June, she'd weaved them into strings for a bow she'd made out of a young oak.

She figured her bow had only a forty-pound draw weight, but it was enough. She took down a boar after a day of tracking. Dried or smoked, it would feed her family for who knew how long.

She fished, too, made a net with dried fiber from inner basswood bark, ready for weaving after two weeks of drying. She dug up worms and affixed them to her net. Barefoot, she swirled her contraption in the river. Though her nightgown was no shield against the icy water, she did not shiver. Obstinately still, Vern had made a pact a long time ago to do the opposite of whatever was expected of her as often as possible. She and Lucy were kin in that regard. They'd done the calculations as small children. Going against tended to end more rightly, more justly, than going with. People were wrong. Rules, most of the time, favored not what was right, but what was convenient or preferable to those in charge.

"Feh," said Howling, pointing downward to the water from his spot on her waist. He was saying *fish*, and it was his first word. "Feh!"

"Don't be thinking it's all for you."

Vern cooked her daily catches over a fire, and, as with all her food, preserved the excess, smoking what remained over hardwood burned down to coal.

Foraging, fishing, hunting, trapping—if she kept at it every day and ignored her body's bids for rest, her little family might survive another winter, fiend be damned.

She hadn't stopped thinking about Reverend Sherman's hound all winter, spring, and summer. His pale, blank face dwelled uninvited in her brain like a haint. She needed to know who he was to her husband and what he had to do with her former home.

As far as Vern knew, the only white people Reverend

Sherman ever spoke to were journalists, IRS types, and social workers, who, despite surely uncovering illegal activities on the compound, never removed any of the children.

Sherman preached that Cainland's untouchability by the law was because of the God of Cain, but Vern was old enough now to know there was no God of Cain. Something else safeguarded the compound. Or someone else. The fiend was as likely a candidate as anyone. Maybe he was a sheriff who'd made a dirty deal with Sherman.

Or a judge? Like the one who gave Lucy back to her father at Cainland after her escape. Her daddy didn't just get full custody. Her mam lost the right to any contact. The way Lucy told it once she'd been forced to return, a judge who could rule in her father's favor had to be in Cainland's pocket.

Vern recalled her last night with Lucy, the few hours they'd spent together before Lucy got away again, this time for good. There was a welcome-back supper for her at Reverend Sherman's house—the year before his house was also Vern's house. It was to be a celebration of the God of Cain's will being done. He'd saved Lucy from the clutches of her mam's heathen hands and the toxicity of the outside world.

Vern had been jumping rope on the porch when Lucy and her dad arrived. Her dress was tied up almost to her knees to allow her more freedom, her handmade leather moccasins discarded somewhere out in the front yard. She was working up a sweat and smelled like what her mam called "outdoors."

"My turn!" said Lucy, running up the porch steps.

"No, ma'am," said Lucy's father sternly, pointing inside.

Reverend Sherman came outside to intervene. "Douglass, let them have their little fun. They aint seen each other in almost half a year. The God of Cain loves Black joy. Come inside while they play."

Reverend Sherman could be like that sometimes. A savior. He gestured for Douglass to come into the house, and Douglass had no choice but to obey.

"Keep it quiet. Grown folks is inside talking," Douglass told Lucy, then let the screen door shut behind him.

As soon as they were alone together on the porch, Lucy told Vern about the judge, her mouth motoring on at a rate Vern struggled to keep up with. "My mama raised money, you know, loads of it. Thousands and thousands of dollars for the best lawyers in the country, but somehow, by some antimiracle, my daddy still got custody of me. We had all the evidence. Mama had been spending months gathering up stuff in secret before she left Cainland. I'm talking photos, recordings, everything. Stuff my daddy done to me. Stuff that happens on the compound. We even had proof of the Ascensions and sleeping strapped down! I went on the stand and said everything that happened here, but it didn't make a lick of difference. Judge said my mam arranged for my kidnapping and because she'd broken the law, lost her rights to me. Bullshit. You know Reverend or somebody had to have paid him off."

Vern did crisscrosses and double jumps as Lucy spoke. At the time, she'd just been glad to have her friend back. "What's wrong with the Ascensions?" she'd asked. "Isn't it a good thing to get cleansed?"

Lucy snorted. "Now, Vern. You are the smartest girl I know. You can't believe that shit is real. It's dangerous. The water could kill you."

Vern shrugged and kept on jumping. "I like them," she said. It was the truth. She always emerged from an Ascension feeling like new, bursting with life and adrenaline and purpose.

Shaking her head, Lucy hoisted herself up on the porch railing. "That's cuz you're a masochist."

Lucy always talked about things Vern knew nothing about. She knew everything about the outside world.

"What's that?"

Lucy grabbed the bottom of Vern's sleeve and scooted it up to reveal the pink scars stretched laterally across Vern's wrist. "Somebody who does shit like this."

Vern wrenched away from Lucy and redid the button of her dress's left cuff.

Douglass, Lucy's daddy, popped his head outside. "Ruthanne needs some help inside. Come on."

"Please, Daddy, five more minutes?" asked Lucy.

His finger pointed inside. "Now. And don't talk back to me again."

"It's all right, Lucy. I'm coming inside anyway," said Vern, flinging the jump rope onto the wooden flooring of the porch before jogging toward the door.

"You pick that thing up right now," said Douglass. "I won't have you disrespecting Reverend Sherman's house."

Vern retrieved it, but when Douglass was turned away, she wrapped it around her neck and pretended it was a noose. She stuck out her tongue dramatically and bugged her eyes wide. Lucy laughed, prompting her father to turn around, but by that point Vern was already wrapping the jump rope up neatly.

"Get inside, both of you," he snapped.

Vern and Lucy grabbed each other's hands and followed Mr. Jenkins inside, making faces behind him. Everyone else was already there, gathered on the couches and chairs.

Carmichael, eight, was reading a thick book all about the ancient civilization of the Maya. He'd been annoying everybody by sharing various facts from the book at all hours.

Vern hated Carmichael for the way he read so effortlessly. Everybody loved him. He was good at school and sweet as syrup.

Vern's mam had made supper tonight, as Reverend Sherman didn't have a wife and the women of Cainland took turns cooking for him on a rotation. Tonight was spicy red beans and rice, corn-and-tomato salad, grilled maple-glazed pork chops, roasted green beans, and sweet rolls with honey butter.

"Vern, baby, set the table," said Mam.

"Lucy, go and help," said Mr. Jenkins. Everything he said was an admonishment, like Lucy should've known what he was thinking long before he even barked it out.

While the adults and Carmichael talked in the living room, Vern and Lucy took their time gathering up dishes, lazily unpacking the open-shelved cabinetry.

"I'm glad you're back," said Vern, smiling at Lucy, who was the prettiest girl in the world, buckteeth and all.

Lucy shrugged. "I aint back really," she said.

"What you mean, you aint back? You're right there, goofy," said Vern, rolling her eyes.

"Well, I'm back now, but not for much longer. Don't tell Reverend Sherman or my daddy, but somebody's coming to get me tonight," she whispered, a big old grin on her face. She didn't care she was ruining Vern's life. "Mama said we was stupid trying to win against Cainland in the courts, so we're just going. Getting new identities and everything."

"That's stupid," said Vern.

"You'd like it out there, Vernie. You can watch TV and movies all the time. And Auntie makes the best corn pudding. She makes the best everything, actually," Lucy said. "And have you ever heard of earrings? I can't remember if I told you about them before. I'm getting me some of those, too. They slit a hole in your ear and you can hang jewelry off it."

Vern carried the finished dishes from the counter to the big dining table, laying down a folded tea towel under each item.

There was sweet tea and lemonade in the icebox, and Vern poured herself a glass of the two mixed together. "Sounds dumb to me," said Vern. "I got enough holes. Too many damn holes. I don't want another way inside me."

"You're just mad because you can't come with me."

"Yes, I can," said Vern.

"How?" asked Lucy.

"I could just leave," she said, tasting a bit of the beans from the large wooden mixing spoon.

"You can't just leave."

"If you can, why can't I?"

"Because nobody's coming to get you," said Lucy.

"I don't need nobody to come get me. I can just walk right out to the gates and go."

"Pshhh," said Lucy, shaking her head. "You too much of a goddamn chicken for that. You can't do anything without me." Lucy lifted the glass top off the cake display tray. Looking Vern right in the eye, she dipped her finger into the glaze of the sock-it-to-me cake and licked it. To prove herself, Vern did the same, taking an even bigger chunk of the sticky white sweetness.

Lucy scooped off more, then Vern did, and back and forth until the cake was light brown and glazeless.

"Girls, what are you doing in there?" called Vern's mam from the other room.

"Nothing!" they both cried in unison as they set the cake tray onto the table, grabbed forks, and ate the whole thing together in a race to the finish.

"You can come with me *if* you promise to make me this cake every day," said Lucy.

"I'll make you whatever you want whenever you want," Vern said.

"I'll make you stuff sometimes, too," said Lucy. "Just don't expect it to be tasting this good."

Vern grinned and Lucy did, too, but when Lucy's daddy came in, he went after his daughter hard, grabbing the same wooden spoon Vern had used to taste the red beans to thwack her several times on the bottom, pushing her out the kitchen toward the front door, all the while Lucy yelling, "It don't even hurt, ugly," to her father.

"See you later, Vern!" Lucy had called, giggling even as her father gave her a whooping. "Don't forget that cake recipe."

Vern never saw her again, her friend whisked away by her mother to a life outside the compound with earrings and movies.

Remembering that night now, she couldn't help but think about that judge. Could he be the same man as the fiend?

"Feh! Feh! Feh!"

"Yes, fish," said Vern, startling, only half an ear to her babe. She couldn't see the wiggling creatures he pointed to below the ambling water, but she felt their slimy bodies slither against her calves. Feral was asleep on her back, oblivious, snoring like an old man.

Whenever Vern was on to something with the fiend, there were the children, reminding her that they could be her only focus. Neither could say the word *Mam* or *Mama*, but they spoke it with their every breath and need. They sweat *Mam*, blinked *Mam*, fussed *Mam*, hungered *Mam*, gurgled *Mam*, spit up *Mam*, shat *Mam*, pissed *Mam*, misbehaved *Mam*.

Their endless demands should've made Vern more sympathetic of her own mother, who bulldozed through life by feigning relentless positivity. It had been clear to Vern from a young age that the life her mam had was not the life she had hoped for growing up.

She never admitted this. She never admitted any untoward feeling. *I guess it's easy to be so positive with a constant blood alcohol level of point-one-five percent,* Lucy had said once about Vern's mother. Vern repeated the remark the next time Mam told her to cheer up, and for two weeks the woman uttered not a word to Vern.

It was the first time Vern understood conclusively that facades could be cracked. When Mam became her mind-numbing cheery self again, Vern didn't mind. Lies could be revealed. What beautiful knowledge.

Whatever Vern managed in the mothering department, it surpassed her mam's approach: alcohol and platitudes. To the woman's credit, Vern was, in fact, *keeping calm and carrying on*. Letting go and letting God. Learning that where there was a will, there was, indeed, a way.

Vern lived. She made gear. Hats to fit her babies' fat yam heads, a linen gown, two wool pullovers and two pairs of knee socks, leggings made of rabbit furs for winter. She did what she could to not die.

In these days, days of endless summer, infinitely lonely days, Vern rarely thought of much but her own vigorous breath. Cainland and the fiend should've been her priority, but with her babes to look after, those questions became accessories. She did no more than what needed doing, a burrowing orphan, digging, digging forward, making her world.

# 4

ONE BRIGHT SEPTEMBER EVENING hot as freshly whipped flesh, Vern tied cloth to Howling and Feral's waists, the other end to a tree. She let them wander in the shallow water near the bank while she fished. As she was hauling her winnings back toward them, she saw Howling, all dark and darker so from sun, rolling away into the water. Her little one, her firstborn, had been taken by the rushing river.

"Howling!" she called, dropping her net and all the fish within it. She waded and waded as fast as she could till the water grew deep and she had to swim. Pondweed, slimy and numerous, glided against her calves. Something thick and tubular slunk between her thighs, either a water moccasin or a fish.

"Howling, where are you?" she called, overwhelmed by the coursing water. It splashed her face and flooded her eyes. It slid into her throat, then sprang back out as she coughed with the burn of it. "Why don't you scream, child?" she called out through stifled breaths. "You know I need you to scream for me! Scream!"

Her gown clung to her skin, pressing her backward and down. She reached forward, praying her finger might grasp Howling's ankle or wrist. Desperately, she pawed a soft mat of curls, thinking it her babe's hair, but it was only star grass. A piece of driftwood lifted her hopes once more, but, softened by water, it dissolved in her hands.

"Howling!" she called again, and she ducked her head under to search. Her voice warbled in the water as she sobbed her child's name. Vern could not make herself stop swimming, no matter how hopeless the cause. This was surely her own sin catching up with her—for hadn't she thought the night he was born to leave him to the mercy of the river?

The cold numbed her, and a cramp knotted her abdomen. She was about to slip under the water into the dark when, finally, she saw him. He'd been caught by a large branch just ahead and to the side. "I'm coming, baby," she called.

Vern swam to him, fighting the current to move toward the bank.

"Howling," she said, coughing up water and rubbing her eyes. "Howling. Baby."

It was not her kin. It was not her babe. This child was older, five or even six, dressed in brown linen rags. She'd seen him back upriver and assumed it was Howling. "Oh, little one," she said, half with guilty relief that it wasn't her babe who was dead. "Where is your mam?"

She wrestled the child's body to the bank and laid it down over a patch of long brown grass. "Oh, sweet thing," she said. Vern thought to give him mouth-to-mouth but the body was already stiff with death. He'd been dead long before she'd first seen him.

Vern shivered. She knew a lot about drowning. Had done it many times back at the compound. "If I'd known you were here, I'd have taught you to swim." She looked around, hopeful a caretaker was close by, a mother, a grandmother, a father, an uncle, someone who might see to the child's burial, someone who might kiss his forehead and dress him properly before laying them to rest.

"Somebody!" she called. "Have you lost your littlun?"

But the child had no one. He'd survived alone in the woods by his wits, much like Vern had done. "I will come back for you," she promised, drawing her thumb across his cheek. "But I got to return to my own children." She kissed him one more time.

By the time she hiked back to her children upriver, they were both napping, curled up into each other like was often the case—and alive. It was not usual for them to nap so late in the day anymore. Seeing her go, they must've cried and fussed until they were spent and collapsed.

She strapped her sleeping babies to her. Goodness, how indecent, to be brought to such stirs of emotion, to be so entrenched. Nothing in this great wide earth was built to last, and life was not a prettiful thing. Her Howling, her Feral, they'd die, and before that have troubles aplenty that would make them wish they would die. Knowing that, why was it not easier to rein her passion for their wellness into something less hot and unkempt?

Once at camp, she crawled into their shelter and put Howling and Feral upon the thicket of compressed leaves. It wasn't a proper bed, was it? It wasn't where babes should sleep, atop composting earth matter, the smell of wet and rot and smoke all around.

Walking out of the Blessed Acres of Cain had seemed a miracle, the compound of little wooden houses surrounding the prayer temple, sad squares in her wake, but maybe Sherman's ravings about the outside world were correct. Everything beyond Cainland's borders was the devil incarnate, and she'd dragged her babes right past the beast's tender uvula into the throat. Vern wrapped herself around her babes, tucking their forms into the C-fold of her body. Their whistling breaths lulled her to sleep, a sleep that dragged on and on, until it was much past dark. She awoke to find both her babes feeding from her, recovered from any earlier distress. Coyotes yipped and howled in the night, merry witches tearing flesh asunder. Was it the dead child they feasted upon?

Vern sat up with a start. She'd forgotten the poor thing in her fatigue. It was too late now to go back, for only ugliness awaited her there. Ants and flies, odors and graying skin.

It was a neglect most uncivilized to leave that wee one to the beasts, but Vern couldn't bear to return to find the child was now missing an arm. Or what if its belly had been opened up by scavengers like a jar of jam? Worse, perhaps the fiend had found him and tied a baby bonnet to his head. There were a thousand ways to defile perfection. Tonight she couldn't handle the whole weight of the nasty universe flooding into her.

"Shh, shh," she said when Feral started to fuss as he fell back to sleep. Howling was already dozing again. It was late enough that they'd likely sleep through till morning, and for that she was glad. Anxious about the drownt child, sick with fear for her own babes, Vern needed to be in her own body.

When the twins were sleeping soundly, she secured their shelter and went outside. There was no fire this evening to light her way, and she liked it like that. She welcomed the dark. She only wished it was colder, wished it was winter. A harsh wind would sweep her back into this world and away from the world of the strange child she'd failed. His spirit seemed to tug at her. He was lonely.

Vern took off her dirty nightgown, still damp, and slung it over a tree branch to air out and dry. She changed into something fresh, then fed herself from her store of berries. She had no appetite, but the seedy tart flesh wakened her mouth, tongue, and throat. So what if each morsel sat like a stone in her stomach? At least she was reminded she had a stomach. She ate until her body threatened to heave it all back up.

Vern tossed the now-empty berry satchel into a pile of dirty linens then rested in a squat next to a tree. Using a long stick, she drew a protective circle around herself. Fidgety and uneasy, she stabbed the dirt with the stick until it snapped, a piece of it scraping against her palm and breaking skin. With the remainder of the splintered wood, she prodded the wound farther open to see if she could get a look at the blood inside. She picked at it the way a child worried at a scab.

As Vern tossed the stick into the brush, she turned toward a new odor in the air. The scent of burning startled her from her grief. She wiped her eyes, which somewhere in the last several minutes had become watery with tears.

The forest air reeked, and Vern retched. She could tell this was the fiend's doing by the smell. He'd thrown rancid meat in a fire to fill the woods with the ripe fetor of death.

Vern hid her shelter and the babies inside with extra branches and leaves, hid her pack, and followed the smoke. "I'll be back soon, babies," she called, though they were too deep in sleep to hear. She'd be safer staying put with them, but she was too uneasy to sit calmly. She needed to move and feel the mass of her legs and the springs of her feet.

Vern cut a path through the bush and bramble. It was as dark now as it had been the night she'd stumbled away from the howling wolves, but she'd been in the woods a year now. While she still struggled to see clearly, experience made her steps more confident. She kept her gait short and her body steady by crouching. Legs bent, half-squatted, she didn't trip so easily.

The bonfire still burned when Vern found the fiend's campsite. It lit the area bright as day. The odor was thick, and Vern bit back a gag. Animal corpses circled the fire, each creature dressed in or arranged with the trappings of infanthood.

As with all summers in the woods, it was a dry night. The bonfire spit flames taller than Vern, and there was a good chance it'd catch and bring the whole woods to ashes. Finally, the fiend had grown tired of his games and had made a plan to burn down Vern's home, her and her babes along with it. At least it was a true move, a real act, something she could respond to properly.

Vern rushed to the fire, hopping over the animals to clear away the nearby brush. Dried kindling and leaves were all around, no doubt placed perfectly for the purpose of causing the most spread. No sparks had caught yet, but there was a warm wind making its way through the trees. It would carry the embers far.

After clearing the immediate area, Vern headed toward a low-hanging branch stooped over the tall flames. It was thicker than her upper arm and would be impossible to remove by force. Vern removed the knife from her boot and sawed the wood near the base of the branch. Once she'd cut an inch or two deep, she put away the knife and pulled down the branch with all her might.

Vern hung from the branch and pulled down, eyes shut. It cracked under her weight with ease, and in the space of a second Vern was on her feet, the amputated branch in her hands. She tossed it to the side away from the fire. Despite its size and heavy weight, it landed twenty feet away.

Vern grabbed a stick and drilled it into the ground, breaking up the earth. The floor of the woods was dry and densely packed. It should've resisted Vern's efforts, but she smashed the ground open in a single strike. She loaded her arms with earth and tossed it onto the fire, then dug more dirt, repeating the sequence until the fire was out. She'd put out a bonfire with a stick.

Vern turned when she caught movement to her side. A rustle of clothing, of leaves. A dark figure in the distance, no doubt the fiend, darted away. Vern stared after him, unmoving. The fire was out. She should go home to her babes.

Where the fiend was running, toward the edge of the woods, was no place for her. This was Vern's world, in the dark. She lived in the place where trees stood as mighty as gods. Hands on her knees, Vern tried to catch her breath. Restless energy darted through her.

She could still hear the patter of the fiend's feet against the ground, the sway of leaves as he brushed against bushes and trees. Vern, her good sense overtaken by desire, gave chase. The air against her face was intoxicatingly bracing. This was the feeling she'd been longing for when gorging herself on berries, when cutting her palm. She was half animal now, only instinct and need.

She leapt over a fallen branch and hopped through a scattering of dead logs. Trees thwacked her face as she ran. Her legs should've been tired, but they felt fresh and unbothered, brand-new legs recently attached. She ran until there was nowhere left to run. Vern had made it to the edge of her world. She'd reached the place where the trees, for just a moment, stopped. A road split their pine kingdom in two. The fiend darted across it, slipping into the woods on the other side. Vern ran after him but stumbled when a long bellow roared in her ears. Someone was honking at her. A pickup truck grazed Vern's side, knocking her to the ground. Dazed, Vern scrabbled up, another car hurtling by, swerving sharply to the right with a loud screech.

Vern jogged on wobbly feet off the road. After a year in the woods, she'd forgotten about cars. She wiped her eyes, still wet and buzzing from the siege of bright white from the headlights.

Down the road, music blared, real music—not one of her damn gospel lullabies, not birdsong, not a nursery rhyme for the twins. Music with instruments and a beat, music you could dance to. Vern closed her eyes and swayed back and forth to the faint noises. Too far away to make out the words, she walked toward it. One step, then another, then another, until her good sense came back to her. She turned toward the woods. That was where she belonged. With her children, where the world made sense. No one lied in the woods. No one charged you money for a decent meal in the woods. No one charged you rent. No one balked at the way you looked or smiled when what they really wanted was to devour you.

Yet it would take Vern ages to locate her camp in the dark. She'd lost track of her whereabouts when chasing the fiend. If she waited until first light, it'd be a quicker trek. Besides, she'd lost all her fish today chasing the drownt child. If she followed the music, maybe there'd be a place to steal food.

Vern hurried again toward the music until she found its source, a small cabin-like structure with a neon sign. It wasn't much more than a shack, its white paint faded. It seemed to Vern, best as she could tell, a white-people sort of place. A row of motorcycles sat in a line outside, a small crowd gathered around it talking. The music playing was country.

There was nothing else around, no convenience stores, no fried-fish joints or barbecue spots. The neon-signed wooden shack was an island in a dark rural wasteland. "You lost, girlie?" somebody asked, and Vern stumbled backward in surprise, barely catching herself before falling.

"I'm fine," said Vern, voice trembling, knowing how she must look. She was wearing one of her Cainite dresses, the sleeves ripped off and the hem cut from ankle-length to be above the knee. Dirt and ash smeared her face. Sweat clung to her. Leaves and seedpods in her hair, which she gave only a cursory comb with her fingers every now and then.

"Something happen to you, honey?" asked a woman dressed in leather, a bottle in one hand.

"I'm fine," said Vern again, voice hard now. She'd not let it shake in front of these strangers again.

Truth was, she was better than fine. She'd just cracked open the ground and put out a bonfire, had torn a thick branch from a tree and tossed it away like it was a ball. She didn't know where that rush of adrenaline had come from, but it was still in her, pulsating.

"I think you might be looking for someplace else," said one of the men. He had a long, dark beard and a shiny bald head.

"How do you know I wasn't looking for you?" Vern asked, walking right up to him. No one had ever once accused her of being sensible. "There someplace I can get cleaned up?" she asked.

"Bathroom's just inside," a woman said, pointing.

Vern opened the creaky door. Sherman would have a fit to know she was at a place like this. She smiled as she pushed into the bathroom and for the first time in a year took a leak in a toilet. It really was like a throne. So high up. No squatting involved. She felt like she should be stealing people's grain and granting pardons to all the wrong people.

The mirrors above the sinks were too scratched and dirty to make sense of her reflection, but she splashed her face and neck with water and scrubbed them with pink gel hand soap until she guessed they were clean. She soaked her hair through and gave it a shake, combing out the caked-in earth and plant matter with her fingers.

Back outside, the crowd had largely cleared, and Vern rubbed her hands along the motorcycles, admiring their size and power, their silver and black sleekness. There was nothing sleek in the woods. Everything had gnarls and knobs.

"You ride?" someone asked.

Vern turned to see a woman leaning against the building, a cigarette in her mouth. She wore high-waisted jeans that seemed too big for her, with a belt cinched tightly, a tucked-in tee. Her red hair was chopped into a bowl cut, and the strands fell into her eyes. Vern stepped closer to get a better look and saw piercings in the woman's nose and in her ears.

"Well?" she asked.

"No," said Vern.

The woman nodded, then flicked ash from her cigarette onto the ground. "That one's mine," she said, pointing. Vern walked up to her bike. Smaller and slimmer than the rest, it stood apart.

"She's vintage, 1966. Honda Super Hawk. You like?"

Vern shrugged as she took the motorcycle in, but inside she was salivating, admiring its shape and form. The bike was a metal mare, moody and unstoppable. She could carry Vern to the other side of the world. On a bike like that, no one would ever think to stop her. You didn't get in the way of a girl on a bike like that. "I call her Lucille. Lucy for short."

Vern whipped her head toward the woman. "What?"

"Lucy, after Lucille Ball, you know? Cause she's a spitfire, and I painted her red."

"Right," said Vern, though she didn't know of any Lucille Ball. Vern knew only one Lucy. Her Lucy. The most important Lucy. And her last name wasn't Ball. It was Jenkins.

"I'm Ollie, by the way," the woman said.

"I'm—" Vern cut herself off. "You can call me V."

Ollie dropped the butt of her cigarette onto the ground. "You want to take a ride, V?"

Vern looked up. "With you?"

"I don't see anybody else offering."

Vern ran her thumb over the bike. "I don't know how," said Vern. "And I don't know you." Though it wouldn't be the first time she'd taken a ride with someone she didn't know. After Lucy left Cainland that second and final time, Vern had thought getting in a car with a stranger was her only course to freedom. Like Lucy had said, nobody was coming for Vern. She had to put her salvation into the arms of a random passerby.

Back when she'd lived in the compound, Vern would amble to the part of the woods that butted up against the road whenever she could get away from her duties. She'd stick her thumb out to passing cars, but only once did someone stop. A patrolling police officer. He'd rolled down his window and asked her, *How much?*

She'd understood the kind of transaction the man was after, and the price she named was escape. *Just take me as far away from here as you can.*

That didn't happen. When they were finished, he drove her to the main gates of the Blessed Acres and called Reverend Sherman. He told him he'd caught her in a man's truck.

Vern had sat with her head bowed in the back of the police cruiser, brow furrowed in consternation.

It wasn't being turned in that had upset her—she was used to being Cainland's black sheep. It was that Reverend Sherman's words about cops had proved true. He'd called policemen treacherous devils sent out to kill, punish, and enslave.

That cop had taken what he wanted from her and for no other reason than cruelty tried to expose her. If he represented the law of the land outside the Blessed Acres, then the sermons were right. Damn the outside world right to hell. What goodness could there be in a place who'd made men like that their kings?

She was thirteen and a half years old the day she'd become certain there was no place on earth free of injustice. Neither in Cainland nor outside it. Wherever Lucy had escaped to, was it any better?

But a woman on a motorcycle didn't have much in common with a police officer.

"I guess I'll see you around, then," said Ollie, and fastened her helmet on. She kicked her leg over the bike so she was straddling it.

Vern stuck her hands into the pockets she'd sewn onto her hemmed dress, rocked back and forth from right leg to left. "Where are you going anyway?"

Ollie leaned forward on the handlebars, squeezing her hands around the leather grips. "Anywhere I want."

Vern raised an eyebrow at the nonanswer. "That's the kind of thing an old friend of mine would've said."

Lucy was always reminding people just how in charge she was of her own life even though it was obviously not true. It wasn't true for anybody at the Blessed Acres. She'd been dragged there by her parents and had gotten to leave only when her mother could orchestrate her escape.

Vern had made her own way out. "If I get on the bike with you, you promise to take me back here when we're all done?"

"Don't know why you'd want me to. It's redneck central. But all right," Ollie said, tucking a strand of short, wavy red hair behind her ear. She looked like someone who'd never once cared about anything.

Vern shifted her gaze back toward the honky-tonk, then toward the woods, then finally back to the woman inviting her on a ride away from it all. "Are you going to hurt me?" Vern asked.

Ollie removed a half-smoked cigarette from a tin case in her side jeans pocket, then placed it between her lips, worrying but not lighting it. "I end up hurting most people," she said, "despite my best efforts."

Vern shivered. She was like a broken windup toy, titillated by the slightest provocation. Ollie need only exude an air of danger to pique Vern's interest. "How old are you?" Vern asked.

"Too old for you," said Ollie. "That a problem?"

Vern licked her bottom lip, took one last breath, then climbed onto the back of the bike. "Put that on," said Ollie, handing Vern a helmet, "and hold on."

"Hold on where?"

Ollie reached around and grabbed Vern's hands, placed them onto her belly. "Tighter," said Ollie.

Vern wiggled herself into the bike seat. Her cheeks warmed.

"You okay?"

"Fine," said Vern.

Ollie turned on the engine and Vern yelped at the rumbling beneath her. She grabbed on more tightly, scooting herself up so their bodies were flush, Vern's front to Ollie's back.

They pulled out the parking lot and onto the pebbled road, Ollie ramping up the speed. Vern, taken over by the glee of it, warm wind and speed and heart racing, shouted and whooped.

They were in the darkness, Vern and Ollie both shooting stars flinging across the black.

On either side of them, trees hovered overhead. The woods had always seemed majestic from the inside. From the road, they seemed nothing but a murky shadow, a dream she'd been lost in for all this time.

Vern didn't mind the smack of bugs against the helmet visor. Ollie had rock music turned up loud, just audible over the engine. Vern bopped her head to it. Even the gaseous odor of exhaust pleased her.

They'd been riding for twenty minutes when Ollie slowed the bike down and pulled it to the side of the road, the neon-signed wooden shack miles in their wake.

"You tell me you can go anywhere in the world, and this is where you choose?" asked Vern, but she followed Ollie off the bike and tore off her helmet. She was still high on music and people, on the rush of wind. What a strange thing, to have a conversation with a person old enough to talk back.

"Didn't want to take you too far from the honky-tonk," Ollie said. She grabbed Vern's hand and pulled her off the roadside into the woods. Vern licked her lips as she tripped over stones and sticks, dragged by this stranger.

Finally, Ollie jolted to a stop and pressed Vern against the thick trunk of a tree. Vern hated the sound of her breaths, fragmented and weak with need. For months and months she'd been alone in the woods, but for her babes and the fiend.

"You want this?" asked Ollie, her forehead against Vern's.

Vern nodded, teeth sunk into her bottom lip. "Sure," she whispered, afraid that if she said so any more loudly, Sherman would hear and track her down. Standing next to the tree, he'd launch into a lecture about how the hormones, antibiotics, and altered genes in food off the compound could stimulate unnatural lesbian attractions.

He'd lament letting her eat too much fast food on their various mission trips in town, and she'd be forced onto a year-long raw food diet to cleanse, like Sister Jay, whose main sin, as far as Vern could tell, was a deep voice. She had what Cainites called a mannish nature: fat, broad, and, though affable, not in a womanly way. *This is not how a woman's body is supposed to look*, Sherman claimed during one of his sermons. To his credit, he did not hold up a picture of Sister Jay, just a picture of a woman who looked like Sister Jay. *If you look at photos of our African ancestors, at our brethren, you see they are lithe, healthy, trim, fit. Hunters who rule over the land with grace and beauty. It is not until we are damaged by the white man's food that our bodies become twisted toward perversion. Disease, fatness, so-called autism, depression, homosexuality. Men who think they're women and women who think they're men.*

"I'll be gentle," said Ollie, leaning in for a kiss.

Vern shook her head. "Don't."

Ollie brushed her lips against Vern's. They were with each other till morning.

⊠

THE SUN HAD BARELY BEGUN TO RISE when Ollie dropped Vern back at the wooden shack. "You're grinning," Ollie said, brushing red hair from her forehead to the side.

"I'm not," said Vern, and if she had been, she wasn't anymore. She schooled her face into its customary frown.

"You sure you got someplace you can go? You can come back to mine if you want."

"Nah, my friend is going to pick me up," said Vern.

"Can I see you again?"

Vern sucked her bottom lip with her teeth. "I don't know."

"If I write down my number for you, will you take it?" Ollie asked, but she was already scrawling it down on a crumpled napkin she'd removed from her jeans pocket. Vern took it and folded it up. "There's a phone inside the Bert's whenever you want to call."

"The Bert's?"

Ollie pointed to the wooden shack. "Call me, if you want."

"They'll let me use the phone? I don't have to pay or nothing?" asked Vern, eyes fastened on the door. There were only a couple of bikes in the parking lot now. She wondered how much longer the place was still open.

Ollie took a wallet out of her back pocket, took out two bills, then handed them to Vern. "It helps if you buy something."

Vern took the money. After a several-second pause, Vern said, "Well, have a good day, I guess."

Ollie pulled the visor of her helmet down. "Bye, V." She got onto her bike and drove off down the road. When she was out of sight, Vern went into the Bert's. "We close in ten," said the barkeep.

"I just want to use the phone," Vern said. Now that she'd returned to civilization, she was tempted by all its fruit.

The barkeep pointed to a sign. "What's it say?" she asked. "I can't see." She couldn't read, either, but he didn't have to know that.

The barkeep looked up at her, pausing to stare. He must've noticed her eyes now, the way the eyeballs had a shake to them. People rarely noticed at first glance, but when they got close enough, they could see the nystagmus clearly. "Does it look like the whole world's moving?" he asked, then swept out his arms to the side and started to move like he was bracing for an earthquake.

"Just tell me what the sign says," said Vern.

The barkeep blew out an annoyed breath. "Bathroom is for customers only. Phone, too. That's not on the sign directly, but it's in the spirit of the sign."

"Can I get some wings, then?" she asked.

The barkeep pointed to another sign. "That one says the kitchen closes at midnight." He pointed to a clock. "And that says it's five forty-five."

"What about a root beer?"

The barkeep grunted but sprayed brown soda into a tall glass and pushed it to her. Next, he set a black cordless phone by her side. She pulled it close to her face to see the numbers, but she didn't really need to. She'd memorized the pattern of Lucy's auntie's number ages ago.

*The number you are trying to reach is no longer in service.*

It always said that. Vern didn't know why she thought that maybe here, from a phone not on the compound, it would work.

"You said it's nearly six, right?" asked Vern. Wake-up on the compound was at 5:00. Morning prayers were at 6:00. Vern's mother often spent that in-between time in Reverend Sherman's office organizing deliveries on and off the compound for the day, using Cainland's single landline phone.

That was a holdover from the Eamon Fields days. In the first year or two of the Blessed Acres' existence, each family home had a line. As Eamon rose in prominence and renown among the settlers, he'd encouraged a paranoia about outsiders destroying their group and the prosperity they'd achieved. He suggested limiting phone access to a select few, the men who made up Claws' loosely organized leadership council. Later, when he invented the position of Reverend and filled it, he took away all the phones but his. Off the back of the group's radical vision, he'd made his own personal theme park to play in. Cainland™. He knew how to maneuver himself into power.

Vern was grateful his megalomania meant there was only one phone number to memorize, at least, and dialed. It rang three times, then: "You've reached the Blessed Acres. You're speaking to Ruthanne. How can I help you this blessed morning?"

Vern closed her eyes upon hearing the familiar refrain. She recognized her mother's voice immediately. It hadn't aged or changed. It wasn't quivery with grief for having lost Vern. It was the voice of a woman who loved Reverend Sherman and loved Cainland. She hadn't changed at all. Here she was as she had been a year ago, doing her duty, sounding chipper to do so.

"Hello?" Ruthanne said when Vern didn't answer. "Anyone there?"

Vern could not breathe, let alone speak. She'd stepped into a pocket of the world outside of time where she was a little girl again back on the compound, sitting under Reverend Sherman's desk while her mam worked the phone.

"Hello?" Ruthanne repeated, this time in a rushed whisper. Though Vern's mam was many, many miles away, she felt the woman's manner shift. "Who is this? Who's there?"

"It's me," said Vern, filled with such abrupt longing for her mother she thought she might disintegrate from the lack of her. Ribbons of brine streaked her cheeks.

"Right. Mrs. Humphrey. Yes, we'd be happy to accept the library's book donations. I'll call you back as soon as I can arrange a good time for drop-off. Have a blessed day."

The line disconnected with an audible click but not a moment later began to ring. Before the barkeep could grab the phone from her, Vern pulled it away from his grasping hand and answered. "Hello?"

Vern let a long, shaky breath stutter through the phone's speaker. "Mam? That you?"

The voice on the other end of the call trembled wordlessly. "Is this a joke?" asked Ruthanne.

Vern exhaled. "It's no joke. It's me. It's Vern."

Ruthanne's breaths cut through the line, loud as death gasps. "No. No. God of Cain, no. They said you were gone. They said God of Cain raptured you in the night."

The relief Vern felt to be talking to her mother was short-lived. "And you believed that?"

"Of course not, Vern. But I thought Reverend Sherman might've—I wondered if he'd killed you. I figured you'd back-talked one too many times and that bastard did what he does." The familiarity with which Ruthanne said *did what he does* revealed a side of Vern's mam previously hidden. This mam knew what the reverend was.

"You really thought there was a chance Sherman could kill me and you let me marry him?" asked Vern.

"I didn't *let* you marry him," Ruthanne protested. She and Vern remembered it very differently.

The proposal happened the day Vern had been with that cop. Sherman sat behind his desk in the temple office and called Vern's mam in. She strode inside and pulled Vern into a posses-sive hug. "Did he—Vern—did he make you do something? Oh Lord, you're all right, baby, you're all right. It's not your fault." She turned to Sherman and pleaded, "She doesn't know no better. You understand that, right?"

Sherman placed a few stray sheets of paper into a stack, then took a sip of coffee. "Of course, Sister Ruthanne. I would not even be surprised if that officer made up the entire incident."

Ruthanne let Vern go and took a seat on the plastic-covered

floral sofa next to her eldest child. "It's not your fault, honey, no matter what happened."

"The police officer is the one I done it with," admitted Vern brazenly. "He was lying about another man."

Vern's eyes shrank away from the beams of midafternoon light coming in through the open window. Sherman adjusted his glasses, then scratched a patch of his cheek covered by beard. "I'm sorry that you had to experience firsthand what we mean when we talk about the nastiness of the white man, and specifically of police."

Ruthanne exhaled, relieved he didn't appear angry at Vern. She grasped her daughter's left hand firmly between both of hers, kissing it over and over. "But I am concerned," said Sherman, "that this was allowed to happen. The point of the Blessed Acres is to spare our citizens the very pain you are feeling right now," he said. His voice boomed like he was up behind the pulpit, and she felt his words fill her.

In that moment, Vern had envied his surety. What a gift it must be to feel always in the right, to walk through life with only specks of doubt, easily dismissed or rubbed out like a smear of pen ink on your finger.

"You're special, Vern. You may think I dislike your rebellious spirit, but I cherish it. You keep me honest. But it also makes you especially vulnerable to outside influences. It is of utmost importance that you are protected from the cruelties and dangers of that world. That's why, even though it's not conventional, I'd like to take you as my wife," said Sherman.

Her mother grunted sharply but covered it quickly with a smile. "Now, Sherman, though I know you only have my baby's best interests at heart, I'm not sure such a young girl should be rushed into marriage and all that entails."

*And all that entails.* Vern's mam was good with words, knew how to layer them so they meant multiple things simultaneously.

Sherman nodded in agreement, but Vern stilled at the look on his face, like he'd just seen three moves ahead in a game of chess and knew he was going to take Ruthanne's queen.

"Age as we tend to think of it today is a very Western concept," he said. "This strict separation of adulthood and childhood in the modern sense was born of whiteness. In Africa, there were nations where boys became men at eleven, girls became women at twelve. We know in Cain that, just as children are full of so much wisdom and perspective, adults can be childish and immature. It's a continuum, and especially considering Vern's spiritual nature, she is older than her years and I think quite ready."

Vern's mother didn't have a ready response. The things Sherman said were so wrong sometimes that one didn't know where to start with a retort. Or everything he said was right, but still a lie.

"I promise I won't do it again," said Vern, standing up.

"I know you won't do it again, because you are a smart woman," Sherman said. "This is not a punishment."

Vern could tell by the lightness of his voice and from context that he was smiling widely, but he looked little more than a blur through the suddenly gathering tears in her spasmodic eyes.

The wedding was held at night under a full moon so the sun posed no hindrance to Vern with her melaninless skin and light-averse eyes. There were fireworks for days. A haze of color that made Vern think of getting raptured. Sometimes, at temple, when the congregation sang after one of Sherman's rousing sermons, Vern could forget she was alive, so taken by the beauty of the music. She wondered if that was what it felt like for everyone else all the time. Not alone. Though a wedding joined people together, Vern had felt none of the sense of communion on that night like she had felt during those temple gospel renditions. On the converse, she could swear everybody was singing on the other side of a glass wall, a soundproof glass wall. They were all making music, and she could not hear.

Not that Sherman Fields was the worst husband. He didn't force her into *marriage and all that entails*. She took care of that all her own. After a few months of endless sadness, she began to want him. To want someone. She craved the hot closeness of coupling, the gutting, vibrant squalor of that time with the cop. The fear. The pain. She wanted it all back. She wanted Lucy. When you can't fill a hole with goodness, fill it with filth. Paint it over.

There. Just like new.

"You could've done more to stop it," Vern said into the receiver now, concealing the notes of bewildered and disappointed sadness in her voice with those of anger. She had asked Ruthanne to fight against the wedding, but her mam had said, *No one said it's easy being a woman, did they? I know you never caught me saying that.*

Ruthanne sighed on the other end of the line. "What do you want me to say? Sorry? Sorry life's absolute shit? Of course I am. I *am*. You want me to say you didn't deserve it? No one does."

Vern was shaking now, every bit as hotheaded as she'd always been accused of being. "You haven't changed. You thought Reverend Sherman actually had killed me, and you're still on his compound playing secretary? What's wrong with you, Mam?"

"I can't click my heels together and be somewhere else, because there is nowhere else. These things always look easy to a child, and that's just what you are. I can't just leave."

"I did."

"And how are you getting by, Vern? Do you have a job? An apartment? I don't even have my birth certificate. Reverend Sherman's got that. I don't have yours, neither. Or Carmichael's.

I don't even exist. Where would I go? How would I survive? Where would I get food?"

"You'd figure it out. Like I did. I'm a mam now, too, did you forget? You best believe I'd never let mine anywhere near the likes of Sherman," Vern snapped, not that she was a good mam herself. She'd forgotten her babes until this very moment when she'd needed to make a rhetorical point against her mother. Last night they'd slipped from her mind—more accurately and less flatteringly, she pushed them from it. Enticed by bright lights, she'd abandoned them in the woods. She'd given in to the exhaustion of caring for them.

"I got to go," said Vern.

"Please. Don't. I didn't mean to start a fight. That's why I called you back, because I want to talk to you. I love you, Vern, so much, no matter what you might think," Ruthanne said.

The bar now was empty aside from Vern, but the barkeep was too busy eavesdropping to want to kick her out. "What was that all about anyway? Why did you hang up on me?"

Mam's voice dropped to a husky whisper. "I'm pretty sure the phone is bugged. Had to call you back on my burner."

Vern couldn't imagine her mother with an illicit phone. "What's Sherman need to tap the phone for? He's up in everybody's business anyway. You can't take a shit without a deacon reporting it to him," said Vern.

"Not him. Outsiders. I don't know who. Feds, maybe. Tryna take the place down, tryna build a case against us."

Vern filed that nugget away. Feds, or Reverend Sherman's goons? Feds, or the fiend?

Or maybe Sherman had done it himself, knowing Vern was weak and would try to call her mother.

"You know it's all lies, don't you?" asked Vern.

"What's lies?"

"Everything. About Cainland."

"Here and everywhere else, baby," Ruthanne said. She sounded sympathetic to Vern's plight, her voice gentle and understanding. Where was all that camaraderie when Vern was back at the compound?

"Do you know what the hauntings are, Mam?"

When Ruthanne didn't answer, Vern checked to make sure the call was still connected.

"Mam?"

"You still getting them?" Ruthanne asked finally. "It's drugs, I suspect. Hallucinogens."

Vern spat out a disgusted, half-formed laugh. Her mam had known all this time, while Vern, falsely branded the skeptic of Cainland, had dumbly believed.

Vern wasn't there in person to see it, but she could imagine her mam's lips pinched into an offended pucker. "It's harmless. A way to bring the community together so we can bond over the shared experience. You don't know what it's like to be without a real home. You've never known what it's like to be truly without a place, a family. Cainland makes homes for people; it just does it in unusual ways."

Something was wrong with Vern's mam if she thought Vern could still be recruited, still be swindled. "You can't really think after all this time I would trust your opinion. Yet here you are, blah-blah-blahing at me. Maybe you think if you can convince me, you can convince yourself you were justified in keeping me there."

Vern felt a surge of petty pride to have rendered her mother silent with that gibe. It served her right. Maybe the guilt of it would drive her to drink yet more. Wallowing in her pain, she'd cry, *If only I'd done better by my kin!*

"It's not like he poisons us," said Ruthanne.

No, Mam was not one to wallow. Not one to linger on past wrong, neither those done to her or those she'd done to others. She picked a place and made it her heaven. "How can you say that when he drugged our food and—"

"I don't know if it's the food. Might be the air." Ruthanne's voice was considered and thoughtful. Her tone gave off the air of a woman deciding whether a stain was best removed with baking soda or dish soap.

"My whole life you made me think I was crazy for hating that place." Vern could do nothing to disguise the dejected quaver in her voice. "I don't think I can ever talk to you again," said Vern, this utterance more resolute.

"Vern, no, please. Lis—"

Vern disconnected the call and slid the phone back to the barkeep. What a strange sadness, to be done with the woman who'd made you.

## 5

THE FOREST LIT UP dimly as the sun rose. The woods were hauntingly quiet this morning. Vern should've felt relief returning to her babes, but she felt only dread. She was back now in the world of the fiend, of the drownt child, of Howling and Feral, who were so full of wanting and need for her she disappeared under the weight of their desires.

Vern walked faster once she reached the river and could follow it back toward her camp. A cool breeze, uncharacteristic of the season, blew against her until the skin over her arms prickled. It felt like a warning.

What if the fiend's intention had never been to burn the woods down but to lure Vern away from her children? Or what

if he'd been peeking through the trees and seen her go off on the
bike with Ollie and taken his chance to track down her camp? It
wouldn't be hard. He'd had to have seen her campfires before.

Vern picked up the pace until she was jogging, breaking into
a run when she was near enough to her camp to know the surroundings by heart. She slowed once she could smell the scents
of her home: old woodsmoke, burnt blackberries she'd stewed
into compote, dried fish. All seemed well, except for a distur-
bance in the shelter. The coverings of leaves and branches had
been tossed to the side. "Howling, Feral!" Vern called. She dove
into the shelter, ready to swoop them both up, but neither was
there.

"Howling! Feral!" Nearby, a short, sharp cry pinged the air,
and Vern ran.

There they both were, laughing hardily as they munched
through stores of dried plums. They'd crawled out of the shelter
by themselves. "Oh, babes," she said, crushing them to her. "I'm
sorry, I'm sorry, I'm sorry. I'm so, so sorry." Both of them cried,
straining out of her embrace.

She kissed them on their heads and stroked them gently, but
their cries didn't calm until she put them to the breast. "I love
you. I promise I do," she said, as much for herself as for them.

Vern resolved never to leave them again. She was a mam
now. Not some little girl who could get carried away with
dreams of women on bikes.

With the babies tethered to her, a rope around her waist, she
fixed herself breakfast, humming merrily to Howling and Feral as they chewed mud, chewed sticks, chewed rocks, chewed
leaves. The babes giggled, smiled, and squidged dirt and dan-
delions between their fingers and mashed overripe fruit onto
their mosquito-ravaged thighs. All the while, Vern watched
over them, dredging every bit of love and attention she could

out of herself and pouring it over them. This was how their lives would be from now on, she'd make sure of it, perfect and quaint.

Vern's fantasy lasted a day.

The next morning, bruises appeared on the babies' backs. Feral's were easy to spot, gulf-water blue and splotched like crumpled tissue paper, reeking of violence. Howling's marks were dark shadows, the faintest navy color hinting toward twilight. In her zeal to hold Howling and Feral close yesterday, she'd split their blood vessels open.

Vern was a strong girl, but no stronger than anyone else who grew up on the compound. Life at the Blessed Acres required endless manual labor. Before breakfast there was milking, shoveling and raking manure, feeding and watering animals. After breakfast: mending, patching, sewing, weaving. School came next, which offered respite, but depending on the time of year, the practical life rotation might involve heavy exertion. Smithing, trapping, and midwifery took a physical toll.

Squeezing a child hard enough that they had trauma to show for it was a different level of strength, however.

Howling, naked, poured water from a hide pouch into a ditch he'd dug. Feral, freshly dressed in a frock to save his skin from burning, dutifully ate breakfast. The accidental beatings the children had taken had not dampened their joy. They were themselves completely.

Had it not been for this fact, Vern might have spent the morning sulking uselessly. Instead, she grabbed a rock about the size of her palm from the ground. Summoning all her might, she squeezed it and waited for the solid gray mineral to become dust in her hands.

No such miracle occurred. "Damn it," she said, and threw the failed experiment out of her hand. Vern waited for the sound of a thunk against the ground or the trunk of a tree but paused when there was only an alarmed squeak.

"Da?" asked Howling.

Until now, Vern thought *feh*, fish, was the child's first spoken word, but knowing that he had it in him to talk, the single syllable Howling had often before blurted became suddenly intelligible. *Da* meant *that*. He was asking, *What's that?*

"Da?" he repeated, and headed toward the noise, crawling with incredible speed. Vern picked up Feral and followed after her eldest until they located the source of the sound. Howling spotted it first. "Beh." Bird.

Vern squatted down. There it was, a dead woodpecker, its little head sunken in on one side, balancing precariously on a twisted neck. Vern had done that, had thrown a rock and killed a bird with the force of it. It wasn't the miracle crushing the stone would've been, but it was something. At Cainland, kids killed birds all the time, though usually with aid of a slingshot. Crows, mostly, who went for the crops. Never with just a throw.

Vern dug a hole in the mud for the bird and placed it inside. She tried to summon up some gentleness for the creature as she covered it in dirt, but the burial was rote, Vern's mind on other matters. Howling reached his hands up. She lifted him so that he was on her shoulders, while Feral remained in place on her hip. Their combined weight, about forty or forty-five pounds, posed no strain. It hadn't in months. The children felt no heavier than two wool-stuffed teddies.

As she walked back to camp, Vern bent down to gather fallen branches for firewood, tucking the long, unruly things under her arm as she did most days. Howling wiggled and pointed from his spot on her shoulders, but she did not struggle to balance him even with her other burdens. She hopped over a fallen tree, the diameter of its dead trunk at least a foot. Over the summer, Vern had grown into a miniature titan, and she was only now realizing it. It hit her with the same calamitous punch that puberty had. Suddenly, nine years old, she'd been unable to escape the animality of her body. Coarse hair and blood.

When she considered it, this change was not so sudden, though. Before the bird, before bruising her babes, before her feats last night putting out the bonfire, there was last winter, when she'd bolted from tree to tree to get away from the fiend.

And before that, of course, before that was her escape from Cainland.

⊠

THE NIGHT OF HER LEAVING, Vern's mam, as usual, had been listening to gospel. Ruthanne had set her favorite song to loop till dawn. *Steal away, steal away home. I aint got long to stay here.*

The music pressed through the mesh of the screen door, making its way to where Vern sat on the porch railing. "Turn that off!" Vern yelled, but there was no point. Mam needed the music to sleep.

Vern stood. With feet clung to the white-painted wood of the porch, she pretended her blowing nightgown was a mast. In the ship of her body, she might sail anywhere.

"Vern, sweet girl, it's time for bed," Sherman called from inside. "You need all the sleep you can get. Little Thurgood needs his mam strong."

"I'm sleeping on the porch tonight," Vern said, though Sherman had already forbidden it.

"Brother Jerome's gonna be by shortly to strap us down," Sherman said. "Your mama and brother are already in bed."

Fog rolled in over the compound like froth spewing from a

devil dog's mouth. Vern wanted to voyage its waves, or sink to her death in it.

At the Blessed Acres of Cain, where no one doubted the dictates espoused in her husband's rousing sermons, Vern stood out as a vapor. It wasn't the albinism that made other Cainites doubt her substance—though in a community built on devotion to Blackness, to African ancestry, it played its part. What rankled them most was her doubt. She did not believe as they believed. Such an uncertain girl, how could she not see herself in the fog's shapelessness?

With Lucy gone, she was but a lone wisp.

This was the real reason Sherman had married her, she suspected: he'd sensed her misgivings about Cainland's mission and wanted to contain them.

"I'm not going upstairs," Vern said.

Her husband opened the screen door. The creaking of its hinges nearly concealed his sigh. "I don't want to get into it tonight," he said.

If she didn't stop her protests soon, he'd send her to the old well. That was the step that preceded an Ascension. She'd be made to stand on the ledge until he'd deemed she'd learned her lesson. Twelve hours, usually. Back in the day, under Eamon Fields's rule, it was longer. If a woman's legs wobbled from weariness, she might very well fall twenty feet down to the water.

Falling showed how weak a woman's spirit was, so she'd be left treading water to strengthen her resolve. And if she hit her head on the well wall tumbling down? Eamon Fields never had anything to say about that. Vern was twelve when she'd gone to the well with Lucy, the two of them calling down to the bottom to see if anyone would call back up. They used to swear they could hear screaming gurgling up from the depths.

"I'm sleeping out here," said Vern.

Mam thought Vern had a death wish, but the truth of it was it was in her nature to poke. She liked to think of what Sherman might do if he finally lost his temper truly and backhanded her so her white cheek erupted blue. What would the folks of Cainland think of him? Some violence could be disguised as a holy cleansing, but wife-beating was wife-beating. Less easy to contort into his narrative.

"What is wrong with you, stupid girl?" he asked, perplexed. It plagued him that he didn't understand her ways. "You're always spoiling for a fight. Aren't you tired? Aren't you just so damn tired of fighting? Come to bed and rest."

Vern squeezed her top row of teeth to her bottom, jaw aching. "What if I don't? You going to kill me?"

"Vern," said Sherman. "I'm not playing with you tonight. Come to bed." The screen door snapped shut behind him as he returned inside.

No matter what people thought, Vern didn't have a death wish. She could leave well enough alone, and for that very reason was about to follow Sherman back inside. She stopped because she saw Brother Jerome approaching. "Evening, sister," he said, and waved.

Vern hopped from the railing onto the porch. The suddenness of the movement startled Brother Jerome and he jumped back. "Shouldn't you be getting upstairs so I can lock you down for the night?" asked Jerome.

Vern sighed loudly and exaggeratedly. "I don't know. Should I? If I was really so dangerous in my sleep, I'd break out my straps, sleepwalk to your house, come in, and strangle you. Now, have I ever done anything of the kind?" Vern said.

Brother Jerome laughed, but the sound was syncopated and unsure.

"Am I joking?" she asked.

"You are something else, Vern."

That was how Cainites politely expressed displeasure in Vern. Lately, it seemed someone said that to her at least once a day. Her small rebellions of yesteryear had turned big and disruptive. It'd been days since she'd done any chores. The goats whined, distended with milk she didn't harvest. Corn bread grew stale on the kitchen counter, untended since the last lunch she made.

Sherman blamed the pregnancy hormones. He laughed gently whenever anyone brought up Vern's troubles. The man was right that being with child had some effect, just not in the ways Sherman asserted. Her new belly made sleep impossible, as did all the talk of the coming child. Little Thurgood this. Little Thurgood that. Vern was nothing but the vessel. In the night, she had visions of Cainites slitting her throat after the birth, her purpose fulfilled.

Vern couldn't worry about being a good little Cainite when her time might well be running out.

Vern paced the porch and breathed in her last taste of the night before following Brother Jerome upstairs. While he went to strap down Mam and Carmichael, Vern went to the master bedroom. Sherman wasn't alone.

"Hello, Vern." It was Dr. Malcolm.

This was Sherman's punishment for the way she'd been acting up lately. She should've known it would be something quiet. Gentle ruinings were Reverend Sherman's style.

"What's he want?" Vern asked, taking a seat on the edge of the bed.

"I want the same thing Reverend Sherman wants. I'm here because this—you acting like you've been acting—can't carry on, sister," said Dr. Malcolm. He knelt close enough in front of her that she could see his face as more than a swipe of color. In his hand he held out a triangle of sedatives, pink, white, and blue. A faded American flag. "I'd like it if we could get you comfortable and settled before Brother Jerome comes in," the doctor said, propagating the illusion that this was for her benefit.

Vern shook her head, right leg curled over her left knee and arms crossed over her chest. "I'm fine," she said.

"Sister," said Dr. Malcolm, "be reasonable."

Vern picked at her cuticles, a tunnel of raw flesh emerging at the border between her nails and skin.

"What have I told you about doing that to yourself, girl?" said Sherman, taking a seat next to her. He grabbed her hand and kissed the back of it.

"I'm not taking those pills," Vern said. Vern didn't believe Mam's adage about picking battles. Everything that could be contested needed contesting. She could wear opponents down by the sheer quantity of escalations.

"You've not been sleeping, sister," Dr. Malcolm stated simply.

Vern doused the yawn she felt coming with a swallow of spit. "There's worse things than being tired." Vern preferred fatigue to the complacency Dr. Malcolm's pills imposed. The sedatives were a glorified lobotomy, and their lulling effect protruded far beyond the sleep hours into the next day.

"Sister Vern—" Dr. Malcolm began, but Sherman held up a hand to stop him.

"It was worth a try, but she says she don't want the damn things, brother," said Sherman. He pretended to be her savior, like he wasn't the one to have brought the doctor up in the first place.

Dr. Malcolm's posture stiffened at Sherman's rebuke. "Of course, Reverend," he said, smiling warily. "But Sister Vern, don't think you can be rid of me altogether. I'll be around in the morning for your blood draws and to give you your vitamin injection.

I don't want to have to come up here and fetch you. I'm an old man and my knees hurt." It was an attempt at humor that Vern had no energy to indulge.

Vern glanced at the bruising on both her right and left arms, blurry blue petals around origins of scabbed black dots. Soon there'd be nowhere left for him to poke the needle. "Have a blessed night, Dr. Malcolm," Vern said.

"You, too, sister. And I hope you get some rest," he said.

"Night, brother," said Sherman, and shut the bedroom door harder than was necessary after the doctor left. She startled but did her best to pay him no mind. Vern plaited her hair into four long stumps. "He's right, you know. You need sleep. Good, hard sleep," Sherman said.

Vern walked to the window and, after shoving the floral-printed curtains to the side, opened it.

"I suggest a compromise," Sherman said.

Vern grasped the window edge and leaned out into the night. The fog beckoned. "What kind of compromise?" she asked, squinting out into the dark. The shadow of a coyote or some other night beast lurked just out of range of her vision.

"I know you hate Dr. Malcolm's pills. I don't blame you. But he's right. He only came here because he cares," said Sherman.

Vern leaned her weight against the shallow windowsill. She felt Sherman approaching from behind and braced herself for his touch. He wrapped his arms around her waist and rested his chin on her shoulder. "Life doesn't have to be as hard as you make it."

Vern pulled from Sherman's grasp and walked to the trunk at the foot of the bed where she sat to rub tallow cream onto her elbows, knees, and feet. "So, what, Sherman, you want me to call Dr. Malcolm back so he can render me brain-dead?"

"What about some cold medicine, honey?" Sherman asked. "Some cough syrup. That stuff always knocks you out good." He whipped it out of the right pocket of his pajama pants. How long had it been there? "Take it, baby. It'll make you feel better," Sherman insisted.

"It tastes like rancid jam," said Vern.

"This isn't a debate," Sherman said.

Vern should've spat at him, or knocked him down with a swipe of her foot across his ankles. She didn't, and with a sigh, she held out her hand. She was no better than anybody here. Nobody knew how to fight. "Give it here."

Sherman handed her the bottle, and Vern opened the Evenyl to take a sip. Afterward, she took another. Took another inch of it until she gulped. She drank it down until it was about empty.

Sherman snatched the bottle from Vern's hands. "Enough."

Every exchange Vern shared with Sherman was one she'd either won or lost. This one she'd almost lost by giving in and taking the medicine, but she'd taken a modicum of power back by drinking more than she should have. The noose he'd slid over her head like a necklace still had a few inches of give, and that made her cocky. "When you were a boy, did you always know you'd be like him?" she asked.

Vern looked toward the strop that hung from the hook drilled into the dresser's side. It once belonged to Sherman's father, Eamon Fields. His initials were branded into the leather.

"Like who?"

But Sherman knew, and the fact that he couldn't bring himself to answer straightaway meant the insult had done its intended damage. "Like your daddy."

Sherman grabbed a three-quarters-full glass of water sitting on the dresser and drained it in a gulp. "Be thankful, child, that I am nothing, nothing, like that man."

"You're right. You're not domineering and controlling at all. Must've had you confused with my other husband." Vern should not have felt so delighted to speak out of turn, but obliterating the narrative Sherman had constructed of himself made her brazen words worth it. "Do you really think you won't do to me what he done to your mam?"

Vern braced for an eruption, but when none came she kept talking. "You know nobody believes it, that what happened to Sister Rainey was an accident. When will you permanently cripple me, too?"

Reverend Sherman slid off his robe and draped it over the foot of the bed. "If you think this track of conversation will rile me, you are sorely wrong, girl. I know my father was a bad man. A hypocrite. To him this place was . . . a game. His treacheries against my mother, God of Cain rest her, do not compare to his treacheries against the compound and its people as a whole. I am not like him. All I have ever wanted is to make you at home among your people. Good night, Vern."

Vern had craved a confrontation. Instead, she'd been quietly dismissed. Instead of adrenaline and pain and hot sparks, she'd gotten more questions, this time about Eamon Fields. But on the compound, questions were pointless. They only dug the hole in her deeper.

"You are like him," she said. It was a pathetic retort and she knew it, but she couldn't let Reverend Sherman have the last word. Vern flipped off the light on her nightstand and joined her husband under the covers, impatient for the cough syrup he'd made her drink to take effect. The sooner she was under its influence, the sooner it'd be over with, her mind her own again.

Brother Jerome arrived moments later. He took the belts already affixed to the bed and crossed all six over Vern's body, attaching them to loops that ran through the middle of the mattress and to the top and bottom posts. She wondered if the belts dated back to Eamon Fields's time, if his wife, Sherman's mother, had slept under these when pregnant with her son.

"No gag tonight," Vern said. "I'm feeling a little sick. Took too much Evenyl," she explained.

Brother Jerome looked over to Sherman, and Sherman nodded his approval. Jerome strapped Sherman down next, pulling the belt taut before looping it through and gagging him.

"Have a blessed night," Jerome said, but Vern wouldn't. The weight of her pregnant belly made that impossible, and while Sherman drifted off quickly, sleep never came for Vern. Instead, she coughed and gurgled up bile. Evenyl glazed a ghostly film of grape-flavored acetaminophen down her tongue and throat, and she turned her head to the side so as not to gag on the sick rising from her gut.

"Sherman!" Vern whispered to her sleeping husband. "Sherman!" She writhed in her bonds. "Sherman, damn it, wake up." He was too lost in a night terror, and he strained against his straps hard enough that the bed shook.

Reflexively, Vern tried to sit up, but her body pressed into the six leather belts securing her to the bed. She strained against them anyway, addled and confused by the syrup. She grunted as she pushed and pushed.

The second strap from the top gave against the pressure of her movement.

Never before had it done that. Pop.

"Huh?" she said out loud, confused, like she'd heard a voice. But nobody was talking to her; it truly was the sound of the strap snapping.

Vern wiggled until she was able to ease her left arm out of the hold to undo the other belts. With such limited mobility and her faculties compromised by the medicine, it took time, but she had that. Sherman and the rest of Cain would be asleep all night. She could strain and fiddle and work her poor fingers sore as much as she wanted, and no one would be the wiser.

She smiled like she never had before once finally free. Just like that, the straps hung limply at the side of the bed. Just like she hadn't tried this same thing a million and one nights before.

Woozy from the cough syrup, Vern wobbled as she stood. "Sherman!" she said. "Look at me!" Vern giggled. "Guess you can't stop me from sleeping on the porch now." She poked his hollow cheeks. "Olly, olly, oxen free!" she yelled. Even if he did wake, he could do nothing but look on.

Vern had no reason to stop at the porch downstairs. She could sleep in the yard. She could sleep on his platform at the center of the compound. She could sleep in the woods. Vern could live in the woods.

Vern packed her bags.

Mam's gospel song played on. *Steal away, steal away.*

Once outside, Vern plowed a path through the bristly browned grass. She walked past the olive grove, past the pecan trees, past the orchard of lemon trees and lime trees and orange trees and peach trees and plum trees and pomegranate trees, toward the woods.

She was a giantess, limbs heavy. Before tonight, this mightiness lay buried. But tonight she walked. Tonight, she left. The Girl Who Went.

Vern's uncanny strength had been with her that very evening. It was why for the first time ever she'd been able to snap the straps and free herself. There was something inside of her making her strong, and it had been with her since Cainland.

# 6

VERN HELD OUT A MONTH before returning to Bert's and calling Ollie.

She had rules now. She'd only go right after putting Howling and Feral down for their night's sleep. After one and a half hours, it was time to come home. That way, when one or the other of the children woke up to complain about how horrible it was being a baby, Vern would be there to tell them it only got worse, as well as to give them milk to make that fact less upsetting. Vern memorized and marked the path to the neon-signed wooden shack so she could make her way back to the children quickly and efficiently even in the dark.

Ollie's apartment was modest and clean. Vern thought a woman as rough around the edges as her would keep a more interesting place, but there was little more to the studio than a gray sofa with a flannel throw, a coffee table, a bookshelf.

"You look disappointed," said Ollie, filling a glass from the tap and handing it to Vern. Vern had forgotten there was water in the world you didn't have to collect from a river and hard-boil for an hour in a covered pot.

"I was just expecting something homier," Vern explained, grateful for the drink. It tasted better than any water she'd had in a year and was delightfully free of sediment.

"I don't actually spend that much time here," said Ollie. "I would've hired a decorator if I figured you for the type to care."

Vern dragged her hand along the bar top of the kitchenette. "It's just the first time I've been . . ." Vern didn't know how to explain that she'd not been inside anywhere at all in a year, not except for the Bert's, and that hardly counted. Nobody lived there. "I guess I'm just homesick or something."

She didn't miss the compound, but she missed chatter, missed blankets that smelled like something other than woodsmoke, missed biscuits and honey, missed Carmichael needling her with his incessant desire to share whatever he was reading about. *Apples are native to the mountains of Central Asia. Xinjiang, China; Kazakhstan; Tajikistan; and Kyrgyzstan specifically.* He'd told her it was possible to hear a blue whale's heartbeat from two miles away, and for a moment Vern had believed in God, the God of Cain and all his creation: Mam, Carmichael, Lucy, candied pecans, the cold lake, deacons smiling at Vern despite her surliness, saying, *Morning, sister, how are you this blessed morning?*

It was a flaw of the human animal that Vern could feel nostalgic for a place like Cainland, but loneliness was the root of all manner of sin. Reverend Sherman exploited it often, fulfilling a wanderer's desire for belonging, validation, and purpose. She'd seen how newcomers to the compound fell into the fantasy of perfect love and perfect truth he offered.

Vern wanted to scream at them. There was no church, no philosophy, no school of thought, no nothing that could be trusted in full. To believe too much in anything was to sacrifice your faculties. The only way forward was to embrace the tussle of it all.

Born with a seething righteousness, Vern looked down on anyone less willing or able to put up a fight than she was. If only people were more like her, she thought, the world could be good. There'd be no Cainlands. There'd be no Lucy's fathers. No Reverends. No fiends.

"Where is home, anyway?" asked Ollie. She'd set a plate of food on the bar top, seedy wheat crackers and some kind of white dip. Vern hoisted herself on a stool and took a bite, letting the dry, bland grains dissolve into her mouth. *Did you know,* Carmichael asked once, *that John Harvey Kellogg believed eating plain foods would prevent people from masturbating? That's why he invented cornflakes. They were marketed as an antimasturbation aid.*

*Please don't use that word at my dinner table,* Vern's mam had said.

"I don't have a home," said Vern, "but I grew up on a commune not too far from here."

"You weren't a fan?"

"That's underselling it," Vern said. Her whole life she'd been drugged and not known it. What else had Reverend Sherman and his goons put inside of her? She thought of the vitamin shots she and other Cainites regularly received. What were they really, and why give them?

Ollie hoisted herself up onto the stool next to Vern. Their shoulders brushed. "I always kind of liked the idea of growing up in a commune. I'm no hippie or anything, but I like the idea of a place to call yours that you can leave and come back to. A home. I had a shit childhood, too, mostly by way of a shit mother. Got shuttled from one uncle or aunt to another. A cousin once. None of them gave a shit about me. Learned to fend for myself, though. There's that."

"There's always that," Vern said, nodding.

Their meetings after that first night at Ollie's place tended to involve less talking, less social throat-clearing. They had an understanding.

Sometimes Ollie would say, "She only wants me for my body," mock-mournfully, the back of her hand on her forehead. "You are insatiable, you know that? What is wrong with you?" Her tone would be teasing, but Vern's face always hardened.

"I'm not insatiable," Vern would say.

"Oh, but you are."

Ollie would climb on top of her, pressing Vern's back into the sofa. "Even now, you're angry, but you want it, don't you?

Want me. It's okay," Ollie assured, sliding up Vern's shirt. "I won't stop."

Vern didn't know what she wanted. She was a girl made of aches and she flung her body at the world in the hopes that something, anything, might soothe the tendernesses.

This was only half metaphor. As Vern's strength grew, so, too, did her discomfort. Frequent headaches. Nausea. Joints hurting. Limbs hurting. Everything hurting. Rarely did a moment pass unmarked by bodily grievance. A doubter and disbeliever, she knew these weren't coincidence. Whatever had made her strong had also made her hurt. She sensed the hauntings, too, were connected. There was a foreign body inside, making her over, and it was no accident.

## 7

HOURS ACCUMULATED into days, into weeks, months, years, and Vern had nothing to show for it but tired joints and two wily almost-three-year-olds, who, as Vern's mother had said of her, had more opinions than sense. Feral, always in woolens and furs because the elements bothered him so, had only just started to speak. She fixed his long, coiled hair into two French braids to keep it from obscuring his vision. He had eyes as shaky and wobbly as Vern's, and a lazy eye, too. He was a watchful child, observant— less sure-footed than his sibling, perhaps, but no less adventurous.

Howling, especially, was bright as blazes. Talking to him was like talking to the taxman. He enunciated ever so clearly and spoke in the longest of sentences. He didn't have the capacity to believe he was ever wrong.

It was a quaint picture, an image from a storybook. How idyllic. How lovely. Jars of bright purple preserves. Sacks of dried fruit hung from trees. Herbs hanging and drying from branches. Chubby babes padding along the soft earth. The smell of pine. The smell of dew.

Everything so pretty as that, Vern should've been happy, but most of the time she felt an all-consuming lust for the end of everything. Every day, wild rages rolled through her, a blaring horn. Only more pain settled her.

How could leaving have so much in common with staying? Cainland had been the source of Vern's unhappiness, ergo, she ought be happy now.

When her babes slept, she'd go to the river and stick her head into the cold rushing stream, hold it there for minutes, hungry for air, just for that feeling of coming back up to the surface to breathe. She'd do it over and over, until her body was rags, dragging herself back to the shelter, collapsing into the deep sleep of the almost-dead.

Back at Cainland, she'd been able to drown properly. Not by herself, but with Reverend Sherman's help. All she need do was get herself in enough trouble, then he'd hold her under the lake until she went still. Seconds later, he'd revive her with his lips to hers. It was a punishment for girls like Vern, the ones who could never get along. Washing away the past, the bad urges, the bad thoughts, the bad inclinations. Whenever she came to on the shore in Reverend Sherman's arms, alive after all, it was hard not to see him as her savior, not to want to do everything to please him.

These were the Ascensions, the name Cainites gave to the redeeming drownings. Vern knew what Lucy meant now when she'd called her a masochist.

Drowning herself until she passed out wasn't an option now. If she held herself under too long, she'd die for good, and there'd be no one to raise her babes. She calmed herself instead with these half drownings. When that didn't work, she'd move on to burnings, holding her hand in the fire until it blistered.

It was always such a shame to awake again in the morn, all—and this was the strangest of it—recovered. Her hands would shine red and raw, bright with new skin, no sign of the burn but for flecks of what looked like moltings on the leaf mattress.

"Mam!" Howling gasped once, seeing her healed arm. A spider had bitten her the day before. There'd been a large, pus-filled rash where its fangs had sunk in. Vern slit the pustule open with her knife to drain the yellow and green muck out, Howling and Feral watching, curious, unafraid.

In the night, the bite and the knife wound had both healed. Her forearm was pristine. "What happen?" Howling asked, pointing. "Where boo-boo?" He had poked at the place where the cut should've been with a long twig.

To test this phenomenon further, Vern held the whole of both of her hands in the fire until she passed out from the pain. She'd put a boulder in the center of the pit, tied a thick belt to it and then to her wrists, so she could not withdraw them from the heat so easily. Her numb hands were swollen, red, and blistered for days, becoming infected, but she fought the rot off with surprising vitality, and weeks and weeks later, her hands were indistinguishable from how they were before the burn. "Special skin," said Howling thoughtfully, for he still had a scar on his arm from the tiny burn he'd sustained months ago.

"Magic Mam."

It wasn't magic. It was the Blessed Acres. A side effect of the poison they'd been giving her from birth. Maybe, when the fiend had brought on the haunting of the wolves on that long-ago night, he hadn't had to put anything in the river water Vern drank. He'd only had to trigger something already inside of her.

Vern shook her head, not knowing how something like that could work. As usual, her attempts to discover the truth butted up against the pervasive ignorance brought on by her upbringing.

When Lucy had come back, she'd said her mother had documented the things that happened at Cainland and showed them to a court. Others might know what was happening, then. Vern had been so lost in her suffering that she'd given up on figuring out the truth, but she could if she actually bothered to look for the answers.

⊠

OLLIE'S APARTMENT didn't smell like much. Even the bathroom, scattered with bottles, did not bear the odor of the products inside those bottles.

This sterility comforted Vern, whose own world was pungent with signs of life.

"What?" asked Ollie one night.

"Thinking," said Vern.

"About?"

"You, I guess, how I don't know nothing about you." Where did she live? Surely not here, not most of the time, anyway. There was never anything in the trash can. There were pans in the cupboard, but they'd never been used.

"I was under the impression that was how you liked it," said Ollie, grabbing snacks from the kitchen. "But I can tell you more if you want."

Vern shook her head. "I was just curious, is all. Aren't you ever curious about me? Where I go when I'm not with you?"

"I figured you were purposefully leaving it out."

"Maybe I was waiting for you to ask me," said Vern, though

she hadn't been. She was only looking for a way to bring up the question she'd been meaning to ask for weeks now.

"Okay. So tell me," said Ollie.

Vern smiled at Ollie's willingness to cooperate. "Remember when I said I grew up on a commune?" Vern asked.

Ollie poured tortilla chips into a big glass bowl and undid the lid from a jar of salsa. "Yeah?"

"It's pretty famous, is all," Vern explained. "Maybe you even heard of it?"

Ollie shrugged, withdrawn. She was like this some nights, cold and uninterested, but Vern couldn't call her on it because it wasn't like she didn't have moods, too. "It's called the Blessed Acres of Cain." Vern waited for a reaction from Ollie, but none came. Ollie collapsed onto the sofa and put chips and salsa onto a paper plate.

"Are you coming to a point?" asked Ollie.

"Do you know anything about it? The Blessed Acres?"

"Probably not as much as you if you grew up there, but yeah, I know of it. Kind of like a whole Black power thing, right?" Ollie put her fist in the air.

"Have you ever seen anything about us on the news? Anything about Reverend Sherman?"

"What kind of thing?"

"I don't know. About him poisoning people or something?" said Vern desperately, perfectly aware it was a ridiculous question. If Sherman was doing things to folks there, it certainly wouldn't be on the news. "Can you look something up for me on that?" Vern asked, pointing to Ollie's laptop. It sat unopened on the bar top of the kitchenette.

"Look up what, V?" Ollie set her paper plate back on the table.

"Cainland. I just—I realize I only know about it from the inside. Maybe if I have some clue from the outside I can figure out . . ."

"Figure out what?"

Vern shifted in her seat. "Can you look it up for me or what?"

Ollie looked wearied by the request of a favor but went to her laptop. "Well?" Ollie asked.

"Can't you just type in *Cainland* and the information comes up on the screen?" asked Vern. That was her impression of how it worked from watching TV at Ollie's house, but she wasn't sure how much of that was based on reality. No one on TV woke before dawn unless they were about to commit a murder. On the compound, everyone did, families gathering around the lake for the morning word and prayers. If there was to be a drowning on that day, it was best to do it before sunup, so the person was resuscitated—reborn—in time for the new day.

On TV, everyone woke around 6:00 or 7:00. They poured their breakfast from a box into a bowl. Alternately, they squeezed breakfast into their mouths from plastic pouches and tubes. Or had yogurt from little plastic containers with pictures of cartoons on the front, or pictures of raspberries or strawberries. They went to work, where they sat, or to school, where they also sat.

Teenage girls on TV shows weren't much like Vern at all. They universally adored boys.

TV spun a web of dreams. Vern was happy to be caught in it. She could get drunk on this place where police were good, always solving crimes and caring about folks, and everyone was so shiny and pretty. A place where you could type words into a computer and get answers.

"Here," Ollie said, gesturing for Vern to come over to the laptop.

"Just read it to me," said Vern. "What's it say?"

"The whole . . . internet?" Ollie asked, but she was being deliberately obstinate.

"Pick one," said Vern, "and read it to me."

Ollie dragged herself back over to the sofa, laptop in tow. She cleared her throat, then began: *"The Blessed Acres of Cain, generally referred to by its shorthand name 'Cainland' or 'Cain,' is a religious and political settlement. Founded by the Black nationalist group Coloreds Against White Supremacy (CLAWS, or Claws) on April third, 1966, Cainland rose to national prominence in the 1960s and 1970s for its strongly antiwhite and anti-American views."* Ollie paused to look up at Vern.

"What else does it say? Keep reading," said Vern.

Ollie sighed but went along. *"The name of the settlement originates from the founders' belief that those with African ancestry were rejected by the White Devil, their interpretation of the Christian God, and were cast out of the Garden of Eden and banned from his bounty. They believe the Cain of Genesis to be their direct forefather, and that the true God, the God of Cain, will provide them untold riches as long as they resist influence from the White Devil and his creation (Europeans and those with European ancestry)."*

The original founders of Claws and later the compound, Harvey Whitmore, Shana Lee Hopkins, Jimmy Jake Jackson, and Barbara "Queen" James, never said those things. In fact, they'd left, not to be heard from again, after Eamon took the stage. It was their mystic talk about dirt and visions that Eamon had latched on to and spun into a mythos. He'd announced himself as a prophet of the God of Cain. The Blessed Acres, named for the sanctity of the land, became the Blessed Acres of Cain. This was what Vern had gleaned from the occasional mutterings of lifers, brothers and sisters who'd been on the compound from the beginning. Harvey, Shana, Jimmy Jake, and Queen were essentially ousted, but everyone went along with it because they weren't willing to abandon their lives at the compound and all it meant for Black liberation.

"Well? What's next? Don't stop," said Vern. Listening to Ollie read was a little like catching someone gossiping about you: uncomfortable, but rewarding to learn what people really thought.

*"Though regarded as a cult by many outsiders and law enforcement because of its socially deviant beliefs and practices, including numerous alleged cases of child abuse, there has never been legal action taken against the group,"* continued Ollie.

Vern perked up. "Does it say why?"

"Why what?"

"Why legal action hasn't been taken against the group," Vern said.

Ollie scanned the article and shook her head. "Not that I see."

"Nothing? Nothing at all?"

Ollie fixed Vern with an impatient glare, but Vern let it slide off her. "It's odd, don't you think? I know for a fact government workers witnessed illegal things on the compound, but we never got in trouble for it. Not once. That means something, surely."

Ollie didn't shrug, but her nonanswer communicated similar levels of disinterest in the topic. Vern supposed that for someone who hadn't grown up in Cainland, none of this was significant, but Vern couldn't let it go.

"Stop pouting. You know what? How about this?" said Ollie, then clicked away at her keyboard. A few seconds later, Vern heard a coughing and whirring noise. "I'm printing it for you, okay? Then you can read as much as you want."

But Vern wouldn't be able to. Didn't Ollie know that? No, Vern supposed she didn't. After all this time, they hardly knew each other. "Fine," said Vern, no closer to figuring out anything about what was inside her or what was going on with the compound.

"I'm sorry, V. I'm just not in the mood tonight, okay?"

"Maybe I'm not in the mood, either," said Vern, rubbing her sore eyes. It was end of day, and her temples throbbed.

"Headache?" Ollie asked. Vern nodded. "I'll get you some pills and we can forget all about this. One second," said Ollie, running off toward the bathroom.

"Get some blankets, too," called Vern. It was October and starting to cool. She'd sneak some of the bedding back with her to the woods.

"What'd you say?" Ollie called.

"I said get me some blanke— Never mind. I'll get them."

Vern stood and went to the trunk positioned as a coffee table in front of the sofa. She removed the chips, salsa, and paper plate and opened it to search inside. There was nothing but old magazines. Vern sighed and headed to the coat closet, fumbling around till she felt a large cardboard box. She tugged it out and lifted the top flaps to the side.

"Bingo," she said, pulling out a small white blanket. Too small. It'd barely cover Vern's knees. She brought it closer to her face when she noticed a print. Little yellow octopuses. It was a baby blanket.

Vern rifled through the box further, holding up each item in front of her. The impulse that made her catalogue every object one by one was self-flagellating in origin—for she knew what she was looking at and understood what it meant.

Baby onesies. Baby jumpsuits. Baby socks. Baby bonnets. Baby bootees. Baby teething rings. Baby swaddlers. Baby burp cloths. Baby diapers. Baby bibs. Baby christening gowns. Baby mittens. Motifs of sailboats, ducklings, clouds, and rainbows. Most of it new, with tags, ready to clothe dead things.

"V." Vern turned to face Ollie. She'd returned with the promised headache pills and a glass of water for washing them down.

"Don't move," said Vern. It would solidify her foolishness to say any of the other things on her mind: that Ollie was a liar, that she was the fiend, that she'd lured Vern out of the woods to play with her, that this was all a part of a game, another way to undo Vern. Vern had fallen right for it.

"Please let me explain. You know me." *Know.* It made Vern gag to think of her body entangled with the fiend's, with the same woman who'd left dead animals for her and chased her through the woods with a rifle.

"I'm gonna kill you," Vern said, tossing a rolled-up pair of baby socks at Ollie. A meager weapon.

"Calm down. Please. *Please.*"

"No!" Vern shouted, and prepared to lunge, but Ollie threw the glass of water she was holding at Vern's face. The vessel shattered over Vern's nose, shards cutting her skin, her cheeks and forehead left throbbing. Vern grabbed the floor lamp in the hall and gripped it. Brandishing it like a lance, she jutted it several times toward Ollie to scare her backward.

"You're a smart girl. I know you are. Smart enough to figure out I know where you live, that you have two kids, Howling and Feral, and they're nearly three years old and sleeping oh so sweetly right now but their dreams won't be so sweet anymore with my knife to their throats. But no matter what you think of me right now, I don't want to do that. That's not who I am. Listen to me, please. Give me a chance."

Vern swung the lamp sideways, hard and fast, and made contact with Ollie's hip. Ollie stumbled but caught herself before she hit the ground. "Please," begged Ollie. Vern swung again, this blow landing against Ollie's temple. Ollie, looking dazed, clutched her now-bleeding head. "If this is how you want to do it—fine. I see your strength has come in, but I don't think your speed has."

Before Vern fully processed Ollie's words, the fiend dashed out the apartment. Vern chased after her down the concrete steps to the main door of the small complex. Ollie hopped onto her motorcycle and sped off. Vern gave chase until Ollie's bike disappeared over an incline.

Vern changed course for the woods, darting off the road into the thicket of trees over the guardrail. There was a well-worn path she'd trodden herself, but she could run only so fast in the dark. It was nearly an hour before she reached camp.

Howling and Feral hung by their ankles from the low branch of a tree over a freshly built fire, screaming and crying out for Vern. Soon the babes would tumble downward into the orange haze.

"Babies, be still, I'm going to get you down," said Vern, but someone grabbed her from behind and pressed a forearm into her throat hard, cutting off her breath.

"We can do this soft and gentle, Vern, or we can do it hard. I can't kill you, but I can kill them, and I will if I have to. Please don't struggle. Just listen to me, for fuck's sake."

"You're nothing but Reverend Sherman's hired dog," Vern croaked as she gasped for air.

"I'm trying to save you. I know you can't see that, but I am. I could've taken you back to Cain at any time. I'm the only thing keeping you in the woods living free. I'm the only thing between you and them."

Vern shifted to wrestle her neck out of Ollie's grip, but a sweaty forearm locked her in place. "Them?" Vern asked, her voice a squeak. The deacon board? Cops? Judges? Who was Reverend Sherman working with?

"I was assigned one task. To bring you back to the compound.

I could have at any time. Don't think for a second there wasn't a moment I didn't know exactly where you were. I lied to them and said I couldn't find your camp. I did that for you. They were satisfied as long as I kept my eye on you in the woods. We can go back to that. This doesn't have to change anything. They don't know yet, they don't know the extent of what you can do."

Vern sniveled uselessly as tears dampened her cheeks. "What about all those stupid dead animals?" Vern asked. It was a small point, considering all Vern had learned, but she couldn't stop thinking about the corpses left as bread crumbs.

If anything Ollie had ever said about her life was true—that she'd had a difficult upbringing, shunted from uncaring family member to the next—Vern could see how that might make her hard. But a sadist? A fiend? What quirk of fate made someone kill a defenseless critter, all for the thrill of dressing it up in bootees?

"All I wanted was to draw you out of the woods," Ollie said. "I didn't think any girl in her right mind would stick around for that. You were braver than I realized."

Vern drew up her lips and nose in recoil at the compliment. Her babes cried out for her. *Mam! Mam! Mam!* She'd neglected them, exposed them to harm. "If you think so much of me, will you tell me what's happening to my body, at least? You know, don't you? Did Reverend Sherman make me this way? Why?"

"I'll tell you all of that and more if you agree to stand down. No one has to know anything. Can't you see I would never hurt you?" said Ollie, her voice cracking with emotion. Her eyes glistened with uncried tears.

Even now, shown the full breadth of Ollie's betrayal, Vern couldn't distinguish the lies from the truth. Where did Ollie's self-delusion end and her attempts to manipulate Vern begin? Was there anything genuine to her? Vern had dark parts, too, but that didn't mean there was no love in her. Was there love in Ollie? What did Vern mean to her?

"Was anything you said to me true?" asked Vern pathetically. She had no reason to trust any answer Ollie gave.

"Every word out my mouth I meant. We're alike, V. Angry and mean and we hurt people. But we aren't liars. Rather than tell you tales I said nothing. I'm sorry. I'm truly sorry."

If Ollie regretted what she'd done then why was she still trying to convince Vern to go back to how it was before? Vern was done crying over this woman. The only thing she ought be feeling was relief. She could finally be free of Ollie's wiles.

"Please, Vern."

Vern jammed her head back, banging her skull into Ollie's face. Ollie cried out and Vern slipped from her grip.

Ollie clutched her nose, which spurted dark blood into the night. In the glow of the fire, Ollie looked as pathetic as Vern felt, her nose mashed flat by Vern's assault. Vern dove for her, expecting to have to struggle, but Ollie went down easy.

Ollie pushed against her, but Vern didn't budge. She couldn't even feel Ollie's attempts to free herself.

Vern socked her in the cheek. Dizzy from the punch, Ollie regarded Vern warily. "That night, the night my babes were born—when you tracked me down—you said you used the wolves to draw me out. What did you mean? How?"

Ollie moaned, too out of it to answer.

"Mam!" called Howling.

"Tell me! Tell me or I'll kill you!" said Vern, ready to lunge toward her babes if she needed to but desperate to get an answer out of the fiend.

"It's not my doing," said Ollie, coughing, eyes now closed. An animal traipsed in the darkness, out of sight, but Vern wouldn't let it distract her. She kept her eyes on Ollie.

"Who, then?" asked Vern as her children cried for her.

"You're in over your head." Ollie's breathing was rapid and off-kilter.

"Shut up," said Vern.

Below her, Ollie gave a weak, barely perceptible shrug. "It's the truth."

"You don't know anything about truth."

"I know that it's the truth that you're making a mistake. Please, for your own sake, let me up. Let me go. And I can tell you all of it. About me. About the hauntings. About Eamon Fields," said Ollie.

Eamon? What was there to know about Eamon? Ollie was still trying to burrow back in. Vern wasn't going to fall for it. "You're in no position to bargain. Tell me now, or I'll kill you."

"You're just a little girl. You're not gonna—"

Was that why Ollie had mistreated her so? Because she was young? Easy to manipulate? She wouldn't be manipulated anymore.

Vern shook Ollie by the shoulders with all her might, slamming the woman's head into the ground over and over until she passed out. Then she picked Ollie up and threw her into the dark. Her limp body made contact with a pine tree, and Vern heard a snap. Her spine breaking? Her neck? Whichever it was, Ollie now lay on the forest floor no more animated than a pile of dirty towels.

Energy pulsed through Vern. She wanted nothing more than to open Ollie sternum to pelvis. Sniff the insides. Eat her till she was empty. Vern licked her lips. Ollie looked like supper.

"Mam!"

Vern shook off the urge and ran to her babes to cut them down, careful not to hug them too tightly for fear of crushing them.

"Did you kill him, Mam?" asked Howling, either afraid or

impressed. Snot dangled from his nose as he sucked in breaths through sobs. Feral cried more quietly.

"She's gone now. She's gone," said Vern, though that was not wholly true. The walloping drum of Ollie's heart still beat. Like a breeze, it floated across the air and brushed against Vern's skin. Despite her distance from Vern, the woman's shallow, skittering breaths were hot on Vern's face. Vern felt the woman begin to die, but she wasn't dead yet.

Vern inhaled. For the first time in a very long while, she felt sensations as they were meant to be felt: sweat dripping down her forehead and along her temples, cool air against her skin, smears of blood on her palm. She was alive, and the veil that was Ollie had been lifted.

The animal lurking in the trees emerged from the shadows, making a course toward Ollie. "Finish her off," said Vern to the hulking beast. She figured it for a stag or an overgrown boar. Maybe a cougar who'd wandered out of its usual territory.

The night Vern first met the fiend, there'd been an animal, too. Was this one the very same? Had a mountain lion latched on to the fiend's scent? Or maybe it had elected itself Vern's guardian.

"Sleep, my babies," Vern said, her mind already plotting. Reverend Sherman and whatever goons he was working with would be coming soon now that his scout was dead. It was time to go.

# 8

THE NEXT NIGHT, when Vern was all packed to leave, the sky slit open like a fish's gut and washed away their home. The winter stores of food drowned, and the grounds of their campsite flooded. The little oasis in the massive woods gave way to the deluge and would soon rot.

Vern shouldn't have wasted time returning to Ollie's apartment. She'd heard the rumbling sky and felt the darkness growing in the woods. She'd known the storm was coming and that she'd have to pack well, but it had been her last time in the area to grab clues. Papers. Ollie's wallet. Her laptop.

Vern whisked Howling and Feral from the sodden forest floor onto a branch. They held fast to it, neither of the two crying despite the wet and the cold. They were only three years old but were strong. Could've climbed the slippery bark of that tree themselves.

"Mam!" Howling called. "Lightning!" He had one arm steady on the branch, the other thrust up to an opening in the treetops to the sky, rain pelting down on him by the bushel. "Look, Mam, look! It's flashing! It looks like veins. Is it full of blood?"

"Quiet, child, let me think," Vern said, arms wrapped around herself. She watched her ruined realm succumb to the rain. She'd packed up most of their belongings, but they wouldn't be able to take them all.

Vern was not a sentimental person. Things had their time. The world rushed and moved. Everything and everyone was forgettable, compostable.

But she was practical, and leaving camp meant leaving any semblance of security, even if that security had been a lie. It meant leaving gear, for she couldn't carry everything as well as the children. Weight wasn't the issue—she was confident she could bear the load of that easily. It was a surface area problem. She had only so many hands and arms, so much back, so much shoulder.

"Here," Vern said to Howling, holding her hands up to him.

He jumped into her grip, and she swung him onto her back, letting him ride low on her hips and fastening him to her tightly with soaking wet linen cloth. Next she held her hands up to Feral, who slid off the branch into her embrace. The lighter of the two, he would go on her shoulders for now. Once steady, she stepped out into night and headed north.

She was sure that was the direction Lucy and her mother had gone after leaving the Blessed Acres, toward Lucy's auntie's place. The phone number to that house was out of service, but maybe they still lived there. Vern wouldn't leave the woods—not with Cainland folks still looking for her—but she'd get herself and her family closer to the only safe place Vern knew. She'd never been there, but Lucy liked her auntie's, and Lucy didn't like anything.

"You ready?" Vern asked the children, checking that they were secure to her.

"Ready," they said.

Both wore thick hooded fur cloaks over their clothes, and Vern swished a wool blanket over the three of them, clasping it at her neck as if her hand were a brooch, then walked.

She wore her knives around her neck, her thread and so on in the pockets of a pair of pants she'd made.

"Mam?" asked Feral. He was still shy with words, his little voice a tinny bell of sweetness in the evening air.

"Not now, baby," Vern said.

"Coyotes," he said in a scared whisper.

"They're all tucked up in their dens. They don't want nothing to do with us."

"Sure?" he asked.

"Sure," said Vern.

"Mean it?" asked Feral.

"I mean it."

"No trick?"

"No trick," said Vern, shaking her head. A person looking on would think she was always teasing him, but Vern never did any such thing. She was not a playful person, and when she said something, she meant it. She didn't have time for foolishness.

"Cross your heart?" Feral asked.

Howling, on the other hand, had a mischievous streak thick as bone. Feral's intense skepticism had developed in response to his sibling's frequent antics.

"I cross my heart," said Vern.

Satisfied that they would be unlikely to run into coyotes, Feral started howling. "Aoooooooooooooooooo!" he called. "Aooooooo! Aoooo!"

Howling joined in. The two of them sang to the sky, enchanted by the dark and the rain. "Our pack roams this here land! We are its brethren! Its subjects! Its children! Its family! Its mams!" said Howling, and though most of his words were verbatim copies of things Vern had said herself, the content of his mimicry revealed a dazzling brightness. Like Vern's brother, Carmichael, had been as a young child, Howling was disgustingly astute, assimilating the makings of his world with an uncanny ease. "And when we die, to the land we will return!"

"Aooooo!" said Feral, content for his sibling to do the speechifying.

"The forest is ours! Aoooo!" Howling said.

"Aoooooooooo! Aoooo!" Feral howled back.

"And we are its!"

"Aooo!"

"She hears us calling!" Howling continued, so young and already a skilled showman. Cynically, she wondered if it was Eamon and Reverend's blood in him but quickly dismissed the thought. Howling was his own entity. "But do we hear her?" he asked.

"Aoooo! Aoooooo!" called Feral, joyful as a firecracker. That was who he was, sweetness, gentle curiosity, and endless cheer. "Do you hear me, coyotes? I love you." Vern heard him blow them a kiss.

"Quiet now, I can't take all that shouting," Vern said, shaking her head.

"Then say a story," demanded Howling. "A scary story."

"Scary story! Scary story!" echoed Feral.

Vern's feet made a squelching slurp noise with each step.

"Please, Mam?" Feral asked.

Sighing, Vern cleared her throat. "I might have a scary story."

"Then say it, Mam!" said Howling and Feral in unison.

"Say what?" she asked.

"A story!"

"A what?"

"A story!"

Vern smiled at the familiar call and response. She'd taught it to her children accidentally, as a matter of reflex. When Howling had just turned two and asked for a story one night, she'd asked, *A what?* And he'd repeated, *I want a story!* And she'd asked, *What?* again, and the cycle had repeated until the child was in a fit of giggles, crying out at the top of his lungs, *A story!*

It mystified Vern to think parts of Cainland were worth keeping, but she couldn't disown all of her upbringing. If she did, there'd be nothing left of her. People aren't born. They're made. Without the Blessed Acres' making of her, she'd be but a baby again, helpless and without form.

"A long time ago, in a little town filled with good, polite folk, lived a man named Brother Jon. He'd built his own house to be a home for himself, his wife, and fourteen babes. Now, this was very special, because he owned the land his house was built on at a time when people like him couldn't own nothing because the white man's greed always has him finding ways to put others down," said Vern, speaking louder than usual to be heard over the storm.

"But Mam!" Howling said. "You said you can't own land. It's for all of us. The land is kin and trying to own it is like trying to own a person."

Vern always rambled at her kids about this and that, trying to figure out what of her upbringing she agreed with and what she didn't. She had no other outlet but the babes for conversation, having never talked to Ollie about these matters.

"Forget all that right now," said Vern. "This man Jon owned a bit of land for him and his, but not so much that he was taking it away from anybody else, all right? He thought he'd found safety, finally. But one morning, he woke up to find his wife altogether different."

"Wife?" asked Howling. "Was that what my pap, Lucy, was to you?"

"Yes," said Vern. "Now hush. Do you want to hear the story or not?"

"Shh!" said Feral to his sibling.

"His wife smiled like she always did, kissed him like she always did, and helped him button on his shirt like she always did, but her smile did not look the same, her kisses did not feel the same, and she buttoned his shirt bottom to top, when before she'd always done it top to bottom. *Woman*, he said, *who is you?* And she said, *I'm your wife.* None of his fourteen children noticed the difference, but Jon could tell this was an impostor. The next morning, his wife still changed, he found his eldest son was now different, too. *You are not my boy*, he said. *For my boy never did a lick of work in his whole life, spoilt ingrate he was, and you've mended the fence and it's not even breakfast yet.* Every day he awoke, and another one of his children was changed. He watched them as they moved through their days, fakes. Whenever he protested, they would state calmly, *I'm your wife*, *I'm your son*, or *I'm your daughter*. The only child who'd not been changed was the youngest. The night he was due to undergo the changing, Jon stayed up and watched over the child's cradle. It was past midnight when he heard noises. He grabbed a fire poker and held it out, ready to fight, but a blow came from behind, knocking him right out."

Howling and Feral both screamed, but Vern went on. "When he woke up, he found himself strapped down. A white man stood over him, metal tools in his hands, a wide grin on his pallid face. *This might smart some*, said the white man, and started to drill into the man's brain while he was awake."

"Was there blood?" asked Howling.

"There was."

"Did it hurt?" Feral whispered.

"Fiercely. Poor Jon was awake as the white man took out pieces of his brain, rearranged them here and there, until, just like his wife and children, he was changed. By the end, there was nothing left of who he was at all. He moved through life like a puppet and could say but one phrase, *I am Jon*, even though he wasn't at all," said Vern, finishing the story.

"That white man was a night doctor, wasn't he?" asked Howling.

"Yes," Vern confirmed. All her scary stories revolved around these semimythological figures: white doctors who came in the night to rob Black people for medical experimentation. Her mam had told her these stories, brought with her from her life before Cainland.

"Was that man who tried to burn us up a white man?" asked Howling.

"Yes," said Vern.

"Are there lots of people somewhere who look like him?"

"There are lots of people all over the place who look all kinds of ways," Vern explained.

"But where?" he asked. "I never seen no one but you, and that white man. Where does Lucy live? And her mam and her pap? Does Lucy have a sibling like Feral?"

Every word out that child's mouth wrought fresh calamity inside of Vern. She'd never be able to sate his ferocious hunger for knowledge . . . "I'm tired, Howl, and we got a ways to go."

"A ways to where?" he asked, his cheek bobbing back and forth against her midback, his voice raspy, nasal, and deep. Everything about Howling, from his compact, lean frame to his jaunty walk and the blooms of black hair emerging like petals from his head, gave Vern the sense of someone to be ready for, to never underestimate. "Home is back that way," he said, leaning his body uncomfortably to point backward.

"But so's that bad white man who was tryna burn us up!" answered Feral.

"That bad man got eated up by a animal. His body wasn't there this morning. I checked all by myself! So we can go back."

"Quiet, I said."

Howling howled and Feral, too, until both of their voices grew hoarse and their bodies slumped against hers, dead weight. Vern took Feral down from her shoulders and tied him to the hip opposite Howling.

How they fell asleep on her with the rain still falling so mightily and the wind gnashing and the trees wild and thrashing and the cold cutting in deep, she didn't understand. Vern was tired, too, but she couldn't think of sleeping, not in this mad tempest. Nor could she think of stopping.

If she kept walking, she could pretend she had a future. Over the next hill, through the next clearing, just this many miles more. Just there, just there. Yonder, a life.

Vern walked twelve hours, then twenty-four. If she'd stopped then, she might've cited adrenaline for her endurance, but she didn't. She carried her children in the woods without sleep for days, with no food and little water. She stopped only so everyone might do their business, to forage for mushrooms, and to let the babes stretch their legs. It wasn't until the tenth day-and-night cycle of walking straight without sleep that she collapsed.

⊠

VERN PULLED HER BABES IN to her chest. They slept one to each side of her, heads crooked between her breasts and underarms. Feral, clingier than Howling, had one leg curled around Vern's body possessively, his heel digging into her belly button. His hand gripped one of her ribs.

She'd not even made them a shelter or a pad of leaves to sleep on when she'd finished her ten-day trek. Just stopped and lay down.

Howling huffed in his sleep, and Feral squeaked softly. A white-tailed kite whistled. Behind Vern was the sound of hooves in dirt, the soft scuffing of mud and fallen leaves. She turned toward the noise, blinking in order to parse the image. Not five feet from Vern and the children was a herd of deer.

Vern's stomach gnawed greedily. She slid out of the embrace of her children, her back flat on the ground and her feet pushing her backward. The two children rolled into each other but made no sound. Vern grabbed her biggest knife, removing it from the sheath that hung from her neck.

She rolled onto her side before moving into a low squat. After a count to three, she lunged at the closest deer and plunged her knife into its neck. Its brethren went running while it buckled under her blade. She jumped onto its back, took the knife out, and jabbed it between the shoulder blades. It went down, poor beast, whimpering all the way.

"Sorry," she said weakly, though it was an apology with little meaning behind it. It was dead, and more of its kind would be dead in the future by her hand, by her knife. She was no sorrier than the endless rain was that had washed away her food stores, than wild boars who rooted for mice.

"Howling, Feral, wake up!" she said. "Wake up now."

"What?" asked Howling.

"Up. Gather some kindling," said Vern.

"Kindling?" asked Feral with his teeny-tiny voice before yawning big and wide. "No more walk?"

"Not today," said Vern. She didn't know about tomorrow. "Now go with Howling and get me some kindling."

Instead, Feral squatted next to the deer. "It cry?" he asked.

"It happened too quick for it to mourn," said Vern.

"You cry?" Feral asked.

"I'm ashamed to say that I did not." Taking the creature's life had been no small thing.

"Shamed?"

"Don't you think this beauty deserves some tears?"

"Cry, then, Mam!" said Howling from up in a tree where he was snagging down thin branches. "You cried after you kilt that man who tried to burn us!"

But Vern hadn't been crying for Ollie. She'd been crying for Vern, feeling sorry for herself and her lot.

Vern laid her hand on the dead deer's cheek and closed her eyes. She willed tears to fall for this perished animal, and they did come in time. "Him so still," said Feral.

She forced herself to stop lest she get lost in it, then wiped her eyes with the back of her hand. Feral's face scrunched up in concentration as he watched her clean the deer.

Howling gathered kindling into a bundle, then asked Vern for her knife so he could make tinder. She handed him her smallest one. She'd been thinking about giving it to him as a present, but then she wouldn't have one to give to Feral.

The children made themselves wooden blades frequently with knives and sticks, which were good enough for dressing fish and squirrels, but they were ready for more. Proper knives, not like the ones you could make crafting in the woods. She'd make them more permanent ones out of rock when she had the energy for it.

Howling scraped the inner bark off one of the surrounding trees. "Can I have the flint stone, Mam?" he asked.

He was always trying to make sparks like Vern did, to start the fire, hitting the knife against the flint. "Go ahead," she said, and fished it out her pocket, tossing it to him before returning to the deer. "Remember what this is called?" she asked Feral, holding out an organ close enough so that he could get a look at it. She let him take his time. Like her, he sometimes needed extra time to process what he was seeing because of his low vision.

"Liver?" he asked.

"And this?" she prompted.

"Intestines."

"Good bear," she said, then swung a glance toward Howling. He was flicking the knife against the stone over and over, but he had yet to make a spark. "That's enough now, Howl. You're gonna hurt yourself. Give it here."

"I almost got it!"

"You're not strong enough yet. Leave it," Vern said.

"I am strong," he said.

"I didn't say you wasn't strong, just not strong enough." Vern sighed anticipating the quarrel coming.

"I can do it."

"You can try again tomorrow," Vern said, and reached for the flint and knife, but Howling took a step back, knife out. "Child. Don't you dare." Howling went running.

Because his vision was so keen compared to hers, she couldn't easily outpace him. She didn't always get her bearings fast enough, especially not in a new woods with unfamiliar ground and un-expected slopes.

She was bigger. Vern grabbed her babe by the hood and yanked him backward. He fell flat to the ground. "You stupid, Mam," he said, lying on his back as he looked up at her, lips shak-ing because he was about to start wailing.

She took the knife and stone from him, then picked him up. He buried his face in her chest. "I want to do it!" he cried out.

"I know."

"I hate you," said Howling.

"It hurts my feelings when you say that."

Howling whimpered. "You don't have feelings," he said. "You killed that deer and didn't even cry. You kill things all the time. And you burn yourself, and it don't even hurt you, even though the fire scorches your skin. I seent it." He writhed in her grip until she put him down. "I bet I could throw this rock at you and it wouldn't even hurt," he said, reaching down to the ground and picking up a hefty stone, big as a skull in his two hands. He hoisted it toward her, but she dodged it.

Howling was an observant child. She'd always thought she'd been private with her burning, but she should've known he'd seen her, had put together the things she'd done to her body.

"I do hurt, Howling, matter of fact," she said. "I hurt think-ing of you cutting yourself with the knife because you get too eager with the flint."

"Nuh-uhn," he said. "You're gonna throw me in the fire till I burn. You aint gonna care at all. You aint gonna cry when I burn up. You was gonna let that man burn us up."

Feral, never sure how to handle it when his sibling unraveled, hugged Vern's thigh and started to cry. She appreciated the heft of him, the feel of his squeezes anchoring her.

"Howling, if you burned away I would never recover," she said.

"You would too cause you like Feral more than me," he cried, his arms crossed over his chest. He was far enough away that she couldn't make out every detail of his face, but she was sure his bottom lip was in full pout, that there were hot tears rolling down the pudgy hills of his cheeks. "Because he's like you."

"I love you both more than breathing. Come here," she said, and squatted. "Right now. Come here."

He dragged his feet toward her. She pulled him in so his nose was to hers. "You're a little me," she said. "Hungry as a wolf."

Howling sniffled. "You think I'm like you?"

"Just like," said Vern, wiping his tears away with her thumbs.

"And me?" asked Feral.

"You, too," she said. Though they both were pleased to hear it, she wasn't sure it was a compliment. They were both her raw parts, her every sensitivity.

⬙

THEY FEASTED ON THAT DEER for weeks. Every morning Vern stewed a different joint over the fire, till the meat and bones were soft. After finishing their fill of meat, the children slurped up the broth greedily and gnawed on the gristle.

She'd chosen a good place to make camp, not far from a river, the ground relatively flat and smooth and not gnarled with tree trunks. She put stakes of different heights around their camp to keep track of which direction was which. The tallest stake, west, toward the river, the next tallest one, east, toward a cliffside where she didn't want the children to wander, and two more for north and south. Northward was a road. She'd heard what she thought was a horn blowing from that way, the sound carried on the wind.

With help from the children, she built a shelter, using the deer hide as a soft bit of flooring. Howling and Feral were eager to participate, and even though they were more hindrance than aid, it was important they be involved. They'd need to know these things, how to live in the woods, how to live at all.

By spring, they were building their own structures. "Look, Mam!" said Feral, showing her his tunnel of sticks and leaves. It wound like a serpent through the trees.

When summer came, they could evade Vern for hours, their shelters so perfectly blended into the environment. It settled her to know how quick her babes were, how strong. She was under no illusion that if she died they'd survive on their own, but it was good to know they could fight. She didn't know how long she had.

Lately, every morning her body erupted with a new agony. The strength and healing remained, but her joints and limbs were now a constant ache. Worse, she itched. She rubbed her body with herbs and tinctures, but they did not soothe. No matter how often she scratched, relief never came. Instead, the itch burrowed deeper, consciously evading her nails.

In the dead of night, her children asleep in the shelter, she crawled out, stripped off her shirt, and scraped her back against the rough bark of a tree until she bled. For once, this harm she did to her body was not intended. She moved up and down as roughly as she could against the bark, moaning as she tore her back to slivers.

"Mam?" she heard Howling call from inside the tent.

"Stay inside," she said.

"You okay?"

"I'm okay. Sleep, baby," she told him.

When dawn came and she'd worried multiple layers of skin away, Vern went down to the river in hopes that the cool, rushing water might numb what discomfort remained. Vern stripped and walked in.

The river was shallow enough that she didn't have to worry about the current carrying her too far away, so she let herself float. The healing waters kissed the inflamed welts on her back. She flipped onto her belly and started to breaststroke, then front crawl. Vern was coming up for air when she saw the body, the little brown body, limp on the current.

Filled to the brim with a dread so horrid her heart did not properly beat its beats, Vern swam after the body of the child. It snagged on a branch, and she carried the body to the bank.

It was the same body she'd seen three years ago, the one she'd left to scavengers when she'd been too cowardly to return to it to give proper burial. That child had not been real, and nor was this one. Like the howling wolves, it was a haunting.

⬚

"MAM?"

"Mam!"

Both her children had come to fetch her.

"I'm down the river, children," she called. "Bring me my clothes."

"Which side you on, Mam?" Feral yelled. His speech was improving rapidly, though it would be a while until he was as adept as Howling.

"Don't worry about which side, just come on!" she called.

"Huh?" they both said.

"Just come on!" she shouted.

When they found her, they handed Vern her summer outfit, a loose linen top and fitted hide pants cropped just above her ankle. Each child looked at her naked body all cockeyed, like they didn't see her without clothing all the time.

"Why you acting like you just seen the dead?" asked Vern.

"What's that, Mam?" Feral asked, his voice so dainty she could barely hear him over the rumbling river.

"What's what?"

Both her babes pointed to her, and she looked down at herself. A great rash had broken out over her arms, chest, and neck. Inflamed patches of red and white, bumpy and pus-filled, covered her.

"You did something to it?" Howling asked.

"I didn't do nothing!" Vern said defensively.

Back at camp she rubbed salve all over. The itching hadn't subsided, but it had lessened with the outbreak of rash. "It's worse on your back," said Howling, rubbing the salve there for her.

"I was scratching it a lot," she said. "Because it was itching," she added hastily, not wanting him to think she'd made those welts on purpose.

"I don't mean that. It looks like . . ." He drew his finger down her spine. "It's all hard, Mam. And white. Like your skin's boiling. You look like your skeleton's on the outside."

Vern couldn't make sense of his description and waved him off. "It's just an allergy. The skin reacting bad to a flower."

"That's one powerful flower," said Howling. "Flowerful." That cracked him up.

He loved rhymes. Loved words. Loved to play with their infinite combinations. Back at Cainland, he'd be reading by now. He'd have inherited her old copy of *Ashanti to Zulu*, an ABC book of cultural traditions from various peoples across the African continent, by a woman named Margaret Musgrove. The copy had belonged to Vern's mam. She should've thought to bring it with her, or other books, at least, when she'd left the compound. Something with pictures and words so her babes could see beyond what was in the woods.

Vern had never learnt to read. It gave her a migraine just to try, with the way it hurt her eyes. Instead, Lucy would read out loud to her. Before Ollie's TV, that was how Vern learned about the outside world, from books. Her favorite was *Giovanni's Room*. In it, two men got together, together-together, like husbands and wives, like Vern with Ollie, though it made her retch now to think of it.

The book had been her and Lucy's secret. Lucy had sneaked it in. Unlike Vern, she hadn't been born on the compound and had only come with her parents when she was seven and already full of the outside world. When she'd left at thirteen with her mam, as abruptly as she'd arrived, she'd left *Giovanni's Room* for Vern in their secret hiding place in the woods, tucked inside a rotting log. But it wasn't like Vern could read it, and she certainly couldn't ask anyone else to read it aloud for her. In it had been the phone number and address for Lucy's aunt's house. Vern knew it was Lucy's way of telling her to come after her.

Vern should've packed the book when she ran away, but her mind, for once, hadn't been on Lucy. It had been on her own two feet, one after the other. Lucy had gotten her chance to leave, had escaped without a second thought about Vern. Now Vern understood why, how intoxicating fleeing was. She'd left her mam and her brother like it was nothing, like they were nothing. Goodness, in that moment, they were.

*Giovanni's Room* was only one book. There were thousands and thousands more. Maybe even a million. Perhaps in one of them there was the answer, the answer to it all. Howling and Feral deserved to read that.

The woods were endless in their own way. There were infinite things to learn in that expanse. But it was not the world, and soon enough they'd all have to say goodbye to it.

There were questions that could not be answered here: questions about Ollie, questions about Vern's body, questions about Cainland, questions about books. She wanted to show her babes the shape of the world, but she couldn't even draw them a map.

She had all those papers and the laptop she'd taken from Ollie's place, and no one to tell her what they said. For all she knew, everything she'd ever wanted to know about where she'd grown up was written on that computer. Everything that was happening to her body.

They'd outgrown this place, and the time for leaving was soon. Her body didn't have long before the woods would not contain it.

⊠

IT WAS AUTUMN, almost winter, when she decided to leave. The children had just turned four, and Howling kept asking about the other half of his parentage. It was a simple question, but its answer was endless and gestured to a world her children didn't know. "Where is this Lucy?" Howling asked.

"All that's important is that you lived in my belly. You grew and grew in there till you were big enough to be bornt. Don't worry about your father."

Howling frowned. "I thought you liked Lucy," he said. "Are people like beavers?"

"What?"

"Like beavers. And bald eagles. And barn owls. Or are they like deer?"

Vern shook her head. "What are you talking about, Howl?"

"Beavers mate for life, and so do bald eagles and barn owls. But not deer."

Several months ago they'd all witnessed a doe give birth to her child. Howling had wondered where the buck was, and she'd explained the species' mating habits. "What about people? You talk about Lucy like she's your mate for life."

Feral turned from his work shelling nuts to look at his mąm, his way of echoing Howling's question.

"It's different for different people," Vern managed.

"Do some people have cloacas?" asked Howling. Her children's perception of the world was so skewed.

"You hurt, Mam?" Feral asked, as Vern shook tree branches with a stick to bring down more nuts.

"I'm fine," she said.

"You limping," said Feral.

Her aches and pains had become more than aches and pains, but doctors didn't do house calls to the woods.

Fear seized Vern to have it put in such simple terms. Nothing had changed about her circumstances, but the starkness of the truth of her world was bracing. There was no medical intervention out here, and if she died from whatever it was Sherman had put into her back at Cainland, her children died with her.

"Mam? You all right? What's wrong?" asked Feral.

Last week Howling had fallen from a tree, losing his footing on a moist patch of moss. He'd not broken anything, but if he had, Vern could set only basic fractures.

"I need to tell you something," Vern said. Sensing the seriousness in her voice, Howling and Feral listened raptly. They were used to abrupt changes in topic when it came to their mam.

"We've got to leave here. We got to leave the woods," she said, forcing herself to spit it out before worry for how they'd take it could set in.

"What do you mean?" said Howling.

"We got to leave the woods," she repeated.

"But how do you leave the woods?" he asked, gesturing all around. "The woods is everywhere."

She shook her head. "You know how sometimes there's a clearing in the trees? There's a place where it's like that everywhere, outside the woods. You've just got to walk far enough in the right direction. That's where Lucy is."

Howling didn't answer back, but he was thinking, brooding, ruminating.

"Why?" asked Feral, sensing his brother's distress and taking over.

"Because I think there's a chance for us out there, and I don't think there's one here. I think I'm sick, babies, and I don't know what's wrong. Out there, there might be a cure for me."

Howling kicked at the small structure of sticks and mud he was building, softly at first, then hard, until it crumbled. "You've never mentioned no outside-the-woods before."

"It was implied," she said, impatient. "Where did you think all my stories took place?"

"In the woods!" cried Howling. "The world!"

"The world is more than woods," she said.

"But will there be sticks for building shelters? If there's a whole place that's only a clearing, where do you get sticks for making a shelter?" asked Howling.

"There are shelters out there prebuilt." She didn't mention that those cost money. It was something else neither of her children could begin to understand. "Haven't you been wondering about what you saw on my back that day at the river? Or why my skin's how it is? Or why I can hardly walk some days? It's only going to get worse. What if I can't take care of you?"

"Then I'll take care of us," said Howling. "I'll take care of you!"

"Oh, baby," she said, and knelt down to Howling's level, squeezed his hands.

Feral watched his mam and sibling carefully, braced. "Why don't you make yourself some medicine, Mam?" he asked, and the naivete of the suggestion made Vern smile and almost tear up simultaneously. "Or tell me how to do it if you can't. I'll do exactly what you say. Tell me what to gather. I'll memorize the list. I'm good at memorizing," he said.

"There's no medicine for this," she said. "Not here."

Feral barreled into Vern's embrace, and she wrapped her arms around him. "You will survive this. You and Howling both. My strong, strong children."

"I like the woods," he said. Sweet child, so did Vern. Not even the fiend had ruined its magic.

"Where is it?" asked Howling, tasked with being the brave sibling, the one who'd sort the details.

Vern pointed. "We'll walk." She tried to sound resolved. She wanted to be someone worth following into the dark.

"Are there hawks there?" Feral asked, sniffling.

"Yes, baby," said Vern. "And there are things there that aren't in the woods. New things. Lions."

"What's lions?" asked Feral.

"They're animals, big and ferocious like a bear. They're in Africa."

"Is that the name of the place we're going to?" asked Howling.

Vern shook her head. "You may get there eventually, if that's where you want to go to. There's rhinos, tigers, gazelles, gorillas, and flamingos, and that's just the beginning. There's millions of species of animals. You hear that now? Millions. That's a big number."

"Bigger than a hundred?"

Vern picked up one of the nuts Feral had shelled. "If this nut was worth one hundred," she said, "you could make a line of them from here all the way down to the riverbank and back probably twenty times, and it still wouldn't be as big as nine million."

"Is the world that big?" Howling asked.

"Bigger," said Vern. She pulled him to her so that he could share her embrace with Feral. She wanted to see his face. "It's bigger than all your imaginings. You could run forever and not get close to the end of it."

Howling cried along with his sibling, but they were silent tears. The wet coiled down his cheeks with each slow blink of his eyes.

"How will I find you? How will I ever find you?" He sucked in breath after breath, but he could not get ahold of himself. His little sobs escaped his throat, where he tried to keep them captive.

"You will survive this, my brave, brave babies," she said.

"When we leave?" Feral asked, his voice a croaky whisper, still caught with mucus.

Vern wanted to spend a few more weeks preparing the children for what they'd find out there, but she hardly knew herself.

They would learn it the same way they'd learned the woods. They'd climb its trees, swim its waters.

Perhaps it was foolish to leave on a whim after all this time, but it was the same impulse that had made her leave Cainland. Sometimes, one's feet knew best, and it was better to ignore one's reasoning mind.

"We leave at nightfall."

PART TWO

# KINGDOM FUNGI

## 9

VERN HAD HOWLING AND FERAL walk the journey to the road. She wanted them exhausted enough that they'd sleep through the excitements of the coming evening. Her children had never seen a streetlight, heard a car's sputtering engine, or been blinded by its searing headlights.

"Soon we'll come upon something called a road," Vern explained. "It's hard and gray. Sometimes black. There's white lines and yellow lines painted on it. You must never go in it without holding my hand, you understand? You stay far to the side of it, either in the dirt or on something called a sidewalk, which is also gray and hard, but it's separated from the road by a curb. The sidewalk is higher than the road part. Usually. That's the part you walk on. Feral, now, you might not be able to see the distinction between—that's why, no matter what, you hold my hand."

The twins weren't used to hearing her talk this much. She hoped the rarity of her lectures meant they understood that when she did give them, they needed heeding.

"What the road for?" Feral asked.

"Cars," said Vern.

"Them those big hard things you talked about?" asked Feral.

"Yes. Bigger than the biggest beast you ever seen, and faster, too. They'll trample you right down."

"Hope it tramples *you* down," Howling said.

"And what's the most important thing?" Vern asked, ignoring Howling's outburst.

"Doing what you say," said Feral.

"Howling, I want to hear you say it, too. I know you're mad, but you listening to me will be the difference between making it or not, you understand? So what do you got to do?" She stopped and knelt in front of him, placed a firm grip on each shoulder.

"I got to do what you say," said Howling, hating it.

"Why?" asked Vern.

"Or I won't make it."

"And what's not making it mean?" she asked.

"I never see you or Feral again."

"Good bear," she said, and stood up to walk. "Come on. Keep up."

Vern brushed her hands against the trees, feeling for the marks she'd made. Soon they'd be beyond her previously explored territory.

"Can you see the stars, Howling?"

The trees, at least, had begun to thin.

"Of course I can, dummy."

"Can you see the very bright star?" she asked.

"The north one?"

"Yes."

"Is it pink?"

Vern shook her head. "That's Mars," she said.

"One of them is moving!" Howling said. "And flashing red."

"Pay no mind to that. Find the bright, bright star, brighter than all the others. Standing still in the sky," she said.

"I can't find it, damn it." That child was already a perfectionist, holding himself to impossible standards.

"Can you find the Drinking Gourd?" she asked.

Howling pranced around, running from tree to tree to get

a good look where there were breaks in the canopy. It took him a moment, but soon he pointed upward. "That's it! That's it! That's it!"

"Now, you see the two stars that form the edge of the bowl part of the ladle, farthest from the tip of the handle?" Vern asked.

"Uh-huh," said Howling.

"Follow those two stars in a straight line down, you should see—"

"I see it! The North Star!"

Vern smiled, struck by Howling's easy nature. That child, mercurial as a Southern winter, could go from cold to hot in moments. "Can you find the Little Drinking Gourd?"

"Of course, Mam. It's right there. Oh! The tip of the Little Drinking Gourd's handle is the North Star!"

"Yes. Exactly," said Vern, confident that he'd found the right star. Based on where he was frantically pointing, Vern had maintained the correct course.

Feral always listened closely as Vern described constellations and asterisms, though, like her, he couldn't see them. When the woods were far behind them, she'd find some paper and draw them out for him from her memory. He'd appreciate their delicate relationships. She would tell him that despite their apparent closeness, they were farther apart than any two things on earth could be.

"Mam?" Feral said.

"Mm?"

"Do you ever wish you could see the stars?" he asked, his voice intrigued rather than regretful.

As a child she had. Folks were always bringing them up and talking about them a great deal. Everybody had a star story, a star memory. "I prefer the moon," said Vern. "Big and glowing. A pupil-less eyeball."

"Blind like us?" asked Feral, his voice ever so serious, this inquiry of utmost importance.

"In its way," Vern said.

"Will I ever see the North Star?" Feral asked. His voice had grown husky with fatigue, sounding lower like his sibling's.

"I don't know," said Vern. "Maybe in a telescope. But even if not, there are many ways to love a thing, to know it deeply. Your uncle, Carmichael, liked to collect facts about things. Did you know the North Star is three stars? Three stars in orbit with each other," she said. "He told me that. All joined up. Like you, me, and Howling. Bound."

CARS WHIRRED BY. "Hear that?" Vern asked. "Like gusts of wind."

"Breaths of a hungry giant," said Feral, intrigued.

Vern led her babes out of the woods onto the shoulder of a backcountry road.

"It's like a river you can't jump into," said Howling, inspecting.

"Hold my hand," she said, reaching her arm out to him. He jumped back from the road and grabbed her hand.

"What now?" asked Feral. "What you do with it? Does it move? You ride in it like a boat? Why's it made of rock?"

"Soon enough more cars will pass by. We'll hear them coming, those gusts of wind. We're going to get into one," she said, holding out her thumb.

She had Howling and Feral stay to the right of her so her body would be a shield against any oncoming vehicles. She walked against traffic to better see cars approach. "One's coming now, get ready," she said, hearing it before seeing it.

When the lights flared and the engine bawled, Howling

screamed his throat raw and Feral yelped before smashing his face into Vern's thigh. Vern crouched and swept them both into her fold, a babe in each arm. "Just a little old car, that's all, children. You don't have to be afraid."

"There was nothing little about it," Howling cried. "You liar. I hate you."

"It's gone now, I promise," she said, squeezing her fingers into the plush bun of coils tied up at the back of his head. "You're right, it's not little. It's big. Big enough to carry us away to where we want to go. They don't mean you harm."

"But it smelled so bad," said Feral. "What was that?" He was covering his nose and mouth with both hands as he gasped for breaths.

"Gas," said Vern. Both children laughed, their fright forgotten. "Not that kind of gas, buttheads. Liquid gas."

"Like diarrhea?" said Howling, still grinning.

Rolling her eyes, Vern shoved Howling away playfully. "Gasoline. I'll explain it later, I promise. You just got to take it all in. The answers are gonna come."

"They should call them skunks instead of cars," said Howling. Feral nodded at his sibling's sage declaration.

Cars, minivans, SUVs, and pickup trucks continued to barrel by, impaling the trio with light. The children shrieked away from the road each time. Though they'd barely left its borders more than twenty minutes ago, they already pined for the woods. "Can the skunks even see us? Why aint they stopping?" asked Howling.

Vern squinted ahead. "What is it, Mam?" the children asked, following her gaze.

A horse-drawn buggy rolled down the road toward them. Vern stumbled backward as two white horses galloped forward, tugging a wood-wheeled wagon. They slowed as they approached. Vern grabbed both her children's hands. The wagon halted. A tall, lanky white man with black hair down to his ears, parted in the middle, stepped down. He held out a lantern in front of him, like he couldn't see her or the children right there in front of him.

Vern held fast to her children and ran. It was a half-realized sprint, her joints sore and unsteady. The children, with their little feet, slowed her down further. She glanced back over her shoulder to get a look. The driver was back in his carriage, whipping the horses to move. "Giddyup!" he snapped.

The whip made a sound like cracking bone as it sliced the air. The horses whinnied and neighed. Their shod hooves trampled the ground. Vern decided to veer back into the cover of the trees, where the horses and wagon could not follow, but the next time she looked back over her shoulder, they were gone.

"Mam! Mam! What is it?" asked Howling, looking back at the direction from which they'd come.

Vern sucked down air. "It was nothing, baby. I thought I— I thought I saw something." It was another haunting. They were increasing in regularity.

"Thought you saw what?" asked Feral.

"A ghost," she said.

Feral nodded. "I hate ghosts," he said, and then, afraid one might have heard him, he corrected himself. "I hate mean ghosts. I love you, other ghosts."

"Leave us alone, mean ghosts!" Howling shouted. He picked up a wad of pebbles from the ground and launched them into the air. Feral joined in. So did Vern. She dug her hand into the hard, packed dirt and fisted a clump of it. She pelted it hard enough that if someone had been in the way, they'd have gotten a nasty bruise.

"Damn, Mam!" said Howling. "Wish I could throw like

that." He picked up a rock and launched it, and while it was a decent throw, it had nothing on Vern's.

"We got to go," said Vern. "That ghost won't be bothering us no more."

## 10

VERN'S BABES weren't good babes in the traditional sense. They'd never needed to be good before, to behave. There was no father or grandfather or uncle looming in the corner with a belt, no mam or grandma or auntie with a hairbrush or wooden spoon waiting to pounce on their bare behinds, no teacher marking their hard work with a red pen, telling them, *Indoor voices.* They could hardly know what indoor was.

Howling and Feral didn't know how to sit still, how not to ask questions, how to smother every impulse, how not to talk back, how to shrink. They didn't know what elders were and that they were to be respected at all costs. They knew only Mam, Mam who they'd decided they liked okay, who seemed in most cases to ensure their pleasure, who rarely dictated how their lives should go on a day-to-day basis. Most elders were not like Mam. In the world beyond the woods, these wild-hearted babes would never get by.

Up ahead, a carnival of lights disrupted the dark. The children's eyes demurred at the flashes of white and yellow and red and pink. Not firelight. Not sunlight. Not starlight. Not moonlight. "Electricity," said Vern, when the children asked if it was hoodoo. "Just stay close."

The road they'd been walking along met with a highway. Cars eased through the gas station like machines on a conveyor belt, and mams rushed frantic children to the toilets. "It smells nice," said Feral, sucking in a wad of cool air through his nostrils. The aromas of a fried-pie shop and barbecue joint scented the evening. "What is that?" asked Feral, tugging her toward civilization, where the blackness dissolved and wires sparked with vitality.

"The smell?" asked Vern. "It's food."

"Can we get some of it?" asked Feral, his natural exuberance for all things novel dwarfing his cautious side.

"I've got some jerky and dried blackberry," she said, fishing into a pouch she carried.

"But I want that food," Feral said, pointing to the lights. "The electricity food."

"Not me," said Howling, being contrary for contrary's sake. "I want the venison." Vern handed him several strips of the berry-sweetened jerky. They'd been out of the woods for only a little while, but the two had declared sides. For Howling, the world would be his adversary, something to conquer. For Feral, it would be a platter of delicacies to try and love.

Judging by the heavy darkness, Vern guessed it was around eleven, maybe midnight. Despite the hour, the rest stop bustled with coffed-up drivers. It was busy enough that she might go unnoticed, even with her getup of hides and furs.

"All right, children. Listen to me carefully. I need you to stay exactly right here," she said. She squatted down and pushed them backward into the bushes.

"You leaving?" asked Feral.

"Just going up ahead to where the electricity is to get us a few things, find us one of those cars that can drive us to our next stop," she said.

"You coming back?" Howling asked. It was more accusation than question.

"What reason would I have not to come back to the two

creatures most precious to me in this big world?" she asked. It came out defensive, not sweetly as she'd intended. She had left them before, abandoned them for Ollie. Maybe Howling remembered that.

"Don't be long," Howling said, grumbling.

"I won't," she said.

"And bring me electricity food," said Feral, excited.

"I will. But you got to swear you won't move an inch."

"Not a one," said Feral.

"And Howling? You swear?" Vern asked.

He shrugged.

"Howling." He turned his head from hers and sat down cross-legged in his designated spot, obscured by the branches. Vern sighed. "I'll be right back."

The food mart surely had bagels and donuts, perhaps foil-wrapped hot sandwiches rotting on a warmer. Vern had been to places like this with Sherman before on their mission trips from the compound, traveling the forty miles into town. Cainites didn't engage with or support the white economy in any way, so instead of buying Vern the machine-made hot cocoa and plastic packet full of six powdered mini-donuts she wanted, he'd encouraged her to steal them or otherwise use her wiles to obtain the items.

It was white people food. *Junk made by robots, no human touch, grown on scorched earth greedy for the sustenance summarily stripped from it.* But he allowed her occasional tastes of the outside world, if only to remind her how good Cainland had it.

Under Sherman's instructions, Vern had walked up to the man at the cash register and told him her mam had passed out in the single-stall bathroom, which was locked. Really, Vern had jammed it. While the man ran down the long hallway to go help, she'd taken what she needed, including a few snacks and drinks for her little brother. Vern had been twelve or thirteen when she'd done that. Older now and rougher-looking, she doubted such a ruse would work for her anymore.

She went into the crowded barbecue joint instead, grabbing leftover scraps from abandoned tables. The place was under-staffed and busy. Easy pickings. Ribs and chopped brisket, sweet rolls, corn on the cob. Potato salad. It was a fast-food place, and everything was already contained in convenient Styrofoam take-away boxes.

Vern tucked her scavengings into her carry pouch, then left, heading toward the side of the rest stop devoted to the trucks. She loitered there, scouting for passersby. "Can I get a ride?" she called to someone several feet away. It could've been a station attendant or a trucker. Could've been someone walking their dog. She couldn't get her bearings in this combination of night, blaring lights, and hurrying people. "I need a lift to Sugar Moun-tain," she said. It was the only touchstone she had, Lucy's auntie's house. She had no idea how close or far it was, but she hoped she was at least in the right state. When she'd made her ten-day trek through the woods, she'd used flora and fauna as a map, finding her way based on geography, but that wouldn't work now.

"Can't help you," the person said.

Vern was thankful for the weariness in her body, for the pain abrading her insides. It made her courageous. Already on the edge, all she had to do was let herself fall. Vern called out to everybody who passed until she got the attention of a trucker. "Sugar Mountain?" he asked.

"That's right. Can you take me there?"

The trucker looked her up and down.

"I can get you pretty close," he said. His voice was re-signed, like he wasn't sure he wanted to be doing this but he was duty bound to.

"How far is it? And how close can you get me?"

"It's about three hundred miles. I can get you two hundred twenty of those. You'll be able to catch a bus from there. Hop in, kid," he said.

Vern smiled and clapped her hands before intertwining her fingers. "Okay. Wait just one second, and I'll be back."

The trucker sighed as he leaned against his rig and shook his head. "I got to get moving," he said.

"I said I'll be right back. I got to get something. Don't go. Please," said Vern, but she didn't like the sound of herself begging and changed tack. "I mean it. Stay right there."

Vern jogged back to her children, counting paces once she stepped from the concrete of the parking lot onto the patchy grass at the side of the road. Twenty-one steps. Left. Just across from the triangular yellow sign. That was where she'd left them.

"Howling?" she said. "Feral?" She called their names again, but neither child answered. "Children." Breathing in to calm herself, she brushed her hands against the trees and bushes along the side of the road. She plunged her arms into the leaves and branches. Her fingers mauled for heat, for flesh.

"Little bears?"

She wrestled twigs and branches on her way back into the woods. Leftward, a scattering of dark trees expanded endlessly before her; rightward, more of the same. Wind pricked her cheeks. "Little bears. Come out. No hiding."

Twigs snapped, but not underfoot. She followed the cracking. There they were, her babes, but not just her babes, a tall woman holding their hands, guiding them into the dark. "Hey!" Vern shouted, and gave chase. She grabbed her children's shoulders to jerk them toward her, but her hands filled with air, not with Howling, not with Feral. They'd gone again, out of her grasp.

"Mam!"

Vern bolted back to the road when she heard the voice. Howling was waving his hands and jumping up and down, shouting to her. "Mam! Mam!" She dove toward him and snatched him into her arms. His legs were there, his feet, his arms, his shoulders, his face, streaked with salt trails from tears. She rubbed her nose along them. "Thank God of Cain," she said, and burrowed her face into his. "Where's Feral?"

Howling pointed to the spot in the bushes where Feral lay sleeping. They'd drifted off and didn't hear her when she called for them. Poor Howling, waking up all alone in the dark, his mam chasing a lie back in the woods.

"We did what you said. Stayed right there," said Howling.

"I know. I'm proud of you. I hid you too well," Vern said. She hoisted Feral, who was still sleeping, up into her arms. The pain of lifting him was immense, a pulse of snapping sensations from the joints in her toes and the tendons in her feet, up through her back, to the vertebrae of her neck. Miles and miles separated Vern from answers, as many miles as were in the universe. On Vern's unsteady legs, a single block proved a marathon. Sugar Mountain or Sri Lanka or Saturn, wherever Lucy was, she was as much a delusion as the howling wolves, the drownt child, the horse and carriage, the tall woman in the night luring her babies off into the dark. She would never find her friend.

# 11

"FUCK," the truck driver said when he saw Vern with her babes.

"You're still here," said Vern. She'd been ready to start the search process all over again.

"Had to finish my cigarette anyway." Vern sniffed. The man didn't smell like smoke.

"They yours?" he asked.

"Course they're mine," she said.

"Of course they're yours, but I mean legally yours."

He was asking if someone in a black robe had told her she couldn't have her kids anymore. That was what had happened to Lucy's mam. The woman who'd snatched Lucy from the compound had been working for Lucy's mam, but Lucy's dad tracked her down. He sued Mrs. Jenkins for custody and won. Lucy came back to the compound, for a time.

"They're mine," Vern assured the trucker. "And they don't know anyone else but me."

"Mhm," he said, in a tone that implied he didn't believe her, but he opened the passenger door for them. She lifted her children inside one by one, then set them up so they were crouched on the floor in front of her seat, between her knees.

"Right," he said.

"I'm armed, just so you know," she said. One knife was in a sheath around her neck, the other two in pockets.

"Wonderful," he said, then wiped the back of his hand over his mustache.

Howling and Feral stared at the man, eyes wide disks. Their mouths flopped open into little puckered Os. The only people they'd ever seen before were themselves and Vern. Ollie, too, though that was a while ago now and they hardly remembered.

"I'm Mitch," the trucker said.

"I'm Feral," volunteered Vern's youngest.

"Shh, child," Vern snapped. She was glad Feral still couldn't say his *f*'s or *r*'s properly. Sounded more like *Pearl*, the way he said it.

"That's a sweet little name for a sweet little girl," said Mitch, starting up the engine.

"Don't call my children *sweet*. Don't call them anything,"

said Vern, and sank into the soft cushion of her seat, lapping up the pleasant darkness. The gentle movement of the truck threatened to lure her to sleep, but she refused to succumb, remaining alert as each hour passed.

"Mam?" Feral said.

"What?"

"Look."

He pointed out the window. Murmurs of light, only just, dabbed the sky. Night was gone. Time slid by and by.

It was a spectacular show, the green of trees, the pink gradient of the sky. Feral crawled up onto Vern's lap and stared out the window. "We're so high and going so fast," he said. "How?"

"It's like rolling your body down a soft grassy hill," Vern said.

He pressed his face and open palms to the glass. "Almost," he said. "Why is the world so big?"

"Everything is always growing, moving," Vern said. "Changing."

That was what was happening to Vern. A stranger was growing inside her.

Vern shivered. She reached into her left sleeve with the opposite hand and picked at an itchy patch of flesh. No amount of scratching made the itch cease. She dug anyway, convinced somehow that if she tore the skin away altogether, made it somehow down to the bone, she could expunge death from inside her.

VERN TILTED HER HEAD an inch to the side to focus her vision. Gray buildings erupted like sorry, prefabricated hills from the street. The only spot of color was a pink stucco cube. A Mexican restaurant, Vern guessed.

"I'm going to need money," said Vern when Mitch pulled off

the highway onto the service road where he planned to drop her off.

He sighed but grabbed his wallet. He took out all the cash in it and handed it to her. Vern brought it close to her eyes so she could count it. Two fives. One ten. Three one-dollar bills. She folded each of the bill types in a different pattern so she'd be able to recognize them quickly. The ten she folded long side to long side, the fives she did shorts to shorts, and the ones she did in thirds. She tucked the money into a thick wad of napkins from the floor, then put it in her carrying pouch.

The trucker stopped at a red light on the service road and gestured to Vern to get out. She slid out the rig and lifted Feral and Howling down with her. She slammed the door behind her, and ran onto the pavement, tripping lightly over the curb. The trucker had already driven off by the time she remembered he was probably owed a thank-you.

"You all right, children?" she asked, setting them down on a spot of brown grass.

Feral rubbed his eyes with his fists. "I don't like it," he said.

"Don't like what?"

"The light's too bright."

Vern nodded and planted a dry kiss on his clammy forehead. "We'll be inside shortly." She picked him up so his legs straddled her right hip, then grabbed Howling's hand.

"Was that man a giant like from a story?" asked Feral, resting his head on Vern's shoulder. Even though he was only an hour younger than Howling, he would always be the baby in a way the elder twin wasn't. "Did you see that fur all over his face? Do all giants have fur? Are there more of him? Are there more of you? Are there littluns like us?"

Vern would be better prepared to handle her children's onslaught of questions if she got some food in her. Hungry as she was, she could eat for five or six. "Like I told Howling last night, you got to take it as it comes. Come on. Let's go get some electricity food."

Vern stopped at the first food place she came to, thankful that even though the drive-through was so long the line extended out onto the street, the inside was empty. A worker in a black-and-white-striped uniform turned to Vern, stumbling backward before composing herself. "Are you all right, honey?" she asked.

Vern took out cash from the napkin in her pouch. "How much food can I get for fifteen dollars?" she asked, sliding the cash over the counter.

The worker hesitated several moments but grabbed the cash before pressing several buttons on the cash register. "That'll be fourteen ninety-one," she said, and handed Vern a nickel and four pennies. "Just give me a minute."

When she returned with a large bag of food and a large cup, Vern directed the children over to a quiet booth in the back next to the emergency exit. Vern laid out the fresh food as well as the scavenged barbecue from last night and started to eat.

"What is it?" Howling asked, looking skeptical. The barbecue, at least, was recognizable. Howling picked at the chopped brisket and ribs, but found it much too sweet. Vern removed the sausage and bacon from one of the breakfast sandwiches and gave it to Howling. Howling ate that gladly, smiling as juice squirted from one of the links onto his chin.

"Try a bite of this," said Vern, handing each of them some biscuit. Feral grubbed his portion down, licking his fingers when he was done, asking for more. Howling nibbled a tiny bite, which he subsequently spat out. The outside world had increased Howling's surliness and transformed Feral's sweet curiosity into spirited adventurousness.

Vern filled the large cup with cola from the drink fountain.
She poked her straw through the plastic lid and slurped a ravenous sip, then gave it to the kids to try. They hated it, so she
guzzled it down herself before filling the cup back up with water
for them.

"You hungry still, Mam?" Feral asked. "I can hear your belly.
It sounds like a river." He then proceeded to mimic the deep
gulping noises in her belly.

"Worry about your own stomach," said Vern. "You done?"
Feral nodded and wiped biscuit crumbs from his mouth with
the back of his hand. "And Howling?"

"I'm done," he said, though he was still chewing. "Mam?"
"What?" she asked, irritable because the two breakfast sandwiches she'd eaten hadn't dented her hunger.

"Where are all the animals here?"

"They're around," she said. "You just got to look a bit closer.
Come on, let's pack up. It's still a long way to Lucy and we'll
need supplies. Different clothes."

"My clothes is fine," said Howling, chewing angrily on the
same mouthful of food he'd had a minute ago. Feral pulled napkins from the dispenser and began tidying up his area, swishing
around the mess rather than effectively cleaning it.

"This cloth is thin as a fallen leaf, damn," said Feral, and
shook his head, but he was more amused than critical. "Look!
It's already broken." The split napkin dangled from his pointer-
and-thumb grip, smeared with honey and a dab of white gravy.

"Why is everything so high up here?" asked Howling, eye-
ing his seat and the table suspiciously. In the woods, they sat
on the ground, occasionally on a log or stump, a boulder. Here,
everything was a throne.

Vern grabbed their tray of trash and dumped it into the can.

"What is that?" asked Feral, pointing to where she'd disposed the food. "Where is all that stuff going?"

"Quiet, for fuck's sake!" said Vern, when Feral asked where he should go piss, and where was an appropriate place to squat to do his other business. Later, she'd take him to the bathroom, but right now she couldn't deal with all their questions. Each one was a reminder of her failure. She might as well not have birthed them at all—kept them wrapped in her womb flesh. She was no better than her own mam, who'd raised her in a den of falsities and ignorance.

THEIR FIRST STOP was Emporium Max, where she and the kids caught stares for their wild dress. Vern, undeterred, walked up to one of the staff members and asked her where the accessories were. With a gulp, the worker pointed to a nearby aisle. "Let me—let me know if you need anything," she stuttered.

Vern followed the woman's finger toward the appropriate area and grabbed pairs of sunglasses for herself and Feral.

"Me, too," said Howling, and he took a pair off the rack and put them on his face, then exhaled. "Much better."

The shop glared, danced, warped, glittered. It possessed very little of value. Racks and rows of garbage. Vern cringed—not at the products, but at herself. The thoughts in her mind seemed ripped right from one of Sherman's sermons.

But where did this stuff come from? Who made it? At the Blessed Acres, all clothes were made from linen that the Cainites processed from flax they grew themselves, or were hand-me-downs, decades old. There seemed enough items here to clothe the whole world multiple times over, yet most of them were so thin and flimsy.

Vern picked out some plain-colored sweaters and tossed them into the cart, gray and rust, forest green, black. Next, black undershirts, socks, underwear. After that, she grabbed black leggings and jeans, the tightest ones she could find, the items Sherman would hate.

On to the babies. She grabbed some clothes and directed them toward the changing room. "Put this on," she told Howling, handing him a pair of black waffle-knit thermals, then a pair of leggings. Some tights, too. They'd need layers, without their hides and furs. Howling stripped and put on the clothes.

"You like it?" Vern asked.

He shrugged but seemed impressed. "They're light. They're soft."

"Very soft," said Feral.

She picked up a few plain black sweaters next, a couple sizes too big so the children could grow into them. They hung on the children like dresses, but the length would keep them warm, their bottoms and thighs nicely covered. All black everything—it was the Cainland uniform. Much as she hated to admit it—and she did, it bent her right out of shape—that place informed every decision she made.

Vern headed toward the shoe aisle next. Neither Howling nor Feral could fit their feet into any of the offerings, their toes too wide and spread from spending so much time barefoot or in nothing but roomy, soft bootees.

"It hurts!" Howling said once his foot was finally jammed into some boots, which lengthwise were too big, but way too narrow for his tree-climbing feet. He tried to walk in them, but tripped and fell. "They're so hard. It's like wearing a rock."

In the end, she found them some velvety slippers, in the shape of bear feet, nice and wide, and one or two sizes too big to give their toes enough room to wiggle. They had Velcro she could tighten over the ankle. For herself, she managed with some wide-fit slip-on snow boots.

The world outside the woods was a strange, shining thing. In this shop filled with luxury and refuse alike, Vern felt she was an actress playing a part. A white suburban mam in tennis shoes and leggings like on one of the commercials or television shows she watched at Ollie's house. Later she'd go running, put her kids Callum and Bruno into the jogger. Find a park. Find a woods. Get lost in it. Never return.

Till her husband called. *Susannah. Where are you?* Some things were the same in Cainland and out, and husbands calling to demand your presence was one of them.

Those women with their travel mugs, bulldog-sized handbags, and yogurt had always attracted Vern's attention. They existed in real life as much as on TV. Vern had seen these Carols and Jens and Caitlins at gas stations and food shops. They had happiness for days. They had lunch plans with strawberry-cheeked friends. Wine. Margaritas! Their cars weren't cars but mini-tanks, which they helmed while drinking green juice.

Problems plagued them, no doubt. Undevoted spouses. Bills. Dental work. But from outside looking in, they didn't have that haunted-glow about them; that aura that came from knowing all the infinite ways the world was colossally fucked. It was a lot to envy, their happiness. When they went to their Jesus churches, she didn't think any of them spent the sermons going, *This is bullshit. Everything anybody has ever said is bullshit, but this, this particularly so.*

"Howling, Feral, come on," she said, though she'd almost let *Callum, Bruno* pop out from her mouth instead. Vern could do that. Slip in and out of people, identities. Think hard enough about a world and be away in it, darting to a reality where she was baking cheesecake-swirl brownies for the school's bake sale. Back when she was a Cainite, it had been a hobby of hers, constructing imaginary worlds out of snippets of conversations she heard from her times off the compound on mission trips.

"What's this, Mam?" said Feral, holding up something or other.

"I don't know."

The children were running through the aisles, climbing up the racks and shelves, making fools of themselves and her, and so be it. Callum and Bruno would've never behaved so unruly, and she hated the imaginary children for that, the way the world had already made them still.

It was time to leave. Vern lifted Howling and then Feral into the cart they'd been filling. They were birds in a nest of cheap clothing.

"Help."

Vern twisted around toward the voice. Clutched in the arms of an adult was a child with fear-struck eyes reaching out a bandaged hand toward Vern. "Hey!" Vern called, turning her cart to chase after them.

Vern gave chase, but when she rounded the corner on the verge of catching them, there was nothing there but an aisle empty of people, dead-ending into a shelf of rubber rain boots. The pair had been a haunting.

Vern gripped the handle of the cart. "Do that again, Mam. Make us fly!" said Feral, but Vern inched back cautiously toward the main aisle to observe her fellow Emporium Max shoppers.

There was a man there and a woman there and a teenager over there, only not. There was a child jumping rope by a large display of yoga balls, only not. A husband and a wife quarreled in the corner, only not. These people dotted the Emporium Max like figures in a painting, their details distressingly vibrant. Vern noted the colors of their irises and the textures of their hair. The faces of her fellow customers were as distinct to her as they would have been had they been standing right in front of her, a foot or less away. She wouldn't be able to see them so well if they were really there, but they were hauntings, not subject to the limitations of her visual acuity.

Vern pushed the cart down the aisle, toward the café at the front of the shop, to the doors. "Ma'am? Miss!" someone snapped. "Miss!"

Vern kept walking. The automatic door swooshed open, as if just for her, nature bending to her will. "Miss!"

Vern sped up. "Run, Mam!" said Feral. "Push us fast!" Vern obliged, leaning into the pain in her back and lower joints. The wind in her face, the gleeful squeals of her babes—running away always felt so good.

## 12

THE WIND slapped Howling icy and mean. His lips, crusty and white with cold, were like fish scales. He peeled them bit by bit like petals from a flower or tines from a pine cone.

Winter suited him. Howling, for all his love of sun, wore an air of godlessness during the cold months. Cheeky abandon turned him preternaturally beautiful, like a girl from one of Mam's stories, daring strangers to hurt her, biting back.

"Aoooooooo!" Feral called as Mam pushed them in the cart. Howling joined in, earning his name.

There was no river in this world to bathe in. No ground to build a fire to heat water for a soak. So Mam took him and Feral to a shelter next to a smelly gasoline place where water came out the mouth of a glinting silver rock. She wet leaf-thin cloths with the water and rubbed herself all over.

"Mam," said Feral, eyes split open wide like a cracked nut. "Your back."

"What?"

"Pretty."

The sides of Mam's back were covered in a white hide of what looked like brain-tanned leather, soft but tough. And there it was down the center. Bone. Like Mam got flipped inside out.

"What is it?" Howling asked.

Mam twisted to see herself. She reached her hand behind her to touch. "Oh, that? That's my—that's my little passenger."

"Huh?" said Howling.

"Like when you get sick."

Howling lit up, remembering. Tiny bugs sometimes took people for rides. That was why people got sick. Mam called the sick bugs *passengers.* "Is that the bug?" He lifted his hand to touch her shoulder blade. Feral ran his fingers down her spine. Her back did look like that of a striped bark scorpion, and that was a bug.

"In a fashion," she said.

After she cleaned herself and dressed, Feral and Howling were next. She squeezed pink goop from a machine all over them. Called it soap but it wasn't nothing like the soap she made in the woods. She dunked their heads into a pool she'd made in a hole—a basin, Mam had called it. *Please stop acting foolish and put your head in the basin.*

Next, Mam slicked tallow in their hair and plaited Howling's hair then Feral's into two braids.

"That's me?" asked Howling, looking in the silver box Mam called a mirror.

He'd seen inklings of his reflection before, caught in bright pools of water, in glass from a jar, but never so clear, as if he had another twin, dark as him, staring right back, about to take him over, start a war.

"It is," said Mam.

Then Feral looked at himself, moving closer to the mirror to get a better look. "I pretty," he said, smiling.

"And silly. Come on, get down," said Mam.

Mam put them in cloths called drawers that covered their privates, then in stretchy cloth called tights, then thicker stretchy cloth called leggings, then an undershirt, a shirt, a sweatshirt, and a sweater.

Howling admired his reflection. "I'm a bear," he said. "Fearsome and beautiful." He loved his new slippers, made to look like bear feet. He stomped and stomped, then roared, beating his chest.

Mam pressed her lips against his ear, then nuzzled it with her nose. "You are. Y'all both look so gorgeous. Damn."

She was about to start crying. Mam was always about to start crying.

Once, Howling had a nightmare where a coyote came in the night and fed on his face and his belly, then started on Feral. He called for Mam over and over, but in the dream she was the coyote.

Sometimes it seemed like there was a creature inside her, lurking, trying to bust through her bones, a demented birth. Mam would be a pile of skin and guts and skeleton, and the creature, clean and bright, would never know that she used to be a mam.

Animals had dead mams all the time. Howling had seen it happen. Orphaned fawns and cubs and hawks. Sometimes orphaned by Howling's own hand. The child could hunt, yes, he could! Slingshot or arrow, he'd take down a mam bunny who surely had baby bunnies back in her den lonesome for milk.

⊠

EVERYTHING WAS NOISES. Everything was colors. It burned, all the smells and the stinks, all the flashing artifacts of the world. There was only one kind of bird here. Pigeons. Only one kind of animal. Squirrels. But what this place lacked in animals, it made up for in people, all sizes and colors and shapes and builds and dispositions. Yelling folks. Staring folks. Pinched-lipped folks. Mouth-open folks. Folks with big hats and folks who whistled at Mam from their big rolling beasts that stampeded along the concrete rivers.

"Why we in these clothes, Mam?" Feral asked. It was a good question. The clothing they'd had before was perfectly service-able, no holes or nothing, and snuggly and warm.

"Because we got to try to blend in. It's like camouflage."

"Like chameleons?" Howling asked, impressed with his own knowledge. Mam had told him about most kinds of animals there were.

"Yes," she said.

There were some pieces of the woods in this outside place. Howling saw them, stalks of wood, like trees without branches, shooting up so high into the sky. When Mam stopped the cart, he jumped and went running toward it and climbed. He needed to move. It had been a thousand years since he'd climbed a tree.

There was nary a branch on which to step up, so he had to shimmy and shimmy all the way to the top, poking his head in the space between the rope. He could hear Feral under him, huffing and puffing. His sibling was always copying him, and they both reached the top together, looking at the whole world. Like Mam had said, it did just go on forever, studded with dazzling, unfamiliar wonders.

"Look, Howling!" said Feral, pointing up, his white hand turned red in the cold. His breaths were white ringlets.

Howling turned his eyes toward the sky, where overhead a plane flew by. He'd heard them before, seen them, even, but never so clear as this, so close. He'd always thought them a kind of bird. It was clear now they were not.

"Children!"

Mam was calling. Had been for some time. In all his lust for the sky, he'd not heard. "What, Mam?" he said. "Come up!"

She couldn't, though, not with her whole body always aching and sore, like a lame deer or a broke-winged bird. She used to chase him and Feral up trees all the time, but not lately.

"Please, God of Cain, come down! Right now!"

Feral groaned, but he worked himself downward. Once he'd made it several yards, Howling slid down after him, stopping himself whenever his feet were about to crash into Feral's head.

It wasn't just Mam there when they made it back down to the ground, but two other people, white people, but not white like Mam-white and Feral-white, a strange skinny white, all their features chiseled into a bony, sticklike sculpture. Hair straight as grass. Shade all wrong. They were white like the man who tried to burn him and Feral up. White like the white people in Mam's stories.

They wore blue clothing, crisp and tight.

"Do you have some kind of ID?" one of them asked Mam.

"Not on me, no, I'm afraid," Mam said, her face stern but calm. Her voice was wrong, stiff and strange and high, a copy of the person talking to her. Howling tucked himself behind her thighs, just like Feral did.

"And your name?"

"Susannah," she said.

"And your children?"

"Callum and Bruno," said Mam, and Howling knew he wasn't supposed to tell these blue-suited people that was a lie. These strangers, they were like bears. Stand still, stay quiet, back away ever so slowly, slower than a snail creeping along your arm, and most important, don't interrupt Mam in the middle of her negotiations. Mam thought Howling never listened, but he did.

One of the blues knelt in front of Howling. "Are you all right, son?" he asked.

Howling looked up at Mam, and she smiled down at him. A fake smile. A tense smile. Yes, these blues were bears.

"I'm all right," Howling said quietly.

"Were you running away from something? Is that why you went up there?"

"I just felt like climbing," said Howling. "I like to climb, and it looked fun to climb, and I wanted to see the city. I never been to this place."

"We live in the country. He's used to having lots of trees to climb," said Mam. "I tried to call for him, but you know children, just running off and pretending not to be able to hear. They both just got away from me."

The blue didn't look at Mam, just kept his eyes steady on Howling. "How old are you, son?"

Howling held up his fingers.

"Four?"

Howling nodded and looked up at his mam, who was still smiling her tight smile.

"Lady, this can't happen again," said the blue, standing back up to talk to Mam.

"Of course not," she said. "And it won't. I'm so sorry. I'm not sure what's gotten into them."

"That right there was extraordinarily dangerous, and letting your children into that situation is tantamount to neglect, you hear? You do what you have to do, simple as that, and if that means getting a leash, get a leash."

"Of course. I'll do that right away," said Mam. Howling didn't like the sound of whatever that was.

"I was joking about the leash," the blue said.

Mam laughed. "Me, too." But Howling knew she hadn't been. She was going along with whatever he said.

When the blue-suits left, Mam grabbed Howling's hand and Feral's, tight, and tugged.

"I'm sorry, Mam," said Feral, but Howling wouldn't say it. Never.

"Don't do it again," said Mam, "unless you want to be taken away from me forever and ever."

Maybe Howling did want to be taken away forever. Howling had only climbed. Nothing wrong with that. She had no right to be angry at him for that.

He waited for her to reprimand him, to ask for his apology, too, but she didn't, and that set him right off. He gritted his teeth together and scrunched his face into a fist. He should be given the chance to say sorry. She shouldn't assume he wasn't going to apologize.

Howling wrestled his hand from Mam's grip but stayed by her side. She needed to know he wasn't happy.

⊠

MAM DRAGGED HOWLING AND FERAL in circles through a maze of ugly. His feet felt strange. The ground was too, too hard, too, too flat. It made him dizzy.

"How many miles we been wandering?" asked Howling.

"Shh," said Mam. "I don't want to hear nothing from you right now." Then she sighed quietly. Mam gave away so much in her breaths—she was about to apologize. Well, Howling wouldn't accept. "I'm sorry for being so grumpy," she said. "Five miles, I'd guess? Bus station is apparently on the edge of town. A ways to go still. But don't tell me you're tired. You've walked three times that in a day, easy." But walking in the woods was nothing like walking on this hard, flat stone spread out everywhere.

To pass the time, he gathered sticks and stones, squirreling them under his arms and in his pocket, picking long grasses when he saw them that he'd weave into twine and make into something good when he had a chance, scavenging interesting objects discarded on the street, until they stopped at a gas station. That was a place where people put special juice into the metal beasts, like the beasts needed water to drink, but it didn't smell like water. Liquid gas, Mam had said. Diarrhea. Howling giggled.

"What?" asked Feral.

"Poop," Howling said, and his sibling laughed.

"Poop, poop, poop," said Feral.

Mam, Howling, and Feral waited near the side of the gas station's mini-mart, Mam watching the comings and goings at the station while Howling and Feral played with rocks, skipping them along the concrete. They bounced so nice. It felt good to be still. Howling wrapped himself up in the quiet of the moment.

The noise of the passing people faded into a filmy haze he could turn away from.

"You two. Stay right here. Don't move a iota, okay? I'm talking to you, especially, Howling. All right, bear?" said Mam.

Howling rolled his eyes. "Last time we didn't move neither, and you still left us behind," he said.

"I didn't leave you behind. I got lost. Mams get lost, too. But I found you in the end because you stayed where you was, didn't I? Now we just got to do that again. I'll be right back." She hurried off without waiting for Howling to answer, which was annoying because he'd been planning to say something extremely mean that would've hurt her feelings.

"Excuse me, miss, miss?" said Mam, running toward the station to leave Howling and Feral by their lonesome. That was the way Howling liked it anyway, like back in the woods, where every piece of its expanse was his domain. He only watched Mam now so when she turned back round to face him, she'd see his frown and know how upset he was at her general foolishness.

The person Mam had shouted at turned toward her. "I was wondering if you could give this to the man inside and tell him to put ten dollars' worth of unleaded on number four," said Mam. "I'd go in myself, but you see, the guy working, he's friends with my husband, and I don't particularly wish to be found by my husband right now."

The person looked at Mam for several moments, then nodded, taking something folded, green, and cloth-like from Mam's outstretched hand.

When the person entered the station, Vern dove into the open door of one of the metal beasts, coming out about a half minute later and running with a hobbled gait back to Howling and Feral.

"Two hundred dollars cash, crisp twenties, can you believe it!" she said, swooping the children in her arms and running faster than Howling had seen her run in a long time away from the station. She didn't put them down until they'd turned several corners. Howling was just glad he'd been holding all his treasures when Mam had picked him up without asking. "Remember that, children. Gas stations are always a good target. People let their guard down. Run into the shop, leaving their purses or wallets inside open cars. And sometimes it takes some to get some. I sacrificed our last bit of money in the hopes we'd get more. She looked rich. Nobody wears a wool cream suit. I expected cash in her handbag but not that much, damn!"

Mam was always talking nonsense. She smiled wide and free, her whole face glinting with it. Whatever two hundred dollars was, it was important if it made Mam look like that. She didn't look like that ever.

"What's two hundred dollars, Mam?" Howling asked. He needed to know whether he was mad at her or not.

"It's a number. Like two or twenty," said Mam. "But it's got one more zero at the end." She'd drawn these figures for Howling and Feral in the mud before. Each symbol meant a different thing. See, if you had thirteen rocks, you wrote one and then a three. The one was on the left side. That was the tens place, so it equaled ten. The three was in the ones place, so it just equaled three. Ten and three was thirteen. "Remember how numbers go on forever? How you could always just go out and collect one more rock?" Mam asked.

"I remember." Of course he remembered.

Mam smiled at him, still gleeful. "Well, two hundred rocks is a lot of rocks. It'll help us get to Lucy."

Mam dragged Feral and him onto a bus, where they sat near the back. Feral got Mam's lap. Howling sat in the empty space beside, watching the world unfurl beside him like a flower from a bud. He watched till it went dark, till sleep claimed him. He dreamed of noise.

## 13

PAIN NUDGED Vern awake.

"Children?" she said, startled by the silence, the lack of breaths. She blinked her eyes several times. "Children?"

She couldn't feel their heat, their weight. "Children!"

"Up here, Mam," called Feral.

Vern walked on lead legs to the front of the bus using the seat backs as leverage. The children were sitting in the driver's seat and playing with the steering wheel as well as the many levers and buttons. As she roused more and more, her awareness sharpening, she pieced the morning together. The bus had arrived some time ago, and the rest of the passengers had disembarked. She'd been deep enough asleep to miss the call, and huddled with her babes tightly enough that the bus driver hadn't seen that they were still there.

Vern peered out the window to the dull conglomerate of concrete and cube buildings. Her eyes weren't doing very well today. It felt like they'd been taken out, squeezed, and plopped back in place. Her back hurt, too. Vern wasn't convinced she'd be able to walk unsupported.

"Howling, Feral, one of you get the backpack," she said, her voice raspy and her throat full of phlegm.

Feral ran to the back of the bus and dragged the backpack to the front, groaning with effort. "Come on," said Vern, and hoisted the backpack over her shoulders with a wince. Grateful to be rid of the reek of bologna, chewed gum, and floral-scented shampoo, Vern exited into the fresh air and walked with her children toward the taxi stand. Pride put a pep in her otherwise impaired step as she navigated the station. She'd never spent more than twelve consecutive hours off the compound or outside the woods, but this world did not intimidate her. She'd brought her children hundreds of miles, from city to city to city.

The final leg of the journey took them down a two-lane road out of town into a terrain of blond grasses and deciduous conifers. Luminous silver mountains edged the horizon, and had Vern not known better, it would've been easy to think there was nothing on the other side of them.

The world was full of false edges, false endings. Vern's mam thought there was nothing for her outside Cainland. For a time, Vern believed there was nothing for her outside the woods, but nothing was ever settled and done, not on this four-point-five-billion-year-old planet. Earth had witnessed the rise, proliferation, and fall of more than five billion life-forms in her time. Vern learned that from one of Carmichael's fun facts.

If Vern could ever be said to have a religion, that would be it: the bigness of it all, the mutability. One article Carmichael read argued one trillion species were alive today and that humankind knew about only one-thousandth of a percent of them. Even conservative estimates—ten million to fourteen million active species—suggested a world too vast for containment. God, if there was one, was that vastness.

COLD SPRINGS was a small town on the edge of Sugar Mountain County. Buildings no higher than five stories lined either side of the main drag. It was a bleak day, the air gelid and the sky gray, but people milled the street undeterred. Vern didn't see anything around that looked like a house.

"Can I help you?" someone asked.

Vern wrapped an arm around Howling and Feral each and pulled them toward her, aware it was unsafe to be someplace where she so readily stood out as a newcomer. "I'm looking for 7131 Osage Road." Vern kept her head bowed, her face disappearing into the generous fabric of her hood.

"Yeah, hon, you found it. It's right there," said the passerby, pointing to a red storefront with large windows, cursive lettering on the glass. Howling and Feral pulled from Vern's grasp to press their faces against the window, and Vern followed suit. Inside, people, patrons presumably, dined at tables and chairs.

"I don't und— Are you sure? This is 7131 Osage Road, Cold Springs, Sugar Mountain?"

"And has been for the last twenty years. Look," they said, pointing to the brass numbers affixed to the top of the door. Vern stood closer so she could see. "Best burgers around, but don't tell Bridget I said so."

"It's a restaurant?"

The passerby mistook Vern's bafflement for disdain. "It may not be fancy, hon, but Auntie's is the real deal. Good, fresh food."

"Auntie's?" Vern felt on the verge of retching.

"Yes. Auntie's Diner, though it's more of a soup kitchen than a restaurant. Flexible pricing, if you get me. It's the only place some folks can get a hot meal in winter. Food is free for those who need it to be."

Vern had stopped listening at *diner*.

"Miss?"

Vern was not a girl easily undone. She'd known it was unlikely that Lucy or even Lucy's auntie lay at the other end of this journey, but she hadn't prepared herself for the possibility that Lucy's auntie, at least the version of her that Vern had conjured in her head, never existed.

"Miss? Are you all right?"

Vern wasn't sure if her memories were distorted or if Lucy had deliberately obfuscated. "Thank you for your time," said

Vern to the person helping her, and pulled the children into Auntie's. A bell dinged as they entered, and Vern waited by the door to be sat down. Across the diner, inside the kitchen, someone called out to Vern. "Yeah, sit where you want. I'll be right with you."

Howling poked Vern's thigh and whispered, "Is that Lucy?" Vern shushed him and led the children to an empty booth.

"Electricity food, electricity food, electricity food," said Feral, banging his fists on the table rhythmically. Vern had only $3.17 left after paying bus fare for her and the children. "Electricity food!"

Howling sat up on his knees, pouring pepper onto the surface of the table before drawing in it with his index finger. Vern wanted to shout at them, *Be good*, but he didn't know a jar of pepper wasn't an art medium. "That's for eating, not for playing," she said. He dipped his finger into it, put it into his mouth, then coughed.

Vern scooped the pepper into her hands, then into a napkin, cleaning the table. "Just try not to do anything unless I tell you it's okay. Please."

The children looked forlorn, but they'd lived lives that required patience. Hunting and fishing weren't for those seeking a quick thrill. They could spend hours sharpening slate into an arrowhead. They could sit still and wait to be served breakfast.

"What can I get you?" asked the waiter brusquely, eyes on her pad of paper. She was in her fifties or sixties and dressed in a pair of overalls. Her long hair, braided in two, was the swirling gray color of a pre-storm sky. "I can come back if you want."

"No, sorry, we'll just have some toast and water, please. Thank you," said Vern, figuring she could afford that.

"Actually," said Feral, either innocently or defiantly—Vern couldn't tell—"I'd like some fried rabbit to go with my toast, please, and also some rabbit stew, some roasted chestnuts, and, oh, also acorn grits, and fried acorn cakes."

Howling, not to be left starving while his sibling feasted, joined in. "And I'll have deer with gooseberry sauce. And for dessert, roasted pecans drizzled with maple syrup."

"And crab apple compote," added Feral. "And some electricity food, too, but I don't know the names of those. Can you bring it all?"

"And blackened fish!"

The children's foolishness made the waiter look up from her pad. "Hmm," she said, examining them. "You boys are awfully big. Are you sure that's going to be enough food?" she asked, revealing a tenderheartedness that otherwise was not immediately apparent in her manner.

"Boys?" asked Feral.

"I'm sorry. *Girls,*" the waiter corrected.

"They're children," Vern said, nervous that she would have to explain what she meant by that. She'd never had to before.

"Ah. Are you sure? They look awfully big to only be children. Surely they are grown-ups," the waiter said without fuss over Vern's correction. Howling and Feral laughed at the teasing. "Why don't I bring you back some of my favorites, then see what you think, huh?"

Vern shook her head. "What can we get for under three dollars?"

"Everything here's on the house, but you can donate over there if you want." The waiter pointed to an area over at the bar counter.

"Really?" asked Vern.

For the first time, the waiter paused her gaze on Vern's face, taking her in. Her head tilted, she stared with eyes too big for her face.

The woman slid her pad into the pocket of her canvas apron. "Vern?"

The plastic saltshaker Vern had been worrying with her right hand slipped from her grasp, landing with a hollow thunk on the table. She hadn't realized she'd been holding it until her palm felt all-at-once bereft, sweaty and desperate for distraction.

Panic-stricken, Vern took hold of a fork, ready to stab the waiter if it came to it. "How do you know my name?" she asked.

The waiter left the table and shouted over to one of her coworkers. "Hey, Buckeye. I got to go. Personal matters. I can count on you to hold the fort?"

"I always do anyway," said Buckeye, rolling his eyes.

"Yeah, yeah," said the waiter, then went back to Vern. "Follow me." The woman flung on a coat and pushed through the double doors of the entryway without checking to see if Vern was behind.

The children looked at Vern for direction, and she nodded. "Come on. Let's go." Howling and Feral bounced up from their seats, each of them slotting the sample-sized jars of jam and honey on the table into their pockets. Vern couldn't move as spryly as they and had to shout at them to stop so they didn't get too far ahead. When she did manage to push herself up onto her legs, it was with much swearing.

"Mam? You all right?" asked Feral.

"Shh," Vern said. Walking demanded potent focus. She grabbed the children's hands and caught up to the waiter outside. There she was, leaning against a light blue hooptie pickup truck.

"Get in," she said.

Vern tightened her grip around Feral and Howling's hands. "The last person to bark orders at me aint around anymore," she threatened.

The waiter did not cower. "Tell me something. You in trouble? Because you look like you might be. What is it you asked back in my diner not five minutes ago? Right, how much food you could get for three dollars. The answer is, besides with me, none, so get in the truck."

Feral tugged at Vern's arm in pain, and Vern remembered to loosen her grip so as not to crush his little fingers. Howling could endure her bruising grips better, but she allowed his hand some give, too. "I've taken care of myself for a long time. I don't need your help."

The woman sighed, fingers fidgety. She looked like she wanted to smoke but in the last six months, regretfully, had quit. "Then why did you come here? To shoot the shit?"

Vern stood still, lips pinched shut.

"No wonder Lucy liked you so much. Birds of a goddamn feather," said the woman, and removed a Zippo lighter from her pocket. She opened the brass lid, flicked the flint wheel, and watched the flame pop up from the metal eyelet like a jack-in-the-box.

Beside Vern, Feral was going wild, pulling toward what to him must have surely seemed an object of sorcery. "Mam! Mam!" he whispered excitedly. Howling, too, was interested, but had maintained his composure.

But the fire held no interest for Vern when considered against the woman's words. Lucy. That name was a spell. Once it was spoken, every alert in Vern's body signaled at once. It'd be maudlin and overly simple to call Lucy her North Star, her beacon. More accurately, she was Vern's trigger.

"You know Lucy?" she asked.

The woman crossed her arms over her chest and closed the Zippo. "The name's Bridget, but a lot of folks call me Auntie. Are you going to get in now or what?"

Vern huffed but opened the door with a yank, lifting Howl-

ing and Feral inside. The truck was an old-style pickup with no
back seat, rips in the upholstery. Vern crawled over the children
so she would be the one forced flush against Bridget.

"You been followed?" asked Bridget.

Vern bristled at the suggestion that she'd been heedless
enough to pick up a tail, but it wasn't an impossibility. Sherman's
power was bolstered by a cabal Vern didn't yet fully compre-
hend. "I don't know. I don't think so."

Bridget grunted. "You never know with Cainland," she said.

"How did you know that I was me?" asked Vern.

Bridget reached into the back pocket of her overalls and pulled
out a brown wallet. She flicked it open and handed it to Vern.
Tucked under cloudy plastic casing was a photo. Vern brought it
toward her face, angling her head until she found the right focal
point for her wobbling eyes.

It was a cut-up Polaroid of Lucy and Vern on the morning of
an Ascension, their hands clutching and their faces as somber
and stiff as gravestones. Sherman didn't allow photography on
the compound, but he took pictures of everyone on the mornings of their rebirths so that the punished could look at the images of their old selves and burn them. Lucy's mother, or Lucy
herself, must've stolen this from Sherman's office.

Vern circled her thumb over the two girls in the picture.
They were strangers now to Vern, these fresh-faced innocents.
Ghosts.

"Here, Mam," said Feral, holding up his arm to her.

"What?"

"You can use my sleeve if you want," he said, worming his
hand inside to create a loose piece of fabric. "For your tears."

Vern handed the wallet back to Bridget and wiped her face
with the back of her hand. "Thank you, Feral, but I'm fine," she
said.

"Are you, Vern?" asked Bridget.

Vern squeezed her eyes shut as a headache teased at her temples. "It was just weird seeing that." Looking at old photos of yourself was like seeing a picture of your own dead body.

"No, I mean physically, are you all right? You look . . . shaky."

Vern sucked snot into her nose and dried off what remained of the fallen tears with the sleeve of her coat. "Been better."

"I'm gonna take you to my place, have my cunksi take a look at you," Bridget said, starting the engine and pulling out onto the street.

"Choonksy?" asked Vern at the unfamiliar word.

"My niece. Gogo."

"Is that Spanish or something?"

Vern caught the note of derision in Bridget's answering laughter. "Lakota, actually."

Vern's cheek flushed to have her ignorance so fully on display. "Like Sitting Bull, right?" she said, desperate to prove she wasn't some hick.

Bridget looked at her with a small smile, and Vern felt redeemed. "Yes, though I'm Oglala myself."

"So, like Crazy Horse?"

This time, Bridget's laugh was husky and sweet, without trace of a gibe. "If you're going to be naming random Natives to save face, you should know his name was Tasunke Witko. And if you want real credit, maybe have a few less famous names under your belt. Though I'll give it to you, don't think I've met a non-Lakota person who'd know what band Tasunke Witko was. Did you learn that at Cainland? Evelyn did say the history Lucy got there was better than anything she learned at school out here." Bridget's bottom lip rippled in and out her mouth restlessly at the mention of Lucy's mother. She tapped her fingers on the steering wheel.

"My little brother, actually." Carmichael was always saving Vern's day, even though she hadn't seen him in over four years. "He reads a lot. Or he did. I don't know if he does now."

Bridget grunted her understanding. "Anyway," she said abruptly, redirecting the conversation, "Gogo will fix you up good."

Vern huffed a breath through her nose. "No offense to her skills, but I doubt I can be fixed up. The stuff that's happening to me—you wouldn't believe it. Nobody would."

Glancing toward the rearview mirror, Bridget changed lanes. "If it's got to do with Cainland, I would," she said, and turned off Cold Springs' main drag onto a gravel road. "Lucy and Evelyn talked a lot about all the medications they had to take there. And the night terrors."

Vern loved having someone in her life who knew Lucy like she did. "Are they back at your place?" she asked.

Bridget shifted gears as she picked up speed, grip firm on the wheel.

"You can tell me the truth," said Vern, voice soft. She was too weakened by sickness to assert her okayness at full volume.

"The truth is I haven't seen either of them in a very long time."

Vern squeezed her left hand with her right. "How long?" she asked.

At least Bridget didn't equivocate. "Seven years. Seven fucking years."

Vern swallowed down a sob. "But that's since she left Cainland for good."

"That's right," said Bridget, nodding her confirmation like this was casual news.

"Do you know where they are? Have you looked for them?"

"Evelyn made it very clear she never wanted to see me

again after what happened with the custody dispute. After I took Lucy—"

"You're the kidnapper," Vern said, remembering that day in the temple's attic, staring out at the stranger through her telescope. "You're the one who picked Lucy up from the compound."

Noticeably stiff, Bridget watched the road ahead. "Anyway, after I got Lucy, Evelyn wanted to go into hiding. I convinced her it wasn't the way. That with all the evidence she had she could win custody of Lucy properly. When that didn't happen, she left here and said she was going back for her girl but for me not to expect to ever see either of them again. And I haven't."

Vern's frustrated sigh filled the pickup's cab. "So they could be dead, for all you know," she said. "Or in trouble. They might need something. They might need my help."

Bridget looked over at Vern, then back at the road. "I don't think you're in any position to help anyone."

Proving Bridget's point, Vern felt too fatigued and light-headed to argue. She let her head loll back onto the seat rest and roll toward the children. Howling and Feral, entranced by the details of the truck's interior—the glove box, the cupholder, the wrappers and papers on the floor—chittered back and forth over each discovery. Feral drew on himself with a discarded ballpoint pen, and Howling flicked through a rumpled newspaper.

"Hello, Mrs. Bear, what you doing?" asked Feral. He'd drawn a beard onto his cheeks and chin.

"Hello, Mrs. Wolf, I am looking at these strange leaves. I think they fell from the kookoo tree," said Howling.

"The kookoo tree?" asked Feral.

"It's a black-and-white tree from far away in the woods. See, it has these special leaves," Howling explained, holding up the newspaper.

"Oh yes. Let's cook some roasted kookoo leaves to be wraps for the deer stew."

Howling roasted the rumpled newspaper pages over a fake fire, then handed a piece to Feral. Feral took a bite. "Most delicious, Mrs. Bear."

"Thank you, Mrs. Wolf." Howling chomped on the newspaper next. "Oh yes. Most delicious."

Somber evergreens buttressed the road. With each mile, the terrain grew hillier, steeper. Bridget forged ahead, her pickup working upward until it turned onto a road up into a mountain. Somewhere along the away, snow had begun falling.

"Shit," Bridget whispered. Her phone buzzed in a rhythm of harsh triplets.

"What is it?" asked Vern.

"Hold on," Bridget said, and pulled to the side of the narrow road into tree cover.

"What's going on?"

"Sheriff's department," said Bridget, and pointed to her phone. "I get an alert whenever they're in range."

"Sheriff's department?" asked Howling.

"Like that man who dressed us down after you climbed up that pole," Vern said, pulling a piece of lint from his hair, instinctively shining him up in case the passing patrol vehicle did notice them.

"A blue-suit," said Howling, nodding, on guard.

The deputy's car sped by, red and blue lights flashing chaotically.

Bridget exhaled, relieved. "All right, looks like we're good to go."

Vern rolled her shoulders forward and backward. The jolty car ride had stiffened her further. "Let's take a five-minute break," said Bridget, assessing Vern. "And when I say five minutes, I mean it. The snow's picking up. We don't want to be out here when it gets worse."

Feral and Howling slid out of the pickup with the same practiced grace they used when hopping from a tree. They each grabbed a stick from the side of the road to play-fight. "I'm gonna take a piss," Vern said, joining her children outside the car. "Howl, Feral, come with me."

Vern limped into the nearby woodland, and the babes scampered behind banging their sticks. "Yah! Aha! You're dead," they shouted to each other. Their exuberant play accentuated the sunless gloom of the woods. There was nothing like the cheer of a child to expose the starkness of a place.

"I'm not dead, you're dead!" said Feral, the volume of his voice quieter now that Vern had pulled farther ahead.

"If I'm so dead, then how can I do this? Aha! Washa! Wabam!" said Howling. Vern couldn't hear what Feral said in reply, the space between her and the children too great.

"Stop dawdling! Keep up!" she yelled back at them, but she appreciated the moment of privacy and partially disrobed before lowering herself into a squat. Cold stung her thighs, her knees, and her ankles, but she was a girl used to the prod of a cruel hand. Perhaps, even, she was a girl who sought out such miseries. She was here now, wasn't she? She could've held it. Vern the masochist. What was it like to feel peace and like it?

The snap of a twig jarred Vern from her self-flagellatory midpiss thoughts . . .

"Children?" she called out.

"What, Mam?" Howling shouted back. His voice came from her left. The noise had come from behind her. Vern closed her eyes and listened. Whispering leaves, scraping earth—it was the unique susurration of a body in motion. Whatever had made the sound was on the move, and it was coming up behind her from a distance away in the trees.

Was it Reverend Sherman? Had he finally caught up? It would please the man to end Vern while she was midsquat. The pool of urine trickling toward the inside edges of her snow boots teased her with its human banality. She might die because she hadn't felt like holding it.

Slowly, Vern turned her head to face the foe behind her. She blinked, eyelids aflutter, and gulped down a spit-wet breath, choking on saliva caught in her trachea. "God of Cain," she said, and coughed. It wasn't Reverend Sherman standing there, or any man.

"Vern! Your five minutes is up," Bridget yelled from afar, but between Vern and the way back to the road was a creature so looming that being next to it was like falling.

"God of Cain, God of Cain," Vern said. Her breaths were stuttered and half-realized.

The creature, bright white, contemplated Vern with curious hunger, its round eyes vast hollows. It was part animal, part god, and antlers twice its size protruded from its back like bone wings or calcified webs. Vern rushed to stand but tripped over her pants and drawers.

"Children!" she cried out for help. "Bridget!" She scooted away from the godanimal, naked ass scraping against the snow that was just beginning to settle on the ground.

The creature regarded Vern's escape attempt with amused nonchalance. It smiled at her, hungry.

"I am pleased to meet you, Vern. I have been waiting," it said, then galloped forward. A sound like a storm siren blared from its lungs, and the antlered beast engulfed her.

Vern flailed. She punched, kneed, and scratched, fighting

mercilessly though impaired by garment-cuffed ankles. With a shudder, she pushed hard against the ground to stand. She threw one last punch, but it landed in the air.

She was alone again, only the ringing in her ears from the creature's scream testifying to its earlier presence. Though nothing remained of its physical form, Vern knew something—something real—had been there with her. That creature was more alive than any of Vern's other hauntings. She'd felt an intelligence, a consciousness. It was a somebody, and it knew her.

Instinct told her the rest. The poison or sickness inside her had finally taken strong enough hold to bring the antlered beast to her.

Vern pulled up her pants and stumbled through the woods toward the sound of her children banging together those damn sticks. "Howling. Feral. Let's go," she said.

They didn't hesitate, chasing after their jogging mam.

"Took you long enough," said Bridget tersely when Vern and the children returned to the truck. She turned the key and pulled back onto the abandoned mountain road.

# 14

BRIDGET'S PLACE was a small cabin on squatted land. It sat in battered defiance at the center of a small clearing in the mountains. "She's sturdier than she looks," said Bridget.

Vern hummed under her breath, arms thrown over the shoulders of her children.

There was no lock on the door, and to open it Bridget slammed her shoulder into the wood as she turned the knob. The hinges creaked like a dying hog.

"Come in. You need to lie down," said Bridget. The children

slipped from Vern's embrace and stepped inside, but Vern hesitated outside.

"What?" asked Bridget. "Do you need some help?"

Vern took in her surroundings. "This place. It's just kind of familiar." She squeezed her arms around herself.

Like corpses, half memories bobbed to the surface from the waters of a past that wasn't hers. A muddy pathway. A solemn girl on a rickety porch swing looking out into the distance with a disapproving frown.

Clear as day, it was Lucy.

"Leave me alone, Mama," she said to Vern.

Vern reached out to touch her best friend, but before her fingers made contact, Lucy was gone.

"Come on. You're letting all the cold in," said Bridget, rubbing her hands together. "Vern?"

"Sorry. I'm coming," said Vern, stuttering. Never before had she had a haunting from someone she knew.

Vern unfixed her eyes from the spot where Lucy had been, then went inside. Shoes lay in a small pile by the door. Among them was a pair of dirty white tennis shoes with pink and red trim, a mud-covered image of Minnie Mouse on the sides. Were there children here?

The entryway opened into a modest living space. A leather couch sat in front of a rickety wood coffee table. There was a wood-burning stove, a buffalo hide on the floor, a few bookshelves. A large weaving over the mantel offered vibrant color in a room that was otherwise dominated by brown. A hunting rifle was mounted by the door.

"You can set your things down there," said Bridget, gesturing to the pile of shoes before starting a fire in the stove. The Minnie Mouse shoes were gone. "Howling? Feral? That's your names, right? How about some food?"

Bridget threw some plastic containers into the microwave, and when it dinged, she served the meal on the coffee table for the children, where they sat on their knees to eat. "Pumpkin-and-beef stew," she said.

"Thank you very much," Feral said politely, grinning wide at remembering his manners.

Prompted by his sibling, Howling grunted something that could've been a thank-you.

Howling finished his food quickly, a glass of water in one hand as he picked up each object in Bridget's living room with the other. The sun shone brightly through the open curtains, and he held up each fascination to the light. A bronze statue head, some coasters, framed photographs, pillow cushions.

"Can I get you something to eat, too, Vern? That's the last of the stew, but I can fry you up some—"

"No, thank you." Her jawbone hurt and her throat felt inflamed.

"Then I'll just get you some water. Anything else you need?"

"Some ibuprofen?" asked Vern. "And acetaminophen, too."

Bridget gave her an encouraging pat. "Just one second. Make yourself at home," she said, and Vern did. She opened every closet, examined every shelf. She'd entered the den of a stranger, but she wouldn't be caught unawares again.

Bridget returned with the pills, and Vern shot down double doses of each. "I'm heating up some frozen chili now on the stove. There's not much left, so I set some venison thawing for later."

A fresh wave of pain dizzied Vern. Now that she'd finally reached her destination, her debility had decided to make room for itself.

Heat from the woodstove had warmed the small cabin enough that Bridget and the children had removed multiple layers of clothing. Howling and Feral were down to their muscle-tee undershirts and leggings. Bundled in her coat, Vern still felt a chill.

"You sure you don't want at least some eggs or something? You look like you need it. When was the last time you ate?"

Vern had waned to a sliver over the last several weeks. The sickness had a ferocious appetite. What it could not gobble up from Vern's belly, it devoured from her physical person.

Too jittery to sit, Vern trod the living room with agitated stiffness while the children played. Feral jumped from the couch down to the buffalo hide, then on top of a chair in front of a desk. He climbed on top the desk, then made the jump back to the couch, giggling as he landed on the soft cushion. Even lost in her sickness, Vern could appreciate his freeness. He was a spirited, buoyant thing. Feral had always been her sweet little bear, but he was more, too. By comparing him to his moody, precocious sibling, she'd underestimated him.

Vern grabbed the throw draped over the back of the sofa and cocooned herself within it. Bridget watched her from the kitchen as she cracked eggs into a skillet.

"Do me a favor, Vern, and sit down. Better yet, lie down," said Bridget.

Vern had exhausted herself with the manic pacing and agreed to Bridget's request. Legs spindly and rigid, she hobbled toward the sofa. In her febrile state, she hardly noticed it when a child appeared before her. She collided with it and stumbled.

"Vern? You okay?" asked Bridget, grabbing her by the elbow. Vern stood in stricken silence. "Vern? What is it?"

Vern's breaths made a sound like a gale wind when they passed through her clenched teeth. "It's Lucy," answered Vern.

Her best friend had returned, though not the version of her

that had been outside on the porch swing. This Lucy looked to be nine years old and was wearing a tank top with a pair of red track shorts, white race stripes down the sides. Minnie Mouse tennis shoes. Red bobbles and white barrettes in her hair. Black knees and black elbows shiny with Vaseline. Smelling like Luster's Pink hair lotion. Smelling like Irish Spring soap. Smelling like a stick of Queen Helene cocoa butter. God of Cain, her lips were glistening with it.

"How is this possible?" Vern croaked.

Lucy's eyes narrowed at Vern, and she spoke: "You're gonna pay for that, asswipe," she said, lunging forward. In the space it took Vern to blink, Lucy's hands had ensnared Vern's neck. Vern tried to gasp but no sound came out, windpipe smashed shut. Lucy laughed all the while.

"Vern? Vern! Vern, what's wrong?" asked Bridget.

Vern closed her eyes and opened them again, released from her best friend's grip and finally able to breathe. Lucy was gone.

"Where the hell did that mark on your neck come from? Jesus Christ," Bridget said. She led Vern to the sofa and forced her to lie back.

"Lucy did it," said Vern. "The hauntings." Fatigue smothered her like an August heat wave. She was on the verge of an epiphany, but she couldn't fully put it together. "They're real. They're real. They're real."

"What's real, Mam?" asked Feral. The children had stopped their play to kneel beside Vern on the sofa. Their cheeks rested against the edge of the seat cushion, the tops of their heads pressed into Vern's rib cage.

"Lucy. The wolves," she said.

They couldn't understand. "Love you, Mam," Feral said, so soft and sweet.

Howling grabbed her hand, then laid his head on her belly. "What's wrong with you, Mam?" he asked. "You want me to rub salve on your back?"

"Shh. Don't worry about me," she said.

"Howling, Feral," Bridget interjected. "I'm gonna set up a movie for you on my computer. Why don't you go pick from one of the DVDs on the bookshelf?" She pointed to a row of children's films.

"It's a story with pictures on a special machine," Vern explained, preempting their questions. "You'll like it. Promise."

"Come on," said Bridget.

"No," Howling snapped.

"It's all right, Howling," said Vern between floundered breaths. "I'm going to be right here. Just having a little rest."

Feral whined, then teared up. "Please don't make us, Mam," he said.

"You're only going to be a little ways from me. I'm still right here," said Vern. "In no time you'll be calling out to me to tell me to stop moaning so loud."

Neither child laughed, but they obeyed. Reluctantly, they let themselves be pulled from Vern's side to a pallet Bridget was making them. Vern tuned her ears closely to their little sounds: their steps against creaking wood and the swish of their cotton-covered thighs touching as they walked. Their breaths were heavy with angst and tears.

Bridget returned to Vern a few moments later with a bag of frozen corn. She laid it on Vern's forehead. "This should cool you down a little," she said. "You're burning up."

Vern nodded. "I need to tell you something before I forget," said Vern. Lucidity was fast leaving her.

"What is it?"

"It's about Lucy. The hauntings," Vern said, panting. Her thoughts outpaced her tongue.

"The what?" asked Bridget.

Vern wasn't sure she'd remember the details of the hauntings on the other side of her fever. "The night terrors. Remind me, if I get better—"

"When you get better."

"Remind me when I get better about the day me and Lucy met, okay?"

"Of course," said Bridget.

"How she sauntered in, in her red-and-white outfit. A boy on the compound saw her and said she was ugly and bald-headed. Lucy strangled him."

Bridget smiled, a tear in the corner of her eye. "Sounds like her."

*You'll have to excuse my Lucy. She's a wild one*, Evelyn had said.

"They're real, Bridget. They're memories." Hers? Lucy's? She wasn't sure.

Vern couldn't have recollected the day she first saw Lucy with such clarity on her own. The exact details of Lucy's outfit, her smells. Until today, she'd forgotten about Brother Carver's son Thelonious calling her names.

The hauntings weren't hallucinations caused by the poisons Reverend Sherman and Dr. Malcolm had injected her with. They were fragments of the past. "Don't let me forget."

Bridget nodded, brows furrowed. "Okay."

"Promise me."

"I promise."

Fever clutched at Vern. She was falling and falling. Her last thought as she faded was that she'd waited too long to leave the woods.

# 15

VERN STARTLED AWAKE at the sound of the front door whapping the wall. Bridget's niece had arrived.

"How bad is she?" Gogo asked, voice stern as she charged inside. She flung the door shut behind her, but not quickly enough to prevent the intrusion of cold and snow from outside.

"Bad," said Bridget. "She's been knocked out the better part of three hours. She's had four Tylenol but she's still on fire."

"You said she had kids?" asked Gogo.

"I moved them to my room when she started moaning and lashing out in her sleep. Didn't want to scare them."

"Any sign of drug use?" asked Gogo as she shed her coat. The heavy fabric fell with a thump to the floor.

"She was talking a little crazy, but I think that was just the fever. I'm guessing she's been sick for a while. Look at her. She's gaunt as a foal."

"Noticeable injuries?"

"Just that on her neck. It came out of nowhere," said Bridget. "Like fucking magic."

Gogo strode over to where Vern lay on the sofa, and knelt down on the floor in front of her.

"I don't do drugs," Vern spat, winded by the effort of speaking.

"I wouldn't care if you did," Gogo said, voice hard, and Vern sensed a reprimand in her tone. "Many of my patients do, and there's no shame in it."

It wasn't what Vern expected, to be chastised for—she wasn't sure exactly—but what she guessed was, in her mam's words, her judgmental nature.

"Whatever you've done or not done, I'm going to take care

of you," said Gogo, the matter closed. She spoke and gestured with such surety of purpose, it was hard not to trust that in her care lay the means to survival.

"I take care of myself," said Vern, panting.

She braced for protest, but Gogo nodded. "It's a job we all have to outsource occasionally. Just for tonight, let me be the one you outsource it to." She grabbed Vern's chin and held her gaze with unblinking ferocity. "Okay?"

Gogo's gaze was hypnotic.

"I don't like doctors," Vern protested, not that the woman kneeling before her looked like any doctor Vern had ever seen. Doctors didn't wear faded jeans, combat boots, and black leather vests over flimsy gray T-shirts. The sides of their heads weren't shaved, and their forearms weren't painted in tattoos.

"I'm not a doctor," Gogo said.

"But she's got medical training from years on the front line," said Bridget, all proud-aunt.

Vern watched Gogo suspiciously. "You're military?" she asked. Even sick as a dog and burning up she could not conceal the contempt in her voice.

"Ina's talking about marches, demos, stuff like that. I do first aid." Gogo removed the pair of fingerless gloves she was wearing.

"First aid? *Psh.* Don't listen to her. Gogo's a trained paramedic. She's got a degree and everything. You should've seen what a proud ina she made me at Iŋyan Wakanagapi Othi," said Bridget.

Vern squinted, not understanding.

"Sacred Stone Camp," Gogo offered mercifully, but those words were no more clear to Vern.

"The pipeline protests," said Bridget, and with a pang Vern resigned herself to not knowing, to accepting she'd missed out on most of the world. "I'm not exaggerating when I say she saved lives, that people who are alive today wouldn't be if she wasn't there. And she was only a teen then. Think about what she can do now. She's even thinking about medical school."

"I'm not. Please ignore my ina," said Gogo, her eyes never once leaving Vern's. If Vern weren't already made breathless by the sickness inside of her, the ardor of Gogo's stare would've done it. "How long have you been sick?" she asked Vern.

"As bad as this? Not long. It's been coming on strong the last day or so. But there's been something wrong with me for a very long time," Vern said. She had to stop talking to make space for herself to gasp for air.

"There's nothing wrong with you," said Gogo.

"I just meant—"

"I know what you meant," Gogo said, and lugged a red bag from the floor onto the coffee table. After stretching on some latex gloves, she removed a thermometer from the bag and pushed the tip of it into Vern's mouth.

"Well?" asked Bridget, but Gogo had eyes only for Vern.

"Going to take your temperature one more time," said Gogo, and tapped the thermometer against her hand several times with a scrunched brow before sliding it between Vern's lips.

Gogo held up the reading for her aunt to see. "How is that even possible?" Bridget asked.

"It's not," said Gogo.

"What's it say?" Vern asked. "What's my temperature?"

Gogo licked her lips. "My training says I should hoist you into my pickup and drive you to the county hospital." Her manner was stern and unyielding.

"No," said Vern, wanting to say more, to object more profusely, but unable to in her state of fevered fatigue.

"I know," Gogo said with the exhausted sigh of a person who'd been in this situation many times before.

Bridget, hovering nervously behind her niece, tapped her foot. "So then what? What the fuck are we going to do?" she asked.

Gogo sat silently as she thought, and Vern knew that whatever she was planning, she didn't believe it had any real chance of working. Vern squeezed her eyelids shut. Death came for all. At least she'd made it this far. At least she'd gotten the children to Bridget.

"Vern, Vern, stay with me," barked Gogo, slapping Vern's cheeks with an insistent hand. Vern's eyes flickered open. She must've drifted off.

"Ina, start the shower running. Cold water," Gogo barked. Bridget nodded curtly and was gone.

"Am I going to die?" asked Vern weakly, embarrassed to admit the possibility frightened her. Vern was the girl who hated all. What folly of human nature possessed her to cling to that which she so despised?

"Vern, Vern." Another slap to the cheek. "You've got to stay with me. You're having a heatstroke, do you understand? We've got to get you cooled down."

Gogo hoisted Vern to a standing position and dragged her to the bathroom. She peeled Vern down to her underwear and lifted her into the tub, the water from the shower spout like a shock of ice pellets. *God of Cain, help me,* Vern thought but did not say, managing only a groan. Pain nested in her throat, and she could not speak through it.

"You see that?" asked Bridget, pointing to Vern's naked torso with a twisted grimace. No one but Howling and Feral had witnessed Vern's passenger before.

"I see it," said Gogo, unbothered as she assessed the ruin that was Vern's back. Vern felt her heartbeat settle from sprint to march under the sedating roll of Gogo's steel voice. Gogo was blues-singer cool, lake-calm. Her composure ran Vern's fears right away.

After several minutes, Gogo plunged the thermometer back into Vern's mouth.

"Any better?" asked Bridget.

"Let's give it a few more minutes," said Gogo, which meant Vern's temperature hadn't gone down.

"Is it cancer?" asked Bridget, eyes on Vern's back. "One of them types of tumors with bones in it?"

Gogo shook her head, then with Bridget's help lifted Vern from the tub onto the toilet to get dry. Vern's bottom sank into the carpeted plush of the seat cover, and Gogo rubbed a rough towel over her skin. "This isn't a teratoma," said Gogo. This is—" she broke off. "This is new."

"Then maybe we have to take her to the hospital. If we don't—"

"What's a hospital going to do for her? Even if I thought there was a chance they could help her—how would we get there? It's an hour and a half away in the snow. We might kill ourselves on the journey."

Vern slipped in and out of lucidity as they discussed her. She felt like Moses in that damn basket, whisked down the river through no choice of her own. When Gogo and Bridget carried her to a bed, she did not once resist. Docile, Vern lay on the mattress, ready to be delivered into Pharaoh's clutches.

"Vern, don't drift off. Not yet. I need you to pay attention," Gogo said. "I'm going to try absolutely everything I can, but just in case, is there anyone we should call?" asked Gogo. "Any family?"

Vern remembered her mother. She remembered Carmichael. Didn't they deserve to know she'd come to the end? The love she had for the two of them felt in this moment distant and vague. The idea of love rather than love itself. Even on the verge of death, Vern was heartless. She could not and would not ever forgive her mam. And Carmichael was nothing more than a boy, a foolish boy who'd one day be a foolish man. There was nothing to say he wouldn't become a Sherman or like any of the other Cainite brothers.

"Just bring me my babies," Vern whimpered.

"Of course."

Vern rolled her head side to side against a pillow as Bridget placed packs of frozen goods and ice over her sheet-covered body. She fell asleep, then awoke, then fell asleep and awoke again in an endless cycle. Her body was a new and different stranger with each waking.

This decline had been a long time coming. For years she'd been teetering on death's edge, and now she was finally falling. The sickness had overwhelmed what meager defenses she had, and good riddance. It was, as far as she could tell, every bit as deserving of life as she. It fed on her with the same enthusiasm she'd fed on swamp hares, deer, and catfish.

Next to her, her children hummed the sweetest, most mournful melody. She didn't know how long they'd been there. Minutes? More likely hours. She reached out to stroke Howling's cheek to find that she'd been hooked to an IV when she wasn't conscious. She shivered as cool liquid from the catheter slid through her. Her body tingled blissfully. Gogo had given her something for the pain.

Vern opened her eyes to see if they'd taken her to the hospital after all, but a dark blur of smoke surrounded her. The tune that Howling and Feral hummed, she didn't recognize it. It wasn't one of the gospels she lullabied them with, but a new song, something Gogo and Bridget were singing, their hands locked together as they sat on either side of her on the bed.

Vern tried to hear the words, to let the music be an anchor, but they were not singing in English.

Her eyelids flitted open and closed, hours slipping by and by. Never once did their fervent, pleading song cease, nor did the smoke, the dark, their skyward-bent faces; and Vern understood, understood that with everything that was inside of them, they were praying for her life.

☒

IT WAS MIDMORNING when Vern awoke. Air, sweet and cool, caressed her lips, tongue, and throat as she rose up out of the dark. She must've been out of it all night.

"Children?" she croaked, unsure if their presence next to her had been a hallucination. She moved her arms, searching for their weight.

"They're sleeping," said Gogo, her voice worn from singing.

Vern opened her eyes, pupils shriveling to tiny specks at the assault of sunlight. As the room came in focus, so, too, did the aliveness of her body, solid and heavy. "I aint dead," she said.

"You're not," Gogo said from where she sat at the foot of the bed. She smelled like coffee and woodsmoke. "How are you feeling?"

Vern flexed, stretched, tensed, cracked, and squeezed, feeling out the possibilities of her body. Everything hurt, but she felt that if she stood up to walk, she'd not immediately topple. "A little better than last night," Vern said, pointing her toes, then turning them in circles to stretch her ankles.

Gogo cleared her throat and scooted up the mattress so she was closer to Vern. "Last night was ten days ago. That's how long you've been in this bed." Gogo's brow furrowed deeply, and Vern swallowed. She blinked away the tear threatening to loose itself from the corner of her eye.

"I guess all the praying worked," she said. "Were you singing that whole time?"

"A lot of it. As much as I could. I fell asleep sometimes but only when Bridget was here to back me up," said Gogo. She sounded tired and no wonder why.

"The only time I've had people pray over me like that was to save me from my sin," said Vern, either self-pityingly or self-mockingly; she couldn't decide.

Snorting, Gogo wiped the back of her hand over her lips, rubbing off dried saliva that had accumulated in the sides. "You're the last woman in the world that needs saving, and I know a lot of women," she said, and proceeded to examine Vern, first with her stethoscope. She pressed the cold metal drum against Vern's chest through the sheet, which was all Vern had in the way of body covering.

"Almost everybody I've ever known would disagree with you," said Vern.

"And are you the type?" Gogo asked.

Vern looked at her questioningly.

"To agree with what everybody's got to say about you?"

Vern raised an eyebrow. No one had ever once accused her of being agreeable. "I'm not the type to agree with what anybody's got to say about anything," she said. She tried to sit up, but buckled under the weight of her body.

"Slowly!" said Gogo. The buzz of a mounting headache forced Vern's eyes briefly shut again. She inhaled and exhaled through a nauseating dizzy spell, needing several moments to regain her bearings.

Gogo held a cup of water to Vern's lips. Though she hated to be babied, Vern sipped greedily. "You don't have to treat me like an invalid. I'm cured now anyway, aren't I?" she asked after swallowing.

"I don't know what you are," said Gogo, as she dabbed away the wetness at the side of Vern's lips with her thumb before offering her more water. "When the snow cleared a couple days ago, I was able to get samples to a friend of mine for testing."

Vern pulled away from Gogo and wiped her own mouth with the back of her hand. "Samples?"

"Blood, urine, saliva, skin," said Gogo, the list sounding like ingredients for a conjure bag. "I took the liberty. I'm sorry." Gogo had reduced Vern to scrapings and fluids.

"What did the tests say?" asked Vern. After four years of not knowing, her desire for answers beat out her indignation at having had her bodily consent violated.

"Best we can conclude, you're a miracle," said Gogo. Despite the grandiosity of the words themselves, she spoke the statement matter-of-factly.

Vern still balked at the drama of it. "That's not a answer at all, unless you're seriously saying you put my blood up under a microscope and there was a divine light glowing through the lens."

Gogo, ever so faintly, smirked as she tossed several strands of black tangled hair behind her ear. Her hair had been unwound from its braid sometime or several times in the last ten days and now hung over to one side, disguising the shaved underbelly. "None of the test results revealed your divinity as such, no," Gogo said but frustratingly did not explain what they did reveal.

"So? What is it?" asked Vern, impatient.

Taking pity, Gogo finally answered. "It's an infection, nothing more . . . and yet everything more. A fungus, one yet to be described by any of the scientific literature we could find. The miracle part is that from the outside looking in, it has ravaged your body, but here you are talking to me like you've got nothing more than a cold."

Vern clutched the damp sheet surrounding her. A fungus.

All this time, that was what had been in her, causing the hauntings, the strength, the endurance. "So you're saying I'm better
now, right?"

Gogo's lips, already full, swelled as she puckered them out in
thought. "You're awake. You're talking. You're drinking. But better? Technically, your condition hasn't changed. Your heart rate
is at thirty beats per minute. Your temperature is still at a level
I'd call heatstroke—one hundred and twelve. But you're not dying. Your body has simply," she said, pausing to think of the right
word, "adapted."

Since leaving Cainland, Vern had lived every moment with
the secret fear that it might be her last, but she had come to the
brink and was, as far as she understood it, fine. "So the fungus
is still in me?"

"Yes. Still in you. Still . . ." Gogo hesitated. "Changing you?
Or your body is changing in response to it? It's only been a few
days, so we've not been able to find out much, but we're working
on it," she said, chewing on the nail of her thumb.

"But how does that explain my passenger?" asked Vern.
Gogo stared at Vern blankly. "You know, the thing. The growth.
What did your aunt call it? A tetra . . ."

Gogo perked in recognition. "Teratoma. A type of tumor
that can have teeth, hair, and, yes, bones. But like I said before.
This isn't that. The tests we took suggest the fungus is—"

Gogo exhaled warily. Vern guessed this wasn't a usual oc-
currence for her, to be confronted with something that left her
speechless.

Vern didn't have time for her reticence. She'd been living
with strangeness for most of her life and didn't have time to
stumble in its presence. "Please, God of Cain, just spit it out."

"It's fruiting. The fungus is fruiting on your back."

Vern felt her eyebrows hitch up at that. She could still be surprised, it turned out.

"It's like a polypore," Gogo said. "I don't know if the placement and design of it is a coincidence—maybe it's that shape because it's primarily drawing nutrients from your bones, breaking them down in order to support itself—but the growth is a conk mushroom forming an exoskeleton around you."

She was explaining to herself as much as to Vern, going by the questioning tone in her voice.

On the way to the cabin, Vern had seen a great antlered beast in her haunting, but it was not a flash of the past the way Lucy was or any of the other visions. That creature had been present, real.

That creature had been like Vern, a picture of her future. A warning.

"I can't stress enough how dead you should be. Part of me is thinking—maybe it's the fungus's enzymes, you know? It should be breaking you down, I mean, it is breaking you down, but maybe it also triggered otherwise dormant genes in your body? There's documented evidence of that happening, though not in humans, that I know of."

There was a haggard beauty to all of this. Fungi consumed and consumed, but Vern's body had refused to be devoured. She was being fed on but not rotting. Together, her body and the fungus had fused into a sickly monstrosity. Would she loom as terrifyingly large as the creature in her haunting one day?

She understood now the ravenous hunger she felt before the worst of the sickness had started. It was everything inside her body trying to hold on to itself despite the fungus's wolfish appetite.

The last ten days had been the peak of the sickness, and her body had come out the other side of it something new. Vern wanted to see exactly who that was. She twisted to her side in order to stand, but grunted upon noticing the IV in her arm and the catheter in her urethra.

"I'll take care of those. Just let me wash my hands," said Gogo, and left the room.

Alone, Vern reveled in her aliveness. All this time she'd thought death was coming for her, but perhaps it was she who was death coming for everyone else.

⊠

VERN WALKED using a pair of crutches Bridget had lying around from an old injury. "Take it slow," Gogo ordered.

Vern stumbled into the living room, then used the arm of the sofa to lower herself to the floor. With what strength she had remaining, she crawled over to the pallet Bridget had made for the children in front of the woodstove and nested herself between Howling and Feral. "Missed you," she whispered, and despite her determination to stay awake—she wouldn't sleep away any more days—in a matter of moments she was passed out again in a cocoon made of her sleeping babes.

Later, their kisses and raucous play awoke her. They were singing their favorite song: *Mam.*

"Mam! You was a goner," said Feral.

"Mam! You was dead meat," said Howling.

"Mam! You was like that dead bird. You remember? The one you killt with the rock?" said Feral, miming the action of throwing a stone.

"Mam, did you hear us singing to you?" asked Howling. "Do you know what a prayer is? We sang you prayers."

"Mam, Mam! Did you know Ina tells stories, too?"

"Mam, I'm hungry."

Vern's eyelids fluttered furiously, trying to keep up, but the children and their chatter raced away ahead of her.

Bridget took pity on Vern and grabbed Howling and Feral each by their hands. "Clean up your stuff. It's almost time for breakfast," she said, referring to the scattered items the children had deposited around the living room: large sticks, pine-cone-doll people, acorns, drawings on the backs of old newspapers.

As the children straightened up their mess, Vern sat up and stretched, rolling her shoulders forward and backward. "Tell me about the last ten days," she said to them, and they gladly narrated the goings-on of their lives here. The magic of real snow, so unlike the occasional icy drizzles they'd been in before. The magic of endless running water. The magic of the refrigerator. The magic of leeks, pistachios, salmon, fennel, yogurt, and a dozen other foods they'd tried.

Feral, as if keenly aware of civilization creeping in on him, ran to jump on the sofa after he'd cleaned up his things, doing somersaults and backflips. Vern shot him a look, and he ceased at once. He apologized for forgetting his manners, as he wouldn't want anyone coming into one of the dens he'd built and jumping on everything and destroying it all. Only, nothing in the woods was as a bouncy as this sofa.

While Feral sat looking shamefaced, Howling lay on the rug thumbing through a book. "What's this letter, Mam?" he asked. Scooting over toward him, Vern tilted her head and brought the book to her face.

"I'm not sure," she said, as she squinted at the intersecting bends, hoops, and loops where Howling pointed.

"Huh?" asked Howling, one eyebrow arched, incredulous. Bless him. He still thought she knew everything.

"What does he mean, letters?" Feral asked from the couch.

"See, look. Come down here. If you get real close, you can see all that smear of black is separate little shapes," said Vern.

Feral jumped up and crashed to the floor with a thud, then crawled over to the book. "They so small," he said, as much in wonder and delight as in intimidation.

"This one's *a*," said Howling. "Ina showed me. It goes *a-a-a*. Like apple. She said there's a song that says all the letters, and I asked her if it went on forever, since if you were to have a song for every number, it'd go on forever, but she said there was only twenty-six. I can count to twenty-six. Easy."

He'd be reading chapter books in weeks, flying ahead of not just Feral, but Vern. "I can count to twenty-six easy, too," said Feral, but he turned to Vern, desperate for reassurance. "Mam, I can learn the letters, too, can't I?"

She nodded, not wanting her doubts in her own abilities to transfer to him. "Yes. You can learn the letters. Of course you can."

"But how, if I can't even see them?"

Gogo entered the room, having freshly showered. Her hair hung in a dark wet plait. She wore a flannel button-up over a black shirt, with black jeans. "We can make the letters easier for you to see with special tools," she said, yawning so widely her jaw clicked. "Or there's Braille. That's where you use your fingers to decode the letters instead of your eyes."

"You got any Braille books here?" Feral asked, casting a jealous eye toward the book Howling was thumbing through.

Gogo shook her head. "But I can look into getting some right away."

Vern cleared her throat to reinsert herself into the conversation. "That's not necessary. Now that I'm better, we won't need to rely on your hospitality. We'll be out of your hair in a few days. I'll get those Braille books myself."

"And special goggles, too? Like the ones Ina said?" asked Feral.

"He means glasse—"

"I know what he means," said Vern. "I can get him glasses. I can get him whatever he needs, like I always have."

Gogo looked at Vern but said nothing.

"What?" Vern asked Gogo, but Bridget stopped further conversation by calling everyone to the kitchen for breakfast.

"Can me and Feral eat down here?" asked Howling. Bridget was already ahead of him, spreading newspaper on the floor before setting their plates on top. The children weren't used to sitting in chairs so high up from the ground. It made their bottoms hurt.

Vern grabbed the crutches and shuffled over to the card table right next to the kitchen. She took a seat in one of the fold-up chairs, and Bridget sat down across from her after laying out the food.

"You coming?" Bridget asked Gogo. Gogo shooed away the question with a flick of her hand. "Don't mind her. That girl lives on black coffee. More for us." She piled food onto a plate for Vern and pushed it in front of her. "Eggs over easy, venison steak, and wild rice risotto. That there on the side is wojapi. Berry sauce, basically. It's good on everything but especially the meat."

Vern shoveled overstuffed forkfuls into her mouth, pausing only for sips of water. Her passenger needed vittles and she did, too. And Howling and Feral, who chomped loudly as they ate, trading stories with each other despite mouths full of food. "They haven't given you too much trouble, have they?"

"The kids? No. No, not at all. They're good kids. Really good kids."

"I know Howling especially can be a handful," said Vern, quietly, not wanting the elder twin to hear the criticism.

"He's smart as blazes, that's all. One of the brightest kids I've ever met. Precocious doesn't really cover it. Gogo used to be like that, you know?" Bridget smiled, wistful. "You don't have to apologize for either of them. You're lucky. Truly lucky."

Vern's face hardened. "I wasn't apologizing. Just, acknowledging the work they can be."

Bridget stirred her coffee. "Fair enough."

Vern was thankful for the lull in the conversation so she could keep eating. It didn't take her long to get through the meal. "You a chef or something?" she asked once her plate was almost clean.

Bridget worked her way through her own plate at a much more reasonable pace. "In a fashion. I run Auntie's, which is part restaurant, part soup kitchen. People around here don't have access to the freshest food, so a couple of us got together to form Auntie's as a cooperative. Almost all of that on your plate was harvested, hunted, or foraged by yours truly. Chanterelles, garlic, sorrel, the wild rice."

Vern finished what remained of her water, and Bridget spooned more food onto Vern's plate. "Lucy talked about your cooking a lot," said Vern. "Her mam wasn't gifted in the kitchen."

Bridget stood from the table with a hardy laugh. "Evelyn had a lot of admirable qualities, but her cooking was not one of them, no. Learned that not long after meeting her. We must've been thirteen, fourteen? She couldn't even scramble eggs. In her defense, foster parents rarely take the time to teach that kind of thing. At least Ms. Franks, that was our foster mother, made sure the supply of Pop-Tarts was consistent and didn't have rules about when we used the toaster. I only learned to cook later when I made it back home as a teen." Bridget removed more food from the freezer to thaw, and Vern was grateful she didn't have to ask for it. Her hunger didn't surprise her—it was the sickness's doing—but it still overwhelmed her with its force. All she could do was surrender to its might.

"Evelyn and I shared the same foster home for four years. The aforementioned Pop-Tart lady. We lost touch, but around the time that Lucy was born she reached out to me because she needed help getting away from Lucy's dad."

The mention of Douglass squashed any cheer Vern had felt to be talking freely about her best friend. "That didn't exactly work," said Vern, disdain creeping into her voice.

Bridget's eyes flicked up but then quickly back down. "It did for a time, but it's not easy, Vern—leaving, staying gone."

"It was easy for me," Vern said, believing it as the thought first occurred to her but doubting it upon hearing the words out loud. When she'd argued the same point to her mam on the phone a few years ago, condemning Ruthanne for her cowardice, Vern was sure her own bravery, good sense, and gumption were the reason for her survival. Later, she learned she'd lived only because Ollie had taken an interest in her.

"Sometimes I still can't wrap my head around what went on there and how the judge just returned custody of Lucy to her father," Bridget said. She switched on the stove and spooned old bacon grease into a cast-iron Dutch oven before adding in a block of frozen food to reheat.

Over in the living room, Gogo folded her book closed. She'd been listening. "It stinks of corruption bigger than one man on an ego trip," Gogo said.

Vern shivered to hear Sherman reduced thus. He was her devil, her personal be-all-end-all of evil, but Gogo was right. He was but one man. "I've known for a long time Cainland's had more power than makes sense," Vern admitted. "I thought until now it was because Sherman was paying people off, but now I wonder, is it people paying *him* off?"

"And if so, which people is it?" asked Gogo.

Vern sifted through what she knew and what she didn't, replaying conversations with Ollie, with her mother, and with Sherman in her head. It was too much to keep straight, but one memory stood out, something Reverend Sherman had said about his father. That he was treacherous. That Cainland had been a game to him. He was dead now, but maybe it was he and not his son who'd been in partnership with an outside power. Ollie had even mentioned Eamon Fields by name.

The children stymied further conversation with their bids to play. Addicted to the excitement of new friends, they coaxed Bridget and Gogo into wrestling, fort-building, and make-believe. When the stew heating on the stove—a concession to Vern's bottomless belly—began to boil over, Vern was the one free to dash over and twist off the gas. She picked up the cast-iron pot to move it to a trivet on the counter so she could clean up. Glops of red broth splattered the burners and surface of the stovetop. She'd have to ask Bridget where the sponges were.

"Vern?" said Gogo from behind.

Stew in hand, Vern turned toward her. "Yeah?"

Gogo swallowed and took two cautious steps forward. "Please put that down." She pointed toward the cast iron in Vern's hands.

Vern frowned, put out by the sudden demand. She did what Gogo requested, but more out of confusion than compliance. She realized what troubled Gogo only when the pot was out of her hands. The scalding-hot iron had burned her palms. It was a sensation Vern was so accustomed to she rarely experienced it as pain anymore.

"Don't worry. It'll heal," Vern said, a deep cleft forming between her eyebrows as she examined her hands.

"Say again?" asked Gogo.

"By tomorrow, it'll be good as new," Vern said, and shrugged.
She'd stopped thinking of her ability to self-heal as extraordinary.

Gogo stood before Vern disbelieving, her mouth a perfect O.

"Mam always heals up," said Howling from the blanket fort
he'd built with Feral in the living room.

"That's not healing up. What you're talking about would be
full-on regeneration," Gogo said.

Vern spooned stew into her mouth and shrugged. "So? Mice
can do it," said Vern dismissively, playing the part of a girl casually in the know, thanking God of Cain for Carmichael and his
endless fact-sharing.

"Exactly *one* genus of rodents and *one* strain of genetically
modified mice," said Gogo. Vern hadn't expected her to know
so much about it, but that had been a foolish miscalculation.
Gogo's interest in biology was deep enough that she had a friend
she could call on to test samples of blood. It was dizzying to
think about what kind of life someone like that had, so much
larger in scope than Vern's own. Upon leaving their forested
home, Vern had told the children that there was more to life
than the woods, but she wasn't sure she'd understood the degree
to which that was true.

"Look, why don't you sit down?" asked Gogo.

Vern's legs had started to wobble from the pain of standing
upright. "Fine," she said, and hobbled over to a chair.

Gogo sat next to her and looked her in the eye. "Tell me what
else you can do," she said.

Vern licked her lips and looked away. "Nothing."

"Whatever Cainland is, it's about you. You get that, right?
It's about what you are. It's got to be," she said, pleading. She

dragged her chair closer to Vern until they were thigh-to-thigh. "Did you mean what you said earlier about leaving in a few days? Don't. Stay here. Take the time to figure this shit out. Let me help. The more you know, the better you can fight, and you better believe it's going to come down to a fight. It always does. What if they come for you?"

The antlered beast. Was it friend? Foe?

Sensing the truth in Gogo's words, Vern willed her distrust and cynicism exorcised. "Okay," said Vern. "I'll start at the beginning." The hauntings and her realization about what they really were, her strength, her endurance, her speed—she'd tell all.

Gogo nodded eagerly, and Vern, after one last steeling breath, began her story.

⊠

EARLY MORNING before the sun rose, Vern crutched herself to the kitchen fridge and ate a half dozen eggs raw. Gnashing shells between her teeth, she sucked down crunchy whites and crunchy yolks.

Frantic with hunger, she sniffed for more. Folded in white butcher paper was a two-pound block of ground venison. Bridget had set it thawing for tomorrow's burger lunch, but Vern tore off the wrapping and drove her teeth into the mass of dark red meat.

"Hungry?"

Vern swung around. Gogo, a shadow in the dark, stood in the kitchen's entrance holding a mug. "There's more in the chest freezer out back if you want it," she said. Vern wiped off her meat-stained mouth with her shoulder.

"Couldn't sleep," said Vern.

Gogo set a kettle on the stove and opened a cabinet. "You hunt?" Gogo asked.

"A little," said Vern, even though it had been her primary source of food for the last four years.

"Good. We took down one buck in the fall, but I don't know if it's going to last us. I hope you like goose. It's what's in season."

"I like anything," said Vern. She didn't have her bow anymore, but she could make a new one from PVC pipe. She'd taken down flying game before, though with her eyesight the conditions had to be just right.

Gogo wet a dishrag under the tap, squeezed, then walked up to Vern with it.

"What?" Vern asked.

Gogo reached up slowly, effectively asking permission, and pressed the wet cloth to Vern's face when Vern did not protest. She cleaned the blood left on Vern's mouth with gentle precision. The kettle whistled and Gogo grabbed it quickly. Vern guessed she didn't want the shrill ringing noise to wake the children.

Gogo moved in silent surety around the kitchen. Vern watched, captivated. The sight of her easy confidence paired with her brusque mannerisms was enough to distract her from the pain of hunger and inflamed joints.

Gogo finished filling her mug, blew into the steaming liquid, took a sip, and winced. Vern lifted an eyebrow. "Dandelion root," Gogo spat. "Bridget keeps telling me I need to drop the caffeine, but how can I if this is her alternative?"

Vern smirked. "You got to have it with cream and sugar."

"If only," said Gogo with a snort. "Bridget doesn't keep food like that in the house. She says if there wasn't some version of it that was a part of our traditional food ways, she's not gonna buy it. When I do, she throws it out."

Vern took a seat in one of the unfolded chairs tucked underneath the card table. "That reminds me of Cainland," said Vern, the memory infused with neither pain nor warmth. She'd risen past hate and nostalgia to a functional acceptance.

"Ouch," said Gogo, and leaned against the counter, her legs crossed and kicked out in front of her.

"I don't mean it in a bad way. It's just after Sister Rita wrote a newsletter about the history of sugar plantations in the Caribbean, we started raising bees and sweetening things only with honey and maple. Of course, then my brother, Carmichael, pointed out that the honeybee is not native to North America, so then we were down to just the maple."

Gogo looked at Vern with that hard gaze of hers. "Do you have a lot of good memories of growing up there?"

Vern couldn't be sure. Even sweet things could be made bitter by the knowledge of hindsight. "Not really, I don't think, but I do think about it all the time. No use denying what was. I was there, I was a part of it. There's a piece of it inside me."

Gogo set her mug down on the counter and filled the coffee percolator sitting on the counter with fresh water and coffee grounds. "The fungus, you mean?" she asked, emptying the dandelion root brew into the sink and rinsing out the mug.

"Not just that," Vern said. Sunlight crept inside inch by inch as the dawn came, and they were both cast in shadow. It made Vern braver, the way the darkness held on despite the encroaching light. "There are parts of it that I still hold dear." Vern couldn't deny the softness of the memory of Sister Rita's newsletter or of Carmichael's presentation about the European honeybee at a picnic after church. "I guess I like the part of Cainland that was a rebellion," Vern admitted. "Before there was the compound, it was just poor Black people pulling together to save themselves. They learned medicine and built clinics. They started schools.

They got people food. Started community farms. They taught people how to defend themselves from the Klan. They armed folk. They were fighters. They made the compound into their home."

Gogo dried the rinsed-out mug with a tea towel. "What changed?"

"Eamon Fields," said Vern, exhaling an angry breath. "I think he just wanted a place where he could act out all his sick desires with the excuse of religion to justify it all. All the rules, he came up with those. Uniforms. Getting rid of the phones. Did you know once upon a time there weren't even leaders? It was all just people cooperating. Getting along. Then he made himself the reverend and never looked back." Vern, disgusted, shook her head. Eamon Fields took a rebellion and turned it into a gated community.

Gogo set her mug down. "You know, given the time frame, it sounds like he could've been a plant," she said, voice plain, like this fact was obvious and any minute now Vern would nod in agreement. "This shit's typical. It was the sixties, right? The American Indian Movement, Black Panthers, and Brown Berets all had government infiltrators. Why would Claws and Cainland be any different?"

Vern slung her arms around her chest and squeezed. She bit her lip raw as she stood to tread a circle around the small kitchen. "You mean like some COINTELPRO shit?" she asked.

Gogo shifted her weight. "I didn't think—"

"We learn about it in school," said Vern. COINTELPRO was a frequent topic in Cainland's history classes. Students did oral presentations on the FBI's dismantling of radical political groups under the program. When they weren't outright murdering and framing dissidents, they were orchestrating their deaths and downfalls using undercover agents.

It was one of the main reasons Eamon started forbidding folks from leaving the compound. It was to protect against spies, informants, and provocateurs. He'd enforced a no- or limited-contact rule with outsiders because feds lurked everywhere. Vern thought of the compound's single phone, the one in his office, so other Cainites wouldn't have their phones bugged.

Vern quaked as the truth of it hit her. His edicts weren't defenses against cops but ways to concentrate power in his hands. Under the guise of keeping government plants out, every one of Eamon's rules had instead kept him, the real plant, in. She couldn't prove it, but she knew it as sure as she could know anything. Eamon was a plant, or he'd been turned into an informant. That was what Reverend Sherman had meant about his father's treacheries.

Vern hated herself for not realizing sooner, when it was so obvious in retrospect. Cainland's prosperity had always been a mystery to her. If the white man was so bent against the Black man—and he certainly was—how had Eamon secured such a large parcel of land in a state deep with KKK roots and racism? How had the police never once brought charges against them for their many illegal activities?

Gogo had said last night that Cainland stank of corruption bigger than one man on an ego trip, and here was Vern's answer. The Blessed Acres of Cain was a psyop.

"But why?" asked Vern, crossing and uncrossing her arms over her chest. "Why go to the trouble of taking over a commune—never mind that, creating a whole goddamn religion?"

But Vern knew the answer. Had known it for some time, in her own way. This was about the fungus. One of its primary effects—the hauntings—was written into Cainland's mythology from the very beginning. The so-called detox. "We're an experiment or something. Test subjects," said Vern, shaking. The vitamin shots and blood draws. All of it had been part of it.

She thought of every horror tale of the night doctors. She was no different than Brother Jon and his disappearing family. Ku Klux scientists messing all up in his brain.

Gogo set her coffee down and clutched Vern's shoulders hard. "Fuck the U.S. government and the horse it rode in on." She tugged Vern into a vise-grip embrace, and Vern let herself be held, let her limbs go slack in Gogo's arms.

"I can't breathe," Vern said, shaking her head.

"I'll breathe for both of us."

Vern wriggled out of Gogo's hold and paced the kitchen, stilling herself when she remembered a long-ago night. "What?" asked Gogo.

Vern tiptoed into the living room and grabbed her bag. She searched inside and then pulled out Ollie's beat-up computer. "This belongs to somebody who's involved in what's going on. Can you get into it?" asked Vern. She wasn't sure the device still worked. More than once it had been accidentally submerged in water.

"Hacking's not really my thing, but I'll try to get somebody on it," said Gogo. Vern nodded gratefully. For the second time since arriving here, she found herself wishing she'd left the woods sooner. It wasn't a thought she'd ever voice aloud, but it turned out other people had their uses.

"Eat up. Get some rest. I'll talk to you later," said Gogo.

## 16

VERN LAY NAKED in the frost-glazed grasses, hungry for who she was becoming. Wet earth coated her bare feet, back, and bottom; it wedged into her creases, and she let it. In the mud, the border between land and body disappeared.

Icy wind lapped Vern all over and she thrummed. Its caress teased her nipples taut and drew blood to the center of her. She gladly indulged the intimacies the mountains offered her. Not since Ollie had Vern given herself over to pleasures of the flesh, but now, out here in the presence of the fresh morn, among the firs, the warblers, and the tufts of herbage, she could put her fingers to herself and feel.

Was it she who was the fiend? Practically rutting the dirt.

She thought of Lucy, of how she must be now, fleshed out and hot-blooded and mean. Like a storm cloud, she'd hover over Vern dark and ready to give. They'd become new things together, outrunning their childhoods.

Vern prayed for a glimpse of her old friend. She couldn't control when the hauntings came, but Gogo thought with practice that might change. If Lucy was out there, she was forming memories all the time, and those memories would make their way to Vern. Vern need only learn how to access them; for the seeds of a thousand hauntings hid dormant in her recesses. Underground, an invisible web of mycelium connected Vern to anyone who had or had ever had the fungus.

But Lucy didn't come when Vern bade, never had—in real life or as a phantasm—and Vern lay alone on the ground with only her base longings for company. She, with the vigor of a young god, fingered herself into oblivion.

She did this every morning. Had done for the last month or two. Since she became well enough to walk without the crutches. Before dawn, she tiptoed outside, undressed, and gave her body over to winter. For three weeks she'd been restricted to the cabin by debilitating pain. Finally free, she was always seeking out moments to taste the outdoors unbridled.

When snow covered the ground, she gobbled packed clumps of it. When the rain made puddles, she sucked up the brown water with lips and tongue. She ate roots and weeds and poisonous berries. Past selves sloughed off, forming a wake of human-shaped pelts behind her. Two months in the mountains, and she was remaking herself anew.

Vern grabbed a fistful of weeds with her left hand as she finished herself off with her right. Her head rocked side to side, and she called out, *God, God, God, God, God*. She was not invoking any known deity. She was calling unto herself, this new being emerging inside of her. As if by her command, the sky opened up and it began to snow.

⊠

SILVER FLAKES dimpled Vern's body like lichen on a tree. She quivered atop the earth and it quivered back. Spanning the underground for thousands of miles pulsed silken rivers of filament. They spoke to Vern in the hauntings, and she wanted to speak to them, too—to the antlered beast she'd seen in the woods.

Experimentally, she closed her eyes. Tendrils of invisible mycelial thread prickled her. She could see the whole shape of its body—her body. She was as big as the continent. The earth.

Vern ate with her skin. Mycelia from the dirt traversed the mycelia of her body and fed her the ground. She absorbed broken-down trees, logs, and animal remains into her cells, and for the first time in months her hunger was sated.

The fungus gave as much as it took. She and it were symbionts. Siblings. Had she no life to tend to, she'd lie out here with the mass of it until she was rot, but she had plans to look for Lucy properly and wanted to get back inside before anyone awoke to ask her what she was doing.

Since Gogo first mentioned the possibility of controlling the hauntings, Vern had tried a number of techniques to summon Lucy to her. She cooked Lucy's favorite meals, gossiped secrets under the blankets that Lucy would've loved, and showed the children how to jump rope to rhymes she and Lucy chanted together as young girls. *Shake it to the east! Shake it to the west! Shake it to the one that you love the best!* These attempts universally concluded in frustration.

But Vern had been keeping track of the days in wait of Lucy's favorite holiday: Valentine's Day. Today she was going to re-create a tradition the two shared when celebrating years past and wanted to be alone to maintain the sanctity of it. She'd go inside to gather her gear, then head for the trees while the household slumbered.

Vern's clothes lay in a pile on the porch swing. She pulled on her drawers and an oversized sweater belonging to Gogo. The cabin didn't have a washing machine, and Gogo and Bridget relied on a laundromat in Cold Springs to clean their clothes. Vern didn't have enough items to last between their weekly trips to Washland, and Gogo had lent her a few items to get by.

When Vern went inside, all was quiet but for the snores of her babes in front of the woodstove and a soft pattering from the kitchen.

Vern stiffened. "Hello?" she whispered.

"It's just me," said Gogo.

"Did I—I didn't wake you, did I?"

"I couldn't sleep," Gogo said, and emerged from the kitchen with a cup of coffee. Her hair was down, and she wore only a ratty old T-shirt and briefs, some thick socks. "Is that all you were wearing out there? Are you cold? I can add wood to the stove." Gogo set her coffee on the side table next to the sofa and grabbed the throw hanging over the back edge of it.

Vern shook her head. "I can't feel it, not anymore. Well, I can. It just doesn't hurt."

"You're soaking wet," Gogo said skeptically, and used the throw to dry Vern's hair, which was sodden with melted snow. "I know you think you're invincible, but you've still got to take care of yourself. Just because you can't feel it doesn't mean it's having no effect. We already know your body runs hot. Think about how much harder that is to maintain in the cold."

Gogo had a tendency to lecture. She was bossy by nature and spoke with authority, ever certain of what was best. In this case, Vern could admit that she was at her tiredest, weakest, and hungriest after her morning jaunts outside and would often sleep in front of the woodstove until early afternoon recovering, missing half the day.

"You're finally starting to put on some weight, but if you keep going out every morning . . ." said Gogo, letting the rest of the sentence finish itself.

Vern's cheeks tingled with sudden warmth. "You know I go out there every morning?" Vern had been less discreet than she'd thought.

Gogo swallowed and glanced downward before returning her eyes to Vern. "I see you sometimes, yeah. Through my window. I keep it open in the night or else I overheat, but by morning I have to close it, and I'll occasionally get a glimpse of you."

"Do you see what I do out there?" asked Vern with a swallow both thick and heavy, aware now of how little she was wearing. The length of the sweater hung only just below her bottom. Its V-neck, designed for a body larger than hers, slit down almost to her tummy, leaving the inside edges of her breasts visible.

Gogo turned away and shrugged. "I hear you sometimes," she said, and refolded the throw she'd used to dry Vern.

Feeling bold, Vern stepped forward and licked her bottom

lip. The thought that her delirious exultations might have carried into Gogo's room through an open window brought out the sinner in her. "Did you hear me today?"

Gogo mumbled a quiet yes as she returned the folded throw to the sofa, and Vern stepped forward once more. "And do you ever—" Vern began, then stopped. "Do you ever watch?"

With breakneck speed, Gogo whipped her gaze toward Vern. She glared, eyes squinted. "No," she said sharply, loudly enough that one of the children briefly stirred under the blankets. "I would never, ever do that, Vern."

The ardor of the denial jolted Vern out of her wanton reverie. Gogo was disgusted by the very thought of Vern's sexuality, and she had every right to be. Vern was not a woman whose body could be trusted. Sherman had often called attention to the specific wickedness of those who lusted after the same sex, and though Vern could see no special reason why this would be so, her aggressive lack of chasteness did seem evidence of her degeneracy. Had it not been her desire that had primed her toward Ollie?

Under the logic that her life was her own business and she didn't hurt anyone by living it according to her own whims, Vern had always fought mightily to make room for herself. But perhaps by merely existing her sexuality was an imposition.

Gogo's disgust was all Vern needed in the way of chastisement. Like an unruly child, she needed to get herself under control.

"I've got to get dressed," said Vern, and grabbed dirty items from the garbage bag she used as a hamper. Inside the bathroom, she whisked off Gogo's sweater and replaced it with her own T-shirt and overlayer. She pulled on leggings and jeans next, then socks and her soft slipper boots.

Vern had to find Lucy. She was the only person who could

see into Vern and understand her. Plus, Vern couldn't offend someone who wasn't really there.

Vern returned to the living room to find the children were awake. Her conversation with Gogo must've nudged them toward consciousness. "Mam!" said Feral. "Come outside with us."

"I was actually going to go on a little walk," said Vern.

"Oh! A walk? Where to?" Feral asked, sounding positively delighted. "Just let me eat my breakfast first, then we can leave. I will keep you company."

Howling yawned and scratched his head. "Unless you prefer to be by yourself," he said in challenge. Vern sighed. It was one of his little tests to make sure she really loved him, and though she didn't often go along with it, it had been a while since she'd spent time outside with them. Generally, they preferred to go on their traipses alone, learning the world at their own speed.

"In fact, I would love company," said Vern. "Thank you for the offer."

☒

THE CHILDREN had come to think of the cabin and its surroundings as home. They moved through the steep woodland with confidence and ease, pointing out treasures to Vern: dissected owl pellets, special stones, sticks in curious shapes. "Mam, it's the letter Y," said Howling, pointing to a fallen branch.

"Do you know the golden ratio, Mam?" Howling asked. "Do you know pi? Did you know that there's negative numbers? It's like digging a hole."

"And imaginary numbers, too," said Feral.

"And do you know who Stephanie Yellowhair is?" Howling asked, as if her knowledge of this person were of the utmost importance.

"Why don't you tell me about her?" she said. He did, repeating almost word for word the things he'd been told by Gogo, who gladly indulged the children's endless questions. She spoke to them about things Vern had only inklings of, like:

"Do you know what the universe is made of?"

"Have you ever wondered if thoughts are real? You can't touch them. You can't feel them," Howling explained.

"And they aint got atoms," Feral finished off.

"A atom is a—"

"I know what an atom is," said Vern.

"You do?" asked Howling. "Can you explain it to me, then?"

"A atom is a dot," Feral offered sagely.

Vern wondered how they would've fared at Cainland. Like her, they were know-it-alls, discontents, and busybodies. Their curiosity was a well as cavernous as time.

Gogo was all too happy to share her knowledge with them, impressed rather than annoyed by their intense precociousness.

Sometimes Vern found herself engaging Gogo, too, though she wasn't sure why she bothered. Gogo's answers to questions as simple as, "What are you reading?" intimidated Vern, for the titles of the books Gogo read contained words like *biosemiotics*, *racial assemblages*, *anthropic mechanism*, and *libidinal economy*.

Vern was a brutish woman with brutish needs. She couldn't parse philosophy, theory, economics, sociology, not the way Gogo could. Vern's realm was that of the purely physical. Bone. Water. Dirt. Viscera. She and Ollie had been perfect for each other. She'd never live up to Gogo's intellect, her propriety.

"Look," said Vern, squinting, relieved to spot a distraction. The children followed her gaze toward a patch of ice-frosted bushes up ahead near the clearing, where the canopy of conifers was at its thinnest and sunlight slid through down to the forest floor.

"What, Mam?" asked Feral, who couldn't see how the bush before them was different than any other.

"I'm not sure," Vern said, and walked toward what she suspected was wild rose based on the size of the bright red blurs.

"Berries!" cried Howling and ran ahead, his sibling chasing after. They squatted and examined the hard ovals spread generously throughout the bush. "Never seen this kind before. Can you eat it?" Howling asked.

"They're rose hips," said Vern as she caught up to the twins and knelt to have a closer look at the bush. Each sphere of orangey-red fruit was cocooned in a shell of cracked ice. "Very rare to see them this late."

"But can you eat it?" Howling pressed.

"Not like this, but yes. We can make jam or syrup. I bet Bridget would like that." It would be a good way to pay back Bridget for how often she helped with the children. Rose hips were difficult and time-consuming to process, and Bridget would appreciate the effort that went into a good jam.

"I will pick fifty-hundred-five-million-and-one," said Howling.

"I will pick fifty-hundred-five-million-and-two," Feral countered.

"You'll do no such thing. We only need a couple pounds," said Vern, and tore off a piece of her shirt and tied it into a bag. "Mind the thorns. They're long and sharp."

"Fine," they said together.

When they'd gathered enough, Vern tied up the cloth into a satisfying bundle and headed back with the children toward the cabin. "I want a turn carrying it," said Feral.

"Then when will I get a turn?" Howling asked.

Vern was about to reason out a compromise, but the matter

was forgotten when the trio reached the clearing. The children headed forward leaving Vern and the rose hip bundle behind.

"Let's build a snow fort," said Howling, and immediately took on a managerial role. "Gather up the snow like this, see? Then pack it." Feral was happy to be directed, and soon the children had forgotten Vern's presence.

Now was her moment for some quiet time with Lucy. "I'll be back soon," Vern called out.

"Where you going?" asked Howling.

"Over there," she said, pointing to the woodland beyond the clearing where she'd spotted some aspens in the mountain's understory of trees.

"Don't be gone long, Mam," said Howling authoritatively. "When we finish, we're going to play a game where we're bears protecting our cubs and you got to be a monster trying to eat them. We'll defend the fort, and you'll attack. Okay?"

"I'll be back, and I'll be the most gruesome monster you ever seen."

Vern sped toward the aspens limberly. These days, especially when she kept on top of taking her naproxen, the hurt in her joints and limbs merely teased. She hadn't needed regular doses of hydromorphone in a month. She took them only at night, when the day's movement caught up with her and even lying down to sleep was agony.

Vern reached the aspen and climbed up along the trunk and branches. Once she found a good place for it, she settled into a perch and slid out her knife. She jammed the point of the blade into the tree and carved her and Lucy's initials the way Lucy had once done herself. A plus sign in the middle. A heart around.

Lucy had told Vern that she was the only person in the world Lucy could stand, and that she guessed that was love. It was childish to cherish so saccharine a memory, but Vern had clung to it because it was the first time she'd felt loving a girl wasn't something grotesque. The moment held special resonance today after a morning that had gone so wrong. Gogo had unequivocally spurned Vern's freak sexuality.

As Vern finished the carving, she scouted her surroundings for signs of Lucy. "You there?" she asked. Nothing but mountains for days.

She was about to give up when she felt a prickle on the back of her neck. An invisible presence. Behind her.

"Lucy?" she whispered as her skin erupted into gooseflesh. She closed her eyes, pressed her palm over the carving, then counted to three.

She flicked her eyes open with the expectation Lucy would be there in front of her, but the presence surrounding her was not that of her best friend. She'd succeeded in bringing on a haunting, but not a kind one.

Instead of Lucy, bodies. They swung from the bare branches of the aspen tree. All moved in unison, pendulums on the same grandfather clock. Vern had summoned a chorus of hangings.

"Stop," she cried out, voice wavering. "Leave me."

But upon hearing her voice, the bodies awoke. At once, their eyes opened, the force of their gaze upending Vern. Screaming, she startled backward, tumbling off the tree.

With a thud and a crack, she landed. Above her, a canopy of the dead hung. One body, writhing in its noose, broke away from the swarm. Gargling and coughing, it squeaked Vern's name.

Vern panted, immobilized by the fall. "Vern," whined the corpse.

"Leave me be," she commanded, though her voice did not convey confidence. "Or else I'll make it so you never come back," she threatened.

Another body disentangled itself from the hanging mass. "Vern," it croaked as it flailed inside of its rope prison.

"I said leave me!" she cried, this time with more conviction. "Leave me now, or perish." These hanging bodies were not mere recordings. Conscious, they called to her. They were echoes of something living, and that meant, as long as Vern wasn't bluffing, her threat of death held power. "Leave!"

The two breakaway bodies dissolved first. Next, all the others. Their decomposed matter rained down in a shroud of dust upon her. She coughed as the ashen particles entered her mouth.

"Vern! Vern!" she heard from the clearing. It was Gogo. The children must've gone to her when they heard Vern screaming. "Vern!"

Groaning, Vern sat up. "I'm here," she said.

"Thank fuck," said Gogo, though she sounded more angry than relieved. She hiked through the debris of leaves, sticks, and shrubs until she was at Vern's side. She knelt down and shook her head as she stared at Vern's arm.

It took Vern several moments to understand what had caught Gogo's attention. A shiny white hunk of radial bone had popped out of place and broken through the flesh.

With a shrieking sob, Vern bent the broken bone back into place. The pain knocked her out cold.

⊠

THE ARM HEALED of its own accord, though Gogo wrapped it in thick gauze as a matter of best practice. "What were you thinking?" she asked on the porch swing next to Vern, a Heineken in her hand. Bridget forbade alcohol in the house, but Gogo kept a stash of beers and "settler" food under the porch.

"I was doing what you told me to do. Figuring out how to control the hauntings," Vern said.

"From up a tree?" asked Gogo, downing the remains of the beer bottle.

"You wouldn't get it," Vern said.

"And why's that?"

"It was something special Lucy and me shared. I thought it might make her come if she remembered it. Remember that, wherever she is now, I used to mean something to her."

"You mean the carving?" asked Gogo.

Vern sipped from her mug of hot chamomile tea. "You saw that?"

Gogo shrugged and blew on the rim of the empty bottle of beer. It whistled and howled like a storm wind.

"It's not what you think," said Vern.

"And what do I think?" asked Gogo. She stretched out her legs and rested her boot-clad feet on top of the plastic coffee table that sat in front of the swing.

"I'm not . . ." said Vern. "You know."

Gogo whistled a melody with the bottle opening, then licked her lips. "What is it I supposedly know, Vern, O Great Mind Reader?"

Wind blew the rusted chimes into a frenzy. "I'm not one of those girls who— You don't have to worry about me. I'm not gay."

In the woods, it had been so easy to assert herself fearlessly, but it was impossible to be a free woman among people. Society demanded a certain level of lying about oneself.

"I am," said Gogo.

Vern turned her head toward Gogo, whose eyes were on the clearing. "I thought—" said Vern, but she didn't know what she thought. Had Gogo's disgust in Vern been more personal?

The growth on her back, her disease—there was a lot to deplore. Perhaps it was something more mundane: her albinism. Or had Gogo sensed her defilement? By Sherman, by Ollie.

"Thought what, Vern?"

"That I'd offended you this morning," said Vern, cheeks flushing with the shame of it.

Gogo looked at her questioningly, her brow a thick knot. "What are you even talking about?"

"When I assumed you might have been looking at me," Vern said, then exhaled shakily. "I wasn't trying to insinuate I was something you'd want to look at. I know I'm not normal. I know the feelings I have aren't exactly pure."

Gogo moved to sit on the plastic coffee table so that she was in front of Vern rather than beside her. She grabbed Vern's hand and squeezed. "First of all, fuck pure," she said. "Second of all, you're right, I was offended, but not at the idea of looking at you. At the idea you thought I'd intentionally violate your privacy in that way. That would be fucked-up."

Gogo hadn't liked the assumption that she was a voyeur, and Vern had been too damaged to realize that. She'd never had sexual dealings with people who had anything like a moral compass.

Vern's eyes met Gogo's. "I understand now," she said, then hesitated before asking her next question in a whisper. "Are you really . . ." Vern couldn't say the final word.

"A dyke? Yeah," she said, still holding Vern's hand. "I prefer winkte, but when I'm talking to non-Natives, yeah, I'm a gay girl."

"Winkte?"

"It's a Lakota thing," said Gogo.

"Lakota for gay?"

Gogo rotated her head side to side, considering. "It can be."

Vern pulled a wisp of hair from in front of her face. "I was with a woman before," she admitted. It was close as she could come to, *I've fucked a woman before, and I liked it*, and, *I'd like to fuck more of them*, and perhaps most pressingly, *I want to fuck you, Gogo.* "We were together for a while."

"You mean Lucy?"

Vern shook her head. "Someone bad."

Acid rose up from Vern's stomach hot and tasting of poison. Chest tight, she swallowed the burning liquid down.

Vern had never hated herself for the way she was, but shame bum-rushed her at the thought that she shared anything in common with the fiend. For who was she to judge her mam, the Cainites, or even Reverend Sherman when Vern, foulest of beasts, had slithered into Ollie's arms not just willingly but eagerly? Desire that strong—wasn't such a thing a sickness?

"Someone who hurt you?"

Vern inhaled. "Yeah."

"Well, fuck her," said Gogo, and stood up.

Smiling, Vern drew up her legs to her chest and rocked the swing with the force of her hips. "Never heard you talk like this before. Usually you're all, you know . . ."

"I'm all what?"

"Words, words, words, words," said Vern with a wry grin.

Gogo snorted and flopped back into the porch swing. "You sure do pretend you're a philistine, for someone with a mind sharp enough to cut the world in half," said Gogo. She wasn't usually so gregarious, and Vern wondered if she'd drunk the beer for exactly this purpose. It was the only way she could get loose.

Gogo didn't have a job, but she was always doing something for somebody. She was a doctor to all the folks in a hundred-mile radius who couldn't or wouldn't go to hospitals. At all hours, she hopped in her pickup and sped toward patients in this county, the next, and the next. She said her grandmother was a healer, and her mother before her. This was her legacy.

"It's not that I'm a philistine. It's that you're all . . . well, I never seen somebody read so many books as you," said Vern. Gogo shrugged the comment away, but Vern persisted, ready to prove her point. "Stand up," she said.

"What? Why?"

"Just do it."

Gogo stood, letting the blanket that was draped around her shoulders drop to the porch floor. She was wearing a black sweatshirt with a gray denim vest over top, sewn with an array of patches. Because Howling and Feral had asked after every single one of them, Vern had memorized the letters on each patch despite not being able to read what they said. Gogo had previously explained all the text. One showed an old rusted cop car overgrown with plants, accompanied by the caption: "Who Said Cops Weren't Good for Anything?"

There was another with the Lakota words "Mni Wiconi," one with a hot pink background embroidered with the text "LAND BACK" in all caps, and another that read: "Silence = Death." There were black flags, black flowers, and black linocut illustrations. Vern's favorite one read "Squat the White House."

Vern ran her eyes over each one, then spoke. "Okay, turn around," she told Gogo.

"What?"

"You heard me. Turn around."

Reluctantly, Gogo turned so she was facing away from Vern. "As predicted," said Vern, and she reached into Gogo's back pocket to remove the battered softcover book stuffed inside of it.

"Be gentle with that; a friend lent it to me," said Gogo, and turned around to snatch it back.

"What's it called? *A Poststructuralist Critique of Embodiment?*" asked Vern, thinking up the most nonsense thing she could based on the titles of other books Gogo read.

Gogo licked her lips as she sat down on the plastic coffee table. "Okay, first of all, that sounds sick as hell, I want to read it. Second of all, it's called *Winter in the Blood.*"

"That doesn't sound like your usual gambit."

"Oh, you think you know me well enough to call out my usual gambit?" she accused ruefully.

"I do," said Vern with a knowing smile.

"Well, I'll have you know, you're exactly right," said Gogo, left eyebrow raised. "Howling and Feral said that I read, and I quote, 'too much of that nonsense stuff,' and suggested I for once read a storybook. So, yeah, I decided to pick up this novel. I just started it, but it's good. Here, listen to the beginning of it," she said, and read the first page out loud. She luxuriated over each word, and Vern appreciated the slowness with which she savored the text. It made it easier to absorb.

The scene opened with a man taking a piss outside, and it sounded like something Vern herself might've written, could she write.

"Thank you," said Vern, meaning it. She'd not been able to experience a book since Lucy had left Cainland. "Lucy used to read to me."

"I'm sorry she didn't come to you today," said Gogo.

Vern closed her eyes and breathed in the early evening air. "It's all right. I learned something all the same," she said, and explained the haunting she'd summoned and how two of the hanging bodies had called out her name. Derailed from their prescribed track, they'd tried to reach out to her, consciousnesses in their own right.

"That sounds heavy. Are you okay?" asked Gogo.

Vern shrugged.

"You can always talk to me about anything, all right?" Gogo said.

"Talk, talk, talk, talk, talk. What does that do?" asked Vern.

"I think of talking like breathing, or eating. You take stuff in, you expel stuff out. It nourishes you. It lets the old leave. Trees talk to each other, you know that? Through their roots."

"And fungi through their mycelia," said Vern.

"Right," Gogo said.

"What the world has to say isn't always so good," said Vern. Breathing heavily, she stood up from the swing. Healing large wounds expended more energy than she had to spare. Fixing the break had worn her, and even though it was only eight, she planned to head to sleep now.

"Sleep in my bed tonight," Gogo offered, seeing Vern's fatigued state.

"I spent ten nights in that janky old thing. Never again," said Vern, but that wasn't her real reason. A night in Gogo's bed was dangerous. An invitation to indulge in feelings best left unfelt.

"You sure? I'm going to be up all night anyway. The bed's no use to me."

"Up all night doing what?"

"Not sleeping," said Gogo.

"You do a lot of that."

"Somebody's got to keep my demons company, you know?" Gogo said with a small smile, but Vern sensed the seriousness of this confession.

"Just for tonight," said Vern.

"Sure," Gogo said, and hopped up from the porch swing to help Vern inside.

Howling and Feral were chopping garlic under Bridget's direction.

"They aren't hassling you, are they?" asked Vern.

"Never," said Bridget.

"We're *helping*, Mam," said Howling, rolling his eyes. Vern smiled and followed Gogo toward her room.

"Hey. Dinner's in fifteen, you two," said Bridget.

"I was actually thinking about retiring early," Vern said. She wasn't one to skip a meal, so Bridget looked immediately concerned. "I'll be fine. Just need some rest."

"She's gonna sleep in my room tonight," said Gogo.

Bridget tossed chopped onions into a frying pan full of browned butter. "You sure that's a good idea?" she asked.

"Why wouldn't it be?" asked Gogo.

Bridget grabbed a handful of mushrooms from the chopping board and threw them in with the caramelizing onions. "You been drinking?" asked Bridget.

"No," said Gogo.

"And are you joining us for dinner?"

Gogo filled a glass of water from the tap. "If Vern can spare me," she said.

"Vern?" asked Bridget.

"Yes, of course," Vern said.

Bridget waved them away reluctantly when the pan started smoking, and Gogo led Vern to her room. "Sorry about that. Sometimes she forgets I'm a grown woman. Seems like the longer I live here, the worse it gets, not better. I'm twenty-two, for fuck's sake," said Gogo, venting.

Vern settled onto Gogo's bed. That was just what family was like, thinking they had a say in your life when they didn't. Back at the compound, Ruthanne had nagged Vern all the time about dressing right, eating right, talking right. That wasn't something that would've changed when Vern turned eighteen.

"Why doesn't she want me to sleep in your room?" Vern asked.

Gogo sighed and collapsed onto the mattress next to Vern. "It's complicated."

"Does she not like me?"

"What? Of course she likes you," said Gogo. "She's worried because you're vulnerable, you know?"

Vern was as close to invincible as a living being got. "What are you talking about? I'm not vulnerable," she said.

"You are," said Gogo. "And the fact that you don't realize that is part of why Bridget's worried. She thinks I'm gonna hurt you."

Vern drew her eyebrows in, curious. "How so?"

Gogo, uncharacteristically hesitant, bit the side of her lip before answering. "I've got a reputation," she said. "And it's well-earned."

"A reputation for what?" asked Vern, her mouth dry.

"You know. Running through girls."

Vern watched Gogo carefully. "Right," she said, doing her best not to react. Vern was in no place to judge who Gogo had or hadn't been with.

"That's not why I invited you in here," assured Gogo as she stood.

"I know," Vern said, and she did. If Gogo wanted something, she would say it outright. She'd offered up her bed because she genuinely thought it would help.

"Are you in any pain?" asked Gogo, in medic mode.

"Always," Vern said, but hopefully she didn't sound too self-pitying. "It's manageable, though. I should probably try to get some rest."

"Do you want me to read you to sleep? We can get through *Winter in the Blood* together," said Gogo.

Vern resented whatever softness she still had in her that made her melt at Gogo's offer. "I don't—not if it's too much."

"It's nothing," Gogo said, and tugged the paperback out from her back pocket. She pulled herself on top of her desk and sat, feet resting on the wooden chair. "Ready?"

"Ready," said Vern, and closed her eyes as her head sank into the pillow. It took her ages to slip under, desperate to hang on to every word. It was a small thing, but she could not remember ever having been pampered so lovingly.

⊠

AFTER THAT NIGHT, Vern and Gogo developed a rapport. They handed pieces of themselves—meager offerings—over to the other.

Vern learned that Gogo's mother died when she was four. Bridget had taken custody, taking her off the rez she'd called home up until that point. That was the central conflict between them: Bridget's belief that she'd rescued Gogo and Gogo's belief that her aunt had stolen away her birthright, her history, her heritage. "I can barely speak Lakota anymore," said Gogo, shaking her head. "All she remembers is the bad, but that was never my story. I had people. History. Who am I without tiospaye, you know?"

Gogo often used Lakota words without explaining them, and Vern rarely felt like breaking the flow of conversation to ask.

"Why not go back?" asked Vern one day.

"And leave Bridget? I'm all she has. Plus, she raised me."

"But you're not responsible for her," said Vern.

"Yeah I am," Gogo said, genuinely perplexed by the idea that she might not be. "When you love someone, you take care of them whether or not it's convenient. Fuck, you do that even when you don't love somebody."

Vern felt no such duty. The only peace she'd found in this life was living for herself, and she'd not be ashamed of it.

"Besides," Gogo continued. "I'm not sure there's anything for me back on the rez, or if I'd even fit in there anymore. Bridget made me into an outsider."

Vern wondered what it must be like to have a claim to a land, to have a relationship with it that stretched back millennia. Cainland was built on the idea of Black people's right to their postslavery forty acres, but forty acres of whose land? There had been talks before about returning to Africa, but it always seemed like Africa didn't belong to them anymore. Maybe Gogo's feelings about the rez paralleled Cainites' feelings about the mother continent.

Gogo also tagged along on walks with the family.

"What you reading?" Howling always asked. Gogo had moved on from *Winter in the Blood* to *Margins of Philosophy, Writing and Difference*, and *Dissemination* by somebody named Jacques Derrida.

Vern stowed away the titles of books like morsels she might snack on later. She liked being reminded of the incomprehensibleness of the world. There was more to life than Cainland, more to earth than its collected sorrows. There was wonder and awe and the allure of nothingness. No one had figured everything out, but there were people who'd made their home in the searching. If they could dwell there, so could Vern.

In quiet moments, Gogo would share less esoteric texts aloud. She'd say, "Vern, isn't this good?" then read a short excerpt for her. *"I hope you live without the need to dominate, and without the need to be dominated,"* Gogo read, pausing to ensure she had Vern's full attention. *"I hope you are never victims, but I hope you have no power over other people."* Gogo's voice, crisp, dulcet, and deep, seemed made for oration. Vern always sprang to alert at the sound of it. *"And when you fail, and are defeated, and in pain, and in the dark,"* Gogo read on, *"then I hope you will remember that darkness is your country, where you live, where no wars are fought and no wars are won, but where the future is."*

It was novel to feel moved by a stranger's words, and Vern regarded this rousing feeling with suspicion. Was this what it was like to be a Cainite? To hear the words of a sage and actually believe them? To find in their message a small truth?

Vern had always loved stories, but years of listening to Sherman disguise lies with rhetoric on the pulpit had made her less generous in her attitude about writing.

"Go on," said Vern, cautiously curious.

Gogo turned the page. *"Our roots are in the dark; the earth is our country. Why did we look up for blessing—instead of around, and down? What hope we have lies there. Not in the sky full of orbiting spy-eyes and weaponry, but in the earth we have looked down upon. Not from above, but from below. Not in the light that blinds, but in the dark that nourishes, where human beings grow human souls,"* said Gogo, finishing.

Darkness was Vern's country. It was all she had by way of a homeland. It pleased her to think it could be a place that nourished. Everyone was always going on about light this and light that, but what of dark?

"Who said all that?" asked Vern.

"Ursula Le Guin," said Gogo. "What I just read is a section from a commencement address she gave in 1983. You would like her work, I think. Anyway, this book is a collection of graduation speeches. I'd be happy to loan it to you if you want to read it yourself. There's a lot of good stuff in here."

Gogo didn't know that Vern couldn't read, and Vern didn't

want to disabuse her of that notion. "All right," she said, swallowing.

"I have most of her novels and collections, though I'd have to dig them up," Gogo said. Vern rarely saw Gogo this excited, and, stupidly, she felt jealous. Jealous of literature and philosophy and how it made Gogo light up. "You'll love her books. I know you will."

Vern turned away and ripped off the white head of a stalk of bear grass. "How do you know what I'll love?"

Gogo became thoughtful. "I suppose I don't know for certain."

"Then why say it? You're always acting like you know everything. You're not better than me," said Vern.

"I'm sorry. I won't presume anymore," said Gogo.

Vern was only bitter because she'd never be able to read these books that she should theoretically love, but that wasn't something she could say to Gogo. Her outburst had succeeded only in cutting off her one access point to books because Gogo had since stopped her read-alouds.

Which was fine. Gogo could be that way if she wanted. Fuck her and her ceaseless pretenses.

Days stumbled one into the other like a toddler into its mother's ankles. Howling learned to read. Bridget found someone to examine Feral's eyes, and soon after that he received glasses. He, too, was starting to read, though the process for him was much slower than it had been for Howling. Mostly he was learning his letters. He used a magnifying glass to practice the sounds, and to figure how to write his name. He drew pictures, occasionally signing them with a giant, distorted *F*. When he was feeling particularly literary, he scribbled along the bottoms of his drawings in pretend writing, then would narrate what he "wrote" to Howling.

Vern was thankful for the part Bridget played in the children's lives. Bridget liked to take them everywhere, to spend every spare moment with them. Vern wondered if she herself was being neglectful, but then she saw how much the twins' world opened up after spending an afternoon in Cold Springs with their adopted aunt. They liked to be doted on by Bridget's friends. They met other children. Some days it seemed Vern hardly saw them. They knew her too well. They wanted to learn about all they didn't yet know.

Besides, after Vern had asked one too many times whether the children were any trouble, Bridget confessed that she couldn't birth children of her own. Sterilized. Something else we can thank Uncle Sam for. Caring for other people's kids was the closest to mothering she ever got, and she cherished it.

As the children softened to civilization, Vern pulled further from it. She continued to waken before dawn for her hour of peace outside, but these days she walked to the wooded areas beyond the clearing, where she didn't have to worry about disturbing anyone. Today, she bathed in a mud puddle before scrubbing herself clean with packed snow. She sat in the high branches of a fir and pretended to be the sky.

And as the sun rose, she lamented her necessary return to the cabin, where she'd be forced to confront her inadequacies. The forest didn't mind illiterates and mad girls. Didn't mind that screaming was sometimes a person's only language.

"Until tomorrow," she whispered, and hopped twenty feet down to the forest floor, her body easily taking the impact.

Back at the cabin, Gogo's pickup truck sat next to Bridget's. It hadn't been there when Vern left this morning. Gogo had been out the whole night. Vern sighed and considered staying outside, but the children didn't like it if they awoke and Vern wasn't there. As winter ambled slowly toward spring, the days were lengthening. Early sunrises meant Howling and Feral were waking up earlier and earlier.

Vern opened the front door gingerly so as to not make a creak. If she was quiet, maybe she could slip to her place in front of the woodstove before Gogo noticed.

"Vern?" whispered Gogo.

It had been a stupid plan anyway. "What?" asked Vern with such hostility it shocked even her.

"You know what? Never mind," said Gogo, shaking her head and leaving the kitchen for her bedroom.

After a minute of internal grousing, Vern followed after her. She knocked lightly on Gogo's door.

"What?" shouted Gogo from inside, with as much unnecessary bitterness as Vern had shown.

"I deserve that," said Vern, and hoped that Gogo wouldn't make her grovel too much. No matter her sin, Vern wasn't built for that. "Can I come in?"

"Fine," said Gogo.

Vern tiptoed inside and shut the door behind her. "Sorry for being a bitch," she said.

"Don't be sorry for being a bitch. That's one of your finer qualities. Be sorry for treating me like shit for weeks over some infraction I don't even understand."

Vern nodded as she exhaled. "Sorry for treating you like shit," Vern said. "There was no infraction. I'm just . . . like that." How else was one to respond to insecurity but with enmity and aggression toward perceived offenders?

"I've missed you," said Gogo, an accusation, not a confession.

"Yeah," Vern said, and though it wasn't in her nature to say it, she sensed she'd break what was between them if she omitted the truth. "I missed you." She rubbed her eye with the butt of her palm.

"Good," said Gogo. "You all right?"

Vern was, until she saw the adolescent girl sitting at Gogo's desk with chalk and slate in hand. Black as earth and pretty as a sunset, she scribbled furiously. Vern, taking a deep breath, walked cautiously over to her.

The writing was recognizable only because it was two of only a very few words Vern knew.

*Hello, Vern.*

Vern tore the tablet from the girl and slammed it into the wall.

"Vern!"

Gogo pulled her from behind. There were indents in the wall where Vern had apparently slammed her fists.

"Fuck, sorry," Vern said, breaking out in shivers. The girl still sat at the desk, a new slate in her hand. She scribbled, and held up her writing.

*Hello, Vern.*

Gogo tugged Vern toward the bed and made her sit. She grabbed Vern's hand and placed it on her chest. "Feel that. You're right here. Nowhere else," she said. "Feel the rise and fall of my breath." Vern's hand moved with Gogo's chest. Calmed by Gogo's steady presence, Vern shut her eyes.

Earlier, she'd railed against the discomforts of the inside world and civilized life, but, touching Gogo, she felt perfect acceptance. When next Vern opened her eyes, the haunting was gone.

Vern's breaths steadied, but she kept her hand on Gogo's chest, absorbing her granite composure.

"Any better?" asked Gogo, but, entranced by brown skin, Vern was only half listening. She rolled her thumb over Gogo's collarbone and dragged it along to the hollow at the bottom center of her neck and downward, toward the neckline of Gogo's shirt.

"Hey," said Gogo in reprimand.

It was times like this that Vern most felt Sherman's influence in her. She could hear him at the pulpit now, preaching about the natural lasciviousness of women. If not controlled by a strong husband, that lasciviousness could be exploited by the white man to break up the Black family. Lesbianism, a proclivity of white women, was but one way Black women's lust could be used to bring down the descendants of Cain.

"I'm sorry," said Vern, jerking her hand from Gogo's chest. "I wasn't thinking."

"Don't be sorry. Please," Gogo said. She reached out to Vern's hand again and squeezed, pulling it toward her lips to kiss the knuckles softly. "It's not that I don't want to," she said.

"Then what?" asked Vern, trying to sound mean, but spit caught in her throat and it came out croaky, unsure.

"You're not in a good place," said Gogo, her grip tight over Vern's hands. "I'm not sure this is the right time."

"I'm fine," said Vern.

"I say this as gently as possible, but no the fuck you're not."

Vern couldn't help the chirp of laughter that escaped her throat. "Well, that's not gonna change anytime soon," she said, biting the tip of her thumbnail.

Gogo tucked her pouty bottom lip into her mouth. "I do want to," she said quietly, only a few notches above a whisper.

"Want to what?" asked Vern, wanting to hear Gogo say it despite knowing the answer perfectly well.

"Touch you."

Vern would've done anything Gogo asked at that moment.

"You are," said Gogo, "distractingly beautiful." Vern's cheeks, neck, and ears rushed with blood. Gogo placed her palm on Vern's face. "You're blushing. Am I making you uncomfortable?"

Vern shook her head hard, shivering.

"And this is what you want?" asked Gogo.

"Yeah," Vern whispered.

"Right now?" asked Gogo, trying to give Vern an out.

Vern nodded, though she still wasn't ready for the dazzling hot rush of sensation that overwhelmed her when Gogo leaned in and kissed her with a gentleness Vern had not ever once been on the receiving end of.

"This okay?" asked Gogo, breaking contact. Vern let out a yelp, bereft. She was as bad as Sherman claimed. Worse. Needing Gogo's touch was another way Vern's body was wrong. "Vern?"

In answer, Vern leaned forward and pressed her tongue into Gogo's mouth. Gogo tangled her fingers into the back of Vern's hair, tugging her close with both hands.

Vern felt the kiss everywhere. Taller and broader than Vern, Gogo had a body to get lost and wrapped up in.

Gogo reached her hand up Vern's shirt and circled her nipple with a thumb before cupping her breast hard. Gogo worked the opposite hand downward, not bothering to take off the long johns Vern was wearing. She pressed her hand to Vern's crotch and rubbed with the heel of her hand. Vern arched her back and ground into Gogo's hand, greedy for her touch.

Vern reached for the zipper of Gogo's jeans, but Gogo pushed her hand away. "Just want to touch you," she said.

They lay down together front to front, lips to lips, legs interlaced. The bed creaked with the movements of their bodies.

As Vern rubbed herself into Gogo's thigh, Gogo touched herself, pushing her fingers beneath the waistband of her jeans and underwear. Self-conscious, Vern didn't moan. To do so would've revealed another weakness: that she was prone to deep feeling, could be rendered to whimpers by it. Gogo was perfectly capable of undoing Vern, and it was better to keep it a secret just how much.

Then Gogo kissed, licked, and bit Vern's neck—Vern's attempts to keep quiet all at once proved futile. Desperate for each other, they clung. Vern reached one hand around to the back of Gogo's head and the other to her ass, squeezing. Legs locked together, they dry-fucked until they both came, moaning into each other's lips.

"You are incredible," said Gogo, like she meant it, trembling and reverent. It was enough to make Vern weep.

## 17

"GET YOUR ASS UP out of bed, girl."

Vern had been staring at the dents she'd made in the wall when his voice called to her. She lay in Gogo's arms, the two of them wrapped up in sheets on the twin-sized bed.

"I said get up. You need to make breakfast. This kind of behavior is beneath you. Get up."

Vern had heard these words before. She rubbed her eyes and looked up, weaving out of Gogo's hold.

Reverend Sherman was here, in the flesh, standing in the corner.

Vern's breaths rushed in and out of her, yet she did not take in air. This was the sensation of dying. Who had let him inside? Bridget? Had she led him to Gogo's room to show him her sin? Were Howling and Feral already gone, whisked away before Vern could awake and have chance to make a scene?

"I've told you time and again, Vern, that if you don't repent and live the life the God of Cain wants for you, I will not be able to protect you from his reign of vengeance," Sherman said. "I saw the way you were looking at that woman in town yesterday. Everybody could." He sounded humiliated, his voice streaked with deep hurt and fear. "They saw you looking, and they knew what you were. You can't let them see that. You can't afford to be this way. Do you understand? The whites don't need an excuse to kill, but they see you looking at one of their women, they will burn you up alive. Don't be fooled by the year. In this county, it's still 1955."

He circuited the room as he did up his tie. "Now, I know your special . . . situation," he said, pointing between her legs, "means it's easy to get confused about what's what. We all have our special burdens, and that's one of yours. You got to keep your eye on the prize. We will make over this world as God intended, but only if we live it according to his laws. Homosexuality is a white man's disease, and you cannot let yourself succumb." He jutted his fist out in the air in her direction. "It's hard at first, but once you get into the routine of your wifely duties, it will become second nature. So get your ass up, and cook breakfast." His nostrils flared angrily as he lorded around the bedroom.

"Gogo!" Vern called, and shook her lover awake.

Gogo's eyes flashed open, and she groaned. "What?" she muttered, voice full of sleep.

"He's here," Vern said, pointing to her husband. "He's here."

"It's just us, baby. Just us. They can't hurt you," rasped Gogo, rubbing each of her eyes with her fist.

"It's Reverend Sherman. Look."

Gogo wrapped her arms around Vern and squeezed with a force only a woman altered by fungus could take. "There's no one there," said Gogo in an understanding whisper.

"Get your ass up out of bed, girl," Sherman said again, intonation identical to before. "I said get up. You need to make breakfast. This kind of behavior is beneath you. Get up."

As he got dressed, he began his upbraiding all over. "I've told you time and again, Vern, that if you don't repent and live the life the God of Cain wants for you, I will not be able to protect you from his reign of vengeance."

He repeated the diatribe from before, and Gogo was frozen in his presence.

"Tell me what's happening. Talk to me," said Gogo, shaking Vern hard.

"It's a memory," said Vern. "I think he's here because—I think he knows what we done." Vern's shame had summoned this haunting.

"Listen to me. Listen to me. Breathe. Blink and think. This will pass. They always pass."

"No," cried Vern. "He knows what I done. He won't leave until I repent, and I will not repent."

Reverend Sherman spoke on. "I saw the way you were looking at that woman in town yesterday. Everybody could." he repeated.

"Stop," she yelled at him. "Stop."

What she wanted didn't matter. He'd play out his track until he was good and ready to stop. Until she was dead.

"Homosexuality is a white man's disease."

Vern sprang out of bed and pounced. "Shut up," she snarled. "Shut up, shut up, shut up." She put her hand on his neck and squeezed, the same way Lucy had squeezed Thelonious's.

Her aggression did not disrupt him. His speech played on. "They knew what you were," he said. "You can't let them see that."

She pleaded with him in her mind to leave her be, to give her the smallest parcel of quiet. "Get your ass up out of bed," he said one last time, then stopped.

His eyes, dazed and twitching, found hers. "Vern?" he asked. "That you?"

She squeezed his neck harder, pressing with all her strength. "You haven't changed," he said with a chuckle, alive in her mind, sentient. "Moody as always. I see the years away have only hardened you more." He licked his lips, grinning. "Please, remove your hands from my neck," he said, and Vern, on reflex, obeyed. Her cells knew his voice, knew how to respond when he was at the limit of how much he could be needled.

"You still got some sense in you," he said.

The dubious compliment reminded Vern of her mother's oft-repeated words. *You got more opinions than sense.* Maybe that was how it should be. Remembering that adage snapped Vern from her docile trance.

She seized his throat once more, calling on the same mental reserves that had kept her and her children alive for years in the forest, and squashed his windpipe. She silenced him to whimpers.

"What's happening?" Gogo asked, her tone coarse and demanding.

"He's talking to me," said Vern. "I'm talking to him."

"He's not real. It's a memory. Come back to me," said Gogo.

"No, he's *here*. Alive. Like the bodies in the tree that called my name." Like that girl writing on her slate.

Reverend Sherman had come alive from the memories, too. He was thinking, feeling, fuming—doing everything a living person did but breathe. "It's him. It's really him."

Gogo touched Vern's arm. "That's not possible."

Vern had surpassed *impossible* when she'd broken those straps and left the Blessed Acres of Cain, surviving in the wood despite everything. Nothing could surprise her more than her own aliveness. Manifesting Reverend Sherman's sentience from memories was small in comparison. Vern's life was the one that was the miracle. Not his.

"Please. Stop," Sherman gasped, begging. Vern loosened her hold.

"When is it?" he asked.

She stared at him, not comprehending the question.

"Come on, girl, damn it. This is not the time for your antics. When is it?"

"What's he want?" asked Gogo.

"To know the date."

"Tell him. See what happens. See what he has to say."

Briefly self-conscious, Vern wondered how she must look to Gogo, rumpled, having slept in her clothes. Braless. She was sweating, because most emotions made Vern sweat. Did it look to Gogo that Vern's hand was squeezing air or that her hand was balled into a fist?

Gogo believed in time Vern would be able to interact with the hauntings in mind only. She'd be able to squeeze Sherman's neck with her hand without ever actually using her hand. Vern wished she could do that now, be simultaneously in bed with Gogo, enmeshed with her body, while her mind tore Sherman in half for making her remember what it felt like to submit.

"It's mid-February," said Vern.

"Year?"

Vern's brow tightened up. "The year?"

"Say it, damn it."

She gave in to his demand but didn't understand how he couldn't know.

The breath he blew out sounded full of regret. "It's three months I've been dead, then." He could've punched her, for how knocked out she felt by this news. "I wonder how long Cainland has left. Everything's already too uncontained. I couldn't control you, and now you're out in the wild," said Sherman. "Judgment Day is upon us. The God of Cain has found us."

"Stop lying," Vern shrieked. "I know you don't believe in that crap."

He leaned to the side, his face strained into an offended

frown. "He's real, Vern. How can you doubt it? How else do you think we've been allowed to flourish? Tell me, child, at the Blessed Acres did you ever know hunger? Homelessness? Do you know what it's like to be sick but not be able to afford a doctor to care for you? These are luxuries not afforded to many. You must know that now. You must've realized the truth since leaving, that the world is as cruel a place as I said it was. Crueler. Tell me, girl. Deny it. Say I'm wrong. My father tried to turn that place over to the feds, but I saved it. I kept to its original promise." Genuine belief suffused his tone.

"You're wrong," Vern said. "None of that stuff has to do with your made-up god."

He winced at her blasphemy. "How is it that you've fallen so far from his light?" asked Sherman, visibly saddened. "I never took you for a gullible girl, yet you've swallowed the lies of the outside."

"You're the one who's swallowed lies. Did you really think it was the God of Cain that gave you all you wanted? You thought the creator of our people would hand back Lucy to an abuser?" asked Vern. She was shaking, but with anger, not fear.

"He was a strong father. A leader. He's what Lucy needed and what many young folk are missing out there, their daddies in prison. He was there for her, damn it. He was there," Sherman cried out, his voice rising.

"Tell me you don't believe that. Tell me there's some part of you that knows better," said Vern. She needed to hear him.

"What I know is that the Blessed Acres of Cain has been a refuge and a land of plenty for decades. If not because of the God of Cain, then who? Of course, I understand it's not him alone. He works through human vessels."

"And just who are those human vessels?" asked Vern. "Eamon's cronies?"

"Just because my father set up those connections doesn't mean they're tainted. We still benefited from them. So what if the God of Cain's got soldiers in every level of government making sure Cain prospers? At least he did. Not anymore. You leaving has disturbed the plan. The beautiful thing we've built will end. You should come back, girl. You should repent. If you don't, it all ends."

Vern breathed, feeling calmer than she ever had in Reverend Sherman's presence. "Then let it end."

"Would you say that if you knew it meant letting them all die? Carmichael. Your mama. Every good brother and sister. Every child. But not just them, the whole dream we've been working toward. Nothing's been the same since you left."

Vern had always imagined everything carrying on once she'd gone. "Carmichael's fifteen. Same age you were when you left. He never said it out loud, but he did always wonder why you didn't take him with you. Of course, there's no chance of that now. God's disciple instructed me to tighten security."

"God's disciple? You mean Ollie? It's the government, Sherman. Come on."

"Very little hope Carmichael can leave," he said, ignoring Vern's words. "Brother Richard and Brother Jerome sit around the compound perimeters with rifles. Did you know that? That's the rules since you left. I once heard Carmichael ask your mama this: *If there had been men with guns willing to fire on Vern that night, do you think she'd still have gone?*" said Sherman.

Vern let go of Sherman and collapsed back onto the bed, exhausted. "Do you want to know what he said next? *I bet she would have. It's just like that song you're always playing, Mam. 'Before I'd be a slave, I'd be buried in my grave, and go home to my Lord and be free.'*"

Vern could hear Carmichael's voice. Another haunting: an echo of Sherman's own memory.

*Is it weak of me that I'd rather be a slave than be free? I don't want to die*, Vern heard him say. She wanted to see him but could not.

"You want to know who my successor was going to be?" Reverend Sherman asked, mocking her, baiting her with tidbits about the life she'd left behind. He was trading on her caring about the people at Cainland despite all they'd done to her in the form of not doing anything at all to fight Sherman.

"Brother Freddy was set to take over leadership. You don't know him. He came in right after you left. A true believer. He even volunteered to preach sometimes. Everybody was surprised a newcomer would get that honor, but they stopped wondering when they heard him up on the pulpit. Now, his sermons weren't as good as mine, but folks liked to listen to what he had to say."

The way Reverend Sherman talked, he was always mid-sermon, even in quiet conversations like these. He couldn't turn off his proselytizing. "Brother Freddy is someone with true vision. He talked about how the white man had corrupted the earth past redemption, and our only chance to make the world the God of Cain wanted is to rebuild somewhere new, in the next life, on the next plane of existence."

Vern covered her ears, desperate to shut him up, but his voice was in her head. She was the one who'd resurrected him. "Brother Freddy sees something in Carmichael. He's even helping him do some self-study courses through a local community college. As I'm sure you remember, your mama has demons when it comes to the drink. It's good that Carmichael has someone solid looking after him, showing him how to be a man. He's too soft. Womanly. I've wondered at times if he has been cursed with an affliction similar to yours."

Tears rolled out of the sockets of Vern's eyes. "Shut up. Please," she said.

"You never wanted to hear the truth, girl."

In Vern's book, there was no greater sin than crying in front of Reverend Sherman, but it poured out of her.

"Are you really dead?" she asked.

Sherman looked surprised. "Of course I am. I'd've thought you would have figured it out by now. Cancer," he said. "The Blessed Acres of Cain *are* blessed. The God of Cain lives in the ground there, and when one of us dies, he takes our memories and spreads them across his body."

Vern felt the sting of fresh tears before fully processing his words. She wiped her cheek with the back of her hand, but more tears fell. If someone had to die for their memories to become hauntings, that meant Lucy was gone. Dead somewhere, and alone.

"You never used to be much of a crier," said Sherman. The taunting in his voice killed her.

She stood up and spit in his face. "I've had enough," she said, her voice wobbling as tears graduated to sobs. "Get out, you disgusting, selfish, pathetic man."

Her words had no impact. Egotism kept him steady. "And go where? I'm in your head, Vern. I live here now."

That was no different than before. Sherman had been an occupant of her psyche for years, since she was a girl. His words, his influence, his touch—the memory of them haunted as much as the visions. "I won't let you destroy me," she said. "And even if somehow you broke me, it'd still always be you who was the broken one. I defeat you just by me being me, and you being you."

Realizing the truth of her words calmed her enough to focus. Vern inhaled and exhaled. Reverend Sherman vanished. "It's just the two of us now," Vern told Gogo, drying what remained of her tears with the collar of her shirt.

"Come here. Sit down," said Gogo, but Vern needed to pace. "Tell me what happened. Are you okay?"

"Lucy's dead," said Vern. A chill passed through her as she admitted the truth aloud. Gogo's silence told Vern she'd already suspected as much.

"How can you know for sure?"

"Reverend Sherman said that's how I get the memories. When someone dies, they go into the land."

All along it had been that simple. The fungus ate the brains of the dead who had hosted it, bringing them back to life in its mycelium.

Gogo sat with her elbows on her knees, her chin on her clasped-together fingers. "I'd been wondering what the mechanism for that was. I'm so sorry about Lucy. I know Ina will be sorry to hear it, too."

"It's not like I didn't know there was a good chance of it."

"Still."

Vern sucked in trailing snot. "Sherman said a lot of stuff."

"Stuff you can trust?"

"I think so."

Vern tried to remember everything he'd said, and Gogo wrote it down in her notebook.

"It doesn't sound good," said Gogo.

"You think they're planning something?" asked Vern. Brother Freddy's talk of a new plane of existence. He was another government plant, I bet, following in Eamon's footsteps. "I should talk to my family. Make sure they're okay."

The thought of this Freddy grooming Carmichael—he was just a child. She'd once called him a foolish boy who'd grow into a foolish man, but that was the thinking of a juvenile. He could not be expected to maintain his dignity in the face of a man deliberately undoing him.

"My little brother might listen to me. He might find a way to leave. I can't not help him."

Gogo grabbed Vern by the hand and pulled her close. "You know I understand."

That morning, Vern called the office of the Blessed Acres from a burner.

"Good morning, this is Ruthanne speaking. How may I help you this blessed day?"

Vern did not hesitate to speak this time. "It's me," she said. Ruthanne hung up, and this time, she did not call back.

# 18

JOY DIDN'T COME EASY amid late March showers. Gushing heavens, gray as a Gulf Coast winter, roused visions of the drownt child.

"Tell me your name," Vern commanded the child with a boldness she did not feel. Was he a Cainite, too? Another test subject? Gogo theorized that the only hauntings to awaken were those in which the fungus had fed on their brains in full. Otherwise, they were mere glimpses.

Brown water spurted from the drownt child's throat, and a stream of river slime dribbled from his eyes. Festering holes sprouted where fish feasted on his flesh.

"Tell me!" Vern cried, more fungus than girl. The day terrors haunted from dawn till dawn till dawn till dawn. From every tree dangled the bodies of the lynched, and from every pit of bubbling mud rang the desperate squeals of corpse-pigs awaiting slaughter.

Vern had left the Blessed Acres more than four years ago, but the hauntings were a reminder she could not wrest herself from the compound's hold.

*The compound.* Vern sneered. *Laboratory* was a name better suited to what was going on there. Cainites weren't victims of humanity gone awry. They were survivors of government experimentation.

"Mam!" Howling called through the cabin's screen door.

"What do you want?" asked Vern, voice shrill. On the porch swing beside her, a woman who was not there was whistling her dogs home. Her shoulder brushed Vern's, and Vern had to hold her breath to keep herself from vomiting.

"Come here, please," Howling said, face pressed up against the screen. The gray mesh distorted his puffy cheeks and lips.

Vern stood from the swing, but the hand of the not-there woman slithered around her wrist. "Why don't you stay out here, John? Aint the sunshine so pretty?" Rain pelted the clearing in thick droves, and blooms of ash-colored clouds darkened the sky.

Trembling, Vern gently tugged her wrist away. "Suit yourself," said the woman.

Inside, Howling and Feral sifted through a box of picture books Bridget had bought for five dollars from the community resale.

"Mam, can you read to me?" asked Howling. His childish request would've been welcome distraction were it not for the four little girls bundled in a blanket in front of the woodstove, lips blue from cold.

"And me, too," Feral said, capping the marker he'd been using to cross out the words on one of the books so he could replace them with his own scribbles.

"This one," Howling said, pressing it into Vern's face. *"Bear and the Princess Potluck,*" said Howling. It sounded like cheerier fare than the shivering girls just across the room.

Tense, Vern licked her lips. "I can try," she said, and opened the cover. Howling hopped into her lap, and she grunted at the impact. The fungus's domain was expanding, and her rib joints hurt. "My vision's not like yours, though. You know that."

"Feral can see the letters just fine," said Howling.

"It's not hard, Mam," Feral agreed, though Vern suspected he was lying to save face in front of his sibling.

Vern flipped to the first page of *Bear and the Princess Potluck.*

"Here, Mam, use my magic jewel," said Feral, handing her his magnifying glass. "Bridget says it's a secret decoder made of a special kind of glass. It's got powers. See? It makes the letters all big." He laid it gently in Vern's palm. "That better, Mam?"

She could see the letters more clearly, but that didn't help her remember the phonics. "Why don't you read it to me?" Vern asked Howling.

"But I like it when someone else reads it, so they can do voices," said Howling, whining. He groaned at the tragedy of it all.

In the corner, the little girls' teeth chattered, and Vern's started to, too. A mean cold dug its way into her bones, and she couldn't stop shaking.

"I can read it," said Gogo, stepping into the living room.

Vern, flushing, forced herself to look away.

"Can you do voices?" Howling asked. "Bridget does voices."

Still in Vern's lap, Howling leaned backward into her abdomen. Her stomach lurched and her ribs clicked painfully, making it difficult to breathe.

"My voices beat the shit out of Bridget's voices," said Gogo.

"Good, cuz Mam can't read," Howling said with a sigh.

"Yes, I can," Vern said.

"Don't lie, Mam," Howling reprimanded.

"Leave her alone," said Gogo, and took a seat next to Vern. The two hadn't spoken since their morning together a few days ago. Not a couple hours after the tryst, Gogo had had to leave to look after one of her patients. She hadn't come back that night or the next morning.

Howling slipped out of Vern's lap and squatted in front of Gogo. "Here," he said, handing her the book.

Gogo nodded and opened it. She placed her free hand on top of Vern's and squeezed. Vern exhaled at the relief of Gogo's touch. Her grip was an anchor.

*"Bear and the Princess Potluck,"* Gogo began.

The children listened, entranced, and Vern, too, tried to get lost in it as Gogo flipped page after page. With concentration, Vern could lessen the impact of the haunting.

*"And what a feast it was, all laid out on the ground, Bear's spot of woods filled with joyous sound. The princess, it seemed, was delighted to attend, and from here on out, would consider Bear her friend,"* Gogo finished. She closed the picture book and handed it back to Howling. "What'd you think?" she asked the children, but Vern spoke before they could respond.

"I don't know why Bear would want the princess to consider him her friend," she said. "She's an agent of the state. Besides, she looks down on Bear. How reformed could she be after one little potluck?"

In the first few pages of the story, the princess had been snooty and judgmental. Bear had no reason to want her at his potluck, but that was how these stories went. Few books for children taught meanness, or how to sit with being forlorn. "It's propaganda." Vern looked at Howling and Feral seriously. "Princesses aren't friends," she said. "They hoard wealth."

Feral volunteered to write a sequel in which the forest animals ate the princess.

"All right, Vern, why don't you choose the next book?" asked Gogo.

"How am I supposed to know what books you got?" Vern complained.

"Name me something. Maybe a book you liked as a child? I can at least check to see if we have it. Or find it online." Gogo stood to walk to the shelf, her flannel shirt riding up and showing her belly before she pulled it down. "Maybe a little *Das Kapital* to counter *Bear and the Princess Potluck*'s anti-revolutionary message?"

Vern tapped her fingers on the cabin floor. "You ever heard of a book called *Giovanni's Room*?" she asked, fearing the only copy in the world was the one she'd left back at Cainland.

Gogo smiled. "I've got about five of that one. Hold on." She left for her bedroom to rummage and returned a few minutes later. "Got it."

Vern looked up. "I can read it myself," she said. Vern cherished honesty more than anything, but, like most, she could lie to herself when her self-protective instinct demanded it.

Shrugging, Gogo opened *Giovanni's Room* to the first page. "I like reading to you."

"Fine, but only if you want," said Vern, but before Gogo began, Vern could already hear the first lines being read.

*"I stand at the window of this great house in the south of France as night falls, the night which is leading me to the most terrible morning of my life."*

Vern turned toward the source of the voice, but she already knew who it was. A haunting of Lucy sat on the couch, her old copy of *Giovanni's Room* in her hands. Dead, but alive again just for Vern.

Vern had always loved that very first line because it was how she felt most every evening of her childhood. She'd stare out her own window as night fell, the night leading her to another terrible morning.

*"I may be drunk by morning but that will not do any good,"* said Vern, joining in as Lucy read. The words tasted as soft and sweet against her tongue as lemon cake.

Next, the narrator described the train he'd be taking with its litany of mundanities, so quotidian that he predicted his morning with the clarity of someone who'd already lived it.

That got Vern, how the future could be identical to the past. *"Someone will offer to share a sandwich with me, someone will offer me a sip of wine, someone will ask me for a match,"* Vern read, though she wasn't really reading. She was remembering.

Vern inhaled the way Lucy always did before reading the last sentence of the paragraph. *"It will all be the same, only I will be stiller."*

Finally Lucy was here. This time she was dressed in her Cainite uniform, though she'd taken off her headscarf. There was a fresh cut on the side of her cheek where her father had gotten her with the belt. She smelled like peaches because she'd spent the whole afternoon canning.

Vern did not touch her, though she longed to. The edges of her hair were shiny with grease, freshly laid with a hard brush and secured into cornrows. Her father hated this look because he said it made her look hard, like she'd just escaped prison. Vern understood in retrospect that he meant the style made her look like a lesbian.

"You *can* read, Mam," said Howling.

Vern turned to him, too dazed by the vision of Lucy to keep the gambit up. "I memorized it," she said. "When I was a girl. My friend read it all the time and the words stuck, I guess."

"You know what happens, then?" asked Gogo.

"I do."

Vern took the book and ran her fingers over the lines of text and watched for Lucy to reappear, if only so she could give her a proper goodbye.

Lucy came again, this time reading from a later section of the book. *"He pulled me against him, putting himself into my arms as though he were giving me himself to carry, and slowly pulled me down with him to that bed. With everything in me screaming No! yet the sum of me sighed Yes."*

Vern shivered the way she had the first time Lucy had read it, and all the times since. It had made the private parts of herself declare themselves, suddenly wishing to make themselves known.

Hearing the details of what Sherman called *the white man's unnatural lifestyles* had awakened a forbidden part of Vern. If it was so unnatural to feel this way, then why did Vern exist? She was a part of nature, too, wasn't she? Humans and their proclivities were as much a part of the earth as trees, as rivers. Loving and fucking and kissing and nuzzling and bucking were more commonplace than sunrise.

Vern reached out to squeeze Lucy's hand. Lucy squeezed back. In her mind, Vern said the words, *I love you, I miss you.* Lucy put down the book, turned to Vern, and said, "I like living inside of you."

Vern expected her to say more, but she returned to the book and read, as if again only a looped memory. This was their goodbye to each other. This was their end.

"It's a good book, isn't it?" Vern asked Gogo.

Gogo smiled. "Yes."

"Have you always known you were . . . like you are?" Vern whispered, but she didn't need to whisper; the children played, oblivious.

"No. I mean, I've always liked girls, but there was nothing

strange about that because I didn't know I was winkte at the time," said Gogo.

"You never told me what that means," said Vern.

Gogo bit the inside of her cheek and shrugged. "It doesn't translate to English."

"Try," said Vern, sensing that Gogo was holding something back. It raised Vern's defenses, and she braced to be lied to.

Gogo looked at Vern, and Vern looked back, their eyes locked fretfully. "For wasicu," began Gogo, "it's simple. There's men, there's women, and that's it. From birth, you're forced into a role, and fuck you if you can't fit into it."

Vern understood this perfectly well. She'd been victimized by this same system.

"For Lakota, there's more flexibility, more than just man and woman. So, me? I'm one of the *more*. When I was born, they guessed from what they saw that I was a boy, but I wasn't a boy. I'm *winkte*. That's the best I can explain it."

Vern, throat dry, took several moments to digest Gogo's words. "You mean you used to be a boy?" she asked, whispering.

Gogo shook her head. "I was never a boy. It's like—like Howling and Feral. One might get one idea from looking at them, but one wouldn't necessarily be right," Gogo said. "I thought you'd understand."

"I do understand," said Vern defensively, taking in Gogo's words. "I guess I thought I'd invented it, is all."

At least that made Gogo laugh, and the tension dissolved between them.

"I'm kind of like you, too," Vern admitted, and Gogo looked at her questioningly. "I don't know if there's a word for it. I was born . . . wrong."

In the woods, Vern's differences were a point of pride, but

she never knew when, among people, they'd reveal themselves as flaws.

"Nothing's wrong with you. *Nothing*. You can tell me anything," said Gogo.

"I'm in-between," said Vern quietly, looking away shyly.

Gogo reached for Vern's chin and turned her face to her. "It's okay," she assured. "There's a word for that, you know. In English."

"I'd rather not know it, then," said Vern.

Gogo nodded. "Why not?"

"Because without a name for it, it's just something I am. A part of life. Once it's got a name, I know that means someone has studied it, dissected it, pulled it apart. When something has a name, they can say it's bad," said Vern, and she didn't want to hear anybody else's thoughts on what was bad anymore.

In fact, the more likely someone was to say something was bad, the more thought Vern would give to its potential goodness. Folks said disease was bad, but the fungus had gifted her a power she'd never had as plain old Vern the Cainite. Even the hauntings had a splendor.

In the living room, the frozen girl-children shivered by the woodstove. Lucy read. A woman chopped onions, and a magpie pecked at the body of a black bear.

Though their presence tore away at Vern's sanity, they were—or would be—a fount of knowledge. She needed only to figure out how to reach them.

Her body existed beneath a veil, but that would've been true without the fungus, too. Every body held something hidden, millions of microbes dwelling inside each person. Babies gathered them at birth and in their early years. For the rest of their lives, they remained. Passengers.

Whatever Eamon Fields and Ollie had done to Vern, that was not the fungus's fault. Complex enough to hold the lives of however many thousands in its cells, it was a living being as much as Vern was.

Vern thought of Howling and Feral, how they'd lived in her body. During that time, she had nourished them, but after their birth, with all their love, they'd been the ones to nourish her.

So, too, would the fungus.

## 19

WINTER SOFTENED into spring, and Vern luxuriated in the damp, golden afternoons. The mountains glistened with light, but the conifers still hid a shadow world.

Vern stood half-naked at the edge of the clearing where snow-speckled grasses transitioned to woodland. Wind washed over her, and her passenger shuddered, alive. It was not lost upon anyone that it was growing. Vern could no longer wear her own tops. She lived exclusively in Gogo's baggy hand-me-downs, but she preferred her nakedness.

Vern's exoskeleton was hard as bone, but it had flex, too, swelling over her shoulder blades and down the sides of her back, connected to bony nodules along her spine.

It was Vern's family. It held several lifetimes of secrets, and it was learning hers.

The passenger stretched from Vern's back around to her front, outlining her ribs. Webbed between the harder sections of carapace was a flexible, leatherlike hide. All of it the fungus's fruit.

"Mam!"

Vern looked up. Howling was calling to her from far up in a

fir, the child swaying back and forth as the wind blew the high branch of the thin-trunked tree.

"What?" she asked.

"I want to see!" he said as he shimmied down expertly. Tall and lithe, he could easily pass for six.

Howling gasped at the sight of Vern's exposed upper body when he hit the ground. "Damn, boo," he said, eyes wide. He ran up to her and touched, hesitating briefly before reaching an index finger to the bony exterior overlaying her ribs.

"Don't be scared," said Vern.

Howling laughed. "Why would I be scared? Is that gonna happen to me? When? How long I got to wait? Do all grown-ups got that? Can you feel this?" he asked, pressing.

"I can feel it," said Vern.

He took a stick and poked it into her back. "Can you feel that?"

"Yes."

"Do it hurt?"

"No," she said.

"It's like dragon skin," he said.

"Where's Feral?" Vern asked.

"Inside trying to find his binoculars," said Howling.

"You mean my binoculars."

"That's what I said, Mam."

Next, Howling pressed his thumb into her sides, then staggered backward with a cry at the passenger's reaction. "Mam!" he shouted, tripping backward into a patch of elk sedge.

The skeleton had unfolded. Expanding, it popped out of Vern's sides like wings.

"It grew," Howling said.

"It does that," Vern said, as she heard the churn of Gogo's pickup revving up the mountain. She breathed in, and the skeleton furled back into hidden slits in the carapace, just in time for Vern to put her flannel button-up back on.

While the skeletal growth appealed to the aesthetics of a four-year-old, neither Vern nor Gogo had seen each other disrobed. Vern was not ready to reveal her monstrous body unclad. Vern's passenger had come far from that night Gogo had first laid eyes on it.

Gogo parked in front of the cabin and hopped out carrying a box. "Picked these up in town," she said.

"You and your damn books," said Howling, speaking Vern's mind. "What are these ones about?"

Gogo had mentioned that she wanted to study Cainland's precedents.

"Precedents?" Vern had asked.

"You know, MKUltra, Project 112, the Edgewood Arsenal human experiments, Tuskegee."

At least Vern knew about Tuskegee.

Gogo slammed the driver's door shut with her hip, then headed into the cabin. She balanced the box in one hand and opened the front door. "Check it out," called Gogo from inside. "Jackpot," she said, smiling as she emptied the box of books on the coffee table in front of the couch.

"Don't worry. I'll read them to you if you want," said Gogo from where she sat on the arm of the sofa.

But Vern was tired of relying on Gogo. She needed to be able to read on her own. What if she wanted to get a letter to Carmichael, warning him? Now that Ruthanne wasn't answering the phone, she didn't have many other choices. What if she found herself alone again, with no Gogo? Vern had made up her mind to fight Cainland, and she wasn't sure she could do that without every resource at her disposal.

"I want to learn to read them myself," Vern declared.

"Sure, I can teach you."

Vern shook her head. Gogo did too much for her already. She'd accept some help, but this she wanted to do by herself. In the following days, Gogo got Vern her very own magnifying glass. A twelve-inch-by-six-inch rectangle, and it had its own stand so Vern didn't have to hold it. It far surpassed the reading glasses she'd been given as a child, which didn't offer enough magnification and fell from her face when she tilted her head to get the right angle. With the magnifier, she could focus on flipping the pages of the books, on running her index finger under the letters.

The days Gogo was home, she chaperoned the children outside, and Vern sat at the kitchen table working.

"One . . . win . . . ter . . . mor . . . n . . . ing—morning—Peh-ter—Peter . . . woke . . . up . . . and . . . looked . . . out the . . . win . . . dow," she read, choosing the book that was a favorite of Howling and Feral's for her first project.

She loved the illustrations, and when her eyes and mind tired after a sentence or two, she rested them on the intricate collage work. Peter, the boy in the book, could've been Howling.

"Snow had . . . fa . . . ll . . . en . . . dur . . . ing the . . . night. It coe-vered—covered—ev . . . er . . . ry . . . thing as far as he . . . could see."

She smacked the book shut, watched it skid across the table and slam into a saltshaker. How naive she'd been to think she'd ever be able to read the sort of books required to know anything real about the world.

"Stupid," a voice sneered.

Hesitating—for she knew a haunting awaited her—Vern looked up. A skeletal woman with soft features and cool gray eyes and hair the color of dead grass stood in front the stove, eyes dead on Vern.

"Leave," said Vern, tensing her chest into a steel plate. Her exoskeleton jolted awake, bracing for a fight, though there was nothing to fight but her own mind.

The woman took a jagged step toward Vern.

"I said leave!"

The woman's bones cracked and contorted as she gained speed jerking forward. She lunged on top of the table in a single motion.

Her dress was from another age, puffed like a hot-air balloon, lacy and ivory. A pair of metal shears in her hand, she crouched into a squat.

Vern pushed herself backward in her chair, nearly toppling it. "Leave," Vern said once more, whispering, but the woman laughed at Vern's command and from her mouth slid that slur as old as this poison nation itself. Vern always thought it apt how it rhymed with *trigger*, for the word was a swift and exploding bullet, and it turned to shrapnel in Vern's chest.

When Vern gasped, openmouthed, the woman took her shears, grabbed Vern by the tongue, and snipped. "Try to sass me now," the woman said.

Pain shocked Vern blind as she asphyxiated on the flesh of her severed tongue. The taste of salt and iron bloomed in her mouth, and Vern was forced to swallow blood, the cavern between her cheeks full up.

Laughing, the woman licked the blood off the shears.

When Gogo returned to the cabin with the children, blood flowed in a stream down Vern's throat, her severed tongue attached by a thread of uncut flesh. She could only moan when Gogo rushed to her aside.

"Vern, you are here," said Gogo. "Nowhere else but here."

But the potency of the haunting was too much for Vern to

fight, and she nearly passed out from lack of air. Gogo carried Vern to her bedroom and put an oxygen mask to her face, but the sensation of drowning in her own tongue did not pass until midnight.

⊠

VERN READ DESPITE.

Each time the woman came, Vern stuttered out the words, severed tongue and all. While the woman—some long-ago plantation mistress—laughed giddily, straw hair falling out of her bonnet, her gray-blue eyes dark bruises above her round, girlish nose, Vern bent her bloody tongue into the proper forms.

She read from the book about the red-suited boy in the snow every day, daring the woman to deride her imperfect articulation. Weeks passed, and Vern moved on to another book and then another, spurred on by the woman's cruelty. Board books and picture books.

Had the plantation mistress not been there, mocking Vern with her scissors and her corded neck that rippled whenever she swallowed, Vern might not have improved as quickly as she did. Defiance would always be Vern's purest and most plentiful resource.

Bitterly, she'd spend afternoons listening to Howling read aloud from his picture books as clearly and fluently as a grown person. A mam, she should've had only gentle thoughts about her babe, but she resented Howling for being so good, and she resented Feral for being as slow as her but more committed than she'd ever been at that age.

But it came in time. Vern thought of how much less lonely her childhood might have been had she been able to read.

By mid-May, she was reading chapter books, and had recently

begun leaving Howling in the dust. A mam shouldn't be proud of surpassing her child, but she was and couldn't help it. Whenever he stuttered over a word as he read aloud, she swooped in and announced it clearly.

*Fri . . . fry . . . frik . . .* Howling would stumble.

*Frightened,* Vern read for him.

He appreciated her interventions, but there was nothing noble about her aid. She was using him to stomp out her insecurities.

Vern knew she should be kinder, but her life was a torrent of hauntings, and they infected her with their pains. Without Gogo there to talk her down, she'd get lost in them indefinitely. During the hauntings that Vern couldn't wish away, Gogo remained by Vern's side, reading aloud to her to remind her where home was.

"*I've known rivers,*" recited Gogo, reading from a poem by Langston Hughes. "*I've known rivers ancient as the world and older than the flow of human blood in human veins.*" Vern imagined it was the fungus speaking this poem. As old as the earth, it had seen all of history unleash.

"Keep reading," Vern said. It was the type of night when she could no longer sleep for fear that she'd wake up with a man's hand mashed against her lips and nose, suffocating her, or a body hanging from a noose tied to the ceiling fan.

Gogo offered up reading after reading like an exorcist banishing away a demon, like words meant something. "Please!" shouted Vern, desperate to hear words that spoke of her life in the woods. Words that reminded her the earth didn't need redeeming. From it flowed infinite beauties.

"*I bathed in the Euphrates when dawns were young. / I built my hut near the Congo and it lulled me to sleep. / I looked upon the Nile and raised the pyramids above it.*"

The poem was called "The Negro Speaks of Rivers," and Vern wondered if it was possible that the fungus was Black. Born in Africa. A watchful spirit looking after her people.

*"I heard the singing of the Mississippi when Abe Lincoln went down to New Orleans, and I've seen its muddy bosom turn all golden in the sunset."*

Muddy bosom turn all golden in the sunset. That image sent Vern's mind home to the forest, to the mud and the wet and the pink sky and the way her skin felt sucking it all in.

"Read about the woods," said Vern.

There was one book that reminded Vern so much of her early days in the forest after she'd left Cainland, her soul's grievances quieted for once as the trees sheltered her and the dirt warmed her skin and the river water licked her clean with its current.

*"Rural Hours?"*

"Yes," Vern said. It was written by a woman in 1850, a recording of a year of her observations.

*"The arbutus is now open everywhere in the woods and groves. How pleasant it is to meet the same flowers year after year!"* Gogo read. Vern followed Gogo's words closely, but there was knocking at the door, thunderous and insistent.

Footsteps creaked along in the corridor outside. Something dragged against the wall, the sound of it groaning, scraping. A stick. An ax.

"It aint real," said Vern, as Gogo read.

*"If the blossoms were liable to change—if they were to become capricious and irregular—they might excite more surprise, more curiosity, but we should love them less."*

"It aint real."

The stranger in the corridor stopped at Vern's door. A fingernail scratched against the wood.

*"They might be just as bright, and gay, and fragrant under other*

*forms, but they would not be the violets, and squirrel-cups, and ground laurels we loved last year,"* Gogo read diligently.

The scratching against the door turned to knocking, then beating, then yelling. "Margaret May, you stupid bitch, let me in."

Poor Margaret May.

*"Whatever your roving fancies may say, there is a virtue in constancy which has a reward above all that fickle change can bestow, giving strength and purity to every affection of life."*

Drunken slurring from outside the door. A crying baby appeared next to Vern in the bed. It screamed with such a great fierceness it drowned out the drunk man yelling outside the door.

*"We admire the strange and brilliant plant of the green-house, but we love most the simple flowers we have loved of old, which have bloomed many a spring, through rain and sunshine, on our native soil."* Gogo always snorted at *native soil*. Rich words from a colonizer, she said.

The man on the other side of the door kept knocking, and the babe still screamed. "Margaret Maaaaay," he drawled tunefully, teasingly. "Margaret Maaaaay. Margaret May. You fucking bitch."

The knob rattled.

Vern's mind was violence upon violence. The crack of a shotgun cocking sounded from the corridor, and the knob of the bedroom door blew off. In came the man, younger than Vern would've guessed, more handsome. Once upon a time Margaret May must've thought him a catch, all slick and doe-eyed. His sleeves were rolled up past his forearms, and the muscles of his biceps pushed through the white fabric of his shirt.

Feeling now what Margaret May must've felt, Vern closed her eyes. Moments passed, and nothing happened, until the gun went off.

Vern let her eyes peek open. She patted her chest, surprisingly whole. The drunk man was on the floor, opened up, leaking blood. A woman stood smugly next to him, a rifle slung over her shoulder. "He's gone now. Don't worry, Mags."

All these people whose lives Vern only ever got snippets of.

Gogo left the candle burning and joined Vern in the bed. "Better now?" she asked. She kissed the back of Vern's neck. Vern was sweaty and sticky, spent from fear. She couldn't even nod.

"I'm here, I'm here, I'm here," said Gogo. She kept on saying it.

The sun was about to rise when Vern finally drifted off to the sounds of a wailing baby and a gun cocking in her ears.

⊠

"READ TO ME, Mam!" Howling said one evening after everyone else had retired. "You can read now, can't you?"

"I'm busy," Vern said. She was working her way through her own book.

"But you've never read to me," he said, and invited himself into her lap.

Vern sighed but relented, trying to make space for her child, lest he pull away from her and find himself searching for love elsewhere, in someone who saw him not as a child but as a vehicle. Like Brother Freddy with Carmichael.

Howling shared much in common with her little brother. They even looked alike. Only difference was Howling was here, and Carmichael was back there.

"It's called *Robin Hood*. Gogo said I would like it, but the words is too big. I can't read it. Can you?"

Vern grabbed the book. *The Adventures of Robin Hood Retold*. "I know about him. He stole from the rich and gave to the poor," said Vern.

"Then read it to me."

Vern always had to resist her urge to bristle at her child's commanding tone. That was just the way kids talked. It didn't represent any real authority. Vern opened the book to the first page and began to read. She smiled at the normality of it. How many places in the world was this scene taking place? They both booed at the part where it said the punishment for killing a deer in the king's wood was torture or imprisonment. Vern, Howling, and Feral would've been dead a hundred times if the repercussions for killing and eating game were so cruel.

Howling burrowed deeper into the front of her body, pressing against the exoskeleton. As she read, he lifted her shirt to comfort himself against her skin as he'd done when he was younger. "It's like claws!" he said in awe, laughing.

"Do you want me to read or not? Then stop interrupting."

Howling pressed a finger against one of the skeleton's shell-like curves, gently exploring, but the pain of it startled Vern in its intensity. She clenched, and her skeleton unfolded, ripping through her shirt.

"Fuck," yelled Vern, standing quickly. When she did, Howling went tumbling out of her lap onto the carpet.

He looked at her with an accusatory pout. "What'd you do that for?" he asked, rubbing his hurt thigh.

Vern's passenger folded inward, and she bent to join her eldest on the floor. "It was a reflex," she said, and forced out an apology. "I'm sorry."

The haunting of the white woman had forced Vern to rely on anger as fuel, and there was little room left for the gentleness motherhood sometimes required.

"I thought you said it didn't hurt. I wouldn't've done it otherwise," said Howling.

Vern curled her finger toward her, gesturing Howling closer.

"This time you poked harder and in a more tender place. Not all of it is the same."

Howling crawled into Vern's arms and rested his cheek on her shoulder. "You still love me, then?" he asked.

"Of course I love you," she said, breathing in Howling's scent. Vern was so used to making herself hard, she struggled to deliberately soften herself. "That will never change," she said, and squeezed Howling tight, embarrassed that she couldn't remember the last time she'd hugged him. "Forever and always," she said, and kissed the top of his head with a smile. For a brief moment, she felt it. That perfect sweetness love could sometimes bring on.

It lasted until she heard the crack and Howling's subsequent yelp.

"Mam!" Howling cried out, and Vern let go of her babe. She'd broken his ribs with the force of her embrace. "Mam," whimpered Howling again, gasping for air.

"Help!" Vern called. "He can't breathe!" Pain stilled him every time he tried to inhale. "I said help!"

Gogo blazed in first, then Bridget.

"I'm too strong," Vern sputtered out in explanation. She was sniffling and crying as much as Howling was. "I didn't mean it."

"Oh, Vern," said Gogo, struck, eyes yawning open at the sight of Vern's unsheathed exoskeleton.

Gogo picked up Howling and laid him on the couch. "Bridget, get me my bag," she ordered, and Bridget quickly complied.

Vern withdrew the skeleton into the scabbard that was her carapace back. "Help him! He can't breathe!" she said.

"He's going to be fine," said Gogo. "Go to the freezer and get out some ice packs. Frozen veg. Ice. Whatever."

Vern rushed to bring back the requested items. By the time she returned with them, Howling's cries had softened to whines. "You're doing great, Howling," said Gogo.

Bridget returned carrying Gogo's medical bag, and Gogo fished inside. She removed a bottle of pills and placed one on the table. "Knife," she said. Bridget brought her a knife. Gogo cut the pill delicately in half. "Permission to give him something a little stronger than Tylenol?"

Vern nodded forcefully. "Yes. Give him anything he needs," she said.

Gogo dissolved half of the pill in a small glass of milk. "I know it might hurt, but do your best to drink," she told Howling, and pressed the cup to his lips.

Face scrunched in a mix of agony and disgust, he sipped the milk until the glass was done.

"It hurts," said Howling.

"Not for much longer," Gogo said, propping several pillows under his back and head until he rested in a more upright position. "Soon you won't feel a thing, and you'll be dreaming away asleep in no time."

Vern paced around the sofa, unwilling to face her firstborn directly.

"Vern?"

She turned toward Gogo's voice.

"Look. He's already drifting off. He's going to be fine."

"What about pneumonia risk?" asked Vern.

"We'll keep an eye on him, but with pain relief, rest, and chest support when he needs to cough, he'll be fine."

"I can't let this happen again," said Vern.

"We won't."

"There's no *we*. This is about me."

"There's always a we," said Gogo. "You hear me? We'll figure this out."

But the scope of Vern's transformation could not be denied. With each passing day she took a step further away from human. Not long ago, Howling had witnessed Vern's passenger as a novelty. Today, he saw the fungus's other side. There was no denying the monster in Vern. There never had been.

"I don't know if I can do this anymore," said Vern, her words left purposefully vague to draw Gogo in.

Gogo's pouty bottom lip wobbled a brief moment before she bit down on it, whipping it into line. "Do what?"

"You know. Me-and-you stuff."

Vern expected Gogo to ask for clarification, but instead she shrugged. "Whatever you say, Vern."

"I got distracted. Nothing like this would've happened had I been paying attention. This is what the world does to you when you look away." Vern despised how self-pitying she felt, but not enough to take back her words. She dreaded the return to constant vigilance and pathological distrust.

"I should get Howling some more pillows," said Gogo, and turned to leave.

Vern was used to pushing people away, less used to them actually going. At Cainland, everyone chased.

"Wait," Vern called out, but Gogo was already out of earshot. Vern had too much pride to call for her again.

## 20

FOR MONTHS NOW Vern had sequestered herself at the cabin, playing house with Gogo like some sitcom newlywed. Vern shook her head at the preposterousness of it. How for months she'd abandoned her vigilant guard. Now her legacy as a mother would be breaking her child.

Between Reverend Sherman's visit and Howling's rib fractures three days ago, Vern could think of little but the devastation the compound had sown and would continue to sow. Carmichael remained in its clutches, oblivious. Lucy, perfect Lucy, had perished. At whose hands? Ollie's? Vern spent her hours skulking outside the cabin in brooding silence.

Her unspooling body, the ravings of the hauntings, summer's sticky-hot approach—each was a clue toward an end Vern could not see or imagine but knew was coming. The antlered beast stalked her with increasing frequency, though she never saw it head-on. Its shadow emerged in the corner of an eye, ballooning as incomprehensibly as the universe, but disappearing by the time Vern worked up the nerve to turn and face it. Only the smell of it belied its presence. Like wet, like mud.

Bridget brought her cups of chamomile tea to calm her. This would've usually been Gogo's job, but she and Vern weren't talking. "So," said Bridget. She was hovering just outside the radius Vern had claimed as her pacing patch.

"Thank you for the tea," Vern said, assuming that was what Bridget was waiting for.

"It's really nothing." Bridget leaned against the side of the cabin she'd built with her own hands, her work boots sliding into dark mud. She had that way about her she sometimes got, like she wanted to smoke. She flicked the lid of her lighter open and closed, eyes on the horizon.

"Friend of mine had a bunch of toys and stuff she was gonna hand in to the Goodwill. I took them off her hands. You wouldn't mind if I let the kids have a look? Don't know what your stance is on toys."

The mundanity of the question tugged Vern from her angst spiral. "That's fine. Go ahead."

"And Gogo wanted to know if she should get anything from the library for them when she next travels to the city."

Had Vern really made such a mess of it that Gogo felt she had to relay messages through Bridget?

"It's not you," said Bridget, speaking to Vern's silent question. "I know you've got this romanticized version of her in your head, but she's got her flaws. The women in my family aren't exactly coolheaded. It's not our way. Besides, she's not used to being the one to get rejected." Bridget slid the lighter back into her pocket. She picked up a rock and skimmed it across the brown puddles forming a pool chain in the clearing. "You're probably the first girl she's had any real interest in, in years."

"I thought she had lots of girlfriends," said Vern, despite herself. She didn't want to be thinking about Gogo.

"I don't know that I'd call them girlfriends," Bridget said with a snort. "But that's kinda what I'm talking about. She's used to getting her way with women, you know? So when she finds one she actually likes . . . Wounded pride, that's all it is. She'll come around. I like you two together. Wasn't sure about it at first, but it's good. Real good."

Vern sat on an abandoned truck tire filled with gravel and rested her chin on her knee. "It's probably better this way."

"There's exactly two flavors of queer drama, far as I can tell. The kind that stems from people like you and Gogo, thinking you're above it all, all chill to the bitter end, and the kind that comes from people that can't help but feel every peccadillo as a tragedy. Always with the waterworks, those people. I'm sure it has to do with astrology or something. My friend Coline is always tryna read my star chart. If somebody asks you your sign, Vern, they're a waterworks queer. Just know it."

Vern looked up at Bridget in amused silence. The two of them rarely talked beyond surface matters. Even though the weather had warmed into the high sixties, Bridget dressed in a thick, wool-lined flannel. She was diabetic and wore an insulin pump, the wallet-sized control mechanism clipped to her belt. Gogo said part of the reason Bridget had gotten so into traditional Native food was her diabetes diagnosis.

Gogo's mom had died from complications related to the disease: pulmonary embolism post–leg amputation. "I love Bridget to death," Gogo had said once, shaking her head, "but she's got it wrong, you know. What's the so-called right food gonna do when you don't have access to good medical care? That's why I do what I do. I wanna be there for people who don't have anyone else to take care of them. Fuck all that eat-a-good-diet shit. What people need to live is other people."

Gogo and Bridget were often at loggerheads, but it was easy to see how they were kin. Seeing their bond, Vern missed Carmichael.

"Anyway," said Bridget, clearing her throat. "You should go to Gogo."

Vern stood from the tire and jammed her hands into the pockets of her jeans. "Right now I got to focus on all this shit that's happening."

"But two heads are better than one, though, right? She's helped you before. Now's not the time to be turning away aid."

What people need to live is other people. Vern had appreciated Gogo's words when she'd first shared them, but pithy adages didn't account for folks like Ollie, Eamon, Sherman, and on and on forever.

"She said she was finally able to get into that computer," said Bridget.

Vern's head snapped toward Bridget, who was smirking now. "You could've led with that," said Vern.

"Then you wouldn't have listened to all that good quality advice I wanted to dispense. Come inside. It's time for lunch."

GOGO SQUINTED at her computer. A friend had been able to get into Ollie's laptop and salvage a few files. He'd emailed them to Gogo this morning.

"What do they say?" asked Vern, trying to keep her tone soft, kind. It didn't come naturally to her.

"It looks like a list of targets," said Gogo, still reading from her perch on her bed, her legs crossed.

"Targets?"

"Potential recruits for Cainland, maybe? They're medical files. Detailed genome maps."

Vern leaned against the bedroom door with crossed arms and tapped her foot on the floor.

Gogo clicked several keys and continued to browse through. "I think they're looking for people vulnerable to the fungus."

Vern released her arms from her chest and let them fall awkwardly to her sides. "Like they wanted us dead?"

Gogo shook her head. "Usually, with a fungus like this, you'd only expect it to infect the severely immunocompromised. Whoever's computer this is, they're looking for the outliers, the people who the fungus can colonize but not kill."

Vern folded her hand into a loose fist. "People like me."

Gogo looked up from the laptop screen to Vern. "And most of the people at Cainland, I'm guessing, all the people that have been recruited over the years."

"You think this is happening to everybody back at the compound?"

Gogo scratched the back of her neck as she continued to read. "No. In reality, they can only search for people who they think might be vulnerable. That doesn't actually guarantee anything."

Vern tilted her head in question, skeptical. "But everybody there gets the hauntings."

"As much as you?"

Vern had to concede that point. "Night terrors, at least. But that's all that used to happen to me, too."

Gogo took everything Vern said in stride, barely reactive. Each answer she gave was calm and considered. Any warmth that had been between them over the last months had gone. "I'd guess there's varying degrees of infection. Most people never get beyond having night terrors. You, on the other hand?"

Gogo read further as Vern strode a short, manic course over the woven carpet on Gogo's floor. "You're in here, Vern. It looks like they recruited you specifically—or your mother, in order to get to you, I guess. Did you know that?"

Vern grabbed Gogo's laptop. "I was born at Cainland."

"I don't think you were. You were chosen based on a particular set of gene markers in your DNA. They wanted someone with a high chance of manifesting the fungus," said Gogo.

So they, Ollie and Eamon and whoever else, had wanted this to happen to Vern. Wanted to use her. Vern was used to her whole world being a lie, but each new learned fabrication jolted her still.

It was a childish thought, perhaps, but she thought it anyway, without shame: she would hurt them for playing with her body like a game of Operation.

Gogo stretched her arms up and yawned, her leather vest, sewn with an array of patches, riding up to reveal the bottom hem of her black, gray, and white plaid shirt.

The two of them were close enough that Vern could examine her properly, lick up the little details of her. She savored these intricacies in people, always had: the way the clock face of her brother Carmichael's watch never faced up, the band too big on his thin wrist despite being set to the tightest notch. Lucy's dark sideburns, the little beads of hair like black pearls. Mam's gospel humming, ever so quiet, so as not to be heard until you were right up close. Even a few feet away, Vern would always have to strain to catch the notes, the words.

Gogo smelled mostly of shampoo, something generic and clean. Rainfall or Spring Zest or Mountain Air. She wore fingerless gloves on her hands, shiny black. There was a paperback book in her back pocket, which made her sit slightly hunched to the left.

"We should probably call it quits for the night," said Gogo. "Bridget will be nagging us about supper soon anyway, yeah?"

Vern was still avoiding the cabin's common areas. She didn't want to see Howling looking happy and carefree, only for his face to fall when she walked in. Nor did she want to see the opposite, him looking sad and upset by the pain, only for his mood to perk when he saw her, forever bound by love to her despite how she'd wronged him.

Howling lay on the sofa most days, Feral bringing him treasures from the woods to play with. He was healing quickly, according to Gogo, and she suspected he was mostly waiting for his spirit rather than his bones to mend.

"I think I'll pass on dinner tonight. I'm pretty tired. Also sore," Vern said.

Gogo shut her laptop and scooted it onto the side table next to a precarious stack of books. "I thought you'd said the pains had mostly settled."

They were nothing like they had been before, but her insides were still in flux, still adjusting. "Just a little here and there," said Vern. "It's not like I was keeping it a secret from you."

Gogo gestured with her head for Vern to come to the bed. Vern hesitated a moment, but took a seat at the edge.

"Where's the pain?" asked Gogo.

This was the Gogo Vern had met that first night at the cabin. Self-assured that she could save the day, exuding perfect confidence. Vern hoped she wasn't playing up the pain too much as a way of manipulating Gogo, of drawing her closer.

"I'm okay. Really. Just growing pains."

"Where's the pain?" Gogo repeated. Her voice had a hardness that made Vern shiver.

"My back, mostly. But honestly it's everywhere."

"Turn around," said Gogo.

Vern flicked a questioning glance toward Gogo. "What for?"

Gogo gave her a look.

"Fine," said Vern, sighing out her resignation. She turned so that her back was to Gogo.

"Can I?" asked Gogo. Her voice was steady with its characteristic edge, but some of the confidence had left it.

"Can you what?"

Gogo was silent, and Vern knew that she was tugging nervously on her braid. When she was ready to speak, she'd throw it back over her shoulder.

"I could rub on the sore parts. It might help with the pain," said Gogo, "but I won't do it if you don't want me to."

Vern let the warmth of the offer flood her, and she smiled. "I don't mind."

"You sure?"

"I'm sure."

"You should lie down," Gogo said.

It was a narrow bed, but Vern did as Gogo suggested, moving about awkwardly till she lay on her side, Gogo to the back of her.

Gogo took off her gloves, then rolled her hands over Vern's neck. Her fingers sank in gently at first, then with great, puncturing force. It hurt soothingly, and Vern relaxed beneath the attention. Gogo moved on to the leathery exoskeleton over the sides of Vern's back.

"That okay?"

Vern tensed at the gentle touch. "Just go slow," she told Gogo.

Gogo pressed harder, and Vern let out a stuttered breath, her whole body turning slack. Vern folded into Gogo's touch. Gogo's hands were a mix of gentle and persistent, with soft, teasing strokes between Vern's ribs, then harder around her neck and shoulders, which were covered in exoskeleton but not as tough.

"You can touch the hard parts," said Vern. "But you don't have to, if you think it's strange," she said.

"I don't," said Gogo.

Gogo ran a finger down Vern's spine, where the exoskeleton was most robust. There was a little give, but not much. Gogo's touch buzzed electrically. It burrowed from the surface deep into Vern's chest, her belly, below her belly.

"Can you feel it?" asked Gogo.

"Yes."

"What's it feel like?"

"Good," said Vern, though that was surely understating it. "Tingly, I guess?" she added, feeling the need to explain the sensations.

For several moments there was only silence as Gogo stroked. Vern bit her lip to stifle her syncopated breaths. She'd become sick with longing in the space of a minute.

"I like feeling you tremble," said Gogo.

Vern licked her lips, about to respond, but what was there to say? That she liked it when Gogo made her tremble? Shouldn't that be obvious?

"Is this too much? What I'm doing now? Do you want me to stop?" asked Gogo.

"Please don't," said Vern.

"Do you want me to do more?"

Vern hated Gogo for making her admit her desires out loud. "Yes."

"I want that, too." Gogo pressed her lips against the base of Vern's neck, where the carapace was most tender. Vern swallowed loudly, and she bit the crochet blanket on top of Gogo's bed to quiet herself.

Gogo's lips were like the prickle of an exposed wire. She started at Vern's neck and worked downward, touching the coarse, hard bits of the exoskeleton and all. Shivering, Vern buried her head into a pillow and squeezed her thighs together.

"Don't hide from me," said Gogo. Gently, she grabbed a section of Vern's hair and tugged.

Next, Gogo kissed back up Vern's spine. She licked the hollow between her shoulder blades. Each sliver of contact startled Vern in its intensity. Gogo hadn't yet touched her anywhere particularly erotic, but, pathetically, she was already approaching a level of desire she'd not yet experienced before. An unappeasable hunger coursed through her.

Gogo drew her tongue along the side of Vern's neck. She grabbed Vern and pulled her around so they were face-to-face.

"Are you okay?" Gogo asked, breathless.

The pause in her attention brought Vern temporarily back to coherence, and in that coherence, doubts and memories asserted themselves. She could see Ollie. Smell Ollie. Reverend, too.

"Vern?"

"Please don't stop." Vern's voice was weak and raspy, and she thought this was what it meant to sound lascivious. The way she keened, was that the noise bad women made? Was this her downfall, this act?

Gogo pinned Vern's lips with her own and threw a possessive leg over Vern's body. She ran her hand up and down Vern's back as the two rocked their hips desperately into each other. Vern, emboldened as raw feeling took over, wedged her hand under the belted waistband of Gogo's jeans so she could get to bare skin.

They pulled each other's pants and underwear down until they were both naked. The throbbing between Vern's legs was desperate to be moved against, and Gogo pressed her fingers there.

"Is it okay if I . . . ?" asked Vern, reaching out to touch Gogo. Gogo nodded. The sound of her moan when Vern's hand gripped her unwound Vern one more revolution. They rubbed each other in furious heat until their finishes rushed them, Vern's first, then Gogo's.

Their breaths came turbulent and frenetic as they grasped each other. Strung out on the feeling of their union, Gogo pressed a final kiss against Vern's forehead, then confessed her eagerness for Vern over and over and over and over in muttering whispers. Vern would call it worshipful, but this thing between them was not god-stuff. They were as two animals, heat, blood, mortal. They were, thank fuck, earthbound, no different than dirt or rotting logs, in no danger of becoming ether, of being raptured and stolen away from this moment.

Vern tried to conjure up some feeling of regret for what just passed between them. She invited shame in, welcomed it into the home of her ill-built heart. But for once, she could not feel bad. She could not view their act, their precious, carnal, desperate act, as anything other than the soft beauty of a kind of living.

◻

THE WORLD took on an easiness after her evening with Gogo. The next day, the unanswered questions she still had beat at her less furiously. She wasn't even angry to find herself in Gogo's bed alone, a note on the bedside table saying she'd gone on an errand with Bridget.

Vern ambled to the living room and sat on the coffee table across from where Howling lay on the sofa. He was still sleeping, his eyelids gently aflutter and his breaths rickety and small. Feral sat in a large velvet chair he'd dragged—scratching the wood floor—from Bridget's room to the woodstove. Two dolls and a stuffed lamb, gifts from Bridget, sat in his lap. He was giving them a make-believe bath.

"Make sure you get behind their ears," said Vern.

"Of *course*," said Feral. "I'm the mam. I know what to do."

"And inside, too, where it's all waxy and crusty."

"Bobo!" Feral cried to his little lamb. "Bobo, stop fooling around! You gonna slip and crack open! Mimi! Stop drinking the soapy water! Chrissy! Don't you dare think about taking a piss in this pristine tub!" He scrubbed them with a scrunched-up piece of paper he was pretending was a sponge. "Mam? You think they clean?" asked Feral.

"What you calling me? I thought you was the mam," she answered back.

He flung his mouth open wide as if he'd made a grave error,

one which he'd not be able to forgive himself for. "You're right," he whispered.

Vern laughed at the poor thing—she couldn't help it.

"It aint funny. I'm responsible for them," he said. "I can't forget I'm their mam."

Feral patted his dolls' heads. "Be still now while I comb this beautiful bird's nest. Chirp! Chirp! Little birdies, fly away now." He was back to his smiling self in no time.

Howling awoke with a groan at his sibling's loud chirping. He blinked his eyes into focus, then stared at his mam.

"Hi, sleepyhead," said Vern. "You're sleeping in late."

"I'm tired, Mam," he returned. His ribs had healed, but not his heart.

"You still angry?" she asked, as she did most days.

"More like . . . jealous," he said, voice gravely serious. "Bridget said you got super-strength. Will I get that, too?"

"Shh! I'm putting my babes to sleep," Feral reprimanded from his spot by the fire.

"I am stronger than I was before," whispered Vern. "So strong I don't know what to do with it."

"How do I know you won't crush me again?" Howling asked, curious, not afraid, his concern appearing to be predominantly intellectual.

"Because I been practicing." Daily, she went outside and explored the ranges and forms of her new body. Gogo threw volleyballs at her. At first Vern couldn't catch them without smashing all the air out of them, busting the hide. Now she could, but it took all her concentration. Soon it would become second nature to have a light hand.

"And you don't got to get near me if you don't want to," said Vern. "No hugs. No holding hands. No kisses. No nuzzles."

"But I like all those things."

"Then we can do it. And I will be careful. I promise."

Howling got up to play with his sibling. He was the Gogo to Feral's Mam. His words.

Vern wanted to live in this scene forever, to suspend herself in its quiet glory, so unlike the rest of her life, but already the moment was ruined. A shadow crossed the room, ephemeral and large. It swallowed the room with its mass.

Vern saw the edge of a haunting, a creature twisted as vine. It was the antlered beast. The mirror of Vern's future.

It spoke a promise. "Found you, Vern," it said, and laughed.

It wasn't long before Vern heard the rumble of an engine.

PART THREE

KINGDOM ANIMALIA

# 21

VERN RAIDED THE KITCHEN drawers and gave her children two knives each. "Strike without hesitation," she said. Carrying the children on either side of her hips, she ran to Bridget's bedroom. She lifted Howling to the shelf at the top of the closet inside, then Feral. "Here!" she said, handing them blankets to cover themselves.

"Who's coming, Mam?" asked Feral.

"Shh!' said Howling, already in hiding mode.

"Listen to Howl," Vern said. "Be quiet. Don't say nothing, *nothing*, unless you hear me, okay? Or Bridget, Gogo. Nobody else. Promise it. Now."

"Promise," whispered Feral.

"Promise," said Howling.

When they were obscured under the blankets and out of sight at the top of the closet, Vern shut the door and ran to Gogo's room, rolling under the bed. She pulled herself up to the underside and clung so no one would see if they casually glanced under.

"Calm," she whispered to herself, "be fucking calm, you foolish girl."

Eyes squeezed shut, she waited. The hum of the engine increased, then stopped altogether. A car door slammed.

*Don't fuck this up, don't fuck this up,* Vern mouthed. She was stronger and faster than anybody knew. She would destroy them, if need be.

Vern opened her eyes at the sound of a knock on the door. She hadn't thought these the kind of folks to ask before entering. *Found you*, the creature had said. Who had it sent after her? Vern's heart sped as the raps continued, her teeth fastened into her bottom lip to force herself quiet.

Somewhere, glass broke. A window? Next, footsteps. Whoever it was must've thought nobody was home. Neither Gogo's nor Bridget's trucks were outside.

"Heel," a woman said quietly, calmly, in a Southern accent, and Vern dug her fingers harder into the metal underside of the bed frame. "I said *heel*."

Vern's skin erupted in goose pimples as she listened for the hound the intruder was ordering around—the tapping of nails against the wood floor or heavy panting—but the only sound beyond the stranger herself was a rasping. Someone drawing labored breaths through a throat ravaged by sickness.

"You feel her?" the intruder asked from the living room.

Growling erupted from the intruder's companion, an animal Vern could not identify by sound.

Vern's head pulsed, bloated by an influx of images. Though her eyes were still slammed shut under the bed, she could see. A room. A sofa. A rocking chair. A woodstove. She was seeing the inside of the cabin's living room through another's eyes.

The beastly husk of the intruder's animal increased in volume until Vern could swear she felt it against her ear, a claw scraping the skin.

Vern's eyes flicked open, not of their own accord. Her face twisted into a wide smile, skin stretching like a sheet of latex until the muscles were sore, a foreign body inside her pressing them up and up, her cheeks bulging uncomfortably.

"She's here?" the stranger asked from the living room.

Vern nodded the same as she would have if the question had been posed to her, her body possessed.

"What a cozy home you've inserted yourself into, Vern," the intruder shouted in that lazy Southern drawl. Vern recognized the cadence of it immediately. Ollie, back from the dead, had come for her.

Vern tried to remain still, but the creature was inside Vern's mind, and she was inside its, seeing what it was seeing. Disorientation threatened the grip she had on the bed frame.

"Have I surprised you?" asked Ollie, her tone genuine rather than taunting as she asked the question, apologetic to be catching Vern unawares. "I supposed I'd be, too, if I were the one who'd left me for dead, barely a pulse or a breath, neck broken, back broken. You couldn't have known at the time that I'm never alone, Vern. You were never my one and only. Queen here predates you, and if you don't listen to me very carefully, she will outlast you."

Vern's chest tightened painfully with understanding. The night of Vern and Ollie's fateful clash, Vern had told the growling animal circling nearby to finish the fiend off, but it had done the opposite and revived her. Ollie's pet.

Vern recalled her children's birthnight and her first confrontation with the fiend. Ollie had stood over Vern, threatening, speaking those words that forever changed Vern's life. *The wolves always flush out the runaways.* Robed in shadow, a creature had skulked out of sight, distracting the fiend long enough for Vern to stab her.

That had been this pet, too. What had Ollie called her? Queen. The name felt familiar, but Vern couldn't place it.

Hindsight sharpened Vern's memory. It hadn't been Ollie who'd put the wolf haunting into Vern's head. It had been this creature.

She was the great antlered creature from Vern's vision. She was the beast Vern was becoming.

Queen had told Vern she was coming, and here she was, true to her word.

"I don't blame you for what you did to me," called Ollie. "I wasn't forthright with you, and you had no reason to trust me. Women like us, hard women, don't take kindly to betrayal, but believe me when I tell you that the only way forward is with me. Queen and I have come here alone. We are the only ones who know your location. I did that for you, Vern, because I want to give you the chance to make the smart decision. Come out," said Ollie.

Vern remained in her hiding spot.

"Come on, Vern. Don't do this. Not again. You must be tired of running. Tired of hiding. Come with me."

Vern could clock a manipulation when she saw one. Ollie presented two choices. Run forever or surrender. But this world was one full of infinite possibility, and even if it wasn't, there was a third option that was such low-hanging fruit, to pretend it didn't exist revealed Ollie's hand. To fight.

Ollie wanted her to forget that Vern had almost killed her. Vern wasn't going to forget.

"Fine, we'll do this the hard way, then," said Ollie, and Vern shivered at the threat.

Feet scraped along the wood floor as Queen snarled and croaked. Vern's nose twitched, and her eyes fluttered open. Smoke. The fume of it overwhelmed the cabin.

"You smell that, Vern? I can't, of course, but I suspect you do by now; smoke pulled from a memory from God knows who and God knows when. But it's yours now. Queen's gift to you."

Vern tried to meditate away the pungent gas of fire. Silently, she chanted, *It's not real, it's not real, it's not real.*

But it was real. Her body's cells didn't distinguish between the physical world and that of the hauntings, her neurons firing identically at the sensory input.

"I admire your endurance," said Ollie, "but Queen's got fifty years on you. She won't lose to a neophyte. She can't lose to anyone. You thought you were singular, Vern? Extraordinary? It is she who is the singular one."

Fifty years. *Think, Vern, think*, mouthed Vern, hastening her mind to remember the name. Who was Queen?

Who was this woman Ollie dragged hither and yonder like a pet? She had to be a Cainite, didn't she? Those were the only ones with the fungus. No one that Vern would remember, someone older. Much older. Someone with fifty years on Vern.

Had Vern not been holding on to the bed for dear life, she'd have snapped her fingers. She remembered. Her full name was Barbara "Queen" James, and she was a founder. Spurred by visions—what Vern now understood as the hauntings—she'd helped create Claws.

Around Vern, Gogo's bedroom lit up with writhing orange flames. Heat engulfed her, hungry, but Vern had been eaten before, picked apart by wolves. Had her guts licked out and stuck between teeth. Her mind would endure this pain.

"Is it getting a little warm in there? You can make this stop. Just say the word," Ollie said. Vern refused to scream. "Queen, darling, turn it up."

A cloud of thick smoke submerged Vern. She breathed it in, every hot, angry, stinking gust of it. Unable to hold out anymore, she coughed, and it wasn't quiet. Desperate for clean air, her chest and throat heaved spasmodically.

She'd given up her position.

Ollie kicked Gogo's flimsy bed to the side, revealing a coughing Vern on the floor. "You held out well," Ollie said with an acknowledging nod.

It pleased Vern how little she recognized the woman. She could be anyone. No one. She'd die one day, and with her all her smugness.

Vern swallowed thick swaths of air while Ollie pressed a gun to Vern's head, finger on the trigger. In the intervening years, she'd learned not to underestimate her opponents.

"Do it," Vern said. Gasping for air, skin still hot and burnt-feeling from fire, Vern faced her stalker. "Kill me, you mother-fucker," she whimpered, shaking. This was life as Vern had always known it, desperate.

"I would never hurt you," Ollie said, pain in her voice as she pulled back the gun. She was about to coldcock Vern, but before she began to swing the gun, she stumbled down to the floor with a grunt.

"Awoooooo!" Howling cried, knife in his hands. He jutted it in and out of Ollie's knee, but he was too small, and she grabbed him by the waist and threw him into the wall, Howling's head bumping against the edge of the fireplace. His body thudded to the floor, but he rolled and pushed himself into a squat. His years in the woods had made him formidable. He was no match for Ollie, but he'd go down fighting.

Feral stampeded into the room next, but he wasn't holding a knife. He had Bridget's hunting rifle. It wasn't loaded—Bridget kept the bullets locked in a cabinet—but Ollie couldn't know that. Feral aimed vaguely in Ollie's direction, little pointer finger on the trigger. "I'll make your head explode" he said. He was an odd sight in his thick glasses and sweater vest pulled over his collared shirt.

It wasn't the first time Vern had been faced with the utter foolishness of her children, but their bravery in this moment rallied her. If she'd been ready to give up a few moments before, now she was ready to fight again.

Ollie wanted her, not them. "Hide!" she called to the children before bounding off in a sprint. She needed them to stay put while she drew Ollie and her creature away from the cabin.

Vern ran, feet skidding across smears of Ollie's blood on the floor before she found her footing and launched herself toward the front door. She jumped off the porch and dashed toward the woods. It was the only advantage she'd have over her chasers. She knew this area by heart.

Behind her, Vern heard the screech of a car as Ollie twisted off the dirt road and onto the grass to chase Vern. She only had to make it to the trees.

Vern wasn't immune to stumbling. The fungus hadn't increased her vision, and though her sensory awareness had been heightened, she still lost her footing when running. She didn't let it slow her down. Whenever she fell, she turned the movement into a roll or a somersault, springing back up onto her feet with ease. She turned it into an advantage.

Vern leapt forward toward the trees, outrunning Ollie's vehicle, but Queen moved on foot.

Vern descended the mountain. She dashed through the firs and slid across mud and skidded down rockslides. With each pace, the distance grew between her and Queen. Vern had lived in the woods for years. Where had Queen lived? In a cage? A laboratory? Vern understood the land. She knew how branches moved, how far her feet sank into mud, and which dirt was loose and which was packed.

Adrenaline fueled Vern. She didn't stop, and she wouldn't. Movement forward was her only goal.

Vern slid down an incline, and Queen let out a heinous cry behind her, a moan as low as rolling thunder. Birds squawked and cawed at the shock of it. The trees, too, seemed to hear it, pine needles spiking outward. White-tailed jackrabbits retreated to their underground hovels.

Vern skidded to a halt. She threw a glance over her shoulder and froze. Queen had come to Vern in a haunting, but her real-life presence could not compare. In the light of day, hot and alive before her, she was a revelation, a marvel, an angel. Queen's carapace put poor Vern's to shame, its massive web of bone unfolded outward nearly four or five feet on either side of her. There were no clothes to cover any aspect of her glory. Exoskeleton covered all but her belly, breasts, and genitals.

Queen growled at Vern and unsheathed herself. The curves of white bone that outlined her rib cage unfurled, creating a set of claws on either side of her torso. It was a threat, one that Vern did not take lightly, and she turned to run again. As she did, Queen screamed another agonized wail, wincing, in pain. Her skeleton folded into itself, and for a moment she looked but a mere woman.

Queen shrank to the ground, crying out, and Vern took a wary step toward her. As Queen rasped and hissed, Vern pressed forward, drawn toward her as if by a magnet. She was a picture of Vern's future, rabid and powerful. Even if it killed her, Vern needed a closer look.

A helicopter whirred nearby. *Run*, Vern told herself. She didn't. Instead, her feet moved one in front of the other toward her future.

Collars made of thick black plastic circled Queen's neck, wrists, and ankles. They buzzed, and Queen cried out again and fell to the ground, convulsing.

"God of Cain," Vern said quietly. "You poor fucking wretch." Queen lay in front of her no mightier than a wounded deer as shocks zapped through the collars and cuffs.

Ollie truly had treated Queen as some inhuman pet: calling her back to heel with an electric leash.

"Don't fucking move," Vern heard from the trees.

She whipped her head to the side, where two figures stood, both armed with rifles pointed at her and Queen. The men were lean and wore red caps, army fatigue pants, and orange vests over indistinct long-sleeved shirts. Hunters.

The sun was heavy in the sky as evening sauntered in. Fading light blessed and cursed in equal turns. The bright glare of midday was gone, and Vern's eyes were thankful for that. But shadows obscured the path down the mountain, her escape route. She'd have to tread more slowly now.

The hunters stalked closer, guns at the ready. Vern straightened herself up into a prettier woman, as much as she could, slicking down the hairs that had escaped the elastic holding together her bun. Sweating and dirt-smudged—as much a monster as Queen—she didn't stand a chance of passing as respectable. But who wanted to be respectable?

One of the men walked up to her, head cocked. There was maybe a smirk on his face. Dead rabbits hung from his belt. He pressed the end of the barrel into Vern's belly and dragged it down just past her navel.

The other man stooped over Queen, who was crouched on the ground, his gun to her head. "What the fuck are you, freak?" he asked.

"You heard him. You, too. What the fuck are you?" asked the man with the rifle jutted into Vern's abdomen.

She wanted to be a girl in an action movie and say, *Your worst nightmare, creep*, then rip him open like a birthday present, but bravery was a finite resource. Like a piece of thread, it frayed in time when tested too heavily. Vern couldn't dodge a rifle bullet at point-blank range.

"Just leave us be," said Vern.

"I don't take orders from freak bitches like you," he said.

"Please," Vern begged. "For your own good."

"Shut up, bitch. Don't talk unless I say talk."

Vern gritted her teeth, not for the first time made helpless by a man who thought the world was made just for him. How could someone think such a thing in the woods? One need only look up at the towering evergreens to be reminded of one's smallness.

With his rifle pressed to Vern's belly, he thought he was King of All. He was king of nothing. Even if he shot her dead, he would be no more a thing than he had been when he woke up this morning.

"If you want to shoot me, then shoot me," said Vern, anger rising. The hunter smacked her across the face with the gun.

Vern laughed. "Was that supposed to hurt?"

He did it again, harder this time, and Vern spit out the blood in her mouth. She wanted to end him right here, right now, but even more than that she wanted to understand what had gone so wrong with his upbringing.

What turned babies, fragile and curious, into Shermans? Into Ollies? Into men who could not interact with a new thing without wanting to dominate it?

What order of events did Vern need to disrupt in the lives of the millions upon millions who woke up every morning proud to be Americans? What made someone love lies?

She saw that cursed flag on the hunter's T-shirt and wondered if he knew about the glut of traumas that defined this nation's founding. Had he fallen so in love with the myth of belonging that he thought the corpses of his imaginary foes were worthwhile sacrifices toward barbecues, megachurches, bandannas, and hot dogs?

The primary freedoms this nation protected were the ones to own and annihilate.

"Why are you like this?" Vern asked weakly.

"You first," he said, glaring hatefully. "Why are you such a freak?"

A few feet away, Queen convulsed, tortured by shocks.

"What's wrong with it, man?" the hunter standing over Queen asked. He shoved the butt of his rifle several times into her shoulder and side.

Vern thought to say, *I wouldn't do that if I were you*, but this man didn't deserve her warning. He dug his foot into Queen's side and twisted. "Check this out, dude. Her skin's like a fucking rhino's," he said.

Though Queen's collar still buzzed electric shocks through her, she'd maintained enough capacity to now grab the hunter's foot and rip it from his leg in a motion so quick and violent Vern wasn't sure her eyes weren't playing tricks.

Vern's hunter turned his rifle toward Queen, cocked, aimed, then fired, but not before Vern lunged and tackled him to the ground. She straddled him, all the power in her hands now. She was the ruler now, queen of him, lord and lady of him, executioner of him.

Metal slid into her thigh. The hunter had swiped a knife from his belt and driven it into her.

Crying out, Vern rolled off him, the blade still in her leg. She gripped its slick wooden handle, damp from palm sweat. She pulled it from her thigh with a grunt, and as he fumbled toward his dropped gun, she walked toward him on her knees, knife in hand.

She held the knife up as he took aim. Her reflexes were fast—maybe she could block the bullet with a fling of the blade.

The hunter pressed his finger against the trigger. The boom made Vern's ears ring and throb. He missed, but she could see him smiling. He was playing with her on purpose, and he fired off another shot as she limped toward him on scraped knees. The round grazed her cheek, and she yelped.

Invigorated by the sport of it, he was laughing, and Vern knew it right away. He'd done this before, she could tell. As a teen, maybe, in these very woods, with a girlfriend, a cousin, a sister, a friend, and him saying, *I'm just playin around, stop being such a pussy*, as he aimed the gun.

"That's right. Crawl," he said.

He reaimed the rifle, this time the barrel centered on Vern's forehead.

The shot didn't come. In the space it had taken Vern to inhale a single breath, Queen had lunged on top of the hunter and laid in.

Vern's eyes were deceiving her. Even as the collar sent shocks through Queen's body, she was eating him alive. Queen glanced up at Vern, blood on her maw. She rasped loudly, and an image of a man running appeared in Vern's mind.

It was a message. Queen was telling her to get out of here.

Vern longed to touch her, to kiss her gently on the forehead. To rip that collar off, and those damn cuffs.

Queen lapped up blood as she forced another image of someone running into Vern's head.

Ollie's control over Queen was far from complete. That had always been Ollie's weakness. Her hubris, her ego, her complete belief in herself, and her underestimation of those over whom she had power.

Vern nodded at Queen, and then, trying something, she imagined the first lines of *Giovanni's Room*. It worked, there Lucy was, sitting on a boulder, reading. Vern didn't know how to make Queen see the haunting, too, but she put all her mind's energy into projecting the vision of Lucy forward. Listening to

Lucy read had always comforted Vern. Maybe it would comfort Queen, too.

The way Queen stopped rasping, the way she paused from her feast of human flesh, made Vern think it had worked.

"I'll be seeing you," said Vern, turning away. It wouldn't be long.

## 22

VERN LIMPED into the wild wind, the hunter's knife wounds not yet healed. A spring storm blew into her, and it took all her strength to remain upright against it.

Vern borrowed the front-desk phone at a motel with aqua-painted doors, a broken signpost, and a parking lot where a woman with waist-length hair leaned against a car, a toddler on her hip, a cigarette in her other hand.

"You got change for a ten?" the woman asked as Vern headed inside. "Linda's being an ass and won't break this for me," she said, holding up the bill.

"Sorry," said Vern, and hurried past her inside.

A gray-haired lady with a black shirt sat behind the desk and answered the phone. "Vital Springs Inn, this is Linda, how can I help you?" she asked, then shortly later, "No, we can't do reservations without credit cards." She hung up.

The woman sighed as she took in Vern's appearance. "I don't see a purse, and those leggings don't have pockets—so no wallet. This isn't a charity," she said.

"It's an emergency," said Vern.

"Then take your ass to the sheriff."

Vern tensed, flexing her muscles. "I don't want to hurt you."

The woman's face broke into a startled smile and she laughed, but her amusement faltered when Vern stepped closer and unsheathed the outer flanks of her carapace.

Vern wasn't unused to being stared at. That came with being Black and albino. But the way this woman's mouth hung open slack was something different.

Vern grabbed the telephone.

"You got to dial nine before the number," said Linda, shaking.

"Go outside and break that woman's ten," Vern commanded.

Linda nodded and rushed outside, leaving her purse behind on the floor by her chair. Vern snagged the wallet from inside, then pressed nine and Gogo's cell. Gogo answered before the first ring finished sounding.

"Vern?" she whispered.

"Yeah. It's me," she said. "Howling? Feral?"

"They're safe. We're all safe," Gogo assured. Vern closed her eyes and let the relief wash over her as Gogo filled her in further. "When Bridget and I got home, we saw the living room all torn up, and thought . . . we thought the worst. Then we heard Feral and Howling hiding in the kitchen cabinets. And you? You're okay? It's so good to hear your voice. I've been praying nonstop."

Vern gripped the plastic of the telephone receiver hard, glossing it up with her sweat. "I'm okay. For now."

"Fuck, don't say shit like that," Gogo said.

"It's the truth, much as I wish it wasn't." Vern didn't know how hot Ollie was on her tail; and though Queen had helped Vern with the hunters, when it was a direct choice between Ollie and Vern, Vern wasn't sure who Queen would choose. Tortured into complying, she was what Vern would be if Ollie and the feds ever found her.

"I wish I was with you. Then I'd know how to act. I could

actually do something instead of sitting here worrying uselessly. Fuck," said Gogo.

"I'm all right, promise—better for hearing your voice," said Vern, and even though it was the truth, her nerves buzzed like she'd just told a lie. It still hurt to reveal her softness. "Where are you now, anyway?" asked Vern. "You can't stay at the cabin."

"Way ahead of you. We didn't even pack, just split. We had go bags in the pickup, anyway. What about you? Where are you calling from?"

"Hell if I know. Some motel. I'm using their phone." Vern looked around to get her bearings, but the place was indistinct.

"You got to pick up a couple burners," said Gogo, sounding more like herself. Now that she knew Vern was safe, she was letting the crisis invigorate her. She was like Vern in that way, more at home in conflict than in peace. Tragedy sharpened you. It was the quickest way to turn yourself into an edge.

"I'll try to find a store and pick some up," said Vern.

The motel manager Linda returned. The woman with the waist-length hair and the toddler followed behind her.

"Can you ask someone at the motel what city you're in?" Gogo asked Vern.

"It doesn't matter where I am. It's not like we can meet up. It's not safe. I gotta put distance between me and the children. Between me and you. Or you'll die. I can't have y'all caught up in this."

"Sorry, but that ship has sailed. We're way beyond caught up already, and I'm not going to leave you stranded alone," said Gogo. "Fuck that. You know, that's your problem. You still think you're the only girl who can solve the world. That's not how it works. Don't shut me out." After a pause, she added more gently, "I need to be with you."

Vern gripped the receiver tightly. "It's just for now. Until this is over."

"It's never going to be over," Gogo snapped, her usual calm gone.

"It will be if I end it," said Vern.

Ollie and those like her wanted people to think their power was eternal, but even gods died. Empires, too. Continents shifted. Nations came. Nations went. Castles became ruins. "I'm going to fight them," said Vern.

Gogo's exasperated breaths were loud through the line. "Fight them how? It's not like they have an office you can walk up to and file a complaint. They'll be operating out of a black site."

"Then I'll figure out where the black site is," said Vern. That would be her next task. She'd sift through hauntings for hours if she had to. There had to be clues in there, flashes from victims kidnapped to their facilities. The raptured.

"Tell me the name of the motel," Gogo said. "This isn't a debate."

Gogo's domineering tone raised Vern's hackles. It was an instinct, her body averse to authority in any form. "Don't talk to me like that. And I said *no*. It isn't safe."

"None of us have been safe since you came into our lives," Gogo spat.

Vern winced. She didn't have a ready reply for that. "That's a fucked-up thing to say."

Gogo exhaled but didn't relent. "Maybe it is, but it's true, and you deciding that you're going to cut us loose harms more than it helps. You're doing this to protect yourself. Not us. Tell me the name of the motel."

Vern would never abide being told what to do. "I'm gonna hang up now," she said.

"Please don't do thi—"

"Take care of my babies," said Vern before disconnecting the call, eyes squeezed shut. She had to catch her breath.

"Man trouble?" asked the long-haired woman who'd asked for cash in the parking lot. Her toddler sat in a chair eating a candy bar from the vending machine. "That a costume or something? Or is it—is it permanent? I watched a documentary about all these crazy body mods you can get. You know, there's a surgery that can make your ears pointy like an elf, and they can split your tongue and shit."

As Vern relaxed, the outer flanks of her exoskeleton shifted back inside, hidden again under her torn shirt. "It's a condition," said Vern.

"Right on."

Linda shuffled excitedly back to her spot behind the front desk. "I'm kind of a UFO nut. My daughter Michelle is, too, but she doesn't like to admit it," she said, gesturing to the woman with the waist-length hair. "Not assuming or nothing, but I do have expertise."

"UFO?" asked Vern.

"Unidentified flying objects. Extraterrestrials, you know?" said Linda's daughter Michelle. "Aliens and all that. You'd be surprised what information is out there if you're willing to dig."

Vern stuffed her hands into her pockets. This was not a side-show she wanted to be a part of. "I've got to go."

"There's nowhere for miles, just FYI. Stay. I put juice and do-nuts out for breakfast, and coffee, too. Fresh," said Linda. "Next town's not for sixty miles, and Storm Rhoda is sweeping in. You know it's bad news when they name them."

"I walk fast," said Vern, headed toward the door.

"Can I get your picture, at least?" asked Linda. Vern pushed her shoulder into one of the double doors.

"You're embarrassing, Ma. Everything you say is so god-damn offensive," said Michelle, filing her nails, the sound of it grating against Vern's ears

"What did you call me?" asked Linda to her daughter.

"Doesn't matter what I called you. You're humiliating me and little Violet-Grace," Michelle said. She slipped the nail file back into her bag.

"You called me Ma. And don't forget it. Lord says you honor your mother."

Michelle rolled her eyes and turned to Vern, who was already halfway out the door. "Please don't mind Linda. She only half means all the stupid shit she says. You should stay here for the night. It aint like people are lining up to spend a night at Vital Springs Inn. She's got vacancies fucking galore, even though she won't let her own daughter sleep here." She looked at her mother pointedly.

"Because if I do, you're gonna leave tomorrow right back to that trash can you call a man."

"He's not a trash can. He's my husband," said Michelle.

The toddler, Violet-Grace, was doing somersaults on the grungy motel carpet, popping up after she finished each one to say, "Ta-da!" as her mother and grandmother argued.

Linda pulled out her cell phone and pretended to read from it. "Michelle's husband, definition. Trash can."

"Fuck you, Ma," said Michelle. "You always do this."

Vern watched their back-and-forth, unable to bring herself to leave and tear away from their drama.

"Pardon me for callin a spade a spade. He slaps you around, I don't have to like him."

"Yeah, but you got to be nice to me, because I'm your fuck-ing kin," said Michelle.

"Fuck kin. You play me again and again. Like that five hundred dollars you took for that bullshit class you lied about when all you were doing was giving it to him to pay down a gambling debt. He aint good. I can't believe you let Violet-Grace around that scum. I raised you better. I raised you to be strong."

Violet-Grace took some coins out of her mam's purse and foisted them into the vending machine, purchasing herself another chocolate bar, then a bag of potato chips, which she handed to her mam before returning to her gymnastics floor routine.

Michelle blitzed through the bag of chips as her mam lectured her. "Half the shit you talk about doesn't make sense," said Michelle, popping the top on her drink and slurping up the bits of fizz liquid that seeped onto the can's surface. "If you don't want me to go back to him, then why won't you let us sleep here?"

Vern, engrossed, spoke up without meaning to. "Maybe she lied because she had to lie," said Vern.

Linda and Michelle both turned toward her. "Maybe her husband said if she didn't find a way to get the money, he'd hurt her, or maybe Violet-Grace. So she told you whatever you needed to hear to give her the money. Or maybe he didn't threaten her, but she knew that if he didn't pay his bookie what was owed, he'd kill him. And if he's dead, he can't work, and she needs that money. Maybe she intended to use it for school, but he stole it, but she told you she gave it to him to protect his image, because having you hate him doesn't help her," said Vern, the words spewing faster than she could think them up.

Michelle slow-clapped before turning back toward her mother. "Take that, Linda. Next time you want to fuck with me, you'll have to go through my knight in shining armor, Ms. Alien Girl," she said, looking at Vern fondly.

"Knights are soldiers of the state," said Vern.

Linda snorted at her daughter. "Maybe she'd have a point if

any of that was true, but the real reason you did it is because you love him. And that's that."

"Maybe she loves him because most of the time he's sweeter to her than you ever were," countered Vern, not sure why it meant so much to her to defend Michelle. Maybe she saw some of herself in her. A mam of questionable quality wed to an aint-shit husband. The world had conspired against Michelle so many times, and now here she was, but the only person anybody wanted to blame was her. Maybe it was hard to give the world your best when the world always gave you its worst.

"I'll stay here at your motel if you let her stay," Vern said to Linda.

Linda looked betrayed and Michelle, hand on hip, looked vindicated.

"I'll even let you take a picture," said Vern.

That changed Linda's mind. She smiled and jutted out her hand for a shake. "Now, that's a deal." Vern didn't take the offered hand, and Michelle snickered at the snub.

"I like you, girl," she said. "I'm gonna go get my suitcase." She grabbed her daughter by the hand and turned to leave.

"Wait," Vern said.

"Yeah?" asked Michelle.

"You got some clothes I can borrow?"

Vern's leggings were holed up from the earlier stabs. Blood had dried the knit fabric into stiff clumps. Her shirt was no better, torn where branches had ripped at the threads, and where the exoskeleton had unsheathed.

"Might not be your style, but absolutely. Just give me a second," said Michelle.

Vern looked warily at Linda, who was waiting excitedly to take the picture, phone already in hand. "I'll go with you," said Vern.

Vern shoved past hauntings to follow Michelle to her car.

Eyes focused in front of her, she could tune out the dramas of the dead.

Michelle opened up the hatchback of her baby-blue two-door. The back seat and trunk of the car were filled with trash bags of clothes and assorted bric-a-brac. There was an open toiletry bag stuffed with soap, deodorant, and makeup. Two hairbrushes, one for Michelle, one for Violet-Grace. Towels. Blankets. A disassembled fishing rod. A cooler. Michelle and her daughter had been living in this car.

"Here, what about this?" asked Michelle, holding up a dark red sweatshirt with an emblem of a brown face in full headdress on it. Above it was the word WARRIORS.

"Who is that?" asked Vern.

"Him? Mascot for my old high school. I think this is the only thing I got big enough to fit your whole . . . situation," said Michelle. When folded in, the exoskeleton wasn't particularly large, but it was enough of a protuberance at two or three inches to make tight tops impossible. Added to that, Michelle was petite, and Vern was not.

"I can't wear this. You should throw it out," said Vern.

Michelle nodded with a nervous smile. "It's offensive, right? I know. But my late boyfriend Cory gave it to me back in eleventh grade before he got killed by a drunk driver senior year, and it's kind of special, you know? I only wear it sometimes."

Vern looked at Michelle hard. "God don't like ugly," she said.

Michelle frowned, visibly shaken by Vern's reproval. "Right," she said. "You know what? I got something else."

She dug around in the car until she pulled out a jacket in the same dark red shade as the sweatshirt. "This was Cory's, too. His letterman jacket." Michelle hugged it. "My husband doesn't even know I have this. I keep it hidden under the seat."

"Thank you," said Vern, snatching it from Michelle.

"Bottoms will be easier," Michelle said, fishing around until she presented Vern with a pair of raw-edged booty shorts. "They're a friend of mine's," said Michelle, explaining their size compared to the rest of her clothing.

"These'll work," said Vern, as she left Michelle to reassemble the bags in her car.

Inside, Linda was waiting with a pair of keys. "Are there others like you? Aliens?" she asked. "I mean, I know there must be, but . . . here. Nearby."

She directed Vern to the stairs. "Elevator's broken."

"I'm not a alien," said Vern.

"Right."

Linda chattered about UFOs and government conspiracies as she walked Vern to her room upstairs. Distracted by explaining the details of the alien lizard race that had infiltrated humanity, she made an easy mark. Vern was able to swipe Linda's old flip phone without notice.

"When you think about it, all the pieces fit," Linda said as she opened the door to the room.

"No. Not when I think about it. Not at all," Vern said, thrust into despair at the depth of human gullibility. Perhaps it was a necessity of the species. To be bent toward believing. For in the wild, a child who did not take to heart the words of its caregivers would easily perish.

Although that had never been the case with Howling and Feral. In the woods, Vern had few rules for them, and the ones she did have, they considered mere recommendations; not sacrosanct. They tested the world on their own terms, drew their own conclusions.

Vern couldn't think of a toddler or small child who didn't butt heads with grown-up rules.

Gogo said it was the world, not the people, who were broken. People believed whatever they needed to, to maintain a thread of power in a society that systematically stripped them of it.

"I've got some printouts at the front desk. You should get some. It's interesting stuff. It might change your mind," said Linda.

Vern hugged the jacket and shorts Michelle had given her, and walked into the room.

"Anyway, it's not much, but the sheets are fresh, and the bathroom's just to your left. Don't leave the shower running too long before you get in. It goes cold quick. Any questions?" Linda asked.

Vern's gut panged wantingly. "Any place round here to get food?" she asked. She remembered earlier today how Queen had stooped over that hunter's body, eating his insides. The memory should've sickened her, but it made Vern lick her lips.

"The vending machines," said Linda. "There's also a pizza place. I don't know if they'll be delivering, with all the weather warnings, but you can call. There's a guidebook with the number in it. Remember. Dial—"

"Nine," Vern said.

"Should we do the picture now or—" Linda cut herself off before finishing when she saw Vern's face. "Sorry, it's just you said that if . . ."

Vern let the woman trail off.

"Tomorrow morning, then," Linda said hopefully.

Vern shook her head. "There won't be any picture, ma'am," she said, "And I'm *not* an alien."

Linda pursed her gray-pink lips. "I—"

"Don't interrupt me."

The force of Vern's scolding made Linda flinch.

"Hear this. The days are coming when your willful ignorance

will no longer be rewarded," said Vern, and shut the door in the woman's face.

Temporarily safe from Linda's foolishness, Vern relaxed her muscles. The day had wrung her dry, and solitude beckoned like a lover.

Vern switched on the overhead light—and switched it off again. Privacy was a gift the fungus was not going to grant her tonight.

A woman lay curled and prone on the concave mattress, bile-green bedspread pulled over herself as she muttered a prayer in Spanish. "A ti clamamos los desterrados hijos de Eva," she said. Despite their foreignness, Vern understood the words.

*To you we cry, banished children of Eve.*

In the window, a teenager hung from a noose made from curtain pulls. It still left Vern stricken at times, the casual way the past flashed back to life in these harrowing glimpses.

"Fuck this," she said, and shut herself in the bathroom. She turned the water as hot as it would go and heeded Linda's advice to hop right in.

The drownt child gurgled for breath as water pooled into the poorly draining tub, but at least he was the devil Vern knew.

The day ran off of Vern's skin in rivulets. Blood and sweat had mixed with dirt to form an itchy paste all over her, but it was no match for the water. She remained under the showerhead long after the water turned lukewarm, then cool, then cold. She sat on the toilet to dry herself off and dressed in the jacket and shorts.

Vern braced as she opened the bathroom door, but when she turned on the light, she was alone. She fell back into the bed in short-lived relief. The telltale prickle of an invading presence brushed her skin.

Next to her, a body appeared in the bed, cool and stiff. On

the other side of her, another. Cold sloughed off the corpses' ashen and blue-tinged skin.

"I thought I was done. Please, not tonight," Vern begged, but the dead were fixtures of Vern's horizon, wishing them away no less futile than bidding away her skin, her eyeballs, her own two feet.

The bodies turned solitude into loneliness. Vern's family was who-knew-where, and her only company was cadavers. She closed her eyes as hard as she could and prayed for sleep. Ten minutes later, the bodies still lay stiff beside her.

Were she back at the cabin, Gogo would distract her by reading aloud. Bridget would make her food. The children would stack books like blocks into structures, and liven the space with their antics.

The cabin had become a home. Vital Springs Inn was a coffin.

Vern the grabbed phone she'd stolen off Linda out of her pocket and dialed Gogo. She didn't answer the first time, so Vern rang again.

"What?" Gogo barked upon answering, knowing it was Vern.

Cautiously, Vern tilted her head to either side to see if her grim companions remained. They did, and this time when she looked, they looked back, their corpses rotated onto their sides to face her whichever way she turned.

"Vern?" asked Gogo. "You okay?"

Vern's breaths quivered out of her. What secret, dark memory would the dead enact on her body tonight? Unfastened from the mortal coil, the beings that walked the haunting realm were as infants in their concern only for self. Only impulse drove them.

"Vern? Vern?" asked Gogo.

Vern gathered the nerve to speak. "I got company," she whispered. "Two dead bodies."

She couldn't disguise the tremble in her voice. It had been some time since she'd had to endure the hauntings alone, without Gogo by her side talking her down. "They're so damn cold."

Through the window, she heard Linda and Michelle fighting, Violet-Grace singing a pop song about *all we do is break up then make up, what we need is a shake up*, out of key. None of it drowned out the haunting.

"Tell me their names," said Gogo.

"Their names?"

"Of the bodies. Who are they?"

Vern had never thought about the names of the people she saw. She closed her eyes, searching. "Peter," she said, "and Samuel." The names were right there, just past the surface of the hauntings. Vern's eyebrows rose in surprise as the specifics of their lives filled her. "They were lovers," she announced triumphantly, pleased by her mastery of the fungus.

For ages, she'd been trying to exert more control over them as Gogo had encouraged, but progress was middling and variable. Seeing Queen in all her unhinged glory must've loosened the necessary screws inhibiting Vern from advancing.

"What happened to them?" asked Gogo, part actually curious, part trying to keep Vern distracted.

"Disease," Vern said, waiting for Gogo to ask more, to give Vern an excuse to look further into the images the fungus had brought forth. But Gogo said nothing. This was on Vern. "They had the same fungus I had." She spoke the thought at the very same moment she'd realized it, no space between the knowing and the saying. "Except it killed them. They had AIDS," Vern said.

"Opportunistic infection?" asked Gogo.

"Yes," Vern said.

"Were they with each other?" asked Gogo. "I mean when it happened. When they died? Say they were."

Vern exhaled and forced herself to turn to her left so she could look at Peter, who was no longer corpse-gray. His dark skin was awash in tattoos so intricate Vern had to squint to make sense of them even through the perfect vision of the fungus. It was a map, a city, drawn in bold, black lines all over him. Vern turned to face the other, Samuel, whose skin was lighter, body thinner.

"Hours apart."

"How old?"

"Thirty-four and twenty-nine," said Vern, opening herself up to their stories. Knowledge rushed through her in a heady haze of images and facts: their mams, Joan Juarez and Patricia Coates, their paps, Ulysses Dominguez-Miron and Jimmy Franks, their siblings, their schools, their favorite books, their first times, their regrets, their favorite ways to fuck (desperately, darkly).

Experimentally, Vern reached out to touch Samuel's dead hand, but jerked it away at the coldness. Counting to three, she tried again. She weaved her fingers with his, then with Peter's.

Their palms warmed in hers, then softened. Samuel's gripped back, then so did Peter's, hard so that Vern felt her bones start to slacken under the pressure.

Vern didn't know what made them appear to her as corpses, awakening only now with her touch. Hauntings were myriad and strange, and their ways resisted complete understanding.

"Vern?" asked Gogo. "Where'd you go?"

Vern's throat had turned dry as sandpaper. Samuel sat up, Peter next. They looked at each other, astounded, seeing each other for the first time since they'd passed, alive in the fungus still.

"Sam," said Peter.

"Peter," said Sam.

Their voices were broken and shrill. Their skin, which

moments ago appeared covered in sores, was smooth and glistened under the flickering overhead light beautifully. Their hands still clasped in Vern's, they reached across her and kissed.

"Vern?"

"They're awake," whispered Vern. "Kissing."

"Awake?"

"Alive. Alive-alive. Like the breakaway bodies in the tree. Like Sherman."

Gogo swallowed loudly. "Wish I could be there with you. Wish I could see them."

Counter to her usual nature, Vern wanted to share this with Gogo, too.

"Peter is—he's the younger one. Twenty-nine. Black. Muscular now, though he wasn't at first when he was lying dead. Tattoos all over. It's a city, but it don't say which one. His hair is buzzed short and flat on the top. And Sam, he's almost—he reminds me of a professor. Glasses. Longish hair just past his ears, black, starting to gray already. Light to medium brown skin. Facial hair."

Vern wished there was a way to plug her brain into Gogo's directly. The description she'd given of the men failed to capture the gentle reverence they had for each other, which in seconds mutated into a rapturing lust. Vern didn't have the vocabulary to articulate their tinny moans as they kissed most viciously, tongues against each other's, their bodies overtaken with quivers. Each held Vern's hand still as they reunited.

"What's happening now?" asked Gogo, whispering.

"Peter's using his free hand to undo his pants. He's—" Vern stopped herself. These two were sharing a private intimacy, and here she was playing voyeur, her own body brought to wanting by their passion.

"Tell me. Tell me about them," said Gogo. She and Vern both

were . . . not touch-starved, precisely, but used to a particular type of emotional isolation that came after years of convincing yourself it was all right, better even, to be alone. As a defense mechanism, such self-delusion had its place, but once the farce faded, it was like your whole body transformed all its years of misbelieving into insatiable hunger for contact.

"They got their hands on each other," said Vern.

"How?"

"They're feeling each other. Taking stock. Relearning. Peter's hand is sliding down Sam's back, reaching beneath the waistband of his jeans, under the drawers, squeezing his ass," she said. Vern squeezed her thighs together as tightly as she could to sate the yearning nested between her legs. Gogo moaned on the other end of the line. "You touching yourself?" asked Vern.

"Yeah."

Vern was already shot through with desire, but hearing Gogo made her weak. She whimpered and said, as if seeing the two men before her weren't enough, "Tell me what you're doing."

"Pressing my hand between my legs through my jeans."

"Where are you?"

"The grungy bathroom of some fucking truck stop, Jesus. I'm leaning against the door to keep it shut cause it doesn't even have a fucking lock."

Peter and Samuel's boldness spread to Vern. If they could touch and kiss and feel right in front of her without shame, she could tell Gogo what she wanted. "Slide your pants down," she said.

"Underwear, too?"

"No," said Vern. "I want you to rub yourself through them." She closed her eyes, embarrassed by her own desires, but she refused to take it back. There was nothing wrong with wanting.

Peter, ever so cautiously, slipped his hand from Vern's. Sam followed suit, and Vern was untethered. She regrounded only when she heard Gogo mumbling, "Want you so bad, wish you were here. I hate how we left things before."

Hands unencumbered, Vern unzipped the jeans shorts she'd borrowed from Michelle and pushed them down to her ankles. Licking her lips, she reached for her clit and pressed her fingers into it.

Peter turned toward her and rested his palm on her thigh. His jeans were off now, and his penis, hard, poked above the band of his boxers, the tip shiny with droplets of pre-semen. His body and Sam's body flexed and moved in startling detail.

Peter's hand slid farther up Vern's thigh till his fingers touched her where she was wet. He hesitated, watching her eyes. She nodded. It didn't matter in this moment that usually her affections belonged to women alone. The need to connect and be a part of this rebirth of lust and love trumped all. Peter shoved two fingers into her as she circled her clit. Sam's mouth descended on Peter's penis, and Gogo was moaning on the phone, rubbing herself through the thin cotton of her underwear, the fabric surely wet and slick by now, friction and fluidity in synchronous harmony.

"So close," Gogo mewled.

"Reach beneath your underwear," said Vern. "Imagine me taking you in my mouth."

Obeying, Gogo moaned as skin touched skin. Vern jerked her hips up into Peter's fingers and into her own as the sound reached into her and pulled her apart. She loved to hear Gogo lose it, and it brought on her finish. She came on the fingers of this stranger and didn't feel bad about it. Cainland had so confused her notions of goodness, pleasure, and degradation that she'd never thought there could be sex without guilt and self-loathing, without a streak of squalor.

Vern breathed rapidly in and out, nerves frenetic. Peter removed his fingers from her, then guided Samuel onto his back, his knees bent and his hips raised. Peter dragged teeth and lips along Samuel's thighs, working his way toward Samuel's ass. Samuel, unable to take more teasing, grabbed Peter's head and drew his partner's mouth to his anus, where Peter gladly placed his tongue.

"What's happening now?" asked Gogo.

"That thing I do for you," said Vern, whispering. Gogo was still touching herself, holding herself at the edge, and Vern bent her legs at the knees and raised her hips up. She reached her fingers to her asshole and pressed inside, using her other hand to rub her clitoris. She narrated each action to Gogo, letting herself be laid bare.

Gogo cried out as she came, and Vern reached her finish a second time, this time in a short, sharp burst. Peter and Samuel continued to fuck, Samuel's hand on his cock as Peter licked his ass.

When the haunting faded, the bedspread smoothed out, and Vern was left by her lonesome, she spoke Gogo's name aloud.

"Yeah?"

Everything Vern could think to say sounded corny or trite. "Nothing."

Gogo sighed and the line became muffled. Vern guessed she was doing up her jeans, the phone wedged between her cheek and shoulder. "I should get back to the others," Gogo said.

"Yeah," said Vern.

The tap water ran, then the hand dryer went off.

"We can . . . I think we should meet up," said Vern. Gogo was silent on the other end of the line. "I mean if you still wa—"

"Yes," said Gogo.

"I'm at a motel called Vital Springs Inn. There's a storm nearby. Storm Rhoda. That enough to find me?"

"Yeah, the storm's coming in here, too. We might not be able to leave until the rain has passed."

"Can I talk to Howling or Feral, at least?"

"You want me to wake them? They're sleeping."

Vern sighed. "No, that's all right," she said, but it wasn't. She was desperate now to reunite with the people in her life.

"Is this the number I should call you back on?"

"Until I can pick up a burner or something," said Vern.

"All right. I'll talk to you soon. And Vern?"

"Yeah?" she asked.

Gogo hesitated a moment, then mumbled an answer. "Love you. Bye." And with that, it was her turn to hang up on Vern.


# 23


THE SKY TONIGHT WAS AN ANEMIC GRAY, and Vern had to turn the TV way up to hear it over the fierce wind kicking up outside. Rain had begun to fall, but only in sprinkles, the worst yet to come.

Vern sat at the foot of the bed, Linda's phone clutched in her hand, waiting for it to buzz. The weather report said the storm wouldn't hit its peak until after nine. Depending on how close they were, there might be time for Gogo to drive here.

Vern—more accurately Linda—received a dozen texts, one of them Michelle's husband: *She with you?*

Vern still wasn't used to all the ways Cainland and the outside were the same. Husbands controlling wives and wives not knowing how to leave them. No one knew how to extricate themselves from pain. Everywhere there were silences that should be replaced with screams. Everywhere there were children who'd taken their care into their own hands.

Vern called the pizza place Linda had told her about as she flipped through channels, pausing on the news. Heart racing, she turned up the volume even higher and stood so she was only a foot in front of the screen.

"The search continues for Vern Fields following the alleged murders of local men Jonathan Leary and Willis Crawford earlier today. She's considered armed and very dangerous. Multiple witnesses place Fields at the scene. Police warn not to apprehend the suspect," the reporter said gravely.

Vern licked her lips and paced in front of the blaring screen. This was Cainland through and through. There had been no witnesses. Only Queen, and she was the one who'd killed the men—which was fine by Vern. She'd have done the same if she'd had the chance.

Vern sat back down on the foot of the bed between a haunting of a woman knitting a blanket for the baby in her pregnant belly and another of a child whittling hardwood into a bird. Vern's knees bounced, and she bit her nails nervously, finally texting Gogo.

I'm on the news.

> No shit.

What they're saying isn't true. I didn't kill those hunters. I didn't kill nobody. But I would've.

> I know.

They're tryna set me up.

> Get a disguise.

When are you gonna get here?

> Maybe not till morning. They're issuing flash flood warnings. The roads are too dangerous.

Please. Hurry.

Vern startled at the sound of knocking on her door. She tossed Linda's phone to the side. "Yeah?" she asked.

"You ordered pizza?"

"You can leave it out there," she said, and slipped two twenties under the bolted door.

"Any change?"

"Nah," she said, and waited for him to go before retrieving her supper. In the space of fifteen minutes she finished both large pizzas.

Vern found Michelle's number in Linda's phone and dialed.

"What the fuck do you want, Linda?"

"It's Vern."

"Who?"

"The one your mam's letting stay at the motel."

"The chick with the costume?"

"It's a condition."

Vern felt the woman's mood soften. "Did you just fucking swipe Linda's phone? Remind me to hug you."

"Her wallet, too. I was wondering if you knew where I could get a wig or something? Some hair dye? I need a hoodie, too."

"Right. Vern. I saw that story about you on the new— Violet-Grace! Stop right now!"

"It's not true."

"Uh-huh," said Michelle.

"You gonna rat me out?"

"Hell, no. I knew Jon-Jon. If anyone had a comeuppance due, it was his ass. Violet. Grace. If I have to say your name one more goddamn time."

Vern tapped her foot impatiently. "So can you help me?"

"With your super-top-secret disguise or whatever? Yeah.

Nothing's open, but I can bring you some shit," said Michelle. "What's your room number?"

"Three twenty-one," Vern said, going to the door to check.

"All right. Cool. Me and Violet-Grace are at the McDonald's drive-through. Once we're done here I'll swing by my friend Nikki's to pick up the stuff. She cams, so she's got a lot of good disguise shit. You want anything else? Any food?"

The whole damn menu. "I wouldn't say no to a burger and fries. Large."

"You got it. Later, chica."

Vern flipped through more channels as she waited for Michelle. She'd get the goods, eat another meal, then go to sleep. All would be fine. Gogo would be here when she awoke.

LIGHT STREAMED INTO THE ROOM early. Vern rubbed her eyes and stretched, unfolding her exoskeleton from its resting place as she stood in front of the mirror on top of the dinged dresser. Though Vern's antler-looking "wings" weren't as large as Queen's, the bone apparatus stretched out magnificently to either side of her, sections branching intricately like veins, like tributaries and rivers.

Vern tried on the various wigs Michelle had dropped off last night. Most were colorful and bright, attracting attention, but one was a short, mousy brown bob with long bangs. Slipping it on, Vern pressed herself close to the mirror to get a good look. She took a photo of herself with Linda's phone and zoomed in. Not too bad. She could almost pass for white with it on, the context of her coarse hair removed.

Last night, Michelle had suggested she wear makeup if she

really wanted to make herself look different. She'd left some
with Vern, but Vern didn't know how to use it.

Can you do my makeup?

> Thought this was my mom
> at first and I was like wtf til
> I remembered. Out getting
> coffee now. You want break-
> fast?

Yeah.

> Coffee, too?

They got smoothies?

> Something like. I'll hook you
> up. Be there soon.

It didn't take long for Michelle to arrive with food and Violet-
Grace. "I hope you like donuts," Michelle said. Vern took one
of the boxes and started in. "Eat all you want. Porter is sweet
on me. Gives me these by the dozen whenever I come into the
shop."

She looked tired, shaky. "You okay?" Vern asked, though she
had little time for another person's troubles, full-up with her own.

"I'm good," she said, smiling. Her knees were bouncing up
and down, though, where she sat in the motel room's desk chair.
"It's just . . ."

"Yeah?"

"Linda might've done something stupid."

Vern swallowed a too-large mouthful of food and dabbed
away the glaze stuck to the side of her mouth with a napkin.
"Stupid like what?" she asked, already standing up and sliding
her feet into her boots.

She straightened her wig and zipped up the letterman jacket to her neck, slipped Linda's phone and wallet into her pocket.

"Like call the local police and ask if there was any kind of reward for turning in information about you. She didn't say where you were, as far as I can tell. She didn't even give a name or anything, but—"

"When'd she make the call?"

"Couple minutes ago? I don't know. She was on the phone when I came in, and I hung it up for her when I realized what she was doing. I'm sure it's nothing to be worried about."

If she was sure about it, she wouldn't be shaking and putting on fake smiles. If she was sure about it, she'd not have told Vern at all. People were always doing this, convincing themselves their bad feelings were nothing. They talked themselves into danger, into Cainland, into Sherman's fold. Was it really so much easier to pretend everything was good than to face the possibility that it wasn't? Folks fell as madly in love with the illusion of truth as they did with truth proper.

Vern went for the door at a run.

"But I still have to do your makeup!"

Vern was down the hall and in the staircase, then in the lobby, stopping only when forced to by the violence of the scene before her. Linda was dead, shot in the head, her body limp over the front desk.

Vern tried to feel sorry for her, but the only thought that really crossed her mind was, *Foolish bitch*, and she hated herself for it. Instead of blood flowing through Vern's veins, there was ceaseless venom, and it turned every thought mean and unforgiving. Vern wasn't the arbiter of these things, but she thought according to most people's standards Linda probably didn't deserve to die.

Aside from Linda's fresh-dead body, the lobby was clear. Ollie must've been searching the rooms for her. If Vern was quick, she could escape. She barreled forward toward the double doors and pushed them open with the force of her body.

Ollie hadn't come alone.

Flanked in formation around the parking lot, twenty men—soldiers—stood with guns at the ready. "Fire!" a voice shouted, and they obeyed.

Vern's exoskeleton popped out on instinct, curling in front of her to deflect the ammunition. It wasn't bullets that bounced off the shield of bone flimsily, but tranquilizer darts. Girded by her exoskeleton, Vern stepped forward, impenetrable. The world around her had never seemed so insignificant. Her body was an entire armory.

Vern unfurled, leaving her front exposed. This was what it was to feel untouchable. Sherman, Eamon, Lucy's daddy—had this same rush of ecstasy surged through them when they imposed their rule?

Vern halted her forward assault when a set of small sticky fingers slid around her legs. Overtaken by sense memory, she looked down, fully expecting to see Howling or Feral at her feet.

It was Violet-Grace, her wispy blond hair blowing in the still-harsh wind. To the left was Michelle, lying on the concrete. She must've come out to help. Now she was stuck with a dose of drugs. Her fate would be no different than Linda's.

Hauntings weaved between the armed soldiers. Forward they marched, an army of the dead desperate for Vern to hear their unfinished business.

"Queen," a voice called. Vern shifted her eyes toward the voice. Ollie lingered at the edges of the formation. Wearing a flannel shirt and faded blue jeans, she stood out easily among the soldiers.

Queen emerged from the back of an armored van. When she didn't immediately run toward Vern, Ollie gave her a shock. Her scream buried the sound of the whistling wind. Vern stumbled backward, the child at her foot clinging to her tightly. Queen trod toward Vern slowly, back hunched under the weight of her exoskeleton. She moved like a praying mantis.

The wind glided across Vern's face, blew the coarse, straw-like strands of her wig in front of her eyes, scratching her nose.

Vern shook her leg, but Violet-Grace held on. "Violet-Grace," said Vern. "I need you to go back inside."

"No," said Violet-Grace.

Vern reached into her pocket, pulling out a couple dollars. She held them to the girl. "Get me some chips and yourself a chocolate bar, okay? Eat it in there, and when I'm all done, I'll come in to get my potato chips, okay?"

Violet-Grace considered the offer on the table and reached her hand up. She snatched the dollar bills and ran inside. Linda's body was still draped over the front desk. Violet-Grace was short. She might not see. She could go do her cartwheels and somersaults on the dirty carpet after finishing her chocolate.

Queen approached methodically. She could've lunged at Vern, pounced and tackled her. She didn't. She was under Ollie's influence, but her mind was still her own. Vern tested her exoskeleton. She moved it experimentally, feeling its boundaries and contours. Queen did the same, copying. She was met with another shock that sent her reeling, her screams so piercing two of the soldiers forgot themselves and dropped their weapons to cover their ears.

Eyes steady on Vern, Queen stilled before entering Vern's mind with a picture of a girl, eleven or twelve, blowing puffs of dandelion as she smiled. The unbridled cheer of the haunting disarmed Vern.

"I don't understand," Vern cried out.

Queen unhunched and spread her exoskeleton out yet farther in an explosion of movement, the complex, webbed network of her bone rearranging. A cloud of fine mist leached from Queen's exoskeleton. It filled Vern's nostrils and mouth, a fragrance akin to woodsmoke and dirt. She swallowed the scent gladly, let it fill her lungs.

The soldiers coughed at the intrusion to their lungs, then dropped their dart guns to the ground, then each removed a gun from his holster. Reflexively, Vern moved her carapace to guard herself, but the soldiers did not aim the guns at her. They brought them up to their own temples and fired. Blood sprayed from each of their brains like fireworks.

Queen laughed, the sound of it startlingly human. It was the laugh of an auntie teasing a nephew about his sweetheart at a Sunday picnic. She was cracking up, her palm pressed to her belly and the other over her lips. "They didn't see that shit coming, did they? Pop. Pop. Splat," she said, and pressed her finger to her temple. "It's easy, Vern, you try," she said, giddy. "Think about spreading it, and you spread it. Try it, Vern. Go ahead. You'll like it."

The child blowing the dandelion—Queen had been telling Vern she was going to spread the fungus. "Think what you want them to think, then hit em with it. You can only do one thought, though. Got to keep it simple. They aint hooked up like us, Vern."

What did that mean, *hooked up*?

Queen heard Vern's thoughts as if she'd spoken them aloud. "All the rivers, girl. They're inside us," she said. She meant the mycelium.

But Vern thought only the thoughts of the dead lived in the hyphae.

"We're special, baby," said Queen, answering Vern's silent question. "They been searching a long time for you. They were starting to think I was the only. I always wanted a sister, Vern, and now I've got her," she said, and again Vern was struck by her apparent joviality, such a contrast to the rasping animal creature Vern had confronted yesterday.

"I'll have you know my mama raised me with manners," said Queen, then tapped her foot on one soldier's body. "Pop, pop, splat!" she said, and erupted into laughter once more.

Vern was shaking. She'd have killed those soldiers dead, too, even laughed at their demise, but to reach into their minds and poison them with untruths, to turn their hands against themselves—that was a violation Vern understood too intimately.

Queen didn't owe those soldiers a damn thing, but Vern couldn't help but think of Sherman's sermons, the way little seeds of thought would be planted in Vern's head, then would spread and consume her.

"Do you understand now?" asked Ollie, emerging from the dispersing mist. "This is what happens to you in the end. The sickness drives you mad." Ollie wore brown hiking boots and a messy bowl cut.

"I reckon you're the one who drove her mad," said Vern. Queen hadn't stopped laughing at what she'd done, staring at the bodies. *Pop, pop, splat*, she sang.

"And yet she spared me. What does that tell you?"

It didn't tell Vern a damn thing. Loving, worshipping, and bowing to folks who harmed you was written into the genes of all animal creatures. To be alive meant to lust after connection, and better to have one with the enemy than with no one at all. A baby's fingers and mouth grasped on instinct.

"She loves me," Ollie said, gloating, threatening: *And one day you'll love me, too.*

Ollie could be right. Maybe in the wake of Queen's various bouts of suffering—the shock collar and whatever other cruelties she'd undergone—she and Ollie had shared a thousand soft kisses. These things weren't marks in Ollie's favor, however, only further proof she needed ending.

While Queen was still laughing, distracted by the massacre she'd orchestrated, Vern dashed toward Ollie. She'd sooner die than be her torture-pet.

Queen's instincts were too quick. She intercepted.

"Vern! Vern!"

Gogo had arrived finally, but at the worst possible moment. Just in time to see Vern's death. She called Vern's name frantically.

"Stay back!" Vern called, hoping her tone expressed the gravity of the situation. Gogo hadn't seen what Queen was capable of. What Vern was capable of.

Vern and Queen circled each other. Queen hissed. Trying it on for size, Vern hissed, too. Thankful to be barefoot, she called on the fungus beneath her feet and let it funnel food into her body, bulking her energy reserves as well as her strength. She'd need every ounce of fortitude if there was any chance—and there wasn't—she was going to win this fight.

Vern stood between Queen and Gogo, poised to fight. They roared at each other, each protectors of their respective lovers. Their eyes met. They regarded each other with cautious respect.

Then Queen darted forward toward Vern.

"No!" cried Gogo.

Her senses keen, Vern felt the events around her transpire in slow motion. Queen, neither fully upright nor on all fours, dragged herself forward at startling velocity, her back stooped. Behind, Vern heard Gogo sprint, deluded into believing she could possibly intervene. And finally, to Vern's side was Ollie, a semiautomatic in one hand, a dart gun in the other.

Vern heard the crack of gunfire. Smelled the smoke. Felt the heat. "No!" Vern called, twisting toward Ollie. A tranquilizer dart hit her in the back. Gogo hit the ground, her chest an expanding red circle of blood. Vern ran toward her. Weakened by the tranq, she fell to her knees and crawled.

Another tranquilizer. This time to the neck. Vern's hand reached out toward Gogo's, but before she could touch her, she passed out in a rush of swarming gray.

## 24

CUFFS BOUND VERN to a metal wall, and she could not move.

"Rise and shine," said Ollie, four or five feet across from Vern. "You've been knocked out for several hours. Time to wake up."

Vern's eyelids were too heavy to lift. She moaned weakly with the effort of it.

"Sorry, Vern," said Queen sheepishly. Her voice, all church-lady-polite again, was enough to rouse Vern that final layer. Vern opened her eyes.

Queen sat to Vern's right, separated from her by a glass wall and locked in cuffs.

Vern's head pulsated with pain and she was mad with the desire to rub her temples. With hands locked in place, she could not. She hummed an agonized wail to keep herself from passing out from the sheer magnitude of the ache. Were she not absolutely certain otherwise, she'd think the fungus was fruiting in her brain, a mass of hard conk erupting through gray and white matter.

"Gogo," she moaned feebly as she recalled the spreading watercolor splash of blood. "Where is she?"

Ollie gestured to Vern's left. "Don't get excited. I expect she won't survive. I've kept her here for now only in the event that I can use her to talk some sense into you. You might not care about your life. Hers? Well. I'm glad you've found love."

Vern rotated her head toward Gogo. She lay on a gurney outside of Vern's cage, bandaged, hooked to an IV, a breathing mask over her face.

Howling and Feral were nowhere to be found, but that was a good thing. They must be with Bridget.

The pain in Vern's head eased as she became more accustomed to consciousness. "Fuck you to pieces, Ollie." She wanted to say the same to Queen—had she not interfered, Gogo and Vern would be free—but she could not bring herself to turn against that wounded woman.

"Good to see you haven't lost your fire," Ollie said, her reaction otherwise frustratingly blank.

Jags and bumps jolted Vern up and down and side to side. They were in the back of a vehicle and it was moving fast.

"Where are you taking me?" asked Vern. "Back to the Blessed Acres?"

"Years ago, had you listened to me, that's where we'd be heading, but that's not an option now." Vern wasn't sure how Ollie could sound so boastful and regretful at the same time.

Vern tested the resistance of her restraints. She was strong, but the metal holding her in place was stronger. "What changed?" she asked, buying herself time to figure out an escape.

"You changed. Literally. Look at you, Vern. All grown up now. The world knows who you are, or they will very soon. We can't have that. I did what I could to keep you safe, but you're hardheaded, aren't you? Can't blame you. I am, too." Ollie leaned back into her seat.

"You'll get to see my home," Queen chimed in with a polite, shy smile.

"Queen, the Blessed Acres is your home," said Vern. "Not that place. Don't you remember? You used to live at the compound. What happened to you? Where are they taking us?"

Queen smiled wordlessly, lost in her mind. Vern wondered how much of her life was spent lost in hauntings.

"You're not gonna get any answers out of her, but you can talk to me. I'll tell you whatever you want to know," said Ollie.

Vern watched Ollie with narrowed eyes. She had that same youthful, devil-may-care look she'd had when Vern first met her. Messy-haired and angular, she was all tomboy.

"Why would you work for the people who did this to me? And Queen?" asked Vern. "Is it just for fun? Do you really get off on hurting people like that?"

"Cainland didn't hurt people. It saved people. Lost souls ended up there, ones who didn't have a place anywhere else in the world. I fought to keep Cainland alive long after everyone else abandoned it and its facilities, wrote it off as a failure like some high school science fair project. My initiative paid off, though, didn't it? I had to carry out a lot of my work in secret— Sherman helped, of course, convinced I was an angel of the God of Cain—and I've got the government's attention now, don't I? They want my guidance. My knowledge. I made you, Vern. Me. I did that. And you didn't have to grow up in a military lab to become the miracle you are."

Vern did grow up in a lab, no matter how Ollie saw it. "It's not like those were the only two choices. You could've fought to cancel the program altogether. You could've freed everyone."

"How could I do that when I believe in the work? How could I abandon it, when it saved me? I'm alive because of it." Ollie had devoted her life so thoroughly to Cainland that she saw it as her reason for living. "I carried on looking after Cainland because I believe in the potential of the remarkable human beings who, like you, for whatever reason the fungus latches on to. Were it up to my colleagues in the military, the happy people of the compound would've been disappeared at black ops sites. So I made Cainland into a place where people could live normal lives, in a town, outside of the confines of a laboratory but where we were still able to learn, understand."

"You mean experiment. Maim. You rip people from their homes," Vern cried out, but appealing to Ollie's moral sense was a fool's errand.

"The problem with your people—and I truly mean no offense when I say that—is a lack of understanding of the bigger picture," said Ollie. Vern hardly recognized her for how calm she sounded. Like Vern, she'd always had a streak of passion. That had been a lie. She was a calculating manipulator who relished asserting her dominance. "Do you know who James Marion Sims is, V? Sorry, Vern," she said with a small, cruel smile. "He was a pioneering doctor in the nineteenth century and the founder of modern gynecology. He innovated a number of techniques and surgeries that would end up becoming foundational to the discipline. But this knowledge did not come out of the ether. He did it by testing on slaves. Of course, today we don't enslave people in that sense, and methods today are not as cruel. He performed surgeries on those women without anesthesia. Today, Cainland itself is the anesthesia. It gives people a purpose, a reason. Of course, there's the added benefit of creating a self-sustaining population with a high susceptibility to the fungus."

There was no talking Ollie and her ilk into believing Vern and her ilk were actually people. They were collateral damage in a useless battle waged to attain more power. Vern wondered what they'd even learned—if it was helpful or necessary. In sixty years of trying to make another Queen, they'd gotten lucky with Vern. Was that all the data they had to show for it? A runaway?

"Cainland is a zoo," said Vern.

"That may be true—certain specifications were necessary for containment, for keeping a collective whole wedded to the space—but let me ask you, would you have rather grown up where Queen lives now?"

"Is that where you killed Lucy?" asked Vern. "At some military lab?"

"Lucy?" Ollie asked, sounding amused. "You mean Lucy Jenkins? The girl who got away. She was a spitfire, wasn't she? Scout's honor, we didn't kill her. We never found her, and I didn't know she was dead until just now. Send her my love when she visits you. She knows me. I drove her back to the compound from court."

The grief of it was endless. Where did it start? Where did it end? Like the horizon, there was no reaching the borders. Yet still Vern wanted to treat it like something small she could hold.

"Did you know what they were going to do to you?" Vern asked Queen, turning her eyes to her.

Queen smiled. "They didn't do nothing to me, Vern. I wanted to help them."

How could a woman be so lost that she couldn't understand the depth of her own suffering?

"Queen, is she not an angel of death in the flesh? Glorious and blazing. A sun. She was the one to catch the military's and the FBI's attention." Queen cooed as Ollie praised her, drunk with giggles. "It was her strength that couldn't be hidden. Everything else came later, but that was the key we wanted to unlock. It was the height of the Cold War, the weapons race. Most departments were focused on nuclear missiles, but that could never be the whole picture. Soldiers strong as Queen? That interested us. How many years of suffering might we have avoided if we'd cracked that?"

Vern couldn't process half of what Ollie was saying. None of it made sense. "That was a long time ago. You can't know all that." Ollie had several years on Vern, but when they'd met, she couldn't have been any older than her midtwenties.

"I'm an essential asset," said Ollie in explanation, "but it was Eamon Fields who was the visionary. Without him, Cainland would never have been. It was never in the plan for him to have a child, but it worked out so well, didn't it? It's a shame that your actions—leaving Cainland—mean it must finally end."

Vern shoved her body as forward as it would go with the restraints holding her back.

"Of course, those showing infection potential will be relocated elsewhere, but everyone else? Your actions, your show of your true form to so many, has brought this on. Some things can only be carried out in secret. When it's no longer secret, it must end. I am truly sorry about what's going to happen to your family, but they are not the first casualties in the pursuit of medical progress. Far from it."

"You can't do this. People will know," Vern cried out, desperate.

"Will they? Or will it just be another sad mass suicide from a sad cult led by a megalomaniac?"

Vern quaked with fury as Ollie blithely discussed a massacre. This was Ollie's hubris, showing itself again. Her certainty that things would always work out in her favor, for they always had before, hadn't they?

"Don't cry, Vern. It doesn't suit you," said Ollie.

Vern's nostrils flared with her wild, angry breaths. "I'm not crying," said Vern. "I'm gathering my strength."

Her bare feet touched the metal flooring of the van. She buzzed with hunger and want. Mycelium, heeding the calling of their distressed symbiont, fed her their nutrients.

"What are you doing?" Ollie asked.

In answer, Vern released her exoskeleton. Its span far out-reached the capacity of the small glass cage. Either the carapace would break against it, or the cage would give.

Vern won out, her exoskeleton denting the glass of the cage and causing the great metal body of the vehicle to shudder back-ward and forward from the impact. She let the exoskeleton click back into its sheath, and released it again, flinging the boned flanks out from her body harder and faster.

The driver swerved, then regained control of the vehicle.

"Don't be stupid!" Ollie called out. "You'll kill your little girlfriend."

Vern glanced sideways. The gurney Gogo was strapped to was fastened to the van's floor. Even if it wasn't, Gogo's fate at the end of this journey would be death. This was Vern's chance to save not just her but everyone back at Cainland.

"Queen!" Ollie shouted, but what could she do, strapped down just as Vern was? If she moved the one part of her body she had control over, the exoskeleton, she'd only be helping Vern.

Vern folded and unfolded her exoskeleton once more. This time, the shake of the vehicle disrupted the driver enough that the vehicle ran off the road, spun, and flipped. Ollie was belted securely in, but her head rattled back and forth and landed in an awkward angle when the vehicle finally stopped. Her eyes were closed.

Gogo groaned awake, still strapped in.

The chains around her wrists and ankles held firm. She tugged and tugged against them, but they didn't budge.

Ollie's eyes opened, alert.

"What are you going to do now?" Vern asked, in threat. If Ollie unbuckled herself, Vern could shake the van again. If she stayed strapped in, what could she do but wait? And for what? Backup?

"Let me out of here, and I'll let you live," said Vern when Ollie didn't answer.

"You will never learn, Vern, will you?" Ollie asked, anger peeking through her composed facade. This was the Ollie of the woods surfacing. She unbuckled her seat belt.

Vern unfolded her exoskeleton hard, shaking the van. Her seat belt unbuckled, Ollie stumbled toward the door, and Vern refolded and unfurled her wings again, knocking the van back and forth so that Ollie couldn't regain footing.

"Let me out, and I'll spare you," said Vern, though she would not. Ollie looked like she was about to protest, but Vern shook the van again, forcing Ollie onto her hands and knees, her cheek crashing onto the floor. It was intoxicating to see her in such a humiliating state. This feeling, this potent high that accompanied the realization and onset of power, had toppled many. It was possible to suffocate on your own ego. "Get up and release me," Vern said. Next to her in her own cage, Queen growled and screeched.

Instead, Ollie reached for her phone. Vern shook the van again, the phone falling out of Ollie's grasp.

"Give up," said Vern.

Ollie held up her hands in surrender. "Okay, okay, okay," she said, and headed for what Vern hoped was the lock that would undo this cage, but then Ollie smiled. She reached for a button, bright green, and pressed. The cage door did not release. Instead, the sound of hissing funneled in. White mist sprayed into Vern's glass cage.

"That would be a nerve agent," said Ollie. They'd devised a way to subdue Vern without direct contact. Vern should've realized they'd have arranged something like this.

Yet Vern didn't feel herself sicken. She breathed in the chemical, no doubt, but her lungs did not burn with it. Her mind was clear.

Ollie, however, fared less well, wobbling, rubbing her eyes, coughing. The glass cage had been compromised when Vern had pounded her exoskeleton against its walls. There was a hole large enough to let the gas out. Unbolstered by the fungus, Ollie was more sensitive to the nerve agent's effects. But Vern had more time before it would harm her. "Let me out, and I'll let you out."

Ollie, trembling, scrabbled to her feet and pressed her hand against the lock. There was another hissing sound and a beep, but no movement. "It's stuck, Vern," she said. The doors leading outside of the van were bent shut and would not open when Ollie tried to wrestle her way out.

"Press it again!" said Vern.

Still shaking, Ollie obeyed. "Shit," she said, when it still didn't work, but the third attempt was a success, Vern's cage door shuddering open a fraction—yet still not the whole way. Ollie slid in. "Don't—don't interfere with my mind."

Vern wiggled her wrists, drawing attention to the restraints. "That depends on you," Vern said in threat. Queen had laughed so drunkenly when she'd reached into those men's minds and tugged, and Vern could understand why. For once, she'd been the one in control. How delicious it must have tasted to usurp those who'd felt so certain of their everlasting reign.

Ollie undid Vern's restraints, but she was lagging. She'd almost passed out by the time the task was finished.

Once free, Vern rushed to Gogo, checking her pulse. She was alive, but just. Vern rammed her shoulders through the warped metal doors at the back of the van and they opened. She unhooked Gogo from the various pieces of medical equipment and carried her outside to fresh air, laying her gently on the road's shoulder. "It's gonna make this okay," she said.

A shot was fired. Ollie had stumbled from the van. Too out of it to aim, she flung her handgun wildly and pulled the trigger over and over. She was surprisingly spry as she army-crawled in Vern's direction.

"Ollie!" Queen cried.

"Stay inside," she called. She'd released Queen from her holds, but she didn't want her interfering with this. Ollie knew Queen didn't have the discipline to subdue Vern without killing her, and the project needed Vern alive. Like Ollie had said, there'd been no perfect vessel for the fungus since Queen herself.

"Give it up, Ollie," said Vern.

Ollie kept firing, and a bullet grazed Vern's shoulder. She hissed, more in annoyance than in pain, then bolted toward the fiend. Let this be finished once and for all.

She tackled Ollie and straddled her at the waist. Ollie's eyes looked beseechingly up into hers, but the ship of mercy and forgiveness had sailed. Fiends didn't get clemency.

While she was poised over Ollie's warm body, the animal lurking inside Vern surfaced. This was who the fungus had turned her into: her true self.

On instinct, she stretched her mouth open wide, leaned down, then clamped her teeth over the fiend's neck. She jostled her head back and forth like a dog, tearing into her victim, her incisors never once breaking contact with Ollie's pale skin. Blood spurted out, soda from a shaken can. It warmed Vern's face with its silky red splendor.

Ollie was dead.

As in their previous altercations—the night the children were born and when Ollie's true identity was revealed—Queen stalked nearby, just out of view and reach. She stood in the van's entrance.

Queen screeched until all her breath was gone. She stared with stricken eyes at her handler. In a fight between Vern and Queen, Vern would lose, and without the advantage of the forest, Vern couldn't outrun her, either. All she could do was remain where she was and hope Queen was more merciful than Vern had just been.

"I'm sorry," said Vern.

Queen convulsed in an anguished fugue, and Vern shuddered as visions poured through her. The early days of Cainland. Queen's gradual transformation. The obviousness of her gifts and afflictions threatening the secrecy of the project. A row of glass cages like those in the van, Queen in one of them. Ollie tending her, feeding her scraps of food when she showed her obedience. Queen wailed. The low tones reached down into Vern and tugged. Melodious and deep with despair, Queen's cries were a funeral song.

Vern waited for the images in her head to become threats, to shift from Queen's archive of pain to the pain she planned to inflict on Vern for killing her progenitor. Ollie had made Queen, just as Reverend Sherman had helped make Vern. Queen looked at Vern, eyes sad and wide.

"I'm sorry," said Vern again.

All speech left Queen. Rasping, shrieking, and moaning were all the language she knew. Vern had been there.

"Come with me," said Vern. "Back to Cainland. Help me save them. Stay with me, and take back what they took from you. Your life. Your dignity. Your whole mind. She didn't love you. She didn't care about you." Queen shook her bowed head as she cried over the dead body. Embarrassed by the viscera still dangling from her lips, Vern wiped the back of her hand over her bloodstained mouth. With her mind linked directly to Queen's, she could see herself through Queen's eyes. Vern looked cruel.

Then, Queen saw herself through Vern's eyes: wild and unkempt, any semblance of sanity worn down by decades of torture. Queen turned away and stood. "Stay with me," Vern repeated.

Queen did not stay. Queen grabbed Ollie's firearm. "It was very nice to meet you, Vern," she said, as kindly as a woman serving up peach cobbler at brunch, and Vern imagined her as she must've been before the fungus, before Cainland, before Ollie.

Queen placed the barrel against her temple and fired. Like a dead, frozen bird, she dropped.

"No!"

Vern crawled over to Queen's body.

"Come back!"

But there was no coming back from this. The fungus had already started feasting. Through the mycelium, Vern fed on Queen's brain.

"Goodbye," said Vern, wishing to linger, knowing she could not. Queen was gone, but Gogo was still there, and so was all of Cainland. Ollie had tried to lay that future tragedy at her feet. Vern wouldn't let her.

Vern was no monster. Nineteen tender years old, she couldn't be said to be much more than a girl. She had changed little since the night she'd birthed Howling and Feral. Just like then, she was not so lost in teenagedom that she thought herself wise.

Dismissing the urge to grab Queen's hand and squeeze, Vern stood. She ran to the van and swiped Ollie's phone, but she couldn't unlock it. It needed Ollie's face.

She looked around her. The sun was bright and the sky was turquoise. To the side of the road, brown and orange dirt. It was a harsh landscape, stark as night, and as merciless, too.

This was the first time in four years that Vern had been without her knife, but she was her own artillery now.

With Ollie's body held firm between her knees, Vern wrapped

her hands around Ollie's jaws, squeezed, and wrenched upward. She beheaded the woman with the ease of her mam uncorking a bottle of wine. She held Ollie's head by the hair and dangled it in front of the phone. It unlocked.

Vern held the screen close to her eyes and found the internet icon. From there, she used the mic to find out where she was and flipped on the setting that made the phone's computer read the text aloud in a robotic voice. Gogo had taught her these settings so she wouldn't have to strain her eyes.

*Gogo.* She needed help if she was going to make it. According to the phone, Gogo and Vern were over a hundred miles away from a hospital. The nearest towns were barely more than gas stations and farm shops. None of these would offer them sanctuary. "Think, think, think, think," said Vern.

Sun stripped her surroundings of color. The world blazed around her bland and beige, as if consumed by fire. Vern stood in the center of the gray road, aching eyes squinted against the punishing light. She spread her exoskeleton out. Ollie's head was still in her hand and hung at her side.

Fifteen minutes later an SUV screeched to a halt in front of her. The span of her exoskeleton covered the width of the road. "Get out the vehicle," Vern said. She needed to get Gogo, and this would all be a waste if the driver simply pressed the pedal and drove away when her body was no longer blocking the road.

A man, Black, young, dressed for high summer in a tank top and bright pink swimming trunks, came out of the SUV with his hands up. "Come here," said Vern, hastily adding, "I'm not going to hurt you." But that was too soft. "If you cooperate."

The man—boy? she couldn't see his face well, but he strode with the arrogance of youth, all limber and fast metabolism. The boy came to her, steps careful. He trembled in fright, but he'd also removed a cell phone from his pocket and began recording her. "This is live," he said.

"Good," said Vern. Wherever she ended up, dead or in a cage, she didn't want her existence to be a secret.

Vern picked up Gogo, who was passed out but moaning, from the side of the road and carried her to the back seat of the SUV and laid her down. Next, she retrieved Ollie's head. She'd need it to work her phone. Finally, Vern got in, lifting Gogo's head onto her lap.

"Come on!" Vern yelled out of the open window.

The boy jogged back to the vehicle and popped into the driver's seat. "I'm not a goddamn chauffeur," he said, but he was still shaking, still afraid. "Is she—"

"She's fine," said Vern. "I need you to take us to the nearest hospital."

"St. Francis is, like, fuck, it's a two-hour drive if I push it. Can she make it that long?"

"She can," said Vern, willing it so.

"Those things that came out of your back? Are those real?"

"Yes."

"And is that head . . . ?"

"She was a bad woman," said Vern.

The boy snapped his head around to look at her. "And what are you supposed to be?" he asked, exasperated. "A good guy? Yeah, that's you, a real fucking saint, huh?"

Vern deserved it, but she rolled her eyes. "Shut up and drive."

The boy hooked his phone into the SUV's system. "Speaking of," he said, flicking. Seconds later, a song played. "I hope you like Rihanna."

Vern did because Lucy did. She used to sing this song all the time at the compound, to her father's dismay as well as Reverend Sherman's.

*"Shut up and drive."* As the pop hit thudded through the speakers, bass-heavy, Lucy appeared at Vern's side, dancing with arms in the air. She swayed, carefree.

"Lucy? Are you there?" asked Vern. "Is it you? Can you help me? Please fucking help me," she yelled to the haunting.

She caught the driver staring at her through the rearview mirror. He probably thought she was talking to herself, that she was crazy. Fine. There was nothing wrong with being crazy.

"Lucy!" Vern cried out to her dead friend.

"Shut up, Vern. I haven't heard this song in forever." Lucy looked about thirteen years old.

"I'll make him play it again. Just talk to me."

"Whatever," Lucy said with an eye roll and a sigh.

"Please, help me. Do you know something?" asked Vern, anything that might help her

"I live in the hyphae of an ancient fungus being. I know everything, Vern, and so do you," she said with a dismissive shrug. "Remember? I bathed in the Euphrates when dawns were young, like Langston said. We both did."

Then she was gone, the only remnant of her the smell of JAM extra-hold gel.

"Come back!" Vern called, but Lucy, as always, was her own spirit. Still a young girl mostly interested in her own whims, she would never come to anybody's beck and call.

Vern cradled Gogo in her arms. She ripped her blood-soaked shirt open so she could put her hand to her chest, warm her up. Gogo's body was cool, and she gasped for air. At least Ollie had bandaged the wound, removed the bullet.

After a sharp intake of breath, Vern kissed Gogo's lips, her eyelids. She closed her eyes and exhaled, blowing into Gogo's mouth.

"Love you," said Vern, and grabbed Gogo's hand, unsure if she meant it, but knowing surely she wanted Gogo to hear it from her. *Love.* She'd only ever thought of that feeling in relation to her babes, and she only supposed that was what it was called. That deep feral caring that made her despair at the thought of their loss. And her Cainland family? Did she love them? Was that what that was? When she thought of not getting to Cainland in time to save them and it was like wind blowing through a gapped tooth, swelling the gums?

Vern stuck to saying things to Gogo she could verify easily. "I'm pathetic with words and feelings both. I'm wretched as a skinned cat," she said. "I want to be with you. I want you to be beside me, alive."

Like all of Vern's attempts at emotional maturity, her affections were too little, too late. Language was like a wedding—speak now or forever hold your peace. Words mattered now, in the moment. They spoiled quickly when held inside, and what did they mean when offered too late but nothing at all?

*I know everything, Vern, and so do you.*

Maybe there was a way for Gogo to hear her now, to put thoughts into her. Remembering Queen, Vern closed her eyes and called to mind the child blowing the dandelion. It was about propagation. Spreading parts of herself into Gogo.

The spores didn't come. She didn't have the ease or command with the fungus that Queen had.

Vern flexed her shoulders and tensed her back, feeling around mentally for the mechanism that would set the mist free. Tendrils of bone and connective tissue sprang like plant shoots outward, tiptoeing in the stuffy air of the SUV's back seat. Despite all she'd learned since the fungus first rooted out her insides and replaced them with its own superior matter, her body would always be a stranger now. It had always been a stranger, the way bodies tended to be, constantly surprising, never being good enough.

Spray, spread, unleash, contaminate. Go forth and multiply. Tell it on the mountain. Vern called every phrase to mind that might bring on the ability to liberate the spores. Queen had unfolded her entire exoskeleton, but Vern couldn't do that now without compromising the vehicle.

Vern spoke to the mycelia. *I know everything, Vern, and so do you.*

The mycelia, as they always did, spoke back. Vern felt the fungus's message through her body. She was to do little more than breathe in and breathe out. When she did, the spores came. They wafted on an invisible current of air. Though the dust cloud was minuscule, too faint for Vern to see, she could feel her body releasing.

*Gogo,* she said, but not with her mouth, with her mind. *I need you. Wake up. Live.*

Queen's spores, once breathed in, had an impact immediately. It hadn't taken long for the fungus to infect and make the soldiers' minds its own.

Yet nothing happened when Vern did it; Gogo's mind as opaque to Vern as ever. Five minutes, ten minutes, half an hour, two hours. They were almost at the hospital now anyway.

"Hey."

Vern looked down into her lap. Gogo's eyes were wide open.

"You aint dead," said Vern, a mirror of her words when she'd awoken from her ten-day sleep under Gogo's care. Vern rested her palm on Gogo's cheek.

"It feels like I am," she said. "What happened?"

"You got shot in the chest. We're on the way to the hospital now."

Gogo blinked as she propped herself up. "Are you sure?" She patted her bare chest where Vern had ripped open the buttons.

There should've been a hole as round as a gaped mouth in her chest, hemorrhaging red rivers. There should've been an opening to the soft, moving parts of Gogo, a peephole to her heart. Gogo should've been spilling.

Though she was blood-slicked, no other evidence remained of Gogo's injury.

"What is it?" Gogo asked, drowsy and frightened by Vern's silence. "Is it bad?"

"It's nothing," said Vern. "It's nothing at all. It's blank. Erased." The spores had saved her.

Just like they'd saved Ollie the night Vern had almost killed her.

The fungus inside Vern was more than an infection. It was the stuff of life itself, some ancient essence from an alien world, foisting itself upon her for its own chance at life. It was a gift, and it had chosen her.

## 25

VERN USED OLLIE'S HEAD to unlock her phone and call Bridget after parting ways with the boy and his SUV, who had almost seemed sad to see them go. Almost. The children, at least, were fine. Bridget had taken them to a friend's trailer in the Muscogee Creek Nation, where they'd all been waiting for word.

"Baby, you all right?" asked Vern.

"I'm fine. Bridget's friend Lloyd made chili and fry bread," said Howling. "He said he's gonna teach me how to make it, too."

"And me, too!" yelled Feral. "When you coming to get us, Mam?"

Vern wanted the answer to be, *Right away.* "I got some business to take care of first, but then I'll be right there."

"What business?" asked Howling. "Has it got to do with the bad man?"

Vern nodded, though they couldn't see her. "Yes. And I'm going to make everything so those people can never hurt us again, or anybody else. I don't want to be worrying about y'all. You promise to behave for Bridget?"

She could feel Howling rolling his eyes. "Are you going to tell *her* to behave for me?"

Vern would never know what to do with this child. "Good point. Just remember to be kind."

"I always am."

"And to fight," she said.

"I always do!"

"Good," she said, her voice tense with emotion. She realized she was giving him a goodbye talk. She had to go to Cainland— didn't have a choice but to save her kin, to save the people scheduled to be massacred in the name of science, efficiency, and a good old-fashioned cover-up. She was stronger than they'd ever know, but this mission was not without risks. There was the possibility she would not return to her babies.

"Put the phone on speaker," she said.

The line clicked. "Feral? You there, too?"

"Yeah, Mam, but Bridget told me not to talk with my mouth full so I can't talk much."

Vern heard Bridget in the background. "I think you can wait to take more bites of food until your mam's done talking to you."

"But it's very good electricity food," said Feral with a soft, pathetic sigh.

"Feral, Howling, listen to me," Vern said, but she had no

more words of wisdom for them. "I love you, whoever you become."

Vern ended the call.

◻

GOGO INSISTED they drum up a plan, but Vern *was* the plan. She was the bullet, the arrow, the poison, the disease.

"You're not invincible," Gogo reminded her. Vern was no longer sure that was true. Queen's death had come only at her own hands. Though approaching ninety, she'd barely aged since the fungus had first found her.

If Gogo was right and Vern had her death to worry over, there was no level of detailed planning that would shield her against the full forces of the occupationist entity that called itself the United States.

Vern had learned something true about herself over all these years. She couldn't not fight. If she died, so be it.

They sped toward Cainland in a pickup truck Gogo had boosted from a strip mall with a Chinese-food buffet, an office supplies superstore, and a Goodwill. On Gogo's recommendation, Vern ditched Ollie's phone, not wanting to be tracked, and picked up a couple of burners. Vern tossed Ollie's head out of the window as they hit the highway.

"I'm gonna send a couple of SOSs out through my network," Gogo said, "see if I can get some media attention at Cainland. It'll help if there's eyes."

Vern shrugged from the passenger seat. People watched others commit atrocities all the time. Seeing didn't transform into doing.

"I know you think it doesn't make a difference," said Gogo, once again revealing that Vern didn't hide her feelings well. "I'm not sure I think it does, either. But it might, and it certainly can't hurt. You have to at least give people the chance to act. People can surprise you."

Vern knew that well, but not how Gogo meant it. Ollie had surprised Vern. So had her mother, revealing she'd known all along about Cainland drugging them. "Do what you want, I'm not going to stop you." Gogo proceeded to use voice-to-text to message friends, acquaintances, and ex-lovers across encrypted channels. She knew people everywhere.

The woods changed shape around them as the truck barreled toward the home Vern had spent years evading. She waited for the fear to set in, but she felt only anticipation. Lucy's words—Langston's words—ignited her. *I bathed in the Euphrates when dawns were young. We both did.* Vern was not alone.

⊠

THEY DIDN'T STOP DRIVING until they reached the Cainland perimeter. Neither had slept, but weariness only made the adrenaline pump harder. Four and a half years ago, Vern had fled, drunk on cough medicine, not yet a mother, a woman, a demigod. She returned now sound of mind and body, fortified. They would meet their creation.

Vern opened the door and leapt from the truck before Gogo had pulled to a stop. "Vern!" Gogo called, swerving to the side of the road and slamming the brakes. She followed Vern out of the pickup, running to keep up.

"So much for eyes," Vern said snidely, more embittered by the lack of spectators than she should've been for a woman who was used to expecting the worst.

Gogo checked her phone, scrolling the screen with her thumb. "Sounds like a few people showed up but cops chased off the ones they could and arrested those they couldn't. There's a contingent hiding out in the woods. Might be useful backup?"

"Maybe you should go wait with them," said Vern.

Gogo shook her head furiously. "I'm going with you. Don't think you can stop me."

Vern plowed ahead through browned grass toward the gates of the Blessed Acres. "You're a liability," she said.

That didn't stop Gogo. "I'd rather I slow you down than you be alone. We fight together."

She was armed, at least, with Ollie's semi and her own hunting rifle. More than a few of the pockets on her leather vest, which she wore over a barely there spaghetti-strap top, had knives.

"Stay close," said Vern. For once, Gogo was entering her world, where Vern was the master, not the student.

"I will not leave your side," assured Gogo.

As they approached, Vern saw armed soldiers, which was unusual. When Ollie didn't check in with whomever she was supposed to check in with, the authorities had sent a small vanguard. There were only three. Vern could take them down easily.

"Stand back!" one called.

"Not another step!" said his buddy. Vern kept walking, Gogo a pace behind her. Motion-activated lights flipped on as they crossed an invisible threshold.

High fluorescent light burst from circular lamps posted on the fence surrounding the borders of the Blessed Acres. Their bright white flare would've slowed down anyone, but Vern, her vision compromised to begin with, was completely blinded. It would take her eyes several moments to adjust.

"Shit, I count at least twenty, thirty. You?"

Vern's estimation of three armed soldiers had apparently been off. "I don't know. I can't see anything. Stand behind me."

Vern pressed forward.

"Halt," they shouted.

When she did not, she heard someone shout the order to fire. She'd been in this position before, and it had ended with her and Gogo's capture, but her will would not be broken. By the time the bullets—and they were bullets this time—launched forward, she'd already flung her exoskeleton in a protective shield around herself and Gogo.

The assault of rifle fire would've blown anyone else to the ground, but the bottom spokes of Vern's carapace punched into the dirt, steadying her. Hundreds of rounds slammed into the white bone sheathed around her, the pain of it rattling.

Vern couldn't break the stalemate without risking Gogo. She needed to find a way to make them stop.

"What the fuck?" said Gogo. "What happened?" The shooting had ceased.

"Let's go," said Vern. She didn't have time to explain that simply by wishing it, she'd released spores into the air that forced the soldiers to enact her will, temporary vessels of the fungus.

She hadn't wanted to do that. A mind was a private thing, and Vern had no business in anyone else's. In the moment, it had been a matter of protecting herself and Gogo. She could forgive herself for using the ability defensively on reflex. It had been as much the fungus's doing as hers. It had been guarding its conked fruit.

"Stay down," Vern said, but for good measure she shoved Gogo toward a massive oak to the side of them for cover.

"Here!" Gogo called, and tossed Vern Ollie's semiautomatic. The lights impaired her sight, but this close, it didn't matter. She shot each soldier one by one, hurrying as fast as she could, not knowing when the spores would wear.

Gogo tossed her another clip after she emptied the first, then followed Vern's lead and fired with her hunting rifle. When the last of the soldiers were dead, Gogo ran toward her. They held each other tight.

Such senseless life-taking did not feel good, but the military had opened fire first. They'd aligned themselves with the nation that had made the Blessed Acres of Cain, and that was one of its smaller sins. They'd been foolish if they'd come out tonight thinking Vern would offer mercy.

"Let's go, more will be coming," said Vern. Gogo chased after her.

Vern tore the metal gate from its hinges. "Carmichael!" she yelled. "Mam!"

A helicopter whirred overhead. "Fuck," said Vern.

"It's KXVTV," said Gogo. She showed Vern the screen of her phone. *Live: Shootout at the Black Power Cult "Cainland"—another Waco?* Gogo's network had come through.

Vern ran toward the buildings that formed the Blessed Acres' main town area. She stopped when she heard a fresh burst of bullets. They came from in front rather than behind, and she ran toward the sound. "Carmichael!" she called.

More bullets.

"No!" Vern shouted. "Carmichael! Mam!"

Another helicopter joined the first, but what did its presence matter right now when inside the very buildings Vern had called home more than half her life, government agents were carrying out a massacre? "They're doing it! They're killing them," Vern cried out.

"You don't know that," said Gogo, but Vern felt it, a cord snapping. It stilled her in her tracks.

Her breaths sounded like sobs, syncopated and shrill as air rushed in and just as quickly rushed out. Gogo's arms wrapped around her, but Vern couldn't stop herself from hyperventilating.

Outside the compound gates, Vern saw the flashing lights of police cars. News vans came next and then finally civilians, each of them with a phone, recording the sight before them. "The cops," Gogo said, shaking Vern, trying to wake her from her stupor. But what did it matter if she died?

"Vern, I'm so sorry," said Gogo, squeezing her hand.

"It's my fault. My leaving caused this."

"No. By leaving you saved yourself. Who knows what would've happened if you'd stayed?"

"If I'd gotten here sooner, I could've stopped it." She was the same stupid girl she'd always been, no wiser for the years she'd lived on the run. How naive she had been to think anything she did mattered.

"You can stop it now. You can shut it down, whoever did this, CIA, FBI, I don't give a fuck," said Gogo.

Ollie and her ilk had wrought generations of pain. It would never stop. Vern was a blip.

With Queen at her side, maybe she could've changed the world. The woman could've taught her the bounds of her power. "Maybe if I had Queen," said Vern, though even as she said it, she recognized it for the romanticization it was, no different than how she'd treated Lucy's memory. It was easy to make someone into a hero when they were gone, to ascribe to them infinite potential. Godlike though Queen's power seemed, she was human and therefore small and imperfect.

"Based on what you told me, Queen was tethered to a leash made of trauma and pain. Ollie had her on reins, a bit in her mouth," said Gogo. "I have no doubt you will surpass what she was capable of. You are limitless. You healed me. No matter what, I'll be right here with you, and so will Bridget, and Feral, and Howling, and anyone you choose. Everyone here who came to bear witness to this. You can do anything, anything but read the future. You can't know how it will turn out. Let your will be," said Gogo. As she said it, Vern felt the rush. Memories sweeping her, new hauntings swelling her brain.

It felt like drowning. She was back at the lake being pushed beneath the surface by Sherman, lungs overwhelmed by the inflow of liquid. It wasn't water, this time, that entered her, but the past. She felt it in her belly, in her chest, her knees, in her fingertips, in her knuckles. For the world, it was a small loss. For her, it was a flood. Vern could feel it. Everybody in Cainland was dead.

# 26

RUTHANNE JOSEPHINE NICOLETTE RILEY—mother of Vern Freddy-Mae Riley and Carmichael Charles Riley—was born to punks.

Her father, Jojo Charles "Frothmouth" Riley, fronted a funk-punk-metal band and was a pioneer in the genre he called hard-core devilpop. Ruthanne's mother, Clarissa Ruth Odette Riley née Buckley, played drums. They were the Afrosapienz and recorded four albums to little commercial but significant underground success. Summers were a barrage of block parties. Burgeoning hip-hop groups sampled their music. Clubs underpaid them to play to sold-out audiences.

They loved Jimi Hendrix more than breathing. They lived in motels and on friends' couches and in vans that stank of vomit and weed. They were Black Panthers. They were dissidents. They were angry. They were afraid.

Nothing was right in Jojo and Clarissa's lives but the music, and they couldn't always get that right. When they did, there was no guarantee folks would understand. They were mad with the grief of living, of being Black, of being artists, of being so goddamn poor, of being failures.

Jojo and Clarissa never planned to have a child, but in 1972 Ruthanne was born, named for one each of Jojo's and Clarissa's grandmothers, Ruth and Anne. They did not make very good parents at all, though, bless them, they did try. Multiple times, though unsupported, Clarissa tried to give up drinking while pregnant, sometimes lasting for weeks at a time before bingeing on gin or cognac. Ruthanne was born small and mostly stayed small. She arrived frighteningly late to every milestone. She drank only formula until twenty months and did not walk until two. She listened, but did not talk.

Clarissa smacked Ruthanne when she cried because that was what you surely did—she'd gotten smacked and turned out all right. She and Jojo both left their daughter at home in front the TV while they played gigs. They needed the money to pay rent on their tiny studio apartment.

Ruthanne ate generic-brand chocolate cereal and not much else, for there was rarely much else to be had. By the age of four, she was wandering the block, hanging around older kids who didn't know what to do with her silent self. Missy Jones, nine, called her dumb and slow. Annie Peterson called her dirty and stinky. Only a girl named Birdy Lamonde was sometimes nice, handing Ruthanne bags of potato chips or bottles of orange soda. Missy and Annie would roll their eyes, call Birdy a high yellow for her light skin, and ride away on their bikes, knee socks sagging down over scabbed-up legs.

Truth was, Birdy was a bit of a high yellow, for she couldn't stop going on about how it wasn't her fault she was so pretty, and it wasn't her fault she had good hair, and it wasn't her fault her dad was an accountant and had money to send her to a fancy school. It was always "woe is me" with Birdy, but Ruthanne was obsessed and followed the girl everywhere. She always had spare dimes to buy Ruthanne chocolate milk and mangoes from the bodega or bagels from the Jewish bakery. It was Birdy who first got Ruthanne talking, as Ruthanne was so enamored of Birdy's white accent. She sounded so proper and silly, and Ruthanne just had to copy it. She had a role model, someone who was good to fixate upon.

Birdy's mama gave Ruthanne hand-me-down dresses and did her hair up with laces and bows.

Not that things were always so bad at home. There were hugs and cuddles occasionally and mornings in bed eating cinnamon-roasted sweet potato and giggles at Ruthanne's attempts to put her father's head into ponytails with bobbles and barrettes and them knowing just what to do sometimes to make her stop crying, but by the time she was twelve, she hated them both, and when Birdy went off to college, Ruthanne couldn't see any good reason to stick around her parents. They were lost souls. She, on the other hand, was full of purpose. She dressed good. She looked good. She spoke good—well. No one would know who her parents were, all crass and uncouth. Drunkards and burnouts.

Ruthanne left to go live with her great-uncle, a Baptist minister in Tennessee who called himself Buck. "Now, what do we have here?" he asked when she turned up at his door, dressed ever so fancily in one of Birdy's old dresses, her hot-combed hair slicked into a bun, her white patent-leather shoes beautiful and unscuffed.

"You're my great-uncle. I'm Clarissa's girl, Ruthanne," she said.

"Get inside, girl," he said, then called for his wife, Freddy-Mae, to heat up some leftovers and make up a bed. "You will call me *sir*, and you will call her *ma'am*. We call you, and we hear you say, *What?* you get popped. So what do you say when Auntie Freddy-Mae calls you?"

"Yes, ma'am," said Ruthanne. She already knew the ropes. Birdy's mother had been the same way. She would answer only to ma'am. Didn't even like to be called Mama.

Ruthanne took to always calling them sir and ma'am instead of Uncle and Auntie, because then people wouldn't know right away she wasn't their daughter or granddaughter, and they'd never give thought to her sad life before she'd come here.

Uncle Buck demanded excellence, and Ruthanne delivered, flourishing under the high expectations. She loved the rules, the strict curfew, church on Sundays, Bible study, picnics, old women pinching her cheeks and telling her to steer clear of this and that boy, but, oh, wasn't he handsome. She liked that Buck checked her homework for errors and made her redo it until it was perfection. He chose her classes for her, made sure that she was taking the most challenging course load possible. Eventually he paid for private school, where she was the only nonwhite student at Woodly Preparatory. Life settled down into an order. She knew that she was loved and cared about always and without question. She knew her future. She'd go to Yale, like Uncle Buck had. She would be the first Black woman Supreme Court justice. She would have children and be the best goddamn mother in the world. She'd never imbibe. She would only ever listen to the same wondrous music Uncle Buck and Aunt Freddy-Mae played. Gospel. The Lord's music. She would be in God's light forever, and she would shine with his love and change the world, and when she talked, folks would listen. Why? Because she talked so good—well. Speech and Rhetoric Competition Champion, 1988, 1989.

She was eighteen when her mother died of an overdose. Two months later her father threw himself off a bridge.

"Focus on the task at hand," her great-uncle had said as she'd cried and cried, not knowing why. She hadn't spoken to them since she was a child. She didn't think they'd even been sad to see her go when she stormed out on a Thursday, suitcase packed.

Ruthanne did focus on the task at hand. She was accepted to Harvard University, where she studied history and linguistics, for a time. When Great-Uncle Buck died, she dropped out to return home to take care of Freddy-Mae, who'd recently been diagnosed with Parkinson's. She died a year later, Ruthanne by her side.

"Ruthie, dear?" asked Freddy-Mae.

"Yes, ma'am?"

"We did right by you, didn't we?" she asked, looking for reassurance.

"Yes, ma'am."

"I never could have children," she said.

Ruthanne nodded. "Yes, ma'am."

"I hope we loved you hard enough. You were our greatest gift." Those were her last words.

Ruthanne lived off her inheritance from Buck and Freddy-Mae, and when that went, she lived off whatever flitty notion she happened to have that month. She dealt weed. She lived in her van. She was a nanny for two years, a time when she learned she truly, completely, and vigorously hated white people.

Without her great-uncle as compass, she was a boat lost at sea. Soon she'd capsize. Feeling wistful and nostalgic one day, she called Birdy's old house, where Birdy's mother and father were still living—though they hadn't heard from Birdy in some time, they said. Still, they gave her the last contact info they had for her.

"Hello?" someone answered on the first ring.

"I'm looking for Birdy," said Ruthanne.

"You found her."

"Birdy? Really? It's me. It's Ruthanne."

They met up together despite their distance. Birdy had always been a beauty, stunning everyone around her, but had now surpassed what seemed humanly possible. She'd cut her hair short. Short! A curly mop on top, the sides gone. Looked like a white girl, with a style like that. The eye makeup she wore was dramatic and bold. Lipstick, dark red. Clothes, fitted and black. She looked like a cat.

It was silly to fall in love with her, but Ruthanne did, and for months they kissed and fucked and read each other poetry and became vegan and watched movies they hated at fancy art houses. That ended, too, when Birdy shriveled like the deferred dream in Langston Hughes's poem "Harlem." It was AIDS, of course. It was always AIDS, Ruthanne had learned. Every disappeared old friend. Every family member who passed under sudden and mysterious circumstances. Every lover.

Ruthanne supposed there was a good chance she was HIV-positive now, too, though she wouldn't get tested. She couldn't write her own death sentence, couldn't let her possibilities end here.

She was glad Uncle Buck was dead because he'd never have to know her immune system was possibly being bludgeoned this very moment. And she was glad her parents were dead for the same reason. For how they always thought her so snotty and snobbish, putting on airs, and they'd feel gratified that her end would be as undignified as theirs.

It did occur to her to end it, like her father had, overwhelmed by grief at the death of his wife, Clarissa, so it was good that she met Andre Wilder one Tuesday at the library. She was researching the best ways to die, and he was studying for his GED. He was trying to get into community college and eventually a four-year university. Then go to seminary school. A clear, bright, well-lit path.

Ruthanne tried her hand at going back to school, too, and eventually they were taking classes together locally. They ate out together. They had fun. Though they'd been fraternizing for nearly a year, they had not yet discussed their respective pasts. Andre wasn't the type to ask, and Ruthanne wasn't the type to offer.

Ruthanne suffered pregnancy patiently and diligently. Absorbed in the task of motherhood, she read every book. There were different opinions, of course, on what was to be done, but all she knew was that she wanted the very opposite of her own girlhood for her new baby, whom she would name Vern after her Great-Uncle Buck (Vernon Buckley).

There would be constancy. There would be a father who worked a good job and a mother who was at home with the baby, tending to its every whim and need. There would be things like Pizza Fridays and Soup Mondays. Back-to-school shopping. Eventually they'd be able to afford a modest home in the suburbs.

The early morning when the doctor laid her baby into her arms and she put it to her breast was the happiest Ruthanne had ever felt. She was made for this. Girl Found. That was what Ruthanne was. There was nothing like a baby to tether you.

"You are white as a ghost," Andre said to the baby, smiling.

"Shh, don't say that," Ruthanne chided. "She's white as the petal of a beautiful flower."

The two of them moved in together, but after six months, it was clear that wasn't going to work. Andre found Ruthanne moody and distant, and Ruthanne found Andre dull and unambitious.

They both stopped taking classes. Had to. Andre got a trucking job, and Ruthanne took care of her baby full-time, until they could afford that no longer. She got work at a fast-food joint, then at a department store, before she was fired for shoplifting baby clothes.

Vern, at least, was smart as a whip. Her first phrase was, *Yes, ma'am*, at ten months old. It made Ruthanne's heart well up with the loveliest memories to hear it, and from then on, she had her daughter call her *ma'am* because it made her think of Freddy-Mae and Buck and the eight years of her life that were utter perfection.

Ruthanne couldn't afford a good day care and had to hire a woman named Sally Dee to look after Vern. She had too many charges and fed the children frosted cereals and red Kool-Aid. It was not the vision of parenthood Ruthanne had.

She started dealing again to make ends meet. She was able to put Vern in a proper preschool when she was two and a half, though it was not the come-up she'd been hoping for. Ruthanne was often late dropping Vern off to school, and late to pick her up. She worked multiple jobs and arrived scattered and un-kempt. Likewise, Vern often looked a mess. Hair undone. Old clothes that were a little too small. Threadbare. Ruthanne rarely had enough extra cash for even shopping at Goodwill. Ms. Katy, Vern's teacher, was the one to call Social Services. What else was there to do with a child so clearly neglected? Certainly not offer resources and support.

A social worker entered Ruthanne's life, a short-haired, red-headed woman with a thick Southern drawl. Her name was Ollie Parks, and she was a mace. How many spikes could a woman have? Infinite, Ollie proved. Never had Ruthanne spoken to someone so lacking in generosity of spirit. Ollie looked in on Vern at school, at the house. Over the next few weeks, it seemed she never wasn't there.

"You are out of options," she told Ruthanne on their final meeting, like Ruthanne didn't know that well. "In cases like this, I tend to recommend immediate removal of the child from the home." Ruthanne was as much a disappointment as a parent as her own mother had been. "However, there's a place you can go where I might be able to ensure your togetherness."

"Where? I'll go anywhere. Do anything," Ruthanne said. She was already pregnant with another. Times were only going to get harder.

"You have to understand that the place we're going to is not one you leave. There's a contract."

"I'm not signing any contract," said Ruthanne.

"Then I can't guarantee Vern can stay with you. In fact, I can assure you that she won't. I hate for things to end in this way. It's obvious that you . . . care. Yet it is obvious to all that you are ill-equipped." Ruthanne signed the papers, content that if she wanted to, she could always run.

But when she arrived, she couldn't understand why she'd ever want to leave. The place Ollie Parks brought her to was not some facility of stainless steel and white walls. It was a wonderland. A utopia made by Black people and for Black people! It was better than the town in *Their Eyes Were Watching God* and so much more bountiful than the one in Toni Morrison's *Paradise*. Uncle Buck would've called it Eden.

Ruthanne had never met folks like she'd met at the Blessed Acres of Cain, dressed smartly in their pressed uniforms and always with smiles and kindness in their hearts. Yet they were learned. Had read the books she'd read, and then some.

There was food aplenty and shelter aplenty and clothing aplenty, all of which cost nothing. There were orchards! Ruthanne had never seen an orchard. Wasn't quite sure what one was at first. There was a range of chores, jobs, and activities she could do, and they didn't mind that it was going to take her some time to figure out what she wanted.

The only rule was to remember that Black Is Beautiful. Vern got her strabismus corrected, and for once, folks weren't talking about how ill and broken she was. Nor did they see her as anything but Black. They were given a small house that was all theirs, with a garden to tend.

On Sundays, they gathered for discussions and community suppers. Here, she could leave every worry behind.

Goodness, she even got married, to a man named Lester Holt. He'd been at Harvard the same time she was, though they'd never linked up. He'd studied physics.

"This is God of Cain's plan for man- and womankind," the leader of the compound said. Reverend Sherman. "This is the power of the Black family when united and whole. Whiteness knows that our togetherness is their destruction, and that is why they have put every effort into locking away our brothers, poisoning our connections with drugs and vice," said Sherman. He wasn't wrong. He sure wasn't.

There were doubts, sometimes, like when her Lester said she had no right to turn down his requests for sex because that would create a rift between them, severing the bonds of family. She disagreed, of course, but didn't know if she had any right to, or if her mind was corrupted by the notions of whiteness, like all their minds were. It was like being on a roller coaster. When the little cars start clicking awake, moving forward ever so slowly at first, you ask the attendant at the machines, "Can I get off?" wary now of what is ahead. It's too late now, though. You are on the track.

At least she never wanted for the necessities, and nor did any of her offspring. What life was waiting for her outside of Cainland?

Thank God of Cain for Ollie, the snake who'd lured her into this particular pit.

## 27

VERN WEPT.

For what? For whom? She didn't know. It was several life-times of tears. Eyes fluttery and lost, she stood limp in Gogo's embrace.

Ollie had been the same age in the haunting with Vern's mother as she had been when Vern met her. She was ageless. Vern should've seen it sooner. Queen's doing. The fungal spores. If they could heal, they could extend youth, too. Ollie had been with Queen, with Cainland, from the beginning. That was what her words had meant back in that van. Queen was what kept her alive literally, not metaphorically.

The fresh wave of hate Vern felt for the fiend wrenched her from her fugue state. "Let's move," she said, pulling from Gogo's hold. She still had time to punish these murderers.

Cameras turned toward her as flocking crowds noticed her presence. Gape-mouthed, they stared at her unsheathed exoskeleton.

The police were ready to release a rain of bullets, but civilians stood between them and Vern.

An army of the dead in the form of fresh hauntings marched behind Vern, and she let their presence embolden her rather than make her afraid. "Follow me if you will, but try and interfere, and you will die. This ends tonight," she said to cop and civilian alike, prepared to release the spores if they did not obey.

They did obey. Crews of news reporters followed, cameras turned to Vern's alien body, but they kept their distance. Citizens filmed. The cops held their guns but did not shoot.

Was it only fear that made them hold their fire? Or was it

wild-eyed marvel? Was their instinct upon seeing this new thing to question and gaze rather than subdue and kill?

"We are filming live at the infamous Cainland compound. A young woman is leading us onto the grounds and appears to be wearing intensely advanced armor," said one reporter in front of a camera.

Vern closed her eyes and listened to the fungus. It led her along even as it disabled her with pulses of fresh memories. Vern's mam was there beside her calling out to the woods, looking for Vern, screaming, sobbing. Brother Jerome played football with a group of boys whose uniform trousers were rolled up in the summer heat. A teenager picked dandelion greens for the night's supper. A little girl threw rocks at a wasp's nest. Sister Alice, Sister Ella, Sister Sonya, and Sister Araminta played spades at a fold-out picnic table, betting each other chores, using peach pits as chips.

Vern walked on, the world behind her. She only stopped once she'd reached the old well, the one she and Lucy had called down to how many thousands of times, certain they'd heard voices calling back. Vern briefly gripped the stone rim of the well to collect herself, then proceeded toward the temple where her family lay dead.

"They're in there," said Vern, pointing to the structure where Carmichael and her mam had spent their final moments. "Be ready to take cover. I don't know how many there are."

Gogo squeezed her hand.

Vern ripped the door that opened into the temple from its hinges. The soldiers who'd carried out the massacre had to know that she was coming for them and were prepared, but she was not afraid. They'd already let loose loss on an unspeakable scale. What more could they do to her? She alternated between fits of rage and a blank numbness as her legs carried her forward by rote, not will, through the temple's entry hall. She could smell smoke and metal. Maybe the fungus was truly divine after all and had made her into a demigod; she already had the indifference that came with being a deity.

At the end of the entry hall was another door. It opened into the sanctuary. "Fuck," said Gogo as she took in the sight before them. Bodies. On instinct, Gogo ran toward them to check for signs of life. "Somebody get the paramedics."

But it was over, and there was no one here to pay back. The jig up, the attackers had fled as quickly as they'd arrived; an elite SEAL team, perhaps, or a private military company.

Vern half laughed, half sobbed. She'd been ready to block bullets, to dodge barbed darts, but those in charge of the Cainland project had denied her the satisfaction of a fight they knew she would win. Running away was their final *fuck you* to her. They must've known how she longed to be the cause of each of their last breaths. Instead, she was left with knowing they were all alive somewhere, and she might well not ever find them. Like the Nazis that the United States had brought here in the forties and fifties to live their lives with their crimes unanswered-for, those who'd carried out the final stage of the Cainland project would be free.

All but Ollie.

At least the fiction of Cainland would die tonight. They wouldn't be able to pass this off as a mass suicide. Vern had ruined that plan.

Perhaps this was the better end. No amount of bloodbath could cleanse this land of sorrow. The deaths of those involved would've felt like a victory, but it wouldn't have been, not as long as the country that'd authorized and carried out the experimentation existed.

"Damn," said Lucy, appearing at Vern's side.

Vern turned toward her dead friend. "Is this how you died?" she asked. "A military op? Did they find you in the end? Assassinate you?"

Lucy shook her head. "Nothing like that. Nothing that would ever make it into a history book."

"Then what happened to you? Tell me."

"You sure you want to see?"

Vern would always prefer a difficult truth to an easy lie. "Please."

Lucy faded away, only to return in a flash in a new set of clothes, a backpack over her shoulders, a smile on her face as she ran back past Vern toward the Cainland gates. This wasn't Lucy-Lucy. This was a haunting proper. A memory.

Lucy cast a glance backward when she heard something behind her. Her father was there. Lucy's face fell, caught, and she catapulted herself toward the gate, trying to outrun him. Her father gave chase, snatching her by the back of her collar when he caught up to her and sending her to the ground.

This part Vern closed her eyes for, knowing where it would lead. She could not watch as Lucy's father killed her, could not watch him land a blow against a soft part of her head. Could not watch him cry once he'd realized what he had done, sobbing over her corpse, begging her to wake up as if it weren't him who put her to sleep for good. He buried her in a shallow grave near the woods like that was a kindness, even though he'd stolen the future she was supposed to have with her mother off the compound.

Lucy had never left. That last night she'd had with Vern, the both of them eating that cake before Lucy's dad came and dragged her away, was her last night altogether. It wasn't even

Cainland that had killed her. It was her dad, the same dad she'd've had anywhere else.

"Don't get too weepy," said Lucy. "Like I said before, I like living in you."

# 28

VERN'S MIRACLES up to now had been happenstance. She'd snapped the straps that bound her to Cainland. She'd walked ten days straight carrying her babes, no sleep, no rest. She'd survived the cold. She'd healed herself, and Gogo, too. By accident, she'd learned the extent of her abilities.

The next thing she'd do would be purposeful, she decided. *I know everything, Vern, and so do you*, Lucy had said.

"I don't know if we have any reason to believe it will work," said Gogo. "The science doesn't necessarily make sense."

"There's no reason to believe I should exist at all," Vern said, squeezing Gogo's hand. This was beyond medicine or science. Life couldn't be broken into discrete parts and studied like counters in a child's math toy. It felt to Vern like the whole universe was inside of her. Whatever this fungus was, she couldn't say for sure it was from this realm, bound by its physics.

Vern could do more than destroy. She could do more than kill. She could heal. And she could bring the people inside her hauntings to life.

If that was the case, maybe she could make them flesh and blood.

It was morning on the former compound of the Blessed Acres of Cain, and everything was ready. Bridget had come in the wee hours with the children, and Gogo had forced Vern to eat a small breakfast. She was prepared as she ever was going to be to face the bodies in broad daylight.

Journalists roamed the area, but Vern had made it clear that there would be no police and no military. Those who tried to test her were warned violently not to do so again, and heeded. She didn't know how long they'd give her carte blanche, but when they stopped, she'd be ready with a defense, an army. Gogo would help her build it.

Last night, a reporter interviewing her had asked if she thought she should be arrested and face charges and a trial. Vern had said, "Why should I, when they never would?" Then, on live television, she declared war against all that was.

Gogo had taken solace in the fact that the tragedy at least had been recorded. It would not be able to be buried. But that didn't matter to Vern. The United States was a catalogue of known wrongs. Cainland was just another Tulsa, another Operation Paperclip, another Tuskegee. Who cared who knew if the knowing didn't prevent future occurrences?

Gogo didn't disagree, of course, but she would always be a woman who appreciated history, who found value in the keeping of it.

"You ready?" asked Gogo. Vern walked over to her.

A medical team sorted the bodies, identifying them, zipping Cainites into black bags. Carmichael looked like a full-grown man, big as he was, his glasses on, holes in his forehead.

"I need you all to leave," said Vern to the milling paramedics, walking to her mother's corpse. She touched her hand to Ruthanne's forehead, though that didn't seem a necessary part of making her plan work. It felt like the right thing to do, though. Touch was essential. It was how she and the mycelia communicated.

Vern released the full span of her exoskeleton and waited

for Gogo to do her part. Her boots fell heavy against the floor as she walked up to each body and pried open the mouth. It was precautionary. If the spores could bring about resurrection, it wouldn't depend on whether the dead had opened or closed mouths. But they knew too little about how the fungus behaved to know its method of transfer. Dead, they could not breathe in the spores themselves.

When every mouth had been tugged into a large O, Vern released her spores. In the same way memories had entered her, she pushed them outward with the spores, pressing them into the bodies they belonged to. The hauntings walked alongside her, alive in her mind, hesitant.

"Is anything happening?" asked Vern, knowing it was silly to hope. Even if the spores mended the holes in their heads, how could that recharge them? Respark them? Life was electricity.

That was what the paddles were for, Vern supposed. Gogo had gotten Bridget to bring an emergency resuscitation kit and travel defibrillator. If there was any sign that the spores could heal the dead, say by reknitting the wounds, then Gogo would apply the paddles to their chests.

"I'm going to try something," said Gogo. She was standing over Carmichael. Nothing had changed in the bodies. They were as dead now as they were before Vern released the spores.

"What are you doing?" Vern asked, when she saw Gogo place the paddles on Carmichael's chest and send electricity through him. It looked too close to defiling, and Vern ran over to push her away from her brother's corpse, which lay at rest.

Gogo, undeterred, set the paddles to Carmichael's chest again. "This was a stupid idea," said Vern, shoving Gogo away, careful to modulate her strength so as not to send her to the ground.

"Look," said Gogo, stumbling to right herself, looking defiant, boastful. Wisps of hair had escaped from the customary French braid down the center of her head and blew in the light summer breeze. The stubble of hair on the sides of her head had grown out, giving her a mullet look.

Vern stood over Carmichael. Gazing upon the brother she barely recognized, she placed an index finger over one of the holes in his chest. She felt it. Felt it moving. Felt the microscopic tugs and pulls. Felt electricity.

Gogo took the defibrillator from body to body, jolting their hearts to beat for even one millisecond so that the fungus spores could work. A moment was all they required. A moment of life to latch on to. It wasn't self-initiated. It was a type of galvanism. For moments, they were all Frankenstein's creatures.

But then they healed. No—they didn't just heal. They'd been resurrected. Vern brought them back to life. She had the capacity for that. To build, nurture.

It took until late afternoon to get through all of the bodies. The Cainites lay asleep but with beating hearts, breathing lungs. Gogo called the paramedics back when Vern had awoken them all.

Ruthanne woke as she was being rolled into an ambulance. She called out Vern's name.

Vern knew she should turn to face her mother, now brought back to life, but she could not. Relief that Ruthanne was alive again did not mean there was any forgiveness. Even knowing all that her mother had gone through did not soften Vern's heart. She walked away.

It was summer, and the world was as bright as a lightning flash. Blue sky. Red dirt. Everything was set alight. Vern tried to cherish it, to turn toward the sun the way bluebells did, but Vern still lusted after the dark of the woods, where she was born, where her true self had been made.

Tomorrow, Vern would exhume Lucy's body—surely too far gone to bring back—and give her a proper burial. Tomorrow, she would introduce Howling and Feral to their uncle. Tomorrow, she would decide how she wanted her little world to look, and she would make it and fight for it with everything inside her.

But today, she would grab Gogo and the children and tug them after her. "Come on," she said to Howling and Feral, who'd arrived this morning with Bridget. She walked with them to the edge of the woods and found the place where *Giovanni's Room* was buried. She dug until her fingers brushed its soft cover. She kissed it, then set it to the side.

"This is Tonkawa land," said Gogo. She touched her palm to the ground, eyes closed, in prayer or gratitude or benediction. Vern joined her. For several minutes, they sat in reverent silence.

Howling spelled out *Tonkawa* in the dirt with a stick before asking how it was spelled in their language. Feral shook unripe crab apples from a tree as he climbed. "It's food for the bunnies," he said.

Vern smiled at all the loves of her life. There was Howling. There was Feral. Now there was Gogo, too. She almost cried, so grateful she was.

"You okay?" asked Gogo.

Vern nodded and wiped away the single tear threatening to fall. "I like the woods," she said. "In them, the possibilities seem endless. They are where wild things are, and I like to think the wild always wins. In the woods, it doesn't matter that there is no patch of earth that has not known bone, known blood, known rot. It feeds from that. It grows the trees. The mushrooms. It turns sorrows into flowers."

They both sat down, sweaty arm to sweaty arm. They remained until the woods were black but for patches of moonlight. They remained until they could hear the night calls of one thousand living things, screaming their existence, assuring the world of their survival. Vern screamed back.

## ACKNOWLEDGMENTS

I wrote this book on a full belly, with shelter over my head and the love and support of friends and family. For many, these things are far from givens, and I wonder what opuses we are missing from people who want to make art but are too preoccupied with basic survival to spare time on it. I could not have written this book without the basic necessities of life, and I'm thankful for the many who supported my family financially when the income I made from writing wasn't enough to keep us afloat and I was unable to work other jobs.

I'm thankful for Bunny, the most wonderful of friends, who's there and there and there, who fights. I'm thankful for Martha, my love, who minds the children, shuttles the children, and feeds the children while I work, who adds joy to dark days with her humor and tenacious spirit.

I'm thankful for my agent, Seth Fishman, who is simply the best and has changed my life in innumerable ways, and for my editor, Sean McDonald, who helped *Sorrowland* metamorphose into its final form with his wisdom and insight. I am thankful for everyone at Farrar, Straus and Giroux and MCD, and for everyone at #Merky Books, especially my UK editor, Jason Arthur. There are many, many more at these respective imprints whose work goes into the business that is making a book, and I'm sorry to not name them all. Suffice it to say, *Sorrowland* was not a solo effort.